THE YEAR OF THE FLOOD

BY THE SAME AUTHOR

FICTION

The Edible Woman
Surfacing
Lady Oracle
Dancing Girls
Life Before Man
Bodily Harm
Murder in the Dark
Bluebeard's Egg
The Handmaid's Tale
Cat's Eye
Wilderness Tips
Good Bones
The Robber Bride
Alias Grace
The Blind Assassin
Good Bones and Simple Murders
Oryx and Crake
The Penelopiad
The Tent
Moral Disorder

POETRY

Double Persephone
The Circle Game
The Animals in That Country
The Journals of Susanna Moodie

Procedures for Underground
Power Politics
You Are Happy
Selected Poems
Two-Headed Poems
True Stories
Interlunar
Selected Poems II: Poems Selected and New 1976–1986
Morning in the Burned House
The Door

NONFICTION

Survival: A Thematic Guide to Canadian Literature
Days of the Rebels 1815–1840
Second Words
Strange Things: The Malevolent North in Canadian Literature
Two Solicitudes: Conversations [with Victor-Lévy Beaulieu]
Negotiating with the Dead: A Writer on Writing
Moving Targets: Writing with Intent 1982–2004
Payback: Debt and the Shadow Side of Wealth

FOR CHILDREN

Up in the Tree
Anna's Pet (with Joyce Barkhouse)
For the Birds
Princess Prunella and the Purple Peanut
Rude Ramsay and the Roaring Radishes
Bashful Bob and Doleful Dorinda

MARGARET
ATWOOD

THE YEAR OF THE FLOOD

BLOOMSBURY
LONDON · BERLIN · NEW YORK

First published in Great Britain 2009

Bloomsbury Publishing, London, Berlin and New York

36 Soho Square, London W1D 3QY

A CIP catalogue record for this book is available from the British Library

ISBN 978 1 4088 0485 8

10 9 8 7 6 5 4 3 2 1

Printed and bound in Great Britain by Clays Ltd, St Ives plc

www.bloomsbury.com/margaretatwood

For Graeme and Jess

CONTENTS

THE GARDEN

Who is it tends the Garden,
The Garden oh so green?

'Twas once the finest Garden
That ever has been seen.

And in it God's dear Creatures
Did swim and fly and play;

But then came greedy Spoilers,
And killed them all away.

And all the Trees that flourished
And gave us wholesome fruit,

By waves of sand are buried,
Both leaf and branch and root.

And all the shining Water
Is turned to slime and mire,

And all the feathered Birds so bright
Have ceased their joyful choir.

Oh Garden, oh my Garden,
I'll mourn forevermore

Until the Gardeners arise,
And you to Life restore.

From *The God's Gardeners Oral Hymnbook*

THE YEAR OF THE FLOOD

1

TOBY

YEAR TWENTY-FIVE, THE YEAR OF THE FLOOD

In the early morning Toby climbs up to the rooftop to watch the sunrise. She uses a mop handle for balance: the elevator stopped working some time ago and the back stairs are slick with damp, so if she slips and topples there won't be anyone to pick her up.

As the first heat hits, mist rises from among the swath of trees between her and the derelict city. The air smells faintly of burning, a smell of caramel and tar and rancid barbecues, and the ashy but greasy smell of a garbage-dump fire after it's been raining. The abandoned towers in the distance are like the coral of an ancient reef – bleached and colourless, devoid of life.

There still is life, however. Birds chirp; sparrows, they must be. Their small voices are clear and sharp, nails on glass: there's no longer any sound of traffic to drown them out. Do they notice that quietness, the absence of motors? If so, are they happier? Toby has no idea. Unlike some of the other Gardeners – the more wild-eyed or possibly overdosed ones – she has never been under the illusion that she can converse with birds.

The sun brightens in the east, reddening the blue-grey haze that marks the distant ocean. The vultures roosting on hydro poles fan out their wings to dry them, opening themselves like black umbrellas. One and then another lifts off on the thermals and spirals upwards. If they plummet suddenly, it means they've spotted carrion.

Vultures are our friends, the Gardeners used to teach. *They purify the earth. They are God's necessary dark Angels of bodily dissolution. Imagine how terrible it would be if there were no death!*

Do I still believe this? Toby wonders.

Everything is different up close.

The rooftop has some planters, their ornamentals running wild; it has a few fake-wood benches. It used to have a sun canopy for cocktail hour, but that's been blown away. Toby sits on one of the benches to survey the grounds. She lifts her binoculars, scanning from left to right. The driveway, with its lumirose borders, untidy now as frayed hair-brushes, their purple glow fading in the strengthening light. The western entrance, done in pink adobe-style solarskin, the snarl of tangled cars outside the gate.

The flower beds, choked with sow thistle and burdock, enormous aqua kudzu moths fluttering above them. The fountains, their scallop-shell basins filled with stagnant rainwater. The parking lot with a pink golf cart and two pink AnooYoo Spa minivans, each with its winking-eye logo. There's a fourth minivan farther along the drive, crashed into a tree: there used to be an arm hanging out of the window, but it's gone now.

The wide lawns have grown up, tall weeds. There are low irregular mounds beneath the milkweed and fleabane and sorrel, with here and there a swatch of fabric, a glint of bone. That's where the people fell, the ones who'd been running or staggering across the lawn. Toby had watched from the roof, crouched behind one of the planters, but she hadn't watched for long. Some of those people had called for help, as if they'd known she was there. But how could she have helped?

The swimming pool has a mottled blanket of algae. Already there are frogs. The herons and the egrets and the peagrets hunt them, at the shallow end. For a while Toby tried to scoop out the small animals that had blundered in and drowned. The luminous green rabbits, the rats, the rakunks, with their striped tails and racoon bandit masks. But now she leaves them alone. Maybe they'll generate fish, somehow. When the pool is more like a swamp.

Is she thinking of eating these theoretical future fish? Surely not.

Surely not yet.

She turns to the dark encircling wall of trees and vines and fronds and shrubby undergrowth, probing it with her binoculars. It's from there that any danger might come. But what kind of danger? She can't imagine.

In the night there are the usual noises: the faraway barking of dogs, the tittering of mice, the water-pipe notes of the crickets, the occasional grumph of a frog. The blood rushing in her ears: *katoush*, *katoush*, *katoush*. A heavy broom sweeping dry leaves.

"Go to sleep," she says out loud. But she never sleeps well, not since she's been alone in this building. Sometimes she hears voices – human voices, calling to her in pain. Or the voices of women, the women who used to work here, the anxious women who used to come, for rest and rejuvenation. Splashing in the pool, strolling on the lawns. All the pink voices, soothed and soothing.

Or the voices of the Gardeners, murmuring or singing; or the children laughing together, up on the Edencliff Garden. Adam One, and Nuala, and Burt. Old Pilar, surrounded by her bees. And Zeb. If any one of them is still alive, it must be Zeb: any day now he'll come walking along the roadway or appear from among the trees.

But he must be dead by now. It's better to think so. Not to waste hope.

There must be someone else left, though; she can't be the only one on the planet. There must be others. But friends or foes? If she sees one, how to tell?

She's prepared. The doors are locked, the windows barred. But even such barriers are no guarantee: every hollow space invites invasion.

Even when she sleeps, she's listening, as animals do – for a break in the pattern, for an unknown sound, for a silence opening like a crack in rock.

When the small creatures hush their singing, said Adam One, it's because they're afraid. You must listen for the sound of their fear.

2

REN

YEAR TWENTY-FIVE, THE YEAR OF THE FLOOD

Beware of words. Be careful what you write. Leave no trails.

This is what the Gardeners taught us, when I was a child among them. They told us to depend on memory, because nothing written down could be relied on. The Spirit travels from mouth to mouth, not from thing to thing: books could be burnt, paper crumble away, computers could be destroyed. Only the Spirit lives forever, and the Spirit isn't a thing.

As for writing, it was dangerous, said the Adams and the Eves, because your enemies could trace you through it, and hunt you down, and use your words to condemn you.

But now that the Waterless Flood has swept over us, any writing I might do is safe enough, because those who would have used it against me are most likely dead. So I can write down anything I want.

What I write is my name, *Ren*, with an eyebrow pencil, on the wall beside the mirror. I've written it a lot of times. *Renrenren*, like a song. You can forget who you are if you're alone too much. Amanda told me that.

I can't see out the window, it's glass brick. I can't get out the door, it's locked on the outside. I still have air though, and water, as long as the solar doesn't quit. I still have food.

I'm lucky. I'm really very lucky. Count your luck, Amanda used to say. So I do. First, I was lucky to be working here at Scales when the Flood hit. Second, it was even luckier that I was shut up this way in the Sticky Zone, because it kept me safe. I got a rip in my Biofilm Bodyglove – a client got carried away and bit me, right through the green sequins – and I was waiting for my test results. It wasn't a wet rip with secretions and membranes involved, it was a dry rip near the elbow, so I wasn't that worried. Still, they checked everything, here at Scales. They had a reputation to keep up: we were known as the cleanest dirty girls in town.

Scales and Tails took care of you, they really did. If you were talent, that is. Good food, a doctor if you needed one, and the tips were great, because the men from the top Corps came here. It was well run, though it was in a seedy area – all the clubs were. That was a matter of image, Mordis would say: seedy was good for business, because unless there's an edge – something lurid or tawdry, a whiff of sleaze – what separated our brand from the run-of-the-mill product the guy could get at home, with the face cream and the white cotton panties?

Mordis believed in plain speaking. He'd been in the business ever since he was a kid, and when they outlawed the pimps and the street trade – for public health and the safety of women, they said – and rolled everything into SeksMart under CorpSeCorps control, Mordis made the jump, because of his experience. "It's who you know," he used to say. "And what you know about them." Then he'd grin and pat you on the bum – just a friendly pat though, he never took freebies from us. He had ethics.

He was a wiry guy with a shaved head and black, shiny, alert eyes like the heads of ants, and he was easy as long as everything was cool. But he'd stand up for us if the clients got violent. "Nobody hurts my best girls," he'd say. It was a point of honour with him.

Also he didn't like waste: we were a valuable asset, he'd say. The cream of the crop. After the SeksMart roll-in, anyone left outside the system was not only illegal but pathetic. A few wrecked, diseased old women wandering the alleyways, practically begging. No man with even a fraction of his brain left would go anywhere near them. "Hazardous waste," we Scales girls used to call them. We shouldn't have been so scornful; we should have had compassion. But compassion takes work, and we were young.

That night when the Waterless Flood began, I was waiting for my test results: they kept you locked in the Sticky Zone for weeks, in case you had something contagious. The food came in through the safety-sealed hatchway, plus there was the minifridge with snacks, and the water was filtered, coming in and out both. You had everything you needed, but it got boring in there. You could exercise on the machines, and I did a lot of that, because a trapeze dancer needs to keep in practice.

You could watch TV or old movies, play your music, talk on the phone. Or you could visit the other rooms in Scales on the intercom videoscreens. Sometimes when we were doing plank work we'd wink at the cameras in mid-moan for the benefit of whoever was stuck in the Sticky Zone. We knew where the cameras were hidden, in the snakeskin or featherwork on the ceilings. It was one big family, at Scales, so even when you were in the Sticky Zone, Mordis liked you to pretend you were still participating.

Mordis made me feel so secure. I knew if I was in big trouble I could go to him. There were only a few people in my life like that. Amanda, most of the time. Zeb, sometimes. And Toby. You wouldn't think it would be Toby – she was so tough and hard – but if you're drowning, a soft squashy thing is no good to hold on to. You need something more solid.

CREATION DAY

CREATION DAY

YEAR FIVE.

OF THE CREATION, AND OF THE NAMING OF THE ANIMALS.

SPOKEN BY ADAM ONE.

Dear Friends, dear Fellow Creatures, dear Fellow Mammals:

On Creation Day five years ago, this Edencliff Rooftop Garden of ours was a sizzling wasteland, hemmed in by festering city slums and dens of wickedness; but now it has blossomed as the rose.

By covering such barren rooftops with greenery we are doing our small part in the redemption of God's Creation from the decay and sterility that lies all around us, and feeding ourselves with unpolluted food into the bargain. Some would term our efforts futile, but if all were to follow our example, what a change would be wrought on our beloved Planet! Much hard work still lies before us, but fear not, my Friends: for we shall move forward undaunted.

I am glad we have all remembered our sunhats.

Now let us turn our minds to our annual Creation Day Devotion.

The Human Words of God speak of the Creation in terms that could be understood by the men of old. There is no talk of galaxies or genes, for such terms would have confused them greatly! But must we therefore take as scientific fact the story that the world was created in six days, thus making a nonsense of observable data? God cannot be held to the narrowness of literal and materialistic interpretations, nor measured by Human measurements, for His days are eons, and a thousand ages of our time are like an evening to Him. Unlike some other religions, we have never felt it served a higher purpose to lie to children about geology.

Remember the first sentences of those Human Words of God: the Earth is without form, and void, and then God speaks Light into being.

This is the moment that Science terms "The Big Bang," as if it were a sex orgy. Yet both accounts concur in their essence: Darkness; then, in an instant, Light. But surely the Creation is ongoing, for are not new stars being formed at every moment? God's Days are not consecutive, my Friends; they run concurrently, the first with the third, the fourth with the sixth. As we are told, "Thou sendeth forth thy Spirit, they are created: and Thou renewest the face of the Earth."

We are told that, on the fifth day of God's Creating activities, the waters brought forth Creatures, and on the sixth day the dry land was populated with Animals, and with Plants and Trees; and all were blessed, and told to multiply; and finally Adam – that is to say, Mankind – was created. According to Science, this is the same order in which the species did in fact appear on the Planet, Man last of all. Or more or less the same order. Or close enough.

What happens next? God brings the Animals before Man, "to see what he would call them." But why didn't God already know what names Adam would choose? The answer can only be that God has given Adam free will, and therefore Adam may do things that God Himself cannot anticipate in advance. Think of that the next time you are tempted by meat-eating or material wealth! Even God may not always know what you are going to do next!

God must have caused the Animals to assemble by speaking to them directly, but what language did He use? It was not Hebrew, my Friends. It was not Latin or Greek, or English, or French, or Spanish, or Arabic, or Chinese. No: He called the Animals in their own languages. To the Reindeer He spoke Reindeer, to the Spider, Spider; to the Elephant He spoke Elephant, to the Flea He spoke Flea, to the Centipede He spoke Centipede, and to the Ant, Ant. So must it have been.

And for Adam himself, the Names of the Animals were the first words he spoke – the first moment of Human language. In this cosmic instant, Adam claims his Human soul. To Name is – we hope – to greet; to draw another towards one's self. Let us imagine Adam calling out the Names of the Animals in fondness and joy, as if to say, *There you are, my dearest! Welcome!* Adam's first act towards the Animals was thus one of loving-kindness and kinship, for Man in his unfallen state was not yet a carnivore. The Animals knew this, and did not run away. So it must have been on that unrepeatable Day – a peaceful gathering at which every living entity on the Earth was embraced by Man.

How much have we lost, dear Fellow Mammals and Fellow Mortals! How much have we wilfully destroyed! How much do we need to restore, within ourselves!

The time of the Naming is not over, my Friends. In His sight, we may still be living in the sixth day. As your Meditation, imagine yourself rocked in that sheltering moment. Stretch out your hand towards those gentle eyes that regard you with such trust – a trust that has not yet been violated by bloodshed and gluttony and pride and disdain.

Say their Names.

Let us sing.

WHEN ADAM FIRST

When Adam first had breath of life
All in that golden place,
He dwelt in peace with Bird and Beast,
And knew God face to face.

Man's Spirit first went forth in speech
To Name each Creature dear;
God called to all in Fellowship,
They came without a fear.

They romped in play, and sang, and flew –
Each motion was a praise
For God's great Creativity
That filled those early days.

How shrunk, how dwindled, in our times
Creation's mighty seed –
For Man has broke the Fellowship
With murder, lust, and greed.

Oh Creatures dear, that suffer here,
How may we Love restore?
We'll Name you in our inner Hearts,
And call you Friend once more.

From *The God's Gardeners Oral Hymnbook*

3

TOBY. PODOCARP DAY

YEAR TWENTY-FIVE

It's daybreak. The break of day. Toby turns this word over: break, broke, broken. What breaks in daybreak? Is it the night? Is it the sun, cracked in two by the horizon like an egg, spilling out light?

She lifts her binoculars. The trees look as innocent as ever; yet she has the feeling that someone's watching her – as if even the most inert stone or stump can sense her, and doesn't wish her well.

Isolation produces such effects. She'd trained for them during the God's Gardeners Vigils and Retreats. The floating orange triangle, the talking crickets, the writhing columns of vegetation, the eyes in the leaves. Still, how to distinguish between such illusions and the real thing?

The sun's fully up now – smaller, hotter. Toby makes her way down from the rooftop, covers herself in her pink top-to-toe, sprays with SuperD for the bugs, and adjusts her broad pink sunhat. Then she unlocks the front door and goes out to tend the garden. This is where they used to grow the ladies' organic salads for the Spa Café – their garnishes, their exotic spliced vegetables, their herbal teas. There's overhead netting to thwart the birds, and a chain-link fence because of the green rabbits and the bobkittens and the rakunks that might wander in from the Park. These weren't numerous before the Flood, but it's astonishing how quickly they've been multiplying.

She's counting on this garden: her supplies in the storeroom are getting low. Over the years she'd stashed what she thought would be enough for an emergency like this, but she'd underestimated, and now she's running out of soybits and soydines. Luckily, everything in the garden is doing well: the chickenpeas have begun to pod, the beananas are in flower, the polyberry bushes are covered with small brown nubbins of different shapes and sizes. She picks some spinach, flicks off the iridescent green beetles on it, steps on them. Then, feeling remorseful, she makes a thumbprint grave for them and says the words for the freeing of the soul and the asking of pardon. Even though no one's watching her, it's hard to break such ingrained habits.

She relocates several slugs and snails and pulls out some weeds, leaving the purslane: she can steam that later. On the delicate carrot fronds she finds two bright-blue kudzu-moth caterpillars. Though developed as a biological control for invasive kudzu, they seem to prefer garden vegetables. In one of those jokey moves so common in the first years of gene-splicing, their designer gave them a baby face at the front end, with big eyes and a happy smile, which makes them remarkably difficult to kill. She pulls them off the carrots, their mandibles chewing ravenously beneath their cutie-pie masks, lifts the edge of the netting, and tosses them outside the fence. No doubt they'll be back.

On the way back to the building, she finds the tail of a dog beside the path – an Irish setter, it looks like – its long fur matted with burrs and twigs. A vulture's dropped it there, most likely: they're always dropping things. She tries not to think of the other things they dropped in the first weeks after the Flood. Fingers were the worst.

Her own hands are getting thicker – stiff and brown, like roots. She's been digging in the earth too much.

4

TOBY. SAINT BASHIR ALOUSE DAY

YEAR TWENTY-FIVE

She takes her baths in the early mornings, before the sun's too hot. She keeps a number of pails and bowls up on the rooftop, for collecting the afternoon-storm rainwater: the Spa has its own well, but the solar system's broken so the pumps are useless. She does her laundry on the rooftop too, spreading it out on the benches to dry. She uses the grey-water to flush her toilet.

She rubs herself with soap – there's still a lot of soap, all of it pink – and sponges off. My body is shrinking, she thinks. I'm puckering, I'm dwindling. Soon I'll be nothing but a hangnail. Though she's always been on the skinny side – *Oh Tobiatha*, the ladies used to say, *if only I had your figure!*

She dries herself off, slips on a pink smock. This one says, *Melody*. There's no need to label herself now that nobody's left to read the labels, so she's begun wearing the smocks of the others: *Anita*, *Quintana*, *Ren*, *Carmel*, *Symphony*. Those girls had been so cheerful, so hopeful. Not Ren, though: Ren had been sad. But Ren had left earlier.

Then all of them had left, once the trouble hit. They'd gone home to be with their families, believing love could save them. "You go ahead, I'll lock up," Toby had told them. And she had locked up, but with herself inside.

She scrubs her long dark hair, twists it into a wet bun. She really must cut it. It's thick and too hot. Also it smells of mutton.

As she's drying her hair she hears an odd sound. She goes cautiously to the rooftop railing. Three huge pigs are nosing around the swimming pool – two sows and a boar. The morning light shines on their plump pinky-grey forms; they glisten like wrestlers. They seem too large and bulbous to be normal. She's spotted pigs like this before, in the meadow, but they've never come this close. Escapees, they must be, from some experimental farm or other.

They're grouped by the shallow end of the pool, gazing at it as if in thought, their snouts twitching. Maybe they're sniffing the dead rakunk floating on the surface of the scummy water. Will they try to retrieve it? They grunt softly to one another, then back away: the thing must be too putrid even for them. They pause for a final sniff, then trot around the corner of the building.

Toby follows the railing, tracking them. They've found the garden fence, they're looking in. Then one of them begins to dig. They'll tunnel under.

"Get away from there!" Toby shouts at them. They peer up at her, dismiss her.

She scrambles down the stairs as fast as she can without slipping. Idiot! She should keep the rifle with her at all times. She grabs it from her bedside, hurries back up to the roof. She holds one of the pigs in the scope – the boar, an easy shot, he's sideways – but then she hesitates. They're God's Creatures. Never kill without just cause, said Adam One.

"I'm warning you!" she yells. Amazingly they seem to understand her. They must've seen a weapon before – a spraygun, a stun gun. They squeal in alarm, then turn and run.

They're a quarter of the way across the meadow when it occurs to her they'll be back. They'll dig under at night and root up her garden in no time flat, and that will be the end of her long-term food supply. She'll have to shoot them, it's self-defence. She squeezes off a round, misses, tries again. The boar falls down. The two sows keep running. Only when they've reached the forest rim do they turn and look back. Then they meld with the foliage and are gone.

Toby's hands are shaking. You've snuffed a life, she tells herself.

You've acted rashly and from anger. You ought to feel guilty. Still, she thinks of going out with one of the kitchen knives and sawing off a ham. She'd taken the Vegivows when she joined the Gardeners, but the prospect of a bacon sandwich is a great temptation right now. She resists it, however: animal protein should be the last resort.

She murmurs the standard Gardener words of apology, though she doesn't feel apologetic. Or not apologetic enough.

She needs to do some target practice. Shooting the boar, missing at first, letting the sows get away – that was clumsy.

In recent weeks she's grown lax about the rifle. Now she vows to cart it around with her wherever she goes – even up to the rooftop for a bath, even to the toilet. Even to the garden – especially to the garden. Pigs are smart, they'll keep her in mind, they won't forgive her. Should she lock the door when she goes out? What if she has to run back into the Spa building in a hurry? But if she leaves the door unlocked, someone or something could slip in when she's working in the garden and be waiting for her inside.

She'll need to think of every angle. *An Ararat without a wall isn't an Ararat at all*, as the Gardener children used to chant. *A wall that cannot be defended is no sooner built than ended.* The Gardeners loved their instructive rhymes.

5

Toby went in search of the rifle a few days after the first outbreaks. It was the night after the girls had fled from AnooYoo, leaving their pink smocks behind them.

This was not an ordinary pandemic: it wouldn't be contained after a few hundred thousand deaths, then obliterated with biotools and bleach. This was the Waterless Flood the Gardeners so often had warned about. It had all the signs: it travelled through the air as if on wings, it burned through cities like fire, spreading germ-ridden mobs, terror, and butchery. The lights were going out everywhere, the news was sporadic: systems were failing as their keepers died. It looked like total breakdown, which was why she'd needed the rifle. Rifles were illegal and getting caught with one would have been fatal a week earlier, but now such laws were no longer a factor.

The trip would be dangerous. She'd have to walk to her old pleeb – no transport would be functioning – and locate the tacky little split-level that had so briefly belonged to her parents. Then she'd have to dig the rifle up from where it had been buried, hoping no one would see her doing it.

Walking that far would be no problem: she'd kept herself in shape. The hazard would be other people. The rioting was everywhere, according to what fitful news she could still pick up from her phone.

She left the Spa at dusk, locking the door behind her. She crossed the wide lawns and made her way to the northern entrance along the woodland walk where the customers used to take their shady strolls: she'd be less visible there. There were still some glowlights marking the pathway. She met no one, though a green rabbit hopped into the bushes and a bobkitten crossed in front of her, turning to stare with its lambent eyes.

The entrance gate was ajar. She slid through cautiously, half expecting a challenge. Then she set out across Heritage Park. People were hurrying past, singly and in groups, trying to get out of the city, hoping to make their way through the pleebland sprawl and seek out refuge in the countryside. There was coughing, a child's wail. She almost stumbled over someone on the ground.

By the time she reached the Park's outer edge, it was pitch-dark. She moved from tree to tree along the verge, hugging the shadows. The boulevard was jammed with cars, trucks, solarbikes, and buses, their drivers honking and shouting. Some of the vehicles had been overturned and were burning. In the shops, the looting was in full swing. There were no CorpSeCorpsMen in sight. They must have been the first to desert, heading for their gated Corporation strongholds to save their skins, and carrying – Toby certainly hoped – the lethal virus with them.

From somewhere there were gunshots. So backyards were already being dug up, thought Toby: hers was not the only rifle.

Up the street there was a barricade, cars wedged together. It had its defenders, armed with what? As far as Toby could see they were using metal pipes. The crowd was screaming at them in fury, throwing bricks and stones: they wanted past, they wanted to flee the city. What did the barricade-holders want? Plunder, no doubt. Rape and money, and other useless things.

When the Waterless Waters rise, Adam One used to say, the people will try to save themselves from drowning. They will clutch at any straw. Be sure you are not that straw, my Friends, for if you are clutched or even touched, you too will drown.

Toby turned away from the barricade – she'd have to circle around it. She held herself back in the darkness, crouching along behind the foliage and skirting the Park's rim. Now she'd reached the open space where the

Gardeners used to hold their markets, and the cobb house where the kids once played. She hid behind it, waiting for a distraction. Soon enough there was a crash and an explosion, and while all heads were turned she ambled across. It's best not to run, Zeb had taught: running away makes you a prey.

The side streets were awash with people; she dodged to avoid them. She'd worn surgical gloves, a bulletproof vest made of silk from a spider/goat splice lifted from the AnooYoo guardhouse a year ago, and a black nose-cone air filter. From the garden shed she'd brought a shovel and a crowbar, both of which could be lethal if used decisively. In her pocket was a bottle of AnooYoo Total Shine Hairspray, an effective weapon if aimed at the eyes. She'd learned a lot of things from Zeb in his Urban Bloodshed Limitation classes: in Zeb's view, the first bloodshed to be limited should be your own.

She headed northeast, through upmarket Fernside, then through Big Box with its tracts of smallish, badly built houses, slipping along the narrowest streets, which were dimly lit and not crowded. Several people passed her, intent on their own stories. Two teenagers paused as if to try a mugging, but she began coughing and croaked out, "Help me!" and they scurried away.

Around midnight, and after a few wrong turns – the streets in Big Box looked so much alike – she reached her parents' former house. No lights were on, the door to the garage was open, and the plate-glass window at the front was smashed, so she didn't think anyone was in there. The current occupants were either dead or elsewhere. It was the same with the identical house next door, the one where the rifle was buried.

She stood for a moment, calming herself down, listening to the blood in her head: *katoush, katoush, katoush.* Either the rifle was still there or it was gone. If it was there, she'd have a rifle. If it was gone, she wouldn't have one. Nothing to panic about.

She opened the neighbours' garden gate, stealthy as a thief. Darkness, no movement. The scent of night flowers: lilies, nicotiana. Mixed with that, a whiff of smoke from something burning, blocks away: she could see the flare. A kudzu moth flickered against her face.

She stuck the crowbar under a patio stone, lifted, grabbed the edge, heaved the stone over. Did it again, and again. Three patio stones. Then she dug with the shovel.

A heartbeat, then another.

It was there.

Don't cry, she told herself. Just cut open the plastic, grab the rifle and the ammunition, and get out of here.

It took her three days to get back to AnooYoo, skirting the worst rioting. There were muddy footprints on the outside steps, but no one had broken in.

6

The rifle is a primitive weapon – a Ruger 44/99 Deerfield. It had been her father's. He was the one who'd taught her to shoot, when she was twelve, back in those days that seem now like some mushroom-induced Technicolour brain vacation. Aim for the centre of the body, he'd said. Don't waste your time with heads. He said he just meant animals.

They'd been living in the semi-country, before the sprawl had rolled over that stretch of landscape. Their white frame house had ten acres of trees around it, and there were squirrels, and the first green rabbits. No rakunks, those hadn't been put together yet. There were a lot of deer; they'd get into her mother's vegetable garden. Toby had shot a couple, and helped to dress them; she can still remember the smell, and the slither of shining viscera. They'd eaten deer stew, and her mother had made soup with the bones. But mostly Toby and her father shot tin cans, and rats at the dump – there'd still been a dump. She'd practised a lot, which had pleased her dad. "Great shot, pal," he'd say.

Had he wanted a son? Perhaps. What he'd said was that everyone needed to know how to shoot. His generation believed that if there was trouble all you'd have to do was shoot someone and then it would be okay.

Then the CorpSeCorps had outlawed firearms in the interests of public security, reserving the newly invented sprayguns for themselves, and suddenly people were officially weaponless. Her father had buried his rifle and a supply of ammunition under a pile of discarded picket fencing and shown Toby where it was in case she ever needed it. The CorpSeCorps could have found it with their metal detectors – they were rumoured to be doing sweeps – but they couldn't look everywhere, and her father was innocuous from their point of view. He sold air conditioning. He was a small potato.

Then a developer wanted to buy his land. The offer was good, but Toby's father refused to sell. He liked it where he was, he said. So did Toby's mother, who ran the HelthWyzer supplements franchise in the nearest shopping area. They turned down another offer, then a third. "We'll build around you," said the developer. Toby's father said that was okay with him: by this time it had become a matter of principle.

He thought the world was still the way it had been fifty years before, thinks Toby. He shouldn't have been so stubborn. Already, back then, the CorpSeCorps were consolidating their power. They'd started as a private security firm for the Corporations, but then they'd taken over when the local police forces collapsed for lack of funding, and people liked that at first because the Corporations paid, but now CorpSeCorps were sending their tentacles everywhere. He should have caved.

First he'd lost his job with the air-conditioning corp. He got another one selling thermal windows, but it paid less. Then Toby's mother came down with a strange illness. She couldn't understand it, because she'd always been so careful about her health: she worked out, she ate a lot of vegetables, she took a dose of HelthWyzer Hi-Potency VitalVite supplements daily. Franchise operators like her got a deal on the supplements – their own customized package, just like the ones for the higher-ups at HelthWyzer.

She took more supplements, but despite that she became weak and confused and lost weight rapidly: it was as if her body had turned against itself. No doctor could give her a diagnosis, though many tests were done by the HelthWyzer Corp clinics; they took an interest because she'd been such a faithful user of their products. They arranged for special care, with their own doctors. They charged for it, though, and even with the discount for members of the HelthWyzer Franchise Family it was a lot of money; and because the condition had no name, her parents' modest health insurance plan refused to cover the costs. Nobody could get public wellness coverage unless they had no money of their own whatsoever.

Not that you'd want to go to one of those public dump bins anyway, thought Toby. All they did was poke at your tongue and give you a few germs and viruses you didn't already have, and send you home.

Toby's father took out a second mortgage and poured the money into the doctors and the drugs and the hired nurses and the hospitals. But Toby's mother continued to wither away.

Her father had to sell their white frame house then, for a much lower price than the one he'd first been offered. The day after the sale closed, the bulldozers flattened the place. Her father bought another house, a tiny split-level in a new subdivision – the one nicknamed Big Box because it was flanked by a whole flotilla of megastores. He'd dug up his rifle from under the picket fencing, smuggled it to the new house, and buried it again, this time under the patio stones in the barren little backyard.

Then he'd lost his thermal-window job because he'd taken too much time off due to his wife's illness. His solarcar had to be sold. Then the furniture disappeared, piece by piece; not that Toby's father could get much for it. People can smell desperation on you, he said to Toby. They take advantage.

This conversation took place over the phone because Toby had made it to college despite the lack of family cash. She'd got a meagre scholarship from the Martha Graham Academy, which she was fleshing out by waiting tables in the student cafeteria. She wanted to come home and help out with her mother, who'd been shipped back from the hospital and was sleeping on the main-floor sofa because she couldn't climb stairs, but her father said no, Toby should stay at college, because there was nothing she could do.

Finally even the tacky Big Box house had to be put up for sale. The sign was on the lawn when Toby came home for her mother's funeral. Her father by that time was a wreck; humiliation, pain, and failure had eaten away at him until there was almost nothing left.

Her mother's funeral was short and dreary. After it, Toby sat with her father in the stripped-down kitchen. They drank a six-pack between them, Toby two, her father four. Then, after Toby had gone to bed, her father went into the empty garage and stuck the Ruger into his mouth, and pulled the trigger.

Toby heard the shot. She knew at once what it was. She'd seen the rifle standing behind the door in the kitchen: he must have dug it up for a reason, but she hadn't allowed herself to imagine what that reason might be.

She couldn't face what was in the garage. She lay in bed, skipping ahead in time. What to do? If she called the authorities – even a doctor or an ambulance – they'd find the bullet wound, and then they'd demand the rifle, and Toby would be in trouble as the daughter of an admitted lawbreaker – one who'd owned a forbidden weapon. That would be the least of it. They might accuse her of murder.

After what seemed hours, she forced herself to move. In the garage, she tried not to look too closely. She wrapped what was left of her father in a blanket, then in plastic heavy-duty garbage bags, sealed him with duct tape, and buried him under the patio stones. She felt terrible about it, but it was a thing he'd have understood. He'd been a practical man, but sentimental under that – power tools in the shed, roses on birthdays. If he'd been nothing but practical he'd have marched into the hospital with the divorce papers, the way a lot of men did when something too debilitating and expensive struck their wives. Left her mother to be tossed out onto the street. Stayed solvent. Instead, he'd spent all their money.

Toby wasn't much for standard religion: none of her family had been. They'd gone to the local church because the neighbours did and it would have been bad for business not to, but she'd heard her father say – privately, and after a couple of drinks – that there were too many crooks in the pulpit and too many dupes in the pews. Nevertheless, Toby had whispered a short prayer over the patio stones: *Earth to earth.* Then she'd brushed sand into the cracks.

She'd wrapped up the rifle in its plastic again and buried it under the patio stones of the house next door, which seemed to be empty: windows dark, no car in evidence. Maybe they'd been foreclosed. She'd taken that chance, trespassing on the neighbours, because if her father's body settled and they dug up the yard, and she'd buried the rifle beside him, it would be found too, and she wanted it to stay where it was. "You never know," her father used to say, "when you might need it," and that was right: you never did know.

It's possible a neighbour or two saw her digging around in the dark, but she didn't think they'd tell. They wouldn't want to draw the lightning down anywhere near their own possibly weapon-filled backyards.

She hosed the blood off the garage floor, then took a shower. Then she went to bed. She lay in the darkness, wanting to cry, but all she felt was cold. Though it wasn't cold at all.

She couldn't sell the house without revealing that she was the owner now because her father was dead, thus unleashing a whole dumpster-load of garbage onto her own head. Where, for instance, was the corpse, and how had it become one? So in the morning, after a sparse breakfast, she put the dishes in the sink and walked out of the house. She didn't even take a suitcase. What was there to pack?

Most likely the CorpSeCorps wouldn't bother tracing her. There was nothing in it for them: one of the Corporation banks would get the house anyway. If her disappearance was of interest to anyone, such as maybe her college – where was she, was she ill, had she been in an accident – the CorpSeCorps would spread it about that she'd been last seen with a cruising pimp on the lookout for fresh recruits, which is what you'd expect in the case of a young woman like her – a young woman in desperate financial straits, with no visible relations and no nest egg or trust fund or fallback. People would shake their heads – a shame but what could you do, and at least she had something of marketable value, namely her young ass, and therefore she wouldn't starve to death, and nobody had to feel guilty. The CorpSeCorps always substituted rumour for action, if action would cost them anything. They believed in the bottom line.

As for her father, everyone would assume he'd changed his name and vanished into one of the seedier pleebs to avoid paying for her mother's funeral with money he didn't have. That sort of thing was happening all the time.

7

The period that followed was a bad time for Toby. Though she'd hidden the evidence and managed to disappear, there was still a chance the CorpSeCorps might come after her for her father's debts. She didn't have any money they could seize, but there were stories about female debtors being farmed out for sex. If she had to make her living on her back, she at least wanted to keep the proceeds.

She'd burned her identity and didn't have the cash to buy a new one – not even a cheap one, without the DNA infusion or the skin-colour change – so she couldn't get a legitimate job: those were mostly controlled by the Corporations. But if you sank deep down – down where names disappeared and no histories were true – the CorpSeCorps wouldn't bother with you.

She rented a tiny room – she had enough money left from her cafeteria savings for that. A room of her own, which might save her few possessions from theft by some dubious roommate. It was on the top floor of a fire-trap commercial building in one of the worst pleebs – Willow Acres was its name, though the locals called it the Sewage Lagoon because a lot of shit ended up in it. She shared the bathroom with six illegal Thai immigrants, who kept very quiet. It was said that the CorpSeCorps had decided that expelling illegals was too expensive, so they'd resorted to the method used by farmers who found a diseased cow in the herd: shoot, shovel, and shut up.

On the floor below her there was an endangered-species luxury couture operation called Slink. They sold Halloween costumes over the counter to fool the animal-righter extremists and cured the skins in the backrooms. The fumes came up through the ventilation system: though Toby tried stuffing pillows into the vent, her cubicle stank of chemicals and rancid fat. Sometimes there was roaring and bleating as well – they killed the animals on the premises because the customers didn't want goat dressed up as oryx or dyed wolf instead of wolverine. They wanted their bragging rights to be genuine.

The skinned carcasses were sold on to a chain of gourmet restaurants called Rarity. The public dining rooms served steak and lamb and venison and buffalo, certified disease-free so it could be cooked rare – that was what "Rarity" pretended to mean. But in the private banquet rooms – key-club entry, bouncer-enforced – you could eat endangered species. The profits were immense; one bottle of tiger-bone wine alone was worth a neckful of diamonds.

Technically, the endangered trade was illegal – there were high fines for it – but it was very lucrative. People in the neighbourhood knew about it, but they had their own worries, and who could you tell, without risk? There were pockets within pockets, with a CorpSeCorps hand in each one of them.

Toby got a job as a furzooter: cheap day labour, no identity required. The furzooters put on fake-fur animal suits with cartoon heads and hung advertising signs around their necks, and worked the higher-end malls and the boutique retail streets. But it was hot and humid inside the furzoots, and the range of vision was limited. In the first week she suffered three attacks by fetishists who knocked her over, twisted the big head around so she was blinded, and rubbed their pelvises against her fur, making strange noises, of which the meows were the most recognizable. It wasn't rape – no part of her actual body was touched – but it was creepy. Also it was distasteful dressing up as bears and tigers and lions and the other endangered species she could hear being slaughtered on the floor below her. So she stopped doing that.

Then she made a lump of quick cash by selling her hair. The hair market hadn't yet been decimated by the Mo'Hair sheep breeders – that happened a few years later – so there were still scalpers who'd buy from anyone, no questions asked. She'd had long hair then, and although it was medium brown – not the best colour, they preferred blond – it had fetched a decent sum.

After the money from the hair was used up, she'd sold her eggs on the black market. Young women could get top dollar for donating their eggs to couples who hadn't been able pay the required bribe or else were so truly unsuitable that no official would sell them a parenthood licence anyway. But she could only pull the egg stunt twice because the second time the extraction needle had been infected. At that time the egg traders were still paying for treatment if anything went wrong; still, it took her a month to recover. When she tried a third time, they told her there were complications, so she could never donate any more eggs, or – incidentally – have any children herself.

Toby hadn't known until then that she'd wanted any children. She'd had a boyfriend back at Martha Graham who used to talk about marriage and a family – Stan was his name – but Toby had said they were far too young and poor to consider it. She was studying Holistic Healing – Lotions and Potions, the students called it – and Stan was in Problematics and Quadruple-Entry Creative Asset Planning, at which he was doing well. His family wasn't rich or he wouldn't have been at a third-rate institution like Martha Graham, but he was ambitious, and fully intended to prosper. On their more tranquil evenings, Toby would rub her flower preparations and herbal extract projects on him, and after that there would be a round of crisp, botanical-remedy-flavoured sex, followed by a shower-off and some popcorn, without salt or fat.

But once her family hit the downdraft, Toby knew she couldn't afford Stan. She also knew her days at college were numbered. So she'd cut off contact. She didn't even answer his reproachful text messages, because there was no future in it: he wanted a two-professionals marriage, and she was no longer in the running. Better to do the weeping sooner rather than later, she told herself.

But it seems she'd wanted children after all, because when she was told she'd been accidentally sterilized she could feel all the light leaking out of her.

After getting that news, she'd blown her hoarded egg-donation money on a drug-fuelled holiday from reality. But waking up with various men she'd never seen before had lost its thrill very quickly, especially when she'd found they had a habit of pocketing her spare change. After the fourth or fifth time she knew she had to make a decision: did she want to live or did she want to die? If *die*, there were quicker ways. If *live*, she had to live differently.

Through one of her single-nighters – a man with the Sewage Lagoon equivalent of a kind soul – she found a job at a pleebmob business. Pleebmob businesses didn't ask for identity and didn't need references: if you dipped into the till they'd simply cut your fingers off.

Toby's new job was with a chain called SecretBurgers. The secret of SecretBurgers was that no one knew what sort of animal protein was actually in them: the counter girls wore T-shirts and baseball caps with the slogan *SecretBurgers! Because Everyone Loves a Secret!* The job paid rock-bottom wages, but you got two free SecretBurgers a day. Once she was with the Gardeners and had taken the Vegivows, Toby suppressed the memory of eating these burgers; but as Adam One used to say, hunger is a powerful reorganizer of the conscience. The meat grinders weren't 100 per cent efficient; you might find a swatch of cat fur in your burger or a fragment of mouse tail. Was there a human fingernail, once?

It was possible. The local pleebmobs paid the CorpSeCorpsMen to turn a blind eye. In return, the CorpSeCorps let the pleebmobs run the low-level kidnappings and assassinations, the skunkweed gro-ops, the crack labs and street-drug retailing, and the plank shops that were their stock-in-trade. They also ran corpse disposals, harvesting organs for transplant, then running the gutted carcasses through the SecretBurgers grinders. So went the worst rumours. During the glory days of SecretBurgers, there were very few bodies found in vacant lots.

If there was a so-called reality TV exposé, the CorpSeCorps would make a pretense at investigation. Then they'd list the case as Unsolved and discard it. They had an image to uphold among those citizens who still paid lip service to the old ideals: defenders of the peace, enforcers of public security, keeping the streets safe. It was a joke even then, but most people felt the CorpSeCorps were better than total anarchy. Even Toby felt that.

The year before, SecretBurgers had gone too far. The CorpSeCorps had closed them down after one of their high-placed officials went slumming in the Sewage Lagoon and his shoes were discovered on the feet of a SecretBurgers meat-grinder operator. So for a while stray cats breathed easier at night. But a few months later the familiar grilling booths were sizzling again, because who could say no to a business with so few supply-side costs?

8

Toby was pleased to learn she'd got the SecretBurgers job: she could pay the rent, she wouldn't starve. But then she discovered the catch.

The catch was the manager. His name was Blanco, though behind his back the SecretBurgers girls called him the Bloat. Rebecca Eckler, who worked Toby's shift, told her about him right away. "Stay off his radar," she said. "Maybe you'll be okay – he's doing that girl Dora, and he mostly does just the one at a time, and you're kind of scrawny and he likes the curvy butts. But if he tells you to come to the office, look out. He's real jealous. He'll take a girl apart."

"Has he asked you?" said Toby. "To the office?"

"Praise the Lord and spit," said Rebecca. "I'm too black and ugly for him, plus he just likes the kittens, not the old cats. Maybe you should wrinkle yourself up, sweetheart. Knock out a few of your teeth."

"You're not ugly," said Toby. Rebecca was in fact beautiful in a substantial way, with her brown skin and her red hair and her Egyptian nose.

"I don't mean ugly like that," said Rebecca. "Ugly to deal with. Us Jelacks, we're two kinds of folks you don't want to mess with. He knows I'd get the Blackened Redfish onto him, and they're one mean gang. Plus maybe the Wolf Isaiahists. Way too much grief!"

Toby had no such backups. She kept her head down when Blanco was around. She'd heard his story. According to Rebecca, he'd been a bouncer at Scales, the classiest club in the Lagoon. Bouncers had status; they strolled around in black suits and dark glasses, looking suave but tough, and they had women swarming all over them. But Blanco had blown it big time, said Rebecca. He'd ripped up a Scales girl – not a smuggled illegal-alien temporary, they got ripped up all the time, but one of the top talent, a star pole dancer. You couldn't have a guy like that around – someone who'd mess up the works because he couldn't keep his cool – so they'd fired him. Lucky for him he had friends in the CorpSeCorps or he'd have ended up minus some body parts in a carbon garboil dumpster. As it was, they'd stuck him in to run the Sewage Lagoon SecretBurgers outlet. It was a big comedown and he was bitter about it – why should he suffer because of some slut? – so he hated the job. But he figured the girls were his perks. He had two pals, ex-bouncers like himself, who acted as his bodyguards, and they got the leavings. Supposing there was anything left.

Blanco was still bouncer-shaped – oblong and hefty – though running to fat: too much beer, said Rebecca. He'd kept the signature bouncer ponytail at the back of his balding head, and he sported a full set of arm tattoos: snakes twining his arms, bracelets of skulls around his wrists, veins and arteries on the backs of his hands so they looked flayed. Around his neck was a tattooed chain, with a lock on it shaped like a red heart, nestled into the chest hair he displayed in the V of his open shirt. According to rumour, that chain went right down his back, twined around an upside-down naked woman whose head was stuck in his ass.

Toby kept her eye on Dora, who'd arrive at the grilling booth to take over when Toby's shift was done. She'd begun as a plump optimist, but over the weeks she'd been shrinking and sagging; on the white skin of her arms, the bruises bloomed and faded. "She wants to run away," Rebecca whispered, "but she's scared. Maybe you should get out of here yourself. He's been looking at you."

"I'll be okay," said Toby. She didn't feel okay, she felt scared. But where else could she go? She lived from pay to pay. She had no money.

The next morning, Rebecca signalled Toby over. "Dora's dead," she said. "Tried to run. I just heard it. Found her in a vacant lot, neck broke, cut to bits. Saying it was some crazy."

"But it was him?" said Toby.

"Course it was him," Rebecca sniffed. "He's bragging."

At noon that same day, Blanco ordered Toby to his office. He sent his two pals with the message. They walked on either side of her, just in case she might get flighty ideas. As they went along the street, the heads turned. Toby felt she was on the way to her own execution. Why hadn't she quit when she had the chance?

The office was through a grimy door tucked behind a carbon garboil dumpster. It was a small room with a desk, filing cabinet, and battered leather couch. Blanco heaved himself out of his swivel chair, grinning.

"Skinny bitch, I'm promoting you," he said. "Say thank you."

Toby could only whisper: she felt strangled.

"See this heart?" said Blanco. He pointed to his tattoo. "It means I love you. And now you love me too. Right?"

Toby managed to nod.

"Smart girl," said Blanco. "Come here. Take off my shirt."

The tattoo on his back was just as Rebecca had described it: a naked woman, wound in chains, her head invisible. Her long hair waving up like flames.

Blanco put his flayed hands around her neck. "Cross me up, I'll snap you like a twig," he said.

9

Ever since her family had died in such sad ways, ever since she herself had disappeared from official view, Toby had tried not to think about her earlier life. She'd covered it in ice, she'd frozen it. Now she longed desperately to be back there in the past – even the bad parts, even the grief – because her present life was torture. She tried to picture her two faraway, long-ago parents, watching over her like guardian spirits, but she saw only mist.

She'd been Blanco's one-and-only for less than two weeks, but it felt like years. His view was that a woman with an ass as skinny as Toby's should consider herself in luck if any man wanted to stick his hole-hammer into her. She'd be even luckier if he didn't sell her to Scales as a temporary, which meant temporarily alive. She should thank her lucky stars. Better, she should thank him: he demanded a thank you after every degrading act. He didn't want her to feel pleasure, though: only submission.

Nor did he give her any time off from her SecretBurgers duties. He demanded her services during her lunch break – the whole half-hour – which meant she got no lunch.

Day by day she was hungrier and more exhausted. She had her own bruises now, like poor Dora's. Despair was taking her over: she could see where this was going, and it looked like a dark tunnel. She'd be used up soon.

Worse, Rebecca had gone away, no one knew exactly where. Off with some religious group, said the street rumour. Blanco didn't care, because Rebecca hadn't been part of his harem. He filled her SecretBurgers place quickly enough.

Toby was working the morning shift when a strange procession approached along the street. From the signs they were carrying and the singing they were doing, she guessed it was a religious thing, though it wasn't a sect she'd ever seen before.

A lot of fringe cults worked the Sewage Lagoon, trolling for souls in torment. The Known Fruits and the Petrobaptists and the other rich-people religions kept away, but a few wattled old Salvation Army bands shuffled through, wheezing under the weight of their drums and French horns. Groups of turbaned Pure-Heart Brethren Sufis might twirl past, or black-clad Ancients of Days, or clumps of saffron-robed Hare Krishnas, tinkling and chanting, attracting jeers and rotting vegetation from the bystanders. The Lion Isaiahists and the Wolf Isaiahists both preached on street corners, battling when they met: they were at odds over whether it was the lion or the wolf that would lie down with the lamb once the Peaceable Kingdom had arrived. When there were scuffles, the pleebrat gangs – the brown Tex-Mexes, the pallid Lintheads, the yellow Asian Fusions, the Blackened Redfish – would swarm the fallen, rooting through their draperies for anything valuable, or even just portable.

As the procession drew nearer, Toby had a better view. The leader had a beard and was wearing a caftan that looked as if it had been sewn by elves on hash. Behind him came an assortment of children – various heights, all colours, but all in dark clothing – holding their slates with slogans printed on them: *God's Gardeners for God's Garden! Don't Eat Death! Animals R Us!* They looked like raggedy angels, or else like midget bag people. They'd been the ones doing the singing. *No meat! No meat! No meat!* they were chanting now. She'd heard of this cult: it was said to have a garden somewhere, on a rooftop. A wodge of drying mud, a few draggled marigolds, a mangy row of pathetic beans, broiling in the unforgiving sun.

The procession drew up in front of the SecretBurgers booth. A crowd was gathering, readying itself to jeer. "My Friends," said the leader, to the crowd at large. His preaching wouldn't go on for long, thought Toby, because the Sewage Lagooners wouldn't tolerate it. "My dear Friends. My name is Adam One. I, too, was once a materialistic, atheistic meat-eater. Like you, I thought Man was the measure of all things."

"Shut the fuck up, ecofreak," someone yelled. Adam One ignored this. "In fact, dear Friends, I thought measurement was the measure of all things! Yes – I was a scientist. I studied epidemics, I counted diseased and dying animals, and people too, as if they were so many pebbles. I thought that only numbers could give a true description of Reality. But then –"

"Piss off, dickhead!"

"But then, one day, when I was standing right where you are standing, devouring – yes! – devouring a SecretBurger, and revelling in the fat thereof, I saw a great Light. I heard a great Voice. And that Voice said –"

"It said, 'Get stuffed!'"

"It said, Spare your fellow Creatures! Do not eat anything with a face! Do not kill your own Soul! And then . . ."

Toby felt the crowd, the way they were poised to surge. They'd stomp this poor fool into the ground, and the little Gardener children with him. "Go away!" she said as loudly as she could.

Adam One gave her a courtly little bow, a kindly smile. "My child," he said, "do you have any idea what you're selling? Surely you wouldn't eat your own relatives."

"I would," Toby said, "if I was hungry enough. Please go!"

"I see you've had a difficult time, my child," said Adam One. "You have grown a callous and hard shell. But that hard shell is not your true self. Inside that shell you have a warm and tender heart, and a kind Soul . . ."

It was true about the shell; she knew she'd hardened. But her shell was her armour: without it she'd be mush.

"This asshole bothering you?" said Blanco. He'd loomed up behind her, as he was in the habit of doing. He put his hand on her waist, and she could see it even without looking at it: the veins, the arteries. Raw flesh.

"It's okay," said Toby. "He's harmless."

Adam One showed no sign of dislodging himself. He carried on as if no one else had spoken. "You long to do good in this world, my child –"

"I'm not your child," said Toby. She was more than aware that she wasn't anyone's child, not any more.

"We are all one another's children," said Adam One with a sad look.

"Scram," said Blanco. "Before I knot you!"

"Please leave or you'll get injured," said Toby as urgently as she could. This man had no fear. She lowered her voice, hissed at him: "Piss off! Now!"

"It is you who will be injured," said Adam One. "Every day you stand here selling the mutilated flesh of God's beloved Creatures, it's injuring you more. Join us, my dear – we are your friends, we have a place for you."

"Get your fuckin' paws off my worker, you fuckin' pervert!" Blanco shouted.

"Am I bothering you, my child?" said Adam One, ignoring him. "I certainly haven't touched . . ."

Blanco came out from behind the booth and lunged, but Adam One seemed used to being attacked: he stepped to the side, and Blanco rocketed forward into the group of singing children, knocking some of them down and falling down himself. A teenaged Linthead promptly hit him over the head with an empty bottle – Blanco wasn't a neighbourhood favourite – and he sank down, bleeding from a gash on his head.

Toby ran around to the front of the grilling booth. Her first impulse was to help him up because she'd be in big trouble later if she didn't. A pack of Redfish pleebrats was mauling him, and some Asian Fusions were working on his shoes. The crowd moved in around him, but now he was struggling to right himself. Where were his two bodyguards? Nowhere to be seen.

Toby felt curiously exhilarated. Then she kicked Blanco's head. She did it without even thinking. She felt herself grinning like a dog, she felt her foot connect with his skull: it was like a towel-covered stone. As soon as she'd done it she realized her mistake. How could she have been so dumb?

"Come away, my dear," said Adam One, taking her by the elbow. "It would be best. You've lost your job in any case."

Blanco's two thug pals were back now, and were beating off the pleebrats. Although he was groggy, his eyes were open and they were fixed on Toby. He'd felt that kick; worse, he'd been humiliated by her in public. He'd lost face. Any minute now he'd haul himself up and pulverize her. "Bitch!" he croaked. "I'll slice off your tits!"

Then Toby was surrounded by a crowd of children. Two of them took hold of her hands, and the others formed themselves into an honour guard, front and back. "Hurry, hurry," they were saying as they pulled and pushed her along the street.

There was a roar from behind: "Get back here, bitch!"

"Quick, this way," said the tallest boy. With Adam One covering the rear they jogged through the streets of the Sewage Lagoon. It was like a parade: people stared. In addition to her panic Toby felt unreal, and a little dizzy.

Now the crowds were becoming thinner and the smells less pungent; fewer shops were boarded up. "Faster," said Adam One. They ran up an alleyway and turned several corners in quick succession, and the shouting faded away.

They came to an early modern red-brick factory building. On the front was a sign saying, PACHINKO, over a smaller one that read, STARDUST PERSONAL MASSAGE, SECOND FLOOR, ALL TASTES INDULGED, NOSE JOBS EXTRA. The children ran around to the side of the building and began climbing up the fire escape, and Toby followed. She was out of breath, but they scampered up like monkeys. Once they'd reached the rooftop, each of them said, "Welcome to our Garden" and hugged her, and she was enveloped in the sweet, salty odour of unwashed children.

Toby couldn't remember being hugged by a child. For the children it must have been a formality, like hugging a distant aunt, but for her it was something she couldn't define: fuzzy, softly intimate. Like being nuzzled by rabbits. But rabbits from Mars. Nevertheless she found it touching: she'd been touched, in an impersonal but kindly way that was not sexual. Considering how she'd been living lately, with Blanco's the only hands touching her, the strangeness must have come in part from that.

There were adults too, holding out their hands in greeting – the women in dark baggy dresses, the men in coveralls – and here, suddenly, was Rebecca. "You made it, sweetheart," she said. "I told them! I just knew they'd get you out!"

The Garden wasn't at all what Toby had expected from hearsay. It wasn't a baked mudflat strewn with rotting vegetable waste – quite the reverse. She gazed around it in wonder: it was so beautiful, with plants and flowers of many kinds she'd never seen before. There were vivid butterflies; from nearby came the vibration of bees. Each petal and leaf was fully alive, shining with awareness of her. Even the air of the Garden was different.

She found herself crying with relief and gratitude. It was as if a large, benevolent hand had reached down and picked her up, and was holding her safe. Later, she frequently heard Adam One speak of "being flooded with the Light of God's Creation," and without knowing it yet that was how she felt.

"I'm so glad you have made this decision, my dear," said Adam One.

But Toby didn't think she'd made any decision at all. Something else had made it for her. Despite everything that happened afterwards, this was a moment she never forgot.

That first evening, there was a modest celebration in honour of Toby's advent. A great fuss was made over the opening of a jar of preserved purple items – those were her first elderberries – and a pot of honey was produced as if it was the Holy Grail.

Adam One made a little speech about providential rescues. The brand plucked from the burning was mentioned, and the one lost sheep – she'd heard of those before, at church – but other, unfamiliar examples of rescue were used as well: the relocated snail, the windfall pear. Then they'd eaten a sort of lentil pancake and a dish called Pilar's Pickled Mushroom Medley, followed by slices of soybread topped with the purple berries and the honey.

After her initial elation, Toby was feeling stunned and uneasy. How had she got up here, to this unlikely and somehow disturbing location? What was she doing among these friendly though bizarre people, with their wacky religion and – right now – their purple teeth?

10

Toby's first weeks with the Gardeners were not reassuring. Adam One gave her no instructions: he simply watched her, by which she understood that she was on probation. She tried to fit in, to help when needed, but at the routine tasks she was inept. She couldn't sew tiny stitches, the way Eve Nine – Nuala – wanted, and after she'd bled into a few salads, Rebecca told her to lay off the vegetable chopping. "If I want it to look like beets I'll put in beets," was what she said. Burt – Adam Thirteen, in charge of garden vegetables – discouraged her from weeding after she'd uprooted some of the artichokes by mistake. She could clean out the violet biolets, though. It was a simple chore that took no special training. So that is what she did.

Adam One was well aware of her efforts. "The biolets aren't so bad, are they?" he said to her one day. "After all, we're strict vegetarians here." Toby wondered what he meant, but then she realized: less smelly. Cow rather than dog.

Figuring out the Gardener hierarchy took her some time. Adam One insisted that all Gardeners were equal on the spiritual level, but the same did not hold true for the material one: the Adams and the Eves ranked higher, though their numbers indicated their areas of expertise rather than their order of importance. In many ways it was like a monastery, she thought. The inner chapter, then the lay brothers. And the lay sisters, of course. Except that chastity was not expected.

Since she was accepting Gardener hospitality, and under false pretenses at that – she wasn't really a convert – she felt she should pay by working very hard. To the violet biolet cleaning she added other tasks. She carted fresh soil up to the rooftop via the fire escape – the Gardeners had a supply of it, gathered from deserted building sites and vacant lots – to be mixed with compost, and with violet biolet by-products. She melted down soap ends and decanted and labelled vinegar. She packaged worms for the Tree of Life Natural Materials Exchange, she mopped the floor of the Run-For-Your-Light Treadmills gym, she swept out the dormitory cubicles on the level below the Rooftop where the single members of the group slept every night on futons stuffed with dried plant materials.

After several months of this, Adam One suggested that she put her other talents to work. "What other talents?" said Toby.

"Didn't you study Holistic Healing?" he asked. "At Martha Graham?"

"Yes," Toby said. There was no point in asking how Adam One knew that about her. He just knew things.

So she set to work making herbal lotions and creams. There wasn't much chopping involved, and she had a strong arm with the mortar and pestle. Soon after that, Adam One asked her to share her skills with the children, so she added several daily classes to her routine.

By now she was used to the dark, sack-like garments the women wore. "You'll want to grow your hair," said Nuala. "Get rid of that scalped look. We Gardener women all wear our hair long." When Toby asked why, she was given to understand that the aesthetic preference was God's. This kind of smiling, bossy sanctimoniousness was a little too pervasive for Toby, especially among the female members of the sect.

From time to time she thought of deserting. For one thing, she was swept with periodic but shameful cravings for animal protein. "You ever feel like eating a SecretBurger?" she asked Rebecca. Rebecca was from her former world: such things could be discussed with her.

"I must admit it," said Rebecca. "I do have those thoughts. They put something in them – it has to be. Some addictive thing."

The food was pleasant enough – Rebecca did her best with the limited materials available – but it was repetitious. In addition to that, the prayers were tedious, the theology scrambled – why be so picky about lifestyle details if you believed everyone would soon be wiped off the face of the planet? The Gardeners were convinced of impending disaster, through no solid evidence that Toby could see. Maybe they were reading bird entrails.

A massive die-off of the human race was impending, due to overpopulation and wickedness, but the Gardeners exempted themselves: they intended to float above the Waterless Flood, with the aid of the food they were stashing away in the hidden storeplaces they called Ararats. As for the flotation devices in which they would ride out this flood, they themselves would be their own Arks, stored with their own collections of inner animals, or at least the names of those animals. Thus they would survive to replenish the Earth. Or something like that.

Toby asked Rebecca whether she really believed the Gardener total-disaster talk, but Rebecca wouldn't be drawn. "They are good people," was all she'd say. "What comes just comes, so what I say is, *Relax.*" Then she'd give Toby a honey/soy doughnut.

Good people or not, Toby couldn't see herself sticking it out among these fugitives from reality for long. But she couldn't just walk away openly. That would be too blatantly ungrateful: after all, these people had saved her skin. So she pictured herself slipping down the fire escape, past the sleeping level and the pachinko joint and the massage parlour on the floors below, and running off under cover of darkness, then hitching a solarcar ride to some other city farther north. Planes were out of the question, being far too expensive and intensely scrutinized by the CorpSeCorps. Even if she'd had the money for it, she couldn't take the bullet train – they checked identities there, and she didn't have one.

Not only that, but Blanco would still be on the lookout for her, down on the pleeb streets – him and his two thug pals. No woman ever got away from him, was his boast. Sooner or later he'd track her down and make her pay. That kick of hers would be very expensive. It would take a publicly advertised gang rape or her head on a pole to wipe the slate.

Was it possible that he didn't know where she was? No: the pleebrat gangs must have picked up such knowledge the way they picked up every rumour and sold it to him. She'd been avoiding the streets, but what was to stop Blanco from coming after her up the fire escape and onto the rooftop? Finally she shared her fears with Adam One. He knew about Blanco and what he was likely to do – he'd seen him in action.

"I don't want to put the Gardeners in danger," was how Toby put it.

"My dear," said Adam One, "you are safe with us. Or moderately safe." Blanco was Sewage Lagoon pleebmob, he explained, and the Gardeners were next door, in the Sinkhole. "Different pleebs, different mobs," he said. "They don't trespass unless they're having a mob war. In any case, the CorpSeCorps run the mobs, and according to our information they've declared us off-limits."

"Why would they bother to do that?" asked Toby.

"It would be bad for their image to eviscerate anything with God in its name," said Adam One. "The Corporations wouldn't approve of it, considering the influence of the Petrobaptists and the Known Fruits among them. They claim to respect the Spirit and to favour religious toleration, as long as the religions don't take to blowing things up: they have an aversion to the destruction of private property."

"They can't possibly *like* us," said Toby.

"Of course not," said Adam One. "They view us as twisted fanatics who combine food extremism with bad fashion sense and a puritanical attitude towards shopping. But we own nothing they want, so we don't qualify as terrorists. Sleep easier, dear Toby. You're guarded by angels."

Curious angels, thought Toby. Not all of them angels of light. But she did sleep easier, on her mattress of rustling husks.

THE FEAST OF ADAM AND ALL PRIMATES

THE FEAST OF ADAM AND ALL PRIMATES

YEAR TEN.

OF GOD'S METHODOLOGY IN CREATING MAN.

SPOKEN BY ADAM ONE.

Dear Fellow Gardeners in the Earth that is God's Garden:

How wonderful to see you all assembled here in our beautiful Edencliff Rooftop Garden! I have enjoyed viewing the excellent Tree of Creatures created by our Children from the plastic objects they've gleaned – such a fine illustration of evil materials being put to good uses! – and I look forward to our coming meal of Fellowship, featuring the turnips we stored from last year's harvest in Rebecca's delicious turnip pie, not to mention the Pickled Mushroom Medley, courtesy of Pilar, our Eve Six. We also celebrate the promotion of Toby to full teaching status. By her hard work and dedication, Toby has shown us that a person can overcome so many painful experiences and inner obstacles once they have seen the light of Truth. We are very proud of you, Toby.

On the Feast of Adam and All Primates, we affirm our Primate ancestry – an affirmation that has brought down wrath upon us from those who arrogantly persist in evolutionary denial. But we affirm, also, the Divine agency that has caused us to be created in the way that we were, and this has enraged those scientific fools who say in their hearts, "There is no God." These claim to prove the non-existence of God because they cannot put Him in a test tube and weigh and measure Him. But God is pure Spirit; so how can anyone reason that the failure to measure the Immeasurable proves its non-existence? God is indeed the No Thing, the No-thingness, that through which and by which all material things exist; for if there were not such a No-thingness, existence would be so crammed full of materiality that no one thing could be distinguished from another. The mere existence of separate material things is a proof of the No-thingness of God.

Where were the scientific fools when God laid the foundations of the Earth by interposing his own Spirit between one blob of matter and another, thus giving rise to forms? Where were they when "the morning stars sang together"? But let us forgive them in our hearts, for it is not our task today to reprimand, but to contemplate our own earthly state in all humility.

God could have made Man out of pure Word, but He did not use this method. He could also have formed him from the dust of the Earth, which in a sense He did, for what else can be signified by "dust" but atoms and molecules, the building blocks of all material entities? In addition to this, He created us through the long and complex process of Natural and Sexual Selection, which is none other than His ingenious device for instilling humility in Man. He made us "a little lower than the Angels," but in other ways – and Science bears this out – we are closely related to our fellow Primates, a fact that the haughty ones of this world do not find pleasant to their self-esteem. Our appetites, our desires, our more uncontrollable emotions – all are Primate! Our Fall from the original Garden was a Fall from the innocent acting-out of such patterns and impulses to a conscious and shamed awareness of them; and from thence comes our sadness, our anxiety, our doubt, our rage against God.

True, we – like the other Animals – were blessed, and ordered to increase and multiply, and to replenish the Earth. But by what humiliating and aggressive and painful means this replenishing frequently takes place! No wonder we are born to a sense of guilt and disgrace! Why did He not make us pure Spirit, like Himself? Why did he embed us in perishable matter, and a matter so unfortunately Monkey-like? So goes the ancient cry.

What commandment did we disobey? The commandment to live the Animal life in all simplicity – without clothing, so to speak. But we craved the knowledge of good and evil, and we obtained that knowledge, and now we are reaping the whirlwind. In our efforts to rise above ourselves we have indeed fallen far, and are falling farther still; for, like the Creation, the Fall, too, is ongoing. Ours is a fall into greed: why do we think that everything on Earth belongs to us, while in reality we belong to Everything? We have betrayed the trust of the Animals, and defiled our sacred task of stewardship. God's commandment to "replenish the Earth" did not mean we should fill it to overflowing with ourselves, thus wiping out everything else. How many other Species have we already annihilated? Insofar as you do it unto the least of God's Creatures, you do it unto Him. Please consider that, my Friends, the next time you crush a Worm underfoot or disparage a Beetle!

We pray that we may not fall into the error of pride by considering ourselves as exceptional, alone in all Creation in having Souls; and that we will not vainly imagine that we are set above all other Life, and may destroy it at our pleasure, and with impunity.

We thank Thee, oh God, for having made us in such a way as to remind us, not only of our less than Angelic being, but also of the knots of DNA and RNA that tie us to our many fellow Creatures.

Let us sing.

OH LET ME NOT BE PROUD

Oh let me not be proud, dear Lord,
Nor rank myself above
The other Primates, through whose genes
We grew into your Love.

A million million years, Your Days,
Your methods past discerning,
Yet through Your blend of DNAs
Came passion, mind, and learning.

We cannot always trace Your path
Through Monkey and Gorilla,
Yet all are sheltered underneath
Your Heavenly Umbrella.

And if we vaunt and puff ourselves
With vanity and pride,
Recall Australopithecus,
Our Animal inside.

So keep us far from worser traits,
Aggression, anger, greed;
Let us not scorn our lowly birth,
Nor yet our Primate seed.

From *The God's Gardeners Oral Hymnbook*

11

REN

YEAR TWENTY-FIVE

When I'm thinking back over that night – the night the Waterless Flood first began – I can't recall anything out of the ordinary. Around seven o'clock I was feeling hungry, so I got a Joltbar from the minifridge and ate half of it. I only ever ate half of anything because a girl with my body type can't afford to blimp up. I once asked Mordis if I should get bimplants, but he said I could play underage in a dim light, and there was heavy demand for the schoolgirl act.

I ran through some chin-ups and did my Kegel floor exercises, and then Mordis called in on my videophone to see if I was okay: he missed me, because no one could work the crowd like me. "Ren, you make them shit thousand-dollar bills," he said, and I blew him a kiss.

"Keeping your butt in shape?" he said, so I held the videophone behind me.

"Chickin' lickin' good," he said. Even if you were feeling ugly, he made you feel pretty.

After that I hit the Snakepit video, to check the action and dance along to the music. It was strange to watch everything going on without me, as if I'd been erased. Crimson Petal was teasing the pole, Savona was subbing for me on the trapeze. She looked good – glittery and green and sinuous, with a new silver Mo'Hair. I was considering one of those myself – they were better than wigs, they never came off – but some girls said the smell was like lamb chops, especially in the rain.

Savona was a little clumsy. She wasn't a trapeze girl, she was a pole girl, and she was top-heavy – she'd blown herself up like a beach ball.

Stick her on stilettos, breathe on her from behind, and she'd do a vertical face-plant. "Whatever works," she'd say. "And, baby, this works."

Now she was doing the upside-down splits move with the one-handed midstroke. She didn't convince me, but the men down there were never much interested in art: they'd think Savona was great unless she laughed instead of moaning, or actually fell off the trapeze.

I left the Snakepit and flipped through the other rooms, but nothing much was going on. No fetishists, nobody who wanted to be covered in feathers or slathered in porridge or strung up with velvet ropes or writhed on by guppies. Just the daily grind.

Then I called Amanda. We're each other's family; I guess when we were kids we were both stray puppies. It's a bond.

Amanda was in the Wisconsin desert, putting together one of the Bioart installations she's been doing now that she's into what she calls the art caper. It was cow bones this time. Wisconsin's covered with cow bones, ever since the big drought ten years ago when they'd found it cheaper to butcher the cows there rather than shipping them out – the ones that hadn't died on their own. She had a couple of fuel-cell front-end loaders and two illegal Tex-Mexican refugees she'd hired, and she was dragging the cow bones into a pattern so big it could only be seen from above: huge capital letters, spelling out a word. Later she'd cover it in pancake syrup and wait until the insect life was all over it, and then take videos of it from the air, to put into galleries. She liked to watch things move and grow and then disappear.

Amanda always got the money to do her art capers. She was kind of famous in the circles that went in for culture. They weren't big circles, but they were rich circles. This time she had a deal with a top CorpSeCorps guy – he'd get her up in the helicopter, to take the videos. "I traded Mr. Big for a whirly," was how she told me – we never said CorpSeCorps or helicopter on the phone, because they had robots listening in for special words like those.

Her Wisconsin thing was part of a series called The Living Word – she said for a joke that it was inspired by the Gardeners because they'd repressed us so much about writing things down. She'd begun with one-letter words – *I* and *A* and *O* – and then done two-letter words like *It*, and then three letters, and four, and five. Now she was up to six. They'd been written in all different materials, including fish guts and toxic-spill-killed birds and toilets from building demolition sites filled with used cooking oil and set on fire.

Her new word was *kaputt*. When she'd told me that earlier, she'd said she was sending a message.

"Who to?" I'd said. "The people who go to the galleries? The Mr. Rich and Bigs?"

"That's who," she'd said. "And the Mrs. Rich and Bigs. Them too."

"You'll get in trouble, Amanda."

"It's okay," she said. "They won't understand it."

The project was going fine, she said: it had rained, the desert flowers were in bloom, there were a lot of insects, which was good for when she'd pour on the syrup. She already had the *K* done, and she was halfway through the *A*. But the Tex-Mexicans were getting bored.

"That makes two of us," I said. "I can hardly wait to get out of here."

"Three," said Amanda. "There's two of them – the Tex-Mexicans. Plus you. Three."

"Oh. Right. You're looking great – that khaki outfit suits you." She was tall, she had that rangy girl-explorer look. A pith-helmet look.

"You're not bad yourself," said Amanda. "Ren, you take care."

"You take care too. Don't let the Tex-Mex guys jump you."

"They won't. They think I'm crazy. Crazy women cut your dong off."

"I didn't know that!" I was laughing. Amanda liked to make me laugh.

"Why would you?" said Amanda. "You're not crazy, you've never seen one of those things wriggling on the floor. Sweet dreams."

"Sweet dreams too," I said. But she'd clicked off.

I've lost track of the Saints' Days – I can't remember which one it is today – but I can count the years. I've used my eyebrow pencil on the wall to add up how long I've known Amanda. I've done it like those old cartoons of prisoners – four strokes and then one through them to make five.

It's been a long time – over fifteen years, ever since she came into the Gardeners. So many people from my earlier life were from there – Amanda, and Bernice, and Zeb; and Adam One, and Shackie, and Croze; and old Pilar; and Toby, of course. I wonder what they'd think of me – of what I ended up doing for a living. Some of them would be disappointed, like Adam One. Bernice would say I was backslidden and it served me right. Lucerne would say I'm a slut, and I'd say takes one to know one. Pilar would look at me wisely. Shackie and Croze would laugh. Toby would be mad at Scales. What about Zeb? I think he'd try to rescue me because it would be a challenge.

Amanda knows already. She doesn't judge. She says you trade what you have to. You don't always have choices.

12

When Lucerne and Zeb first took me away from the Exfernal World to live among the Gardeners, I didn't like it at all. They smiled a lot, but they scared me: they were so interested in doom, and enemies, and God. And they talked so much about Death. The Gardeners were strict about not killing Life, but on the other hand they said Death was a natural process, which was sort of a contradiction, now that I think about it. They had the idea that turning into compost would be just fine. Not everyone might think that having your body become part of a vulture was a terrific future to look forward to, but the Gardeners did. And when they'd start talking about the Waterless Flood that was going to kill everybody on Earth, except maybe them – that gave me nightmares.

None of it scared the real Gardener kids. They were used to it. They'd even make fun of it, or the older boys would – Shackie and Croze and their pals. "We're all gonna diiiiie," they'd say, making dead-person faces. "Hey, Ren. Want to do your bit for the Cycle of Life? Lie down in that dumpster, you can be the compost." "Hey, Ren. Want to be a maggot? Lick my cut!"

"Shut up," Bernice would say. "Or you're going into that dumpster yourself because I'm shoving you in!" Bernice was mean, and she stood her ground, and most kids would back off. Even the boys would. But then I'd owe Bernice, and I'd have to do what she said.

Shackie and Croze would tease me, though, when Bernice wasn't around to push back at them. They were slug-squeezers, they were beetle-eaters. They tried to gross you out. They were trouble – that's what Toby called them. I'd hear her saying to Rebecca, "Here comes trouble."

Shackie was the oldest; he was tall and skinny, and he had a spider tattoo on the inside of his arm that he'd punched in himself with a needle and some candle soot. Croze was a stumpier shape, with a round head and a missing side tooth, which he claimed had been knocked out in a street battle. They had a little brother whose name was Oates. They didn't have any parents; they'd had some once, but their father had gone off with Zeb on some special Adam trip and had never come back, and then their mother had left, telling Adam One she'd send for them when she'd got herself established. But she never had.

The Gardener school was in a different building from the Rooftop. It was called the Wellness Clinic because that's what used to be in there. It still had some leftover boxes full of gauze bandages, which the Gardeners were gleaning for crafts projects. It smelled of vinegar: across the hallway from the schoolrooms was the room the Gardeners used for their vinegar making.

The benches at the Wellness Clinic were hard; we sat in rows. We wrote on slates, and they had to be wiped off at the end of each day because the Gardeners said you couldn't leave words lying around where our enemies might find them. Anyway, paper was sinful because it was made from the flesh of trees.

We spent a lot of time memorizing things and chanting them out loud. The Gardener history, for instance – it went like this:

> *Year One, Garden just begun; Year Two, still new; Year Three, Pilar started bees; Year Four, Burt came in the door; Year Five, Toby snatched alive; Year Six, Katuro in the mix; Year Seven, Zeb came to our heaven.*

Year Seven should have said that I came too, and my mother, Lucerne, and anyway it wasn't heaven, but the Gardeners liked their chants to rhyme.

Year Eight, Nuala found her fate; Year Nine, Philo began to shine.

I wanted Year Ten to have Ren in it, but I didn't think it would.

The other things we had to memorize were harder. Mathematical and science things were the worst. We also had to memorize every saint's day, and every single day had at least one saint and sometimes more, or maybe a feast, which meant over four hundred of those. Plus what the saints had done to get to be saints. Some of them were easy. Saint Yossi Leshem of Barn Owls – well, it was obvious what the answer was. And Saint Dian Fossey, because the story was so sad, and Saint Shackleton, because it was heroic. But some of them were really hard. Who could remember Saint Bashir Alouse, or Saint Crick, or Podocarp Day? I always got Podocarp Day wrong because what was a Podocarp? It was an ancient kind of tree, but it sounded like a fish.

Our teachers were Nuala for the little kids and the Buds and Blooms Choir and Fabric Recycling, and Rebecca for Culinary Arts, which meant cooking, and Surya for Sewing, and Mugi for Mental Arithmetic, and Pilar for Bees and Mycology, and Toby for Holistic Healing with Plant Remedies, and Burt for Wild and Garden Botanicals, and Philo for Meditation, and Zeb for Predator-Prey Relationships and Animal Camouflage. There were some other teachers – when we were thirteen, we'd get Katuro for Emergency Medical and Marushka Midwife for the Human Reproductive System, whereas all we'd had so far was Frog Ovaries – but those were the main ones.

The Gardener kids had nicknames for all of the teachers. Pilar was the Fungus, Zeb was the Mad Adam, Stuart was the Screw because he built the furniture. Mugi was the Muscle, Marushka was the Mucous, Rebecca was the Salt and Peppler, Burt was the Knob because he was bald. Toby was the Dry Witch. Witch because she was always mixing things up and pouring them into bottles and Dry because she was so thin and hard, and to tell her apart from Nuala, who was the Wet Witch because of her damp mouth and her wobbly bum, and because you could make her cry so easily.

In addition to the learning chants, the Gardener kids had rude ones they made up themselves. They'd chant softly – Shackleton and Crozier and the older boys would start, but then we'd all join in:

Wet Witch, Wet Witch,
Big fat slobbery bitch,
Sell her to the butcher, make yourself rich,
Eat her in a sausage, Wet Wet Witch!

It was especially bad about the butcher and the sausage, because meat of any kind was obscene as far as the Gardeners were concerned. "Stop that," Nuala would say, but then she'd sniffle, and the older boys would give each other a thumbs-up.

We could never make Dry Witch Toby cry. The boys said she was a hardass – she and Rebecca were the two hardest asses. Rebecca was jolly on the outside, but you did not push her buttons. As for Toby, she was leathery inside and out. "Don't try it, Shackleton," she would say, even though her back was turned. Nuala was too kind to us, but Toby held us to account, and we trusted Toby more: you'd trust a rock more than a cake.

13

I lived with Lucerne and Zeb in a building about five blocks from the Garden. It was called the Cheese Factory because that's what it used to be, and it still had a faint cheesy smell to it. After the cheese it was used for artists' lofts, but there weren't any artists left, and nobody seemed to know who owned it. Meanwhile the Gardeners had taken it over. They liked living in places where they didn't have to pay rent.

Our space was a big room, with some cubicles curtained off – one for me, one for Lucerne and Zeb, one for the violet biolet, one for the shower. The cubicle curtains were woven of plastic-bag strips and duct tape, and they weren't in any way soundproof. This wasn't great, especially when it came to the violet biolet. The Gardeners said digestion was holy and there was nothing funny or terrible about the smells and noises that were part of the end product of the nutritional process, but at our place those end products were hard to ignore.

We ate our meals in the main room, on a table made out of a door. All of our dishes and pots and pans were salvaged – gleaned, as the Gardeners said – except for some of the thicker plates and mugs. Those had been made by the Gardeners back in their Ceramics period, before they'd decided that kilns used up too much energy.

I slept on a futon stuffed with husks and straw. It had a quilt sewed out of blue jeans and used bathmats, and every morning I had to make the bed first thing, because the Gardeners liked neatly made beds, though they weren't squeamish about what they were made of. Then I'd take my clothes down from the nail on the wall and put them on. I got clean ones every seventh day: the Gardeners didn't believe in wasting water and soap on too much washing. My clothes were always dank, because of the humidity and because the Gardeners didn't believe in dryers. "God made the sun for a reason," Nuala used to say, and according to her that reason was for drying our clothes.

Lucerne would still be in bed, it being her favourite place. Back when we'd lived at HelthWyzer with my real father she'd hardly ever stayed inside our house, but here she almost never went out of it, except to go over to the Rooftop or the Wellness Clinic and help the other Gardener women peel burdock roots or make those lumpy quilts or weave those plastic-bag curtains or something.

Zeb would be in the shower: *No daily showers* was one of the many Gardener rules Zeb ignored. Our shower water came down a garden hose out of a rain barrel and was gravity-fed, so no energy was used. That was Zeb's reason for making an exception for himself. He'd be singing:

Nobody gives a hoot,
Nobody gives a hoot,
And that is why we're down the chute,
Cause nobody gives a hoot!

All his shower songs were negative in this way, though he sang them cheerfully, in his big Russian-bear voice.

I had mixed feelings about Zeb. He could be frightening, but also it was reassuring to have someone so important in my family. Zeb was an Adam – a leading Adam. You could tell by the way the others looked up to him. He was large and solid, with a biker's beard and long hair – brown with a little grey in it – and a leathery face, and eyebrows like a barbed-wire fence. He looked as if he ought to have a silver tooth and a tattoo, but he didn't. He was strong as a bouncer, and he had the same menacing but genial expression, as if he'd break your neck if necessary, but not for fun.

Sometimes he'd play dominoes with me. The Gardeners were skimpy on toys – *Nature is our playground* – and the only toys they approved of were sewed out of leftover fabric or knitted with saved-up string, or they'd be wrinkly old-person figures with heads fashioned from dried crabapples. But they allowed dominoes, because they carved the sets themselves. When I won, Zeb would laugh and say, "Atta girl," and then I'd get a warm feeling, like nasturtiums.

Lucerne was always telling me to be nice to him, because although he wasn't my real father he was *like* my real father, and it hurt his feelings if I was rude to him. But then she didn't like it much when Zeb was nice to me. So it was hard to know how to act.

While Zeb was singing in the shower I'd get myself something to eat – dry soybits or maybe a vegetable patty left over from dinner. Lucerne was a fairly terrible cook. Then I'd go off to school. I was usually still hungry, but I could count on a school lunch. It wouldn't be great, but it would be food. As Adam One used to say, Hunger is the best sauce.

I couldn't remember ever being hungry at the HelthWyzer Compound. I really wanted to go back there. I wanted my real father, who must still love me: if he'd known where I was, he'd surely have come to take me back. I wanted my real house, with my own room and the bed with pink bed curtains and the closet full of different clothes in it. But most of all I wanted my mother to be the way she used to be, when she'd take me shopping, or go to the Club to play golf, or off to the AnooYoo Spa to get improvements done to herself, and then she'd come back smelling nice. But if I mentioned anything about our old life, she'd say all that was in the past.

She had a lot of reasons for running off with Zeb to join the Gardeners. She'd say their way was best for humankind, and for all the other creatures on Earth as well, and she'd acted out of love, not only for Zeb but for me, because she wanted the world to be healed so life wouldn't die out completely, and didn't it make me happy to know that?

She herself didn't seem all that happy. She'd sit at the table brushing her hair, staring at herself in our one small mirror with an expression that was glum, or critical, or maybe tragic. She had long hair like all the Gardener women, and the brushing and the braiding and the pinning up was a big job. On bad days she'd go through the whole thing four or five times.

On the days when Zeb was away, she'd barely talk to me. Or she'd act as if I'd hidden him. "When did you last see him?" she'd say. "Was he at school?" It was like she wanted me to spy on him. Then she'd be apologetic and say, "How are you feeling?" as if she'd done something wrong to me.

When I'd answer, she wouldn't be listening. Instead she'd be listening for Zeb. She'd get more and more anxious, even angry; she'd pace around and look out our window, talking to herself about how badly he treated her; but when he'd finally turn up, she'd fall all over him. Then she'd start nagging – where had he been, who had he been with, why hadn't he come back sooner? He'd just shrug and say, "It's okay, babe, I'm here now. You worry too much."

Then the two of them would disappear behind their plastic-strip and duct-tape curtain, and my mother would make pained and abject noises I found mortifying. I hated her then, because she had no pride and no restraint. It was like she was running down the middle of the mallway with no clothes on. Why did she worship Zeb so much?

Now I can see how that can happen. You can fall in love with anybody – a fool, a criminal, a nothing. There are no good rules.

The other thing I disliked so much at the Gardeners was the clothes. The Gardeners themselves were all colours, but their clothes weren't. If Nature was beautiful, as the Adams and the Eves claimed – if the lilies of the field were our models – why couldn't we look more like butterflies and less like parking lots? We were so flat, so plain, so scrubbed, so dark.

The street kids – the pleebrats – were hardly rich, but they were glittery. I envied the shiny things, the shimmering things, like the TV camera phones, pink and purple and silver, that flashed in and out of their hands like magician's cards, or the Sea/H/Ear Candies they stuck into their ears to hear music. I wanted their gaudy freedom.

We were forbidden to make friends with the pleebrats, and on their part they treated us like pariahs, holding their noses and yelling, or throwing things at us. The Adams and the Eves said we were being persecuted for our faith, but it was most likely for our wardrobes: the pleebrats were very fashion-conscious and wore the best clothes they could trade or steal. So we couldn't mingle with them, but we could eavesdrop. We got their knowledge that way – we caught it like germs. We gazed at that forbidden worldly life as if through a chain-link fence.

Once I found a beautiful camera phone, lying on the sidewalk. It was muddy and the signal was dead, but I took it home anyway, and the Eves caught me with it. "Don't you know any better?" they said. "Such a thing can hurt you! It can burn your brain! Don't even look at it: if you can see it, it can see you."

14

I first met Amanda in Year Ten, when I was ten: I was always the same age as the Year, so it's easy to remember when it was.

That day was Saint Farley of Wolves – a Young Bioneer scavenging day, when we had to tie sucky green bandanas around our necks and go out gleaning for the Gardeners' recycled-materials crafts. Sometimes we collected soap ends, carrying wicker baskets and making the rounds of the good hotels and restaurants because they threw out soap by the shovelful. The best hotels were in the rich pleebs – Fernside, Golfgreens, and the richest of all, SolarSpace – and we'd hitch rides to them, even though it was forbidden. The Gardeners were like that: they'd tell you to do something and then prohibit the easiest way to do it.

Rose-scented soap was the best. Bernice and me would take some home, and I'd keep mine in my pillowcase, to drown out the mildew smell of my damp quilt. We'd take the rest to the Gardeners, to be simmered into a jelly in the black-box solarcookers on the Rooftop, then cooled and cut up into slabs. The Gardeners used a lot of soap, because they were so worried about microbes, but some of the cut-up soaps would be set aside. They'd be rolled up in leaves and have strands of twisted grass tied around them, to be sold to tourists and gawkers at the Gardeners' Tree of Life Natural Materials Exchange, along with the bags of worms and the organic turnips and zucchinis and the other vegetables the Gardeners hadn't used up themselves.

⁙

That day wasn't a soap day, it was a vinegar day. We'd go to the back entrances of the bars and nightclubs and strip joints and pick through their dump boxes, and find any leftover wine, and pour it into our Young Bioneer enamel pails. Then we'd lug it off to the Wellness Clinic building, where it would be poured into the huge barrels in the Vinegar Room and fermented into vinegar, which the Gardeners used for household cleaning. The extra was decanted into the small bottles we'd gather up during our gleaning, which would have Gardeners labels glued onto them. Then they'd be offered for sale at the Tree of Life, along with the soap.

Our Young Bioneer work was supposed to teach us some useful lessons. For instance: Nothing should be carelessly thrown away, not even wine from sinful places. There was no such thing as garbage, trash, or dirt, only matter that hadn't been put to a proper use. And, most importantly, everyone, including children, had to contribute to the life of the community.

Shackie and Croze and the older boys sometimes drank their wine instead of saving it. If they drank too much, they'd fall down or throw up, or they'd get into fights with the pleebrats and throw stones at the winos. In revenge, the winos would pee into empty wine bottles to see if they could trick us. I never drank any piss myself: all you had to do was smell the opening of the bottle. But some kids had deadened their noses by smoking the butt ends of cigarettes or cigars, or even skunkweed if they could get it, and they'd upend the bottle, then spit and swear. Though maybe those kids drank from the peed-in bottles on purpose, to give themselves an excuse for the swearing, which was forbidden by the Gardeners.

As soon as they were out of sight of the Garden, Shackie and Croze and those boys would take off their Young Bioneer bandanas and tie them around their heads, like the Asian Fusions. They wanted to be a street gang too – they even had a password. "Gang!" they'd say, and the other person was supposed to say, "Grene." So, gangrene. The "gang" part was because they were a gang, and the "grene" stood for "green," like their head scarves. It was supposed to be a secret thing just for their gang members, but we all knew about it anyway. Bernice said it was a really good password for them, because gangrene was flesh rot and they were totally rotten.

"Big joke, Bernice," said Crozier. "P.S., you're ugly."

We were supposed to glean in groups, so we could defend ourselves against the pleebrat street gangs, or the winos who might grab our pails and drink the wine, or the child-snatchers who might sell us on the chicken-sex market. But instead we'd break up in twos or threes because that way we could cover the territory faster.

On this particular day I started out with Bernice, but then we had a fight. We squabbled constantly, which I took as a sign of our friendship because no matter how viciously we fought we'd always make up afterwards. Some bond held us together: not hard like bone, but slippery, like cartilage. Most likely we both felt insecure among the Gardener kids; we were each afraid to be left without an ally.

This time our fight was over a beaded change purse with a starfish on it that we'd picked out of a trash pile. We coveted finds like that and were always looking for them. The pleeblanders threw a lot of stuff away, because – said the Adams and Eves – they had short attention spans and no morals.

"I saw it first," I said.

"You saw it first last time," said Bernice.

"So what? I still saw it first!"

"Your mother's a skank," said Bernice. That was unfair because I thought so myself and Bernice knew it.

"Yours is a vegetable!" I said. "Vegetable" shouldn't have been an insult among the Gardeners, but it was. "Veena the Vegetable!" I added.

"Meat-breath!" said Bernice. She had the purse, and she was keeping it.

"Fine!" I said. I turned and walked away. I loitered, but I didn't look around, and Bernice didn't hurry after me.

This happened at the mallway, which was called Apple Corners. This was the official name of our pleeb, though everyone called it the Sinkhole because people vanished into it without a trace. We Gardener kids walked through the mallway whenever we could, just looking.

Like everything else in our pleeb, this mallway had once been classier. There was a broken fountain full of empty beer cans, there were built-in planters with a lot of Zizzy Froot cans and cigarette butts and used condoms covered (said Nuala) in festering germs. There was a holospinner booth that must once have spun out suns and moons, and rare animals, and your own image if you put money in, but it had been trashed some time ago and now stood empty-eyed. Sometimes we went inside it and pulled the tattered star-sprinkled curtain across, and read the messages left on the walls by the pleebrats. *Monica sucks. So does Darf only betr. UR $? 4 U free, baBc8s! Brad UR ded.* Those pleebrats were so daring, they'd write anywhere or anything. They didn't care who saw it.

The Sinkhole pleebrats went into the holospinner to smoke dope – the booth reeked of it – and they had sex in there: we could tell because of the condoms and sometimes the panties they'd leave behind. Gardener kids weren't supposed to do either one of those things – hallucinogenics were for religious purposes, and sex was for those who'd exchanged green leaves and jumped the bonfire – but the older Gardener kids said they'd done them anyway.

The shops that weren't boarded up were twenty-dollar stores called Tinsel's and Wild Side and Bong's – names like that. They sold feather hats, and crayons for drawing on your body, and T-shirts with dragons and skulls and mean slogans. Also Joltbars, and chewing gum that made your tongue glow in the dark, and red-lipped ashtrays that said, Let Me Blow It For You, and In-Your-Skin Etcha-Tattoos the Eves said would burn your skin down to the veins. You could find expensive stuff at bargain prices that Shackie said were boosted from the SolarSpace boutiques.

Tawdry rubbish, all of it, the Eves would say. If you're going to sell your soul, at least demand a higher price! Bernice and I paid no attention to that. Our souls didn't interest us. We'd peer in the windows, giddy with wanting. *What would you get?* we'd say. *The LED-light wand? That's baby! The Blood and Roses video? Gross, that's for boys! The Real Woman Stick-on Bimplants, with responsive nipples? Ren, you suck!*

After Bernice had left that day, I wasn't sure what to do. I thought maybe I should just go back, because I didn't feel too safe, alone. Then I saw Amanda, standing on the other side of the mallway with a group of Tex-Mexican pleeb girls. I knew that group by sight, and Amanda had never been with them before.

Those girls were wearing the sort of clothes they usually wore: miniskirts and spangled tops, candyfloss boas around their necks, silver gloves, plasticized butterflies clipped into their hair. They had their Sea/H/Ear Candies and their burning-bright phones and their jellyfish bracelets, and they were showing off. They were playing the same tune on their Sea/H/Ear Candies and they were dancing to it, swivelling their bums, sticking out their chests. They looked as if they already owned everything from every single store and were bored with it. I envied that look so much. I just stood there, envying.

Amanda was dancing too, except she was better. After a while she stopped and stood a little apart, texting on her purple phone. Then she stared straight at me and smiled, and waved her silver fingers. That meant *Come here.*

I checked that no one was looking. Then I crossed the mallway.

15

"You want to see my jellyfish bracelet?" Amanda said once I got there. I must have seemed pathetic to her, with my orphanish clothes and chalky fingers. She held up her wrist: there were the tiny jellyfish, opening and closing themselves like swimming flowers. They looked so perfect.

"Where did you get it?" I asked. I hardly knew what to say.

"Lifted," said Amanda. That was how the pleebrat girls mostly got things.

"How do they stay alive in there?"

She pointed to the silver knob where the bracelet fastened. "This is an aerator," she said. "It pumps in oxygen. You add the food twice a week."

"What happens if you forget?"

"They eat each other," said Amanda. She gave a little smile. "Some kids do that on purpose, they don't add the food. Then it's like a miniwar in there, and after a while there's just one jellyfish left, and then it dies."

"That's horrible," I said.

Amanda kept the same smile. "Yeah. That's why they do it."

"They're really pretty," I said in a neutral voice. I wanted to please her, and I couldn't tell whether she thought *horrible* was good or bad.

"Take it," said Amanda. She held out her wrist. "I can lift another one."

I wanted that bracelet so badly, but I wouldn't know how to buy the food and the jellyfish would die. Or else the bracelet would be discovered, no matter how well I hid it, and I'd be in trouble. "I can't," I said. I took a step back.

"You're one of *them*, aren't you?" said Amanda. She wasn't taunting, she seemed merely curious. "The Goddies. The Godawfuls. They say there's a bunch of them around here."

"No," I said, "I'm not." The lie must have stood out all over me. There were a lot of shabby people in the Sinkhole pleeb, but they weren't shabby on purpose the way the Gardeners were.

Amanda tilted her head a little to one side. "Funny," she said. "You look like them."

"I only live with them," I said. "I'm just more or less visiting them. I'm not really like them at all."

"Of course you aren't," said Amanda, smiling. She gave my arm a little pat. "Come over here. I want to show you something."

Where she took me was the alleyway that led to the back of Scales and Tails. We Gardener kids weren't supposed to go there, but we did anyway because when we were collecting you could get a lot of vinegar wine if you were early enough to beat out the winos.

That alleyway was dangerous. Scales and Tails was a dirt den, said the Eves. We should never, ever go into it, especially not girls. It said, ADULT ENTERTAINMENT in neon over the door, which was guarded at night by two enormous men in black suits who wore sunglasses even though it was dark. One of the older Gardener girls claimed these men had said to her, "Come back in a year and bring your sweet little ass." But Bernice said she was just bragging.

Scales had pictures on either side of the entrance – light-up holophotos. The pictures were of beautiful girls covered completely with shining green scales, like lizards, except for the hair. One of them was standing on a single leg with the other leg hooked around her neck. I thought that it must hurt to stand like that, but the girl in the picture was smiling.

Did the scales grow or were they were pasted on? Bernice and I disagreed about that. I said they were pasted, Bernice said they grew because the girls had been operated on, like getting bimplants. I told Bernice that was nuts because nobody would have such an operation. But secretly I sort of believed her.

One day we'd seen a scaly girl running down the street in daytime, with a black-suited man chasing her. She sparkled a lot because of her shiny green scales; she'd kicked off her high heels and she was running in her bare feet, dodging in and out among the people, but then she hit a patch of broken glass and fell. The man caught up with her and scooped her up, and carried her back to Scales with her green snakeskin arms dangling down. Her feet were bleeding. Whenever I thought of that, a chill went all through me, like watching someone else cut their finger.

At the back of the alleyway beside Scales there was a small square yard where the trash bins were kept – the ones for the carbon garboil trash and the other kind. Then there was a board fence, and on the other side of it there was a vacant lot where a building had burned down. Now it was just hard earth with pieces of cement and charred wood and broken glass, and weeds growing on it.

Sometimes the pleebrats hung out around there, and they'd jump us when we were emptying the wine bottles. They'd yell, "Goddie, goddie, stinky body" and snatch the pails and run off with them or empty them onto us. That happened to Bernice once and she reeked of wine for days.

Sometimes we went into that vacant lot with Zeb on our Outdoor Classroom days: he said it was the closest thing to a meadow we'd ever find in our pleeb. When he was with us, the pleebland kids didn't bother us. Zeb was like having your own private tiger: tame to you, savage to everyone else.

Once, we found a dead girl there. She didn't have any hair or clothes: she only had a few green scales left clinging to her. *Pasted on*, I thought. *Or something. Anyway, not growing. So I was right.*

"Maybe she's sunbathing," said one of the older boys, and the rest of them snickered.

"Don't touch her," said Zeb. "Have some respect! We'll have our lesson on the Rooftop Garden today." When we came back for our next Outdoor Classroom, she was gone.

"I bet she's carbon garboil," Bernice whispered to me. Carbon garboil was made from any sort of carbon garbage – slaughterhouse refuse, old vegetables, restaurant tossout, even plastic bottles. The carbs went into a boiler, and oil and water came out, plus anything metal. Officially you couldn't put in human corpses, but the kids made jokes about that. Oil, water, and shirt buttons. Oil, water, and gold pen nibs.

"Oil, water, and green scales," I whispered to Bernice.

At first glance the vacant lot was empty. No winos, no pleebrats, no dead naked women. Amanda led me over to the far corner, where there was a flat slab of concrete. A syrup bottle was leaning against it, the squeeze kind.

"Look at this," she said. She'd written her name in syrup on the slab, and a stream of ants was feeding on the letters, so that each letter had an edging of black ants. That was how I first learned Amanda's name – I saw it written in ants. Amanda Payne.

"Cool, huh?" she said. "Want to write your own name?"

"Why are you doing that?" I said.

"It's neat," said Amanda. "You write things, then they eat your writing. So you appear, then you disappear. That way no one can find you."

Why did this make sense to me? I don't know, but it did. "Where do you live?" I asked.

"Oh, around," said Amanda carelessly. That meant she didn't really live anywhere: she was sleeping in a squat somewhere, or worse. "I used to live in Texas," she added.

So she was a refugee. A lot of Texas refugees had turned up after the hurricanes and then the droughts. They were mostly illegal. Now I could see why Amanda would be so interested in disappearing.

"You can come and live with me," I said. I hadn't planned that, it just came out of my mouth.

At that moment Bernice squeezed through the gap in the fence. She'd relented, she'd returned to collect me, except now I didn't want her.

"Ren! What're you *doing*!" she yelled. She came clomping across the vacant lot in that purposeful way she had. I found myself thinking she had big feet, and her body was too square and her nose too small, and her neck ought to be longer and thinner. More like Amanda's.

"Here comes a friend of yours, I guess," said Amanda, smiling. I felt like saying, *She's not my friend*, but I wasn't brave enough to be that treacherous.

Bernice came up to us, red-faced. She always got red when she was mad. "Come on, Ren," she said. "You're not supposed to talk to her." She spotted Amanda's jellyfish bracelet, and I could tell she wanted it as much as I did. "You're evil," she said to Amanda. "Pleebrat!" She stuck her arm through mine.

"This is Amanda," I said. "She's coming to live with me."

I thought Bernice would fly into one of her rages. But I was giving her my stony-eyed stare, the one that said I wasn't going to give in. She'd risk losing face in front of a stranger if she pushed too hard, so instead she gave me a silent, calculating look. "Okay then," she said. "She can help carry the vinegar wine."

"Amanda knows how to steal things," I said to Bernice as we trudged back to the Wellness Clinic. I meant this as a peace offering, but Bernice only grunted.

16

I knew I couldn't really take Amanda home with me like a stray kitten: Lucerne would've told me to put her back where I found her, because Amanda was a pleebrat and Lucerne hated pleebrats. According to her they were ruined children, thieves and liars all, and once a child had been ruined it was like a wild dog, it could never be trained or trusted. She was afraid to walk along the street from one Gardener place to another because of the pleebrat gangs that could swarm you and run off with anything they could grab. She never learned about picking up stones and hitting back and yelling. It was because of her earlier life. She was a hothouse flower: that's what Zeb called her. I used to think this was a compliment, because of the word *flower.*

So Amanda would be sent packing, unless I got Adam One's permission first. He loved people joining the Gardeners, especially kids – he was always going on about how the Gardeners should mould young minds. If he said Amanda should live with us, Lucerne wouldn't be able to say no.

The three of us found Adam One at the Wellness Clinic, helping to bottle the vinegar. I explained that I'd picked up Amanda – "gleaned" her, I said – and that she wished to join us, having seen the Light, and could she live at my house?

"Is that true, my child?" Adam One asked Amanda. The other Gardeners had stopped work and were eyeing Amanda's miniskirt and silver fingers.

"Yes, sir," said Amanda in a respectful voice.

"She'll be a bad influence on Ren," said Nuala, who had come over. "Ren is too easily led. We should place her with Bernice."

Bernice gave me a triumphant look: *See what you've done!* "That would be fine," she said neutrally.

"No!" I said. "I found her!" Bernice glared at me. Amanda said nothing.

Adam One considered the three of us. He knew a lot of things. "Perhaps Amanda herself should decide," he said. "She should meet the families in question. That will help to settle the matter. That would be fairest, no?"

"My place first," said Bernice.

Bernice lived in the Buenavista Condos. The Gardeners didn't exactly own the building, because ownership was wrong, but somehow they controlled it. It had "Luxury Lofts for Today's Singles" on it in faded gold lettering, but I knew it wasn't Luxury: the shower in Bernice's apartment was clogged, the tiles in the kitchen were cracked and gap-toothed, the ceilings oozed when it rained, the bathroom was slick with mildew.

The three of us went into the lobby, past the middle-aged Gardener lady on security duty there – she was busy with some snarled-up macramé craft object and hardly noticed us. We had to climb six flights of stairs to get to Bernice's floor because the Gardeners didn't believe in elevators except for old people and paraplegics. There were forbidden objects in the stairwell – needles, used condoms, spoons, candle ends. The Gardeners said pleeb crooks and thugs and pimps got in at night and used the stairwell for nasty parties; we'd never seen any of these, though we'd once caught Shackie and Croze and their pals drinking wine dregs in there.

Bernice had her own plastikey; she unlocked the door and let us in. The apartment smelled like unwashed clothes left under a dripping sink, or like other kids' plugged sinuses, or like diapers. Through these odours drifted another one – a rich, fertile, spicy, earthy aroma. Maybe it was wafting up through the hot-air vents from the Gardener mushroom beds in the basement.

But this smell – all the smells – seemed to be coming from Bernice's mother, Veena, who was sitting on the worn plush-covered sofa as if rooted there, staring at the wall. She had on her usual shapeless dress; her knees were covered with an old yellow baby blanket; her pale hair hung limply on either side of her round, soft, whitish face; her hands lay curled slackly, as if her fingers were broken. On the floor in front of her was a scattering of dirty plates. Veena didn't cook: she ate what Bernice's father gave her; or else she didn't eat it. But she never tidied up. She hardly ever spoke, and she didn't speak now. Her eyes flickered as we went past her though, so maybe she saw us.

"What's the matter with her?" Amanda whispered to me.

"She's Fallow," I whispered back.

"Yeah?" Amanda whispered. "She just looks really stoned."

My own mother said Bernice's mother was "depressed." But my mother wasn't a real Gardener, as Bernice was always telling me, because a real Gardener would never say *depressed*. The Gardeners believed that people who acted like Veena were in a Fallow state – resting, retreating into themselves to gain Spiritual insight, gathering their energy for the moment when they would burst out again like buds in spring. They only appeared to be doing nothing. Some Gardeners could remain in a Fallow state for a very long time.

"This is my place," said Bernice.

"Where would I sleep?" said Amanda.

We were looking at Bernice's room when Burt the Knob came in. "Where's my little girl?" he called.

"Don't answer," said Bernice. "Close the door!" We could hear him moving around in the main room; then he came into Bernice's room and scooped her up. He stood there holding her under the armpits. "Where's my little girl?" he said again, which made me cringe. I'd seen him do this before, not only to Bernice. He just loved girls' armpits. He'd corner you in behind the bean rows when you were doing slug and snail relocation and pretend to be helping you. Then along would come the hands. He was such a knob.

Bernice was scowling and wriggling. "I'm not your little girl," she said, which could mean: *I'm not little*, or *I'm not yours*, or even *I'm not a girl*. Burt took this as a joke.

"Then where's my little girl gone?" he repeated in a woebegone voice.

"Put me down," Bernice shouted. I felt sorry for her, and also I felt lucky – because whatever I felt about Zeb, it wasn't embarrassment.

"I'd like to look at your place now," said Amanda. So the two of us went back down the stairs, leaving Bernice behind us, redder and angrier than ever. I did feel bad about that, but not bad enough to give up Amanda.

Lucerne wasn't pleased to find that Amanda had been added to our family, but I told her that Adam One had ordered it; so what could she do? "She'll have to sleep in your room," she said crossly.

"She won't mind," I said. "Will you, Amanda?"

"No, indeed," said Amanda. She had a very polite manner she could put on, as if she was the one doing you the favour. It grated on Lucerne.

"And she'll have to get rid of those flashy clothes," said Lucerne.

"But they aren't worn out yet," I said innocently. "We can't just throw them away! That would be wasteful!"

"We'll sell them," said Lucerne tightly. "We can certainly use the money."

"Amanda should get the money," I said. "They're her clothes."

"It's okay," said Amanda, softly but regally. "They didn't cost me anything." Then we went into my cubicle and sat on the bed, and laughed behind our hands.

When Zeb got back that evening, he had no comment at first. We all ate dinner together, and Zeb chewed away at the soybit and green bean casserole and watched Amanda with her graceful neck and silver fingers picking daintily away at what was on her plate. She hadn't yet taken off her gloves. Finally he said to her, "You're a sly little operator, aren't you?" It was his friendly voice, the one he used for saying, "Atta girl" at dominoes.

Lucerne, who was dishing him out a second helping, stiffened in mid-motion, the big spoon straight up in the air like some kind of metal detector. Amanda gazed at him straight-faced, with her eyes wide open. "Excuse me, sir?"

Zeb laughed. "You're very good," he said.

17

Having Amanda living with me was like having a sister, only better. She had Gardeners' clothing now, so she looked like the rest of us; and pretty soon she smelled like the rest of us too.

In the first week I showed her all around. I took her to the Vinegar Room, the Sewing Room, and up to the Run-For-Your-Light Treadmills gym. Mugi was in charge of that; we called him Mugi the Muscle because he only had one muscle left. Amanda made friends with him, though. She made friends with everyone by asking them the right way to do things.

Burt the Knob explained how to relocate the slugs and snails in the Garden by heaving them over the railing into the traffic, where they were supposed to crawl off and find new homes, though I knew they really got squashed. Katuro the Wrench, who fixed the leaks and took care of the water systems, showed her how the plumbing worked.

Philo the Fog didn't say much to her; he just smiled at her a lot. The older Gardeners said he'd transcended language and was travelling with the Spirit, though Amanda said he was just wasted. Stuart the Screw, who made our furniture out of recycled junk, didn't like people much, but he liked Amanda. "That girl's got a good eye for wood," he'd say.

Amanda didn't like sewing, but she pretended to, so Surya praised her. Rebecca called her *sweetheart* and said she had good food taste, and Nuala cooed over her singing in the Buds and Blooms Choir. Even Dry Witch Toby would brighten up when she saw Amanda coming. She was the hardest nut to crack, but Amanda took a sudden interest in mushrooms, and helped old Pilar stamp bees on the honey labels, and that pleased Toby, though she tried not to show it.

"Why are you sucking up so much?" I asked Amanda.

"It's how you find stuff out," she said.

We told each other a lot of things. I told her about my father and my house in the HelthWyzer Compound, and how my mother ran off with Zeb.

"I bet she had hot panties for him," said Amanda. We were whispering all of this in our cubicle, at night, with Zeb and Lucerne right nearby, so it was hard not to hear the sex noises they'd make. Before Amanda came I'd found all of that shameful, but now found it funny because Amanda did.

Amanda told me about the droughts in Texas – how her parents had lost their Happicuppa coffee franchise and couldn't sell their house because no one would buy it, and how there were no jobs and they'd ended up in a refugee camp with old trailers and a lot of Tex-Mexicans. Then their trailer was demolished in one of the hurricanes and her father was killed by a piece of flying metal. A lot of people drowned, but she and her mother held on to a tree and got rescued by some men in a rowboat. They were thieves, said Amanda, looking for stuff they could lift, but they said they'd take Amanda and her mother to dry land and a shelter if they'd do a trade.

"What kind of trade?" I said.

"Just a trade," said Amanda.

The shelter was a football stadium with tents in it. There was a lot of trading going on: people would do anything for twenty dollars, Amanda said. Then her mother got sick from the drinking water, but Amanda didn't because she traded for sodas. And there was no medicine, so her mother died. "A lot of people shat to death," said Amanda. "You should have smelled that place."

Amanda snuck away after that because more people were getting sick and no one was taking away the crap and garbage or bringing food. She changed her name, because she didn't want to be put back in the football stadium: the refugees were supposed to be farmed out to work in whatever job they were told to. "No free lunch," people were saying: you had to pay for everything, one way or another.

"What did you change it from?" I asked her. "Your name."

"It was a white-trash name. Barb Jones," said Amanda. "That was my identity. But I don't have an identity now. So I'm invisible." It was one more thing I could admire about her – her invisibility.

Amanda walked north, along with thousands of other people. "I tried to hitch, but I only got one lift, with a guy who said he was a chicken farmer," she said. "He pushed his hand between my legs; you can tell that's coming when they breathe funny. I stuck my thumbs in his eyes and got out of there fast." She made it sound like thumbs in the eyes was normal in the Exfernal World. I wanted to learn how to do it, but I didn't think I could work up the nerve.

"Then I had to get past the Wall," she said.

"What wall?"

"Don't you watch the news? The Wall they're building to keep the Tex refugees out, because just the fence wasn't enough. There's men with sprayguns – it's a CorpSeCorps wall. But they can't patrol every inch – the Tex-Mex kids know all the tunnels, they helped me get through."

"You could've been shot," I said. "Then what?"

"Then I worked my way up here. For food and stuff. It took a while."

In her place I would have just laid down in a ditch and cried myself to death. But Amanda says if there's something you really want, you can figure out a way to get it. She says being discouraged is a waste of time.

I worried that there might be trouble with the other Gardener kids: after all, Amanda was a pleebrat – one of our enemies. Bernice hated her, of course, but she didn't dare say so because like everyone else she was in awe of her. First of all, no Gardener kid could dance, and Amanda had excellent moves – it was like her hips were dislocated. She'd teach me when Lucerne and Zeb weren't there. We'd get the music off her purple phone, which she kept hidden in our mattress, and when the card was used up she'd lift another one. She had some flashy pleeblander clothes hidden away as well, so when she needed to lift something she'd put those clothes on and go off to the Sinkhole mallway.

I could see that Shackleton and Crozier and the older boys were in love with her. She was very pretty, with her tawny skin and her long neck and her big eyes, but you could be pretty and still get called a carrot-sucker or a meat-hole on legs by those boys; they had a bunch of sick names for girls.

Not for Amanda, though: she had their respect. She had a piece of glass with duct tape along one edge to hold it with, and she said this glass had saved her life more than once. She showed us how to ram a guy in the crotch or trip him up and then kick him under the chin and break his neck. There were lots of tricks like that, she said – ones you could use if you had to.

But on Festival days or at Buds and Blooms Choir practice, no one was as pious as her. You'd think she'd been washed in milk.

THE FESTIVAL OF ARKS

THE FESTIVAL OF ARKS

YEAR TEN.

OF THE TWO FLOODS AND THE TWO COVENANTS.

SPOKEN BY ADAM ONE.

Dear Friends and Fellow Mortals:

Today the Children have built their little Arks and launched them on the Arboretum Creek to carry their messages of respect for God's Creatures to other children who may happen to find them on the seashore. In an increasingly endangered world, what a caring act that is! Let us remember: It is better to hope than to mope!

This evening we will share a special Festival meal – Rebecca's delicious lentil soup, representing the First Flood, with Noah's Ark dumplings stuffed with vegetable Animal forms. One of those dumplings contains a turnip Noah, and whoever finds that Noah will get a special prize – thus teaching us not to gobble our food in a heedless manner.

That prize is a picture painted by Nuala, our talented Eve Nine: Saint Brendan the Voyager, shown with the essential items we must include in our Ararat storerooms in preparation for the Waterless Flood. In this artwork, Nuala has given the tinned soydines and the soybits their due prominence. But let us remind ourselves to refresh our Ararats regularly. You wouldn't want to open that tin of soydines on the day of need and find that the contents have gone bad.

Burt's worthy wife, Veena, is in a Fallow state and cannot be with us for this Festival, but we look forward to welcoming her among us very soon.

Now let us turn to our Devotion for the Festival of Arks.

On this day we mourn, but we also rejoice. We mourn the deaths of all those Creatures of the land that were destroyed in the First Flood of extinctions – whenever those occurred – but we rejoice that the Fishes and Whales, and the Corals, and the Sea Turtles and the Dolphins, and the Sea Urchins, yea, also the Sharks – we rejoice that they were spared, unless a change in ocean temperature and salinity caused by the great downpour of fresh waters did harm to some Species unknown to us.

We mourn the carnage that took place among the Animals. God was evidently willing to do away with numerous Species, as the fossil records attest, but many were saved until our times, and these are the ones He bequeathed anew to our care. If you had composed a splendid symphony, would you want it to be obliterated? The Earth and the music thereof, the Universe and the harmony therein – these are God's works of Creativity, of which Man's creativity is but a poor shadow.

According to the Human Words of God, the task of saving the chosen Species was given to Noah, symbolizing the aware ones among Mankind. He alone was forewarned; he alone took upon himself Adam's original stewardship, keeping God's beloved Species safe until the waters of the Flood had receded and his Ark was beached upon Ararat. Then the rescued Creatures were set loose upon the Earth, as if at a second Creation.

At the first Creation all was rejoicing, but the second event was qualified: God was no longer so well pleased. He knew something had gone very wrong with his last experiment, Man, but that it was too late for him to fix it. "I will not again curse the ground any more for man's sake; for the imagination of man's heart is evil from his youth; neither will I again smite every thing living, as I have done," say the Human Words of God in Genesis 8:21.

Yes, my Friends – any further cursing of the ground would be done not by God but by Man himself. Consider the southern shores of the Mediterranean – once fruitful farmland, now a desert. Consider the ruinations wrought in the Amazon River basin; consider the wholesale slaughter of ecosystems, each one a living reflection of God's infinite care for detail . . . but these are subjects for another day.

Then God says a noteworthy thing. He says, "And the fear of you" – that is, Man – "and the dread of you shall be upon every beast of the earth, and upon every fowl of the air . . . into your hand are they delivered." Genesis 9:2. This is not God telling Man that he has a right to destroy all the Animals, as some claim. Instead it is a warning to God's beloved Creatures: *Beware of Man, and of his evil heart.*

Then God establishes his Covenant with Noah, and with his sons, "and with every living creature." Many recall the Covenant with Noah, but forget the Covenant with all other living Beings. However, God does not forget it. He repeats the terms "all flesh" and "every living creature" a number of times, to make sure we get the point.

No one can make a Covenant with a stone: for a Covenant to exist, there must be a minimum of two live and responsible parties to it. Therefore the Animals are not senseless matter, not mere chunks of meat. No; they have living Souls, or God could not have made a Covenant with them. The Human Words of God affirm this: "But ask now the beasts," says Job 12, "and they shall teach thee; and the fowls of the air, and they shall tell thee . . . and the fishes of the sea shall declare unto thee."

Let us today remember Noah, the chosen caregiver of the Species. We God's Gardeners are a plural Noah: we too have been called, we too forewarned. We can feel the symptoms of coming disaster as a doctor feels a sick man's pulse. We must be ready for the time when those who have broken trust with the Animals – yes, wiped them from the face of the Earth where God placed them – will be swept away by the Waterless Flood, which will be carried on the wings of God's dark Angels that fly by night, and in airplanes and helicopters and bullet trains, and on transport trucks and other such conveyances.

But we Gardeners will cherish within us the knowledge of the Species, and of their preciousness to God. We must ferry this priceless knowledge over the face of the Waterless Waters, as if within an Ark.

Let us construct our Ararats carefully, my Friends. Let us provision them with foresight, and with canned and dried goods. Let us camouflage them well.

May God deliver us from the snare of the fowler, and cover us with his feathers, and under his wings may we trust, as it says in Psalm 91; and thou shalt not be afraid of the pestilence that walketh in darkness, nor for the destruction that wasteth at noonday.

May I remind you all about the importance of hand-washing, seven times a day at least, and after every encounter with a stranger. It is never too early to practise this essential precaution.

Avoid anyone who is sneezing.

Let us sing.

MY BODY IS MY EARTHLY ARK

My body is my earthly Ark,
It's proof against the Flood;
It holds all Creatures in its heart,
And knows that they are good.

It's builded firm of genes and cells,
And neurons without number;
My Ark enfolds the million years
That Adam spent in slumber.

And when Destruction swirls around,
To Ararat I'll glide;
My Ark will then come safe to land
By light of Spirit's guide.

With Creatures all, in harmony
I'll pass my mortal days,
While each in its appointed voice
Sings the Creator's praise.

From *The God's Gardeners Oral Hymnbook*

18

TOBY. SAINT CRICK'S DAY

YEAR TWENTY-FIVE

In the northern meadow the dead boar is still lying. The vultures have been at it, though they can't get through the tough hide: they're limited to eyes and tongue. They'll have to wait until it rots and bursts before they can really dig in.

Toby turns her binoculars skyward, at the crows racketing around. When she looks back, two liobams are crossing the meadow. A male, a female, strolling along as if they own the place. They stop at the boar, sniff briefly. Then they continue their walk.

Toby stares at them, fascinated: she's never seen a liobam in the flesh, only pictures. Am I imagining things? she wonders. No, the liobams are actual. They must be zoo animals freed by one of the more fanatical sects in those last desperate days.

They don't look dangerous, although they are. The lion-sheep splice was commissioned by the Lion Isaiahists in order to force the advent of the Peaceable Kingdom. They'd reasoned that the only way to fulfil the lion/lamb friendship prophecy without the first eating the second would be to meld the two of them together. But the result hadn't been strictly vegetarian.

Still, the liobams seem gentle enough, with their curly golden hair and twirling tails. They're nibbling flower heads, they don't look up; yet she has the sense that they're perfectly aware of her. Then the male opens its mouth, displaying its long, sharp canines, and calls. It's an odd combination of baa and roar: a bloar, thinks Toby.

Her skin prickles. She doesn't relish the thought of one of those creatures leaping on her from behind a shrub. If it's her fate to be mangled and devoured, she'd prefer a more conventional beast of prey. Still, they are astounding. She watches them while they gambol together, then sniff the air and saunter away to the edge of the forest, vanishing into dappled shade.

How Pilar would have enjoyed seeing those, she thinks. Pilar, and Rebecca, and little Ren. And Adam One. And Zeb. All dead now.

Stop it, she tells herself. Just stop that right now.

She sidesteps carefully down the stairs, using her mop handle for balance. She keeps expecting – still – that the elevator doors will open, the lights blink on, the air conditioning begins to breathe, and someone – who? – will step out.

She goes down the long hall, walking softly on the increasingly spongy carpet, past the line of mirrors. There's no shortage of mirrors in the Spa: the ladies needed to be reminded by harsh light of how bad they looked, and then by soft light of how good they might yet appear with a little costly help. But after her first few weeks alone she'd covered the mirrors with pink towels to avoid being startled by her own shape as it flitted from one frame to the next.

"Who lives here?" she says out loud. Not me, she thinks. This thing I'm doing can hardly be called living. Instead I'm lying dormant, like a bacterium in a glacier. Getting time over with. That's all.

She spends the rest of the morning sitting in a kind of stupor. Once, this would have been meditation, but she can hardly call it that now. Paralyzing rage can still take hold of her, it seems: impossible to know when it will strike. It begins as disbelief and ends in sorrow, but in between those two phases her whole body shakes with anger. Anger at whom, at what? Why has she been saved alive? Out of the countless millions. Why not someone younger, someone with more optimism and fresher cells? She ought to trust that she's here for a reason – to bear witness, to transmit a message, to salvage at least something from the general wreck. She ought to trust, but she can't.

It's wrong to give so much time over to mourning, she tells herself. Mourning and brooding. There's nothing to be accomplished by it.

During the heat of the day, she naps. Trying to stay awake through the noontime steambath is a waste of energy.

She sleeps on a massage table in one of the cubicles where the Spa clients took their organic-botanic treatments. There are pink sheets and pink pillows, and pink blankets too – soft cuddly colours, pampering infant colours – though she doesn't need the blankets, not in this weather.

She's been having some difficulty waking up. She must fight against lethargy. It's a strong desire – to sleep. To sleep and sleep. To sleep forever. She can't live only in the present, like a shrub. But the past is a closed door, and she can't see any future. Maybe she'll go on from day to day and year to year until she simply withers, folds in on herself, shrivels up like an old spider.

Or she could take a shortcut. There's always the Poppy in its red bottle, there are always the lethal amanita mushrooms, the little Death Angels. How soon before she sets them loose inside herself and lets them fly away with her on their white, white wings?

To cheer herself up, she opens her jar of honey. It's the last one remaining from the honey she extracted so long ago – she and Pilar – up on the Edencliff Rooftop. She's been saving it all these years as if it's a protective charm. Honey doesn't decay, said Pilar, as long as you keep water out of it: that's why the ancients called it the food of immortality.

She swallows one fragrant spoonful, then another. It was hard work collecting that honey: the smoking of the hives, the painstaking removal of the combs, the extracting. It took delicacy and tact. The bees had to be spoken to and persuaded, not to mention temporarily gassed, and sometimes they'd sting, but in her memory the whole experience is one of unblemished happiness. She knows she's deceiving herself about that, but she prefers to deceive herself. She desperately needs to believe such pure joy is still possible.

19

Gradually, Toby stopped thinking she should leave the Gardeners. She didn't really believe in their creed, but she no longer disbelieved. One season blended into the next – rainy, stormy, hot and dry, cooler and dry, rainy and warm – and then one year into another. She wasn't quite a Gardener, yet she wasn't a pleeblander any more. She was neither the one nor the other.

She'd venture out onto the street now, though she didn't go far from the Garden, and she'd cover herself well and wear a nose cone and a wide sunhat. She still had nightmares about Blanco – the snakes on his arms, the headless women chained to his back, his skinless-looking blue-veined hands coming for her neck. *Say you love me! Say it, bitch!* During the worst times with him, during the most terror, the most pain, she'd focus on those hands coming off at the wrists. The hands, other parts of him. Grey blood gushing out. She'd picture him stuffed into a garboil boiler, alive. Those had been violent thoughts, and since joining the Gardeners she'd sincerely tried to erase them from her brain. But they kept coming back. She was told by those in nearby sleeping cubicles that she sometimes made what they called "signals of distress" in her sleep.

Adam One was aware of these signals. She had come, over time, to realize it would be a mistake to underestimate him. Though his beard had now turned an innocent feathery white and his blue eyes were round and guileless as a baby's, though he seemed so trusting and vulnerable, Toby felt she would never encounter anyone as strong in purpose. He didn't wield this purpose like a weapon, he simply floated along inside it and let it carry him. That would be hard to attack: like attacking the tide.

"He's in Painball now, my dear," he told her one fine Saint Mendel's Day. "He may not ever be released. Perhaps he will return to the elements there."

Toby's heart fluttered. "What did he do?"

"Killed a woman," said Adam One. "The wrong kind of woman. A woman from one of the Corps who was seeking excitement in the pleeblands. I wish they wouldn't do that. The CorpSeCorps were forced to act, this time."

Toby had heard about Painball. It was a facility for condemned criminals, both political ones and the other kind: they had a choice of being spraygunned to death or doing time in the Painball Arena, which wasn't an arena at all, but more like an enclosed forest. You got enough food for two weeks, plus the Painball gun – it shot paint, like a regular paintball gun, but a hit in the eyes would blind you, and if you got the paint on your skin you'd start to corrode, and then you'd be an easy target for the throat-slitters on the other team. For everyone who went in was assigned to one of two teams: the Red, the Gold.

Woman criminals didn't choose Painball much, they chose the sprayguns. So did most of the politicals. They knew they wouldn't stand a chance in there, they preferred to just get it over with. Toby could understand that.

For a long time they'd kept the Painball Arena secret, like cockfighting and Internal Rendition, but now, it was said, you could watch it onscreen. There were cameras in the Painball forest, hidden in trees and built into rocks, but often there wasn't much to see except a leg or an arm or a blurry shadow, because the Painballers were understandably stealthy. But once in a while there'd be a hit, right on screen. If you survived for a month, you were good; longer than that, very good. Some got hooked on the adrenalin and didn't want to come out when their time was up. Even the CorpSeCorps professionals were scared of the long-term Painballers.

Some teams would hang their kill on a tree, some would mutilate the body. Cut off the head, tear out the heart and kidneys. That was to intimidate the other team. Eat part of it, if food was running low or just to show how mean you were. After a while, thought Toby, you wouldn't just cross the line, you'd forget there ever were any lines. You'd do whatever it takes.

She had a quick vision of Blanco, headless, hanging upside down. What did she feel about that? Pleasure? Pity? She couldn't tell.

She asked to do a Vigil, and spent it on her knees, attempting to mind-meld with a plantful of green peas. The vines, the flowers, the leaves, the pods. So green and soothing. It almost worked.

One day, old walnut-faced Pilar – Eve Six – asked Toby if she wanted to learn about bees. Bees and mushrooms – these were Pilar's specialties. Toby liked Pilar, who seemed kind, and who had a serenity she envied; so she said yes.

"Good," said Pilar. "You can always tell the bees your troubles." So Adam One wasn't the only person to have registered Toby's worry.

Pilar took her to visit the beehives, and introduced her to the bees by name. "They need to know you're a friend," she said. "They can smell you. Just move slowly," she cautioned as the bees coated Toby's bare arm like golden fur. "They'll know you next time. Oh – if they do sting, don't slap them. Just brush the sting off. But they won't sting unless they're frightened, because stinging kills them."

Pilar had a fund of bee lore. A bee in the house means a visit from a stranger, and if you kill the bee, the visit will not be a good one. If the beekeeper dies, the bees must be told, or they will swarm and fly away. Honey helps an open wound. A swarm of bees in May, worth a cool day. A swarm of bees in June, worth a new moon. A swarm of bees in July, not worth a squashed fly. All the bees of a hive are one bee: that's why they'll die for the hive. "Like the Gardeners," Pilar said. Toby couldn't tell whether or not she was joking.

The bees were agitated by her at first, but after a while they accepted her. They allowed her to extract the honey by herself, and she got stung only twice. "The bees made a mistake," Pilar told her. "You must ask permission of their Queen, and explain to them that you mean them no harm." She said you had to speak out loud because the bees couldn't read your mind precisely, any more than a person could. So Toby did speak, though she felt like a fool. What would anyone down there on the sidewalk think if they saw her talking to a swarm of bees?

According to Pilar, the bees all over the world had been in trouble for decades. It was the pesticides, or the hot weather, or a disease, or maybe all of these – nobody knew exactly. But the bees on the Rooftop Garden were all right. In fact, they were thriving. "They know they're loved," said Pilar.

Toby doubted this. She doubted a lot of things. But she kept her doubts to herself, because *doubt* wasn't a word the Gardeners used much.

After a while, Pilar took Toby down to the dank cellars below the Buenavista Condos and showed her where the mushrooms were grown. Bees and mushrooms went together, said Pilar: the bees were on good terms with the unseen world, being the messengers to the dead. She tossed that crazed little factoid off as if it was something everyone knew, and Toby pretended to ignore it. Mushrooms were the roses in the garden of that unseen world, because the real mushroom plant was underground. The part you could see – what most people called a mushroom – was just a brief apparition. A cloud flower.

There were mushrooms for eating, mushrooms for medicinal uses, and mushrooms for visions. These last were used only for the Retreats and the Isolation Weeks, though sometimes they might be good for certain medical conditions, and even to ease people through their Fallow states, when the Soul was refertilizing itself. Pilar said that everyone had a Fallow state sometime. But it was dangerous to stay Fallow too long, "It's like going down the stairs," she said, "and never coming back up. But the mushrooms can help with that."

There were three kinds of mushrooms, said Pilar – Never Poisonous, Employ with Caution and Advice, and Beware. They all had to be memorized. Puffballs, any species: Never Poisonous. The psilocybins: Employ with Caution and Advice. All amanitas, and especially amanita phalloides, the Death Angel: Beware.

"Aren't those very dangerous?" said Toby.

Pilar nodded. "Oh yes. Very dangerous."

"Then why do you grow them?"

"God wouldn't have made poisonous mushrooms unless He intended us to use them sometimes," said Pilar.

Pilar was so mild-mannered and gentle that Toby couldn't believe she'd just heard this. "You wouldn't poison anyone!" she said.

Pilar gave her a straight look. "You never know, dear," she said. "When you might have to."

Now Toby spent all her spare hours with Pilar – tending the Edencliff beehives and the crops of buckwheat and lavender grown for the bees on adjacent rooftops, extracting the honey and storing it in jars. They stamped the labels with the little bee stamp that Pilar used instead of lettering, and set some jars aside to add to the preserved foods in the Ararat that Pilar had built behind a moveable cinder block in the Buenavista cellar wall. Or they cared for the Poppy plants and collected the thick juice from their seed pods, or pottered among the mushroom beds in the Buenavista cellar, or simmered elixirs and remedies and the honey-and-rose liquid skin emulsion they'd sell at the Tree of Life Natural Materials Exchange.

Thus the time passed. Toby stopped counting it. In any case, time is not a thing that passes, said Pilar: it's a sea on which you float.

At night, Toby breathed herself in. Her new self. Her skin smelled like honey and salt. And earth.

20

New people kept arriving among the Gardeners. Some were genuine converts, but others didn't stay long. They'd be there for a while, wearing the same baggy, concealing clothes as everyone else, working at the most menial tasks, and, if they were women, weeping from time to time. Then they'd be gone. They were shadow people, and Adam One was moving them around in the shadows. As he'd moved Toby herself.

This was guesswork: it hadn't taken Toby long to realize that the Gardeners did not welcome personal questions. Where you'd come from, what you'd done before – all of that was irrelevant, their manner implied. Only the Now counted. Say about others as you would have them say about you. In other words, nothing.

There were a lot of things Toby remained curious about. For instance, had Nuala ever got laid, and if not, was that why she flirted so much? Where had Marushka Midwife learned her skills? What exactly had Adam One done before the Gardeners? Had there ever been an Eve One, or even a Mrs. Adam One, or any child Adam Ones? If she came too close to such territory Toby would be granted a smile and a change of subject, and a hint that she might try avoiding the original sin of desiring too much knowledge, or possibly too much power. Because the two were connected – didn't dear Toby agree?

Then there was Zeb. Adam Seven. Toby didn't believe Zeb was a true Gardener, any more than she was. She'd seen a lot of men of that general shape and hairiness during her SecretBurger days, and she'd bet that he had some game going; he had that kind of alertness. Now what was a man like that doing at the Edencliff Rooftop?

Zeb came and went; sometimes he'd vanish for days, and when he turned up again he might be wearing pleeblander clothes: solarbiker fleather gear, groundsman's coveralls, bouncer black. At first she'd worried that he was a Blanco affiliate, come to spy her out, but no, it wasn't that. Mad Adam, the kids nicknamed him, but he appeared sane enough. A little too sane to be hanging out with this clutch of sweet but delusional eccentrics. And what was the bond between him and Lucerne? Lucerne had pampered Compound wife written all over her: every time she broke a nail she went into a pout. She was an unlikely choice of partner for a man like Zeb – a bullet-spitter, he'd have been called in Toby's childhood, back when bullets were common.

Though maybe it was the sex, Toby thought. A mirage of the flesh, a hormone-fuelled obsession. It happened to a lot of people. She could remember a time when she herself might have been part of such a story, given the right man, but the longer she stayed with the Gardeners, the more that time receded.

She'd had no sex recently, nor did she miss it: during her immersion in the Sewage Lagoon she'd had far too much sex, though not the kind anyone would want. Freedom from Blanco was worth a lot: she was lucky she hadn't ended up fucked into a purée and battered to a pulp and poured out onto a vacant lot.

There had been one sex-linked incident at the Gardeners: old Mugi the Muscle had leapt on her when she was putting in an hour on one of the Run-For-Your-Light Treadmills in the former party room at the top of the Boulevard Condos. He'd pulled her off the treadmill and tussled her to the floor, then fallen heavily on top of her and groped under her denim skirt, wheezing like a faulty pump. But she was strong from all the soil-hauling and stair-climbing, and Mugi wasn't as fit as he must have been once, and she'd dug her elbow into him and levered him off, and left him sprawled and gasping on the floor.

She'd told Pilar about it, as she now told her everything that puzzled her. "What should I do?" she said.

"We never make a fuss about such things," said Pilar. "There's no harm in Mugi really. He's tried that on more than one of us – even me, some years ago." She gave a dry little chuckle. "The ancient Australopithecus can come out in all of us. You must forgive him in your heart. He won't do it again, you'll see."

So that was that, as far as sex went. Maybe it's temporary, thought Toby. Maybe it's like having your arm go to sleep. My neural connections for sex are blocked. But why don't I care?

It was the afternoon of Saint Maria Sibylla Merian of Insect Metamorphosis Day, said to be a propitious time for working with bees. Toby and Pilar were extracting the honey. They had on their wide veiled hats; for the smoke they used a bellows, and a smudge of decaying wood.

"Your parents – are they living?" said Pilar, from behind her white veil.

Toby was surprised by such a question, uncharacteristically direct for a Gardener. But Pilar wouldn't have asked such a thing without good reason. Toby couldn't bring herself to discuss her father, so instead she told Pilar about her mother's mysterious illness. What was so odd, she said, was that her mother had always been so keen on health: by weight she would have been half vitamin supplement.

"Tell me," said Pilar. "What supplements was she taking?"

"She ran a HelthWyzer franchise, so she took those."

"HelthWyzer," said Pilar. "Yes. We've heard of this before."

"Heard of what?" said Toby.

"This kind of illness, coupled with those supplements. No wonder the HelthWyzer people wanted to treat your mother themselves."

"What do you mean?" said Toby. She felt chilly, even though the morning sun was hot.

"Did it ever occur to you, my dear," said Pilar, "that your mother may have been a guinea pig?"

It hadn't occurred to Toby, but it occurred to her now. "I kind of wondered," she said. "Not about the pills, but . . . I thought it was the developer who wanted Dad's land. I figured maybe they'd put something in the well."

"In that case you'd all have been ill," said Pilar. "Now, promise me that you will never take any pill made by a Corporation. Never buy such a pill, and never accept any such pill if offered, no matter what they say. They'll produce data and scientists; they'll produce doctors – worthless, they've all been bought."

"Surely not all of them!" said Toby, shocked by Pilar's vehemence: she was usually so calm.

"No," said Pilar. "Not all. But all who are still working with any of the Corporations. The others – some have died unexpectedly. But those still alive – those with any shred of the old medical ethic left in them . . ." She paused. "There are doctors like that, still. But not at the Corps."

"Where are they?" Toby asked.

"Some of them are here, with us," said Pilar. She smiled. "Katuro the Wrench used to be an internist. He does our plumbing now. Surya was an eye surgeon. Stuart was an oncologist. Marushka was a gynecologist."

"And the other doctors? If they aren't here?"

"Let's just say they're safe, elsewhere," said Pilar. "For the moment. But now you must promise me: those Corporation pills are the food of the dead, my dear. Not our kind of dead, the bad kind. The dead who are still alive. We must teach the children to avoid these pills – they're evil. It's not only a rule of faith among us, it's a matter of certainty."

"But how can you be so sure?" Toby asked. "The Corps – nobody knows what they're doing. They're locked into those Compounds of theirs, nothing gets out . . ."

"You'd be surprised," said Pilar. "No boat was ever built that didn't spring a leak eventually. Now, promise me."

Toby promised.

"One day," said Pilar, "when you're an Eve, you'll understand more."

"Oh, I don't think I'll ever be an Eve," said Toby lightly. Pilar smiled.

Later that same afternoon, when Pilar and Toby had finished the honey extraction and Pilar was thanking the hive and the queen for their co-operation, Zeb came up the fire-escape stairs. He was wearing a black fleather jacket of the kind favoured by solarbikers. They slashed those jackets to let the hot air circulate while they were riding, but there were extra slashes in this one.

"What happened?" said Toby. "What can I do?" Zeb's tree-stump hands were clutched to his stomach; blood was coming out from between his fingers. She felt a little sick. At the same time she felt an urge to say, "Don't drip on the bees."

"Fell down and cut myself," said Zeb. "Broken glass." He was breathing heavily.

"I don't believe that," said Toby.

"Didn't think you would," said Zeb, grinning at her. "Here," he said to Pilar. "Brought you a present. SecretBurger special." He reached a hand into the pocket of his fleather jacket and brought out a fistful of ground meat. For a moment, Toby had the horrible impression that this was part of Zeb himself, but Pilar smiled.

"Thank you, dear Zeb," she said. "I can always rely on you! Come with me, now, we'll fix it up. Toby, could you find Rebecca and ask her to bring some clean kitchen towels? And Katuro. Him too." She didn't seem at all flustered by the sight of blood.

How old will I be, thought Toby, before I can be that calm? She felt cut open.

21

Pilar and Toby carried Zeb over to the Fallows Recovery Hut on the northwest corner of the Rooftop, which was used by Gardeners on Vigils, or those emerging from a Fallow state, or those who were moderately ill. As they were helping him to lie down, Rebecca came out from the enclosed shed at the back of the Rooftop, carrying a stack of dishtowels. "Now who did that?" she said. "That's a glass job! Bottle fight?"

Katuro arrived, peeled the jacket off Zeb's stomach, took a professional look. "Stopped by ribs," he said. "Slash, not stab. No deep punctures – lucky."

Pilar handed the ground meat to Toby. "It's for the maggots," she said. "Could you take care of it this time, dear?" The meat was already going off, from the smell of it.

Toby wrapped it in gauze from the Wellness Clinic as she'd seen Pilar do, and lowered the bundle over the edge of the rooftop on a string. In a couple of days, after the flies had laid their eggs and the eggs had had time to hatch, they'd haul it up again and harvest the maggots, because where there was rotting flesh, maggots were sure to follow. Pilar kept a supply of maggots always on hand for therapeutic use in case of need, but Toby had never seen them in action.

According to Pilar, maggot therapy was very ancient. It had been discarded as out of date along with leeches and bleeding, but during the First World War the doctors had noticed that soldiers' wounds healed much faster if maggots were present. Not only did the helpful creatures eat the decaying flesh, they killed necrotic bacteria, and were thus a great help in preventing gangrene.

The maggots created a pleasant sensation, said Pilar – a gentle nibbling, as of minnows – but they needed to be watched carefully, because if they ran out of decay and began to invade the living flesh there would be pain and bleeding. Otherwise, the wound would heal cleanly.

Pilar and Katuro sponged Zeb's cuts with vinegar, then rubbed on honey. Zeb was no longer bleeding, though he was pale. Toby got him a drink of Sumac.

Katuro said that pleebland street-fight glass was notoriously septic, so they should apply the maggots right away to avoid blood poisoning. Pilar used tweezers to place her stored maggots inside a fold of gauze, taping the gauze to Zeb. By the time the maggots had chewed through the gauze, Zeb would surely be festering enough to be attractive to them.

"Someone has to stay on maggot watch," said Pilar. "Twenty-four hours a day. In case the maggots start to eat our dear Zeb."

"Or in case I start to eat them," said Zeb. "Land shrimp. Same body plan. Very nice fried. Great source of lipids." He was keeping up a good front, but his voice was weak.

Toby took the first five hours. Adam One had heard about Zeb's accident and came to visit. "Discretion is the better part of valour," he said mildly.

"Yeah, well, there were too many of them," said Zeb. "Anyway I put three of them in the hospital."

"Not a thing to be proud of," said Adam One. Zeb frowned.

"Foot soldiers use their feet," he said. "That's why I wear boots."

"We'll discuss this later, when you're feeling better," said Adam One.

"I'm feeling fine," Zeb growled.

Nuala bustled in to take over from Toby. "Have you made him some Willow?" she said. "Oh dear, I hate those maggots! Here, let me prop you up! Can't we raise the screening? We need a breeze through!

Zeb, is this what you mean by Urban Bloodshed Limitation? You are so naughty!" She was twittering, and Toby felt like kicking her.

Lucerne arrived next, blotting tears. "This is terrible! What's happened, who did . . ."

"Oh, he's been so bad!" said Nuala conspiratorially. "Haven't you, Zeb? Fighting with the pleeblanders," she whispered delightedly.

"Toby," said Lucerne, ignoring Nuala, "how serious is it? Will he . . . is he . . ." She sounded like some old-time TV actress playing a deathbed scene.

"I'm fine," said Zeb. "Now buzz off and leave me alone!"

He didn't want anyone fiddling with him, he said. Except Pilar. And Katuro, if absolutely necessary. And Toby, because at least she was silent. Lucerne went away, weeping angrily, but there was nothing Toby could do about that.

Rumour was the daily news among the Gardeners. The older boys heard quickly about Zeb's battle – it had now become a battle – and the next afternoon Shackleton and Crozier came to see him. He was asleep – Toby had slipped some Poppy into his Willow tea – so they tiptoed around him, speaking in low voices and trying for a peek at his wound.

"He ate a bear once," said Shackleton. "When he was flying for Bearlift, that time they were trying to save the polar bears. His plane crashed and he walked out – it took months!" The older boys had many such heroic tales about Zeb. "He said bears look just like a man when they're skinned."

"He ate the co-pilot. After he was dead, though," Crozier said.

"Can we see the maggots?"

"Has he got gangrene?"

"Gang! Grene!" shouted little Oates, who'd tagged along after his brothers.

"Shut up, Oatie!"

"Ow! You meat-breath!"

"Off you go now," said Toby. "Zeb – Adam Seven needs his rest."

Adam One persisted in thinking that Shackleton and Crozier and young Oates would turn out just fine, but Toby had her doubts. Philo the Fog was supposed to be their stand-in father, but he wasn't always mentally available.

Pilar took the night watches: she didn't sleep much at night anyway, she said. Nuala volunteered for the mornings. Toby took over during the afternoons. She checked the maggots every hour. Zeb had no temperature, and there was no fresh blood.

Once he began healing he was restless, so Toby played dominoes with him, then cribbage, and finally chess. The chess set was Pilar's: black was ants, white was bees; she'd carved it herself. "They used to think the queen of the bees was a king," Pilar said. "Since if you killed that bee, the rest lost their purpose. That's why the chess king doesn't move around much on the board – it's because the queen bee always stays inside the hive." Toby wasn't sure this was true: did the queen bee always stay inside the hive? Except for swarming, of course, and for nuptial flights . . . She stared at the board, trying to see the pattern. From outside the Fallows Recovery Hut came the sound of Nuala's voice mingling with the chirping of the smaller children. "The five senses, through which the world comes to us . . . seeing, hearing, feeling, smelling, tasting . . . what do we use for tasting? That's right . . . Oates, there is no need for you to lick Melissa. Now pop your tongues back into your tongue containers and close the lids." Toby had an image – no, a taste. She could taste the skin of Zeb's arm, the salt on it . . .

"Checkmate," said Zeb. "Ants win again." Zeb always played Ants, to give Toby an opening advantage.

"Oh," said Toby. "I didn't see that." Now she was wondering – unworthy thought – whether there was something going on between Nuala and Zeb. Though overblown, Nuala was lush, and oddly babyish. Some men found that quality alluring.

Zeb swept the pieces from the board and began to set them up again. "Do me a favour?" he said. He didn't wait for a yes.

Lucerne was having a lot of headaches, he said. His voice was neutral, but there was an edge to it, by which Toby understood that the headaches might not be real; or else that they were real enough, but Zeb found them boring anyway.

Could Toby stop by with some of her bottles the next time Lucerne had a migraine, he said, and see what she could manage? Because he himself sure as hell couldn't do anything for Lucerne's hormones, if that's what it was. "She's been giving me a lot of grief," he said. "For being away too much. Makes her jealous." He grinned like a shark. "Maybe she'll hear sense, from you."

So. The bloom is off the rose, thought Toby. And the rose doesn't like it.

22

Saint Allan Sparrow of Clean Air: not a Day that had so far lived up to its name. Toby picked her way through the crowded pleebland streets, carrying her bag of dried herbals and bottled medicinals hidden under her loose coverall. The afternoon thunderstorm had cleared the fumes and particulate somewhat, but she was wearing a black nose cone anyway, in honour of Saint Sparrow. As was the custom.

She felt safer on the street since Blanco had been put into Painball; still, she never strolled or loitered, but – remembering Zeb's instructions – also she didn't run. It was best to look purposeful, as if you were on a mission. She ignored the passing stares, the anti-Gardener slurs, but she was alert to sudden movement or to anyone coming too close. A pleebrat gang had once grabbed her mushrooms; luckily for them, she hadn't been carrying anything lethal that time.

She was heading towards the Cheese Factory building to fulfil Zeb's request. This was the third time she'd gone. If Lucerne's headaches were real and not just a bid for attention, an over-the-counter double-strength painkiller/soporific from HelthWyzer could have handled the problem, either by curing her or killing her. But Corps pills were taboo among the Gardeners, so she'd been using extract of Willow, followed by Valerian, with some Poppy mixed in; though not too much Poppy, as it could be addictive.

"What's in this?" Lucerne would say each time Toby had treated her. "It tastes better when Pilar makes it."

Toby would refrain from saying that Pilar had in fact made it, and would urge Lucerne to swallow the dose. Then she'd put a cold compress on her forehead and sit by her bedside, trying to tune out Lucerne's whining.

The Gardeners were expected to avoid any broadcasting of their personal problems: foisting your mental junk on others was frowned on. For drinking Life there are two cups, Nuala taught the small children. What's in each of them might be exactly the same, but my, oh my, the taste is so different!

The No Cup is bitter, the Yes Cup is yummy –
Now, which one would you *rather have in* your *tummy?*

This was a basic Gardener credo. But though Lucerne could mouth the slogans, she hadn't internalized the teachings: Toby could tell a sham when she saw one, being a sham herself. As soon as Toby was locked into the ministering position, everything that was festering inside Lucerne would come roiling out. Toby would nod and say nothing, hoping to convey the impression of sympathy, though in reality she'd be considering how many drops of Poppy it would take to knock Lucerne unconscious before she, Toby, gave in to her worst impulses and throttled her.

As she quick-stepped through the streets, Toby anticipated Lucerne's complaints. If true to pattern, they'd be about Zeb: why was he never there when Lucerne needed him? How had she ended up in this unsanitary septic tank with this clutch of dreamers – *I don't mean you, Toby, you've got some sense* – who didn't understand the first thing about how the world really worked? She was buried alive here with a monster of egotism, with a man who cared only about his own needs. Talking to him was like talking to a potato – no, to a stone. He didn't hear you, he never told you what he was thinking, he was hard as flint.

Not that Lucerne hadn't tried. She wanted to be a responsible person, she really did believe that Adam One was right about so many things, and nobody loved animals more than she did, but really there was a limit and she did not believe for one instant that slugs had any central nervous system, and to say they had souls was to make a mockery of the whole idea of souls, and she resented that, because nobody had more respect for souls than she did, she'd always been a very spiritual person. As for saving the world, nobody wanted to save the world as much as she did, but no matter how much the Gardeners deprived themselves of proper food and clothing and even proper showers, for heaven's sake, and felt more high and mighty and virtuous than everyone else, it wouldn't really change anything. They were just like those people who used to whip themselves during the Middle Ages – those flagrants.

"Flagellants," Toby had said, the first time this came up.

Then Lucerne had said she didn't mean it about the Gardeners, she was just feeling gloomy because of the headache. Also because they looked down on her for coming from a Corps, and for ditching her husband and running away with Zeb. They didn't trust her. They thought she was a slut. They made dirty jokes about her behind her back. Or the children did – didn't they?

"The children make dirty jokes about everyone," Toby had said. "Including me."

"You?" Lucerne had said, opening her large eyes with their dark lashes. "Why would they make dirty jokes about you?" Nothing sexual about *you*, was what she meant. Flat as a board, back and front. Worker bee.

There was a plus to that: at least Lucerne wasn't jealous of her. In that respect, Toby stood alone among the Gardener women.

"They don't look down on you," Toby had said. "They don't think you're a slut. Now just relax and close your eyes and picture the Willow moving through your body, up to your head, where the pain is."

It was true that the Gardeners didn't look down on Lucerne, or not for the reasons she thought they did. They might resent the way she slacked off on chores and could never learn how to chop a carrot, they might be scornful of the messiness of her living space and her pathetic attempt at windowsill tomato-growing and the amount of time she spent in bed, but they didn't care about her infidelity, or her adultery, or whatever it had once been called.

That was because the Gardeners didn't bother with marriage certificates. They endorsed fidelity as long as a pair-bonding was current but there was no record of the first Adam and the first Eve going through a wedding, so in their eyes neither the clergymen of other religions nor any secular official had the power to marry people. As for the CorpSeCorps, they favoured official marriages only as a means for capturing your iris image, your fingerscans, and your DNA, all the better to track you with. Or so the Gardeners claimed, and this was one claim of theirs that Toby could believe without reservation.

Among the Gardeners, weddings were simple affairs. Both parties had to proclaim in front of witnesses that they loved each other. They exchanged green leaves to symbolize growth and fertility and jumped over a bonfire to symbolize the energy of the universe, then declared themselves married and went to bed. For divorces they did the whole thing in reverse: a public statement of non-love and separation, the exchange of dead twigs, and a swift hop over a heap of cold ashes.

A standing complaint of Lucerne's – which was sure to come up if Toby wasn't quick enough with the Poppy – was that Zeb had never invited her to do the green-leaf and bonfire-leaping ceremony with him. "Not that I think it means anything," she'd say. "But he must think it does, because he's one of them, right? So by not doing it, he's refusing commitment. Don't you agree?"

"I never know what anyone thinks," Toby would say.

"But if it was you, wouldn't you feel he was shirking his responsibility?"

"Why don't you ask him?" Toby would say. "Ask why he hasn't . . ." Was *proposed* the right word?

"He'd just get angry." Lucerne would sigh. "He was so different when I first knew him!"

Then Toby would be treated to the story of Lucerne and Zeb – a story Lucerne never tired of telling.

23

The story went like this. Lucerne met Zeb at the AnooYoo Spa-in-the-Park – did Toby know the AnooYoo? Oh. Well, it was a fantastic place to unwind and get yourself resurfaced. This was right after it was built and they were still putting in the landscaping. The fountains, the lawns, the gardens, the bushes. The lumiroses. Didn't Toby just love lumiroses? She'd never seen them? Oh. Well, maybe sometime . . .

Lucerne loved to get up at dawn, she was an early riser then, she liked to watch the sunrise; it was because she'd always been so sensitive to colour and light, she'd paid so much attention to the aesthetic values in her homes – the homes she'd decorated. She loved to include at least one room in sunrise colours – the sunrise room, she would think of that room.

Also she was restless in those days. She was really very restless, because her husband was cold as a crypt, and they never made love any more because he was too busy with his career. And she was a sensual person, she always had been, and her sensual nature was being starved to death. Which was bad for the health, and especially for the immune system. She'd read the studies on that!

So there she was, prowling around at dawn in her pink kimono and crying a little, and contemplating a divorce from her HelthWyzer Corp husband, or a separation at least, though she realized it would not be the best thing for Ren, so young then and fond of her father, not that he paid enough attention to Ren either. And suddenly there was Zeb, in the rising light, like a – well, like a vision, all by himself, planting a lumirose bush. One of those roses that glow in the dark, the scent was so divine – had

Toby ever smelled them? – she didn't suppose so because the Gardeners were death on anything new, but those roses were really pretty.

So there was a man, in the dawn, kneeling on the ground and looking as if he was holding a bouquet of live coals.

What restless woman can resist a man with a shovel in one hand and a glowing rose bush in the other, and a moderately crazed glitter in his eyes that might be mistaken for love? thought Toby. On Zeb's part there must have been something to be said for an attractive woman in a pink kimono, a loosely tied pink kimono, on a lawn in a pearly sunrise, especially when tearful. Because Lucerne was attractive. Simply from a visual point of view, she was very attractive. Even if whining, which was the way Toby saw her mostly.

Lucerne had wafted across the lawn, aware of her bare feet on the damp cool grass, aware of the brush of fabric across her thighs, aware of the tightness around her waist and the looseness below her collarbone. Billowing, like waves. She'd stopped in front of Zeb, who'd been watching her come towards him as if he'd been a sailor dumped into the ocean by mistake and she'd been either a mermaid or a shark. (Toby supplied these images: Lucerne said *Fate.*) They were both just so *aware*, she told Toby; she'd always been aware of other peoples' awareness, she was like a cat, or, or . . . she had that talent, or was it a curse – that was how she knew. So she could feel from the inside what Zeb was feeling as he watched her. That was overwhelming!

It was impossible to explain this in words, she'd say, as if nothing of the sort could ever have happened to Toby herself.

Anyway, there they stood, though they'd already foreseen what was about to happen – what had to happen. Fear and lust pushed them together and held them apart, equally.

Lucerne did not call it lust. She called it longing.

At this point, Toby would have an image of the set of salt and pepper shakers that used to be on the kitchen table in her long-ago childhood home: a little china hen, a little china rooster. The hen had been the salt, the rooster had been the pepper. Salty Lucerne had stood there in front of peppery Zeb, smiling and looking up, and she'd asked him a simple question – how many rose bushes would there be or something, she couldn't remember, so mesmerized was she by Zeb's . . . (Here Toby would turn off her attention because she didn't want to hear about the biceps, triceps, and other muscular attractions of Zeb. Was she herself immune to them? No. Was she therefore jealous of this part of the story? Yes. We must be mindful of our own animal-nature tendencies and biases at all times, said Adam One.)

And then, Lucerne would say, hooking Toby back into her story – and then a strange thing had happened: she'd recognized Zeb.

"I've seen you before," she'd said. "Didn't you used to be at HelthWyzer? But you weren't working on the grounds then! You were –"

"Mistaken identity," said Zeb. And then he'd kissed her. That kiss had gone right into her like a knife, and she'd crumpled into his arms like – like a dead fish – no – like a petticoat – no – like damp tissue paper! And then he'd picked her up and laid her down on the lawn, right where anyone could have seen, which was an unbelievable turn-on, and then he'd undone her kimono and pulled the petals off the roses he was holding and scattered them all over her body, and then the two of them . . . It was like a high-speed collision, said Lucerne, and she'd thought, How can I survive this, I'm going to die right here and now! And she could tell he felt the same.

Later – quite a lot later, after they were living together – he'd told her she'd been right. Yes, he'd been at HelthWyzer, but for reasons he wouldn't go into he'd had to leave in a hurry, and he trusted her not to mention that earlier time and place he'd once inhabited, not to anybody. Which she hadn't mentioned. Or not very much. Except right now, to Toby.

Back then, though, during her Spa sojourn – thank god she hadn't been having any skin procedure that would have made her scabby, she'd just been there for a tuneup – back then, they'd had several more appetizer-sized helpings of each other, locked into one of the showers in the Spa pool's changeroom, and after that she was stuck to Zeb like a wet leaf. As he was to her, she added. They couldn't get enough of each other.

And then, after her Spa sessions were over and she was back at her so-called home, she'd slip out of the Compound on one pretext or another – shopping errands, mostly, the things you could buy in the Compound were so predictable – and they'd met secretly in the pleeblands – it was so exciting at first! – such funny places, junky little love hotels and rent-a-rooms, you took them by the hour, so far away from the buttoned-down ambiance of the HelthWyzer Compound; and then, when he'd had to travel in a hurry – there was some trouble, she'd never understood why, but he needed to get away very fast – and, well, she couldn't bear to be apart from him.

So she'd left her so-called husband, not that it didn't serve him right for being so inert. And they'd moved around from one city to another, from one trailer park to another, and Zeb had bought a few black-market procedures, for his fingers and his DNA and so on; and then, when it was safe, they'd come back, right here, to the Gardeners. Because Zeb had told her he'd been a Gardener all along. Or so he'd said. Anyway, he seemed to know Adam One quite well. They'd been to school together. Or something like that.

So Zeb was forced into it, Toby thought. He was ex-Corps, on the run; maybe he'd been black-marketing some proprietary item, such as a nanotechnology or a gene splice. That could be fatal if you were caught. And Lucerne had put face and ex-name together, and he'd had to distract her with sex, then take her with him to ensure her loyalty. It was either that or kill her. He couldn't leave her behind: she would have felt scorned, she'd have set the CorpSeCorps dogs on him. Still, what a risk he'd taken. The woman was like an amateur car bomb: you never knew when she'd blow up or who she'd take down with her when she did. Toby wondered whether Zeb had ever thought of stuffing a cork down her epiglottis and slotting her into a carbon garboil dumpster.

But maybe he loved her. In his way. Hard though that was for Toby to picture. However, perhaps the love had run out, because he wasn't doing enough maintenance work on her at the moment.

"Hasn't your husband looked for you?" Toby had asked the first time she'd heard this tale. "The one at HelthWyzer?"

"I don't consider that man to be my husband any more," Lucerne said in an offended tone.

"Excuse me. Your former husband. Haven't the CorpSeCorps . . . did you leave him a message?" The trail of Lucerne, if followed, would lead right to the Gardeners – not only to Zeb, but to Toby herself, and to her own former identity. Which could be uncomfortable for her: the CorpSeCorps never wrote off skipped debts, and what if anyone had dug up her father?

"Why would they spend the money?" said Lucerne. "I'm not important to them. As for my former husband" – she gave a little grimace – "he ought to have married an equation. Maybe he doesn't even notice I've gone."

"What about Ren?" said Toby. "She's a lovely little girl. Surely he misses her."

"Oh," said Lucerne. "Yes. He probably does notice that."

Toby wanted to ask why Lucerne hadn't simply left Ren behind with her father. Stealing her away, leaving no information – it seemed like a petty act of spite. But asking such a question would simply make Lucerne angry – it would sound too much like criticism.

Two blocks away from the Cheese Factory, Toby ran into a pleebrat street fight – Asian Fusions versus Blackened Redfish, with a few Lintheads shouting around the edges. These kids were only seven or eight, but there were a lot of them, and when they spotted her they stopped yelling at one another and started yelling at her. *Goddie goddie, whitey bitch! Get her shoes!*

She swivelled so her back was against a wall and prepared to fend them off. It was difficult to kick them really hard when they were that young – as Zeb had pointed out in his Urban Bloodshed Limitation class, there was a species inhibition against hurting children – but she knew she'd have to, because they could be deadly. They'd aim for her stomach, ram her with their hard little heads, try to pull her down. The smaller ones had a nasty habit of hoisting the Gardener women's baggy skirts and diving in under them, then biting whatever they could find once they were in there. But she was ready for them: when they got close enough, she'd twist their ears or chop their necks with the side of her hand, or bang two of their little skulls together.

Suddenly, however, they swerved like a school of fish, rushed past her, and disappeared into an alleyway.

She turned her head, saw why. It was Blanco. He wasn't in Painball at all. He must have been let out. Or got out, somehow.

Panic gripped her heart. She saw his red-and-blue flayed hands, she felt her bones crumbling. This was her worst fear.

Take hold, she told herself. He was across the street, and she was inside her baggy coverall and had her nose cone on, so maybe he couldn't recognize her. And he'd given no sign yet that he'd noticed her. But she was alone, and he wasn't above a random stomp-and-rape. He'd drag her up that very same alleyway, the one where the pleebrats had gone. Then he'd rip off the cone and see who she was. And that would be the end, but it wouldn't be a quick end. It would be as slow as he could make it. He'd turn her into a flesh billboard – a not-quite-living demonstration of his rank finesse.

She turned quickly and marched away as fast as she could, before he'd had a chance to focus his malevolence on her. Breathless, she turned the corner, went half a block, glanced back. He wasn't there.

For once she was more than happy to reach the door of Lucerne's apartment. She raised her nose cone, twitched the muscles of her professional smile, and knocked.

"Zeb?" Lucerne called. "Is that you?"

SAINT EUELL OF WILD FOODS

SAINT EUELL OF WILD FOODS

YEAR TWELVE.

OF THE GIFTS OF SAINT EUELL.
SPOKEN BY ADAM ONE.

My Friends, my Fellow Creatures, my dear Children:

This day marks the beginning of Saint Euell's Week, during which we will be foraging for the Wild Harvest gifts that God, through Nature, has put at our disposal. Pilar, our Eve Six, will lead us in a ramble through the Heritage Park, hunting for Fungi, and Burt, our Adam Thirteen, will aid us with the Edible Weeds. Remember – if in doubt, spit it out! But if a mouse has eaten it, you can probably eat it too. Though not invariably.

The older children will have a demonstration by Zeb, our respected Adam Seven, concerning the trapping of small Animals for survival food in times of pressing need. Remember, nothing is unclean to us if gratitude is felt and pardon asked, and if we ourselves are willing to offer ourselves to the great chain of nourishment in our turn. For where else lies the deep meaning of sacrifice?

Burt's esteemed wife, Veena, is still in her Fallow state, though we hope to welcome her back among us very soon. Let us wish Light around her.

Today we meditate upon Saint Euell Gibbons, who flourished upon this Earth from 1911 to 1975, so long ago but so close to us in our hearts. As a boy, when his father left home to seek work, Saint Euell provided for his family through his Natural knowledge. He went to no high school but Yours, oh Lord. In Your Species he found his teachers, often strict but always true. And then he shared those teachings with us.

He taught the uses of Your many Puffballs, and the other wholesome Fungi; he taught the dangers of the poisonous species, which however can also be of Spiritual value, if taken in judicious quantities.

He sang the virtues of the wild Onion, of the wild Asparagus, of the wild Garlic, that toil not, neither do they spin, nor do they have pesticides sprayed upon them, if they happily grow far enough away from agribusiness crops. He knew the roadside medicines: the bark of the Willow in respect of pains and fevers, the root of the Dandelion as a diuretic in the shedding of excess fluid. He taught us not to waste; for even the lowly Nettle, so often wrenched up and thrown away, is a source of many vitamins. He taught us to improvise; for if there is no Sorrel, there may be Cattails; and if there are no Blueberries, the wild Cranberry may perhaps abound.

Saint Euell, may we sit with you in Spirit at your table, that lowly tarpaulin spread upon the ground; and dine with you upon wild Strawberries, and upon spring Fiddleheads, and upon young Milkweed pods, lightly simmered, with a little butter substitute if it can be obtained.

And in the time of our greatest need, help us to accept whatever Fate may bring us; and whisper into our inner and Spiritual ears the names of the Plants, and their seasons, and the locations in which they may be found.

For the Waterless Flood is coming, in which all buying and selling will cease, and we will find ourselves thrown back upon our own resources, in the midst of God's bounteous Garden. Which was your Garden also.

Let us sing.

OH SING WE NOW THE HOLY WEEDS

Oh sing we now the Holy Weeds
That flourish in the ditch,
For they are for the meek in needs,
They are not for the rich.

You cannot buy them at the mall,
Nor at the superstore,
They are despised because they all
Grow freely for the poor.

The Dandelion shoots, for spring,
Before their flowers burst;
The Burdock root is best in June
When it is fat with juice;

When autumn comes, the Acorn's ripe,
The Walnut black is too;
Young Milkweed pods are sweet when boiled,
And Milkweed shoots when new.

The inner bark of Spruce and Birch
For extra Vitamin C –
But do not take too much of each,
Or you will kill the tree.

The Purslane, Sorrel, Lamb's Quarters,
And Nettles, too, are good;
The Hawthorn, Elder, Sumac, Rose –
Their berries wholesome food.

The Holy Weeds are plentiful
And beautiful to see –

For who can doubt God put them there,
So starved we'll never be?

From *The Gods' Gardeners Oral Hymnbook*

24

REN

YEAR TWENTY-FIVE

I remember what the dinner was, that night in the Sticky Zone: it was ChickieNobs. I couldn't deal with meat very well ever since the Gardeners, but Mordis said that ChickieNobs were really vegetables because they grew on stems and didn't have faces. So I ate half of them.

Then I did some dancing to keep in practice. I had my own Sea/H/Ear Candy, and I sang along. Adam One said music was built into us by God: we could sing like the birds but also like the angels, because singing was a form of praise that came from deeper than just talking, and God could hear us better when we were singing. I try to remember that.

Then I looked in on the Snakepit again. There were three guys from Painball in the Snakepit – ones who'd just got out. You could always tell because they were freshly shaved, with new haircuts, and new clothes too, and they had a stunned look, like they'd been kept in a dark closet for a long time. Also they had a little tattoo at the base of their left thumb – a round circle, red or bright yellow, depending on whether they were Red Team or Gold Team. The other customers were sort of moving back from them, giving them room, but respectfully – as if they were webstars or sports heroes instead of Painball criminals. Rich guys loved to imagine themselves as Painball players. They gambled on the teams as well: Red against Gold. A lot of money changed hands over Painball.

There were always two or three CorpSeCorps guys minding the Painball vets – they could go berserk and do a lot of damage. We Scalies were never allowed to be alone with them: they didn't understand make-believe, they never knew when to stop, and they could break a lot more than the furniture. It was best to get them wasted, but it had to be fast or they'd go into full rage mode.

"I'd bar those assholes myself," said Mordis. "Nothing much human left inside that scar tissue of theirs. But SeksMart pays us a big-time extra bonus when it's them."

We'd feed them drinks and pills, with a shovel if we could. There was something new they'd started using just after I went into the Sticky Zone – BlyssPluss, it was called. Hassle-free sex, total satisfaction, blow you right out of your skin, plus 100 percent protection – that was the word on it. Scales girls weren't allowed to do drugs on the job – we weren't paid to enjoy ourselves, said Mordis – but this was different, because if you took it you didn't need a Biofilm Bodyglove, and a lot of customers would pay extra that way. Scales was testing the BlyssPluss for the ReJoov Corp, so they weren't handing it out like candy – it was mostly for the top customers – but I could hardly wait to try it.

We always got huge tips on Painball nights, though none of us regular Scales girls had to do plank duty with the new vets because we were skilled artists and any damage to us would be pricey. For the basic bristle work they brought in the temporaries – smuggled Eurotrash or Tex-Mexicans or Asian Fusion and Redfish minors scooped off the streets because the Painball guys wanted membrane, and after they were finished you'd be judged contaminated until proved otherwise, and Scales didn't want to spend Sticky Zone money either testing these girls or fixing them up. I never saw them twice. They walked in the door, but I don't think they walked out. In a shoddier club they'd have been used for the guys acting out their vampire fantasies, but that involved mouth-to-blood contact, and as I said, Mordis liked to keep it clean.

That night one of the Painball guys had Starlite on his lap, giving him the signature twist. She was in her peagret-feather outfit with the headdress, and maybe she was terrific from the front, but from my angle of vision it looked like the guy had a big blue-green duster working him over – like a dry carwash.

The second guy was gazing up at Savona with his mouth open and his head so far back it was almost at right angles to his spine. If her grip slips, she'll snap his neck. If that happens, I thought, he won't be the first guy to be carted out the back door of Scales and dumped in a vacant lot with no clothes on. He was an older guy, bald on top, with a ponytail at the back, and a lot of arm tattoos. There was something familiar about him – maybe he was a repeat – but I didn't get a very good look.

The third one was drinking himself into mud. Maybe he was trying to forget what he'd done inside the Painball Arena. I never watched the Painball Arena website myself. It was too disgusting. I only knew about it because men talk. It's amazing what they'll tell you, especially if you're covered with shiny green scales and they can't see your real face. It must be like talking to a fish.

Nothing else was happening, so I called Amanda on her cell. But she wasn't answering. Maybe she was asleep, rolled up in her sleeping bag out there in Wisconsin. Maybe she was sitting around a campfire and the two Tex-Mexicans were playing their guitars and singing, and Amanda was singing too because she knew the Tex-Mex language. Maybe there was a moon up above and some coyotes howling in the distance, just like an old movie. I hoped so.

25

Things changed in my life when Amanda came to live with me, and they changed again in the Saint Euell's Week when I was almost thirteen. Amanda was older: she'd already grown real tits. It's strange how you measure time that way.

That year, Amanda and I – and Bernice as well – would be joining the older kids for Zeb's Predator-Prey Relationship demonstration, when we'd have to eat real prey. I had a faint memory of meat-eating, back at the HelthWyzer Compound. But the Gardeners were very much against it except in times of crisis, so the idea of putting a chunk of bloody muscle and gristle into my mouth and pushing it down inside my throat was nauseating. I vowed not to throw up, though, because that would embarrass me a lot and make Zeb look bad.

I wasn't worried about Amanda. She was used to eating meat, she'd done it lots of times before. She used to lift SecretBurgers whenever she could. So she'd be able to chew and swallow as if there was nothing to it.

On the Monday of Saint Euell's Week, we put our clean clothes on – clean yesterday – and I braided Amanda's hair, and then she braided mine. "Primate grooming," Zeb called it.

We could hear Zeb singing in the shower:

Nobody gives a poop.
Nobody gives a poop;

And that is why we're in the soup,
Cause nobody gives a poop!

I'd come to find this morning singing of his a comforting sound. It meant things were ordinary, at least for that day.

Usually Lucerne stayed in bed until we were gone, partly to avoid Amanda, but today she was in the kitchen area, wearing her dark-coloured Gardener dress, and she was actually cooking. She'd been making that effort more often lately. Also she was keeping our living space tidier. She was even growing a raggedy tomato plant in a pot on the sill. I think she was trying to make things nice for Zeb, though they were having more fights. They made us go outside when they were fighting, but that didn't mean we couldn't listen in.

The fights were about where Zeb was when he wasn't with Lucerne. "Working," was all he'd say. Or "Don't push me, babe." Or "You don't need to know. It's for your own good."

"You've got someone else!" Lucerne would say. "I can smell bitch all over you!"

"Wow," Amanda would whisper. "Your mom's got a foul mouth!" and I didn't know whether to be proud or ashamed.

"No, no," Zeb would say in a tired voice. "Why would I want anyone but you, babe?"

"You're lying!"

"Oh, Christ in a helicopter! Get off my fucking case!"

Zeb came out of the shower cubicle, dripping on the floor. I could see the scar where he'd got slashed that time, back when I was ten: it gave me a shivery feeling. "How're my little pleebrats today?" he said, grinning like a troll.

Amanda smiled sweetly. "Big pleebrats," she said.

For breakfast we had mashed-up fried black beans and soft-boiled pigeon's eggs. "Nice breakfast, babe," Zeb said to Lucerne. I had to admit that it was actually quite nice, even though Lucerne had cooked it.

Lucerne gave him that syrupy smile of hers. "I wanted to be sure you all get a good meal," she said. "Considering what you'll be eating the rest of the week. Old roots and mice, I suppose."

"Barbecued rabbit," said Zeb. "I could eat ten of those suckers, with a side of mice and some deep-fried slugs for dessert." He leered over at Amanda and me: he was trying to gross us out.

"Sounds real good," said Amanda.

"You're such a monster," said Lucerne, giving him her cookie eyes.

"Too bad I can't get a beer with it," said Zeb. "Join us, babe, we need some decoration."

"Oh, I think I'll sit this one out," said Lucerne.

"You're not coming with us?" I said. Usually during Saint Euell's Week, Lucerne would trail along on the woodland walks, picking the odd weed and complaining about the bugs and keeping an eye on Zeb. I didn't really want her to come this time, but also I wanted things to stay normal, because I had a feeling that everything was about to be rearranged again, as it was when I'd been yanked out of the HelthWyzer Compound. It was just a feeling, but I didn't like it. I was used to the Gardeners, it was where I belonged now.

"I don't think I can," she said. "I've got a migraine headache." She'd had a migraine headache yesterday too. "I'll just go back to bed."

"I'll ask Toby to drop around," said Zeb. "Or Pilar. Make that mean ol' pain go away."

"Would you?" A suffering smile.

"No problem," said Zeb. Lucerne hadn't eaten her pigeon's egg, so he ate it for her. It was only about the size of a plum anyway.

The beans were from the Garden, but the pigeon's eggs were from our own rooftop. We didn't have any plants up there, because Adam One said it was not a suitable surface, but we had pigeons. Zeb lured them with crumbs, moving softly so they felt safe. Then they'd lay eggs, and then he'd rob their nests. Pigeons weren't an endangered species, he said, so it was okay.

Adam One said that eggs were potential Creatures, but they weren't Creatures yet: a nut was not a Tree. Did eggs have souls? No, but they had potential souls. So not a lot of Gardeners did egg-eating, but they didn't condemn it either. You didn't apologize to an egg before joining its protein to yours, though you had to apologize to the mother pigeon, and thank her for her gift. I doubt Zeb bothered with any apologizing. Most likely he ate some of the mother pigeons too, on the sly.

Amanda had one pigeon's egg. So did I. Zeb had three, plus Lucerne's. He needed more than us because he was bigger, Lucerne said: if we ate like him we'd get fat.

"See you later, warrior maidens. Don't kill anyone," said Zeb as we went out the door. He'd heard about Amanda's knee-in-the-groin and eye-gouging moves, and her piece of glass with the duct tape; he made jokes about them.

26

We had to pick up Bernice at the Buenavista before school. Amanda and I had wanted to quit, but we knew we'd get in trouble from Adam One if we did, for being un-Gardener. Bernice still didn't like Amanda, but she didn't exactly hate her either. She was wary of her the way you might be of some animals, like a bird with a very sharp beak. Bernice was mean, but Amanda was tough, which is different.

Nothing could change the way things were, which was that Bernice and I had once been best friends and we weren't any longer. That made me uneasy when I was around her: I felt guilty in some way. Bernice was aware of this, and she'd try to find ways to twist my guilt around and turn it against Amanda.

Still, things were friendly on the outside. The three of us walked to and from school together, or did chores or Young Bioneer collecting. That sort of thing. Bernice never came over to the Cheese Factory, though, and we never hung out with her after school.

On the way to Bernice's that morning, Amanda said, "I've found out something."

"What?" I said.

"I know where Burt goes between five and six, two nights a week."

"Burt the Knob? Who cares!" I said. We both felt contempt for him because he was such a pathetic armpit-groper.

"No. Listen. He goes to the same place Nuala goes," said Amanda.

"You're joking! Where?" Nuala flirted, but she flirted with all men. It was only her way, like giving you the stone-eye was Toby's way.

"They go into the Vinegar Room when no one's supposed to be there."

"Oh no!" I said. "Really?" I knew this was about sex – most of our jokey conversations were. The Gardeners called sex "the generative act" and said it was not a fit subject for ridicule, but Amanda ridiculed it anyway. You could snigger at it or trade it or both, but you couldn't respect it.

"No wonder her bum's so wobbly," said Amanda. "It's getting worn out. It's like Veena's old sofa – all saggy."

"I don't believe you!" I said. "She couldn't be doing it! Not with Burt!"

"Cross my heart and spit," said Amanda. She spat: she was a good spitter. "Why else would she go there with him?"

We Gardeners kids often made up rude stories about the sex lives of the Adams and Eves. It took away some of their power to imagine them naked, either with each other or with stray dogs, or even with the green-skinned girls in the pictures outside Scales and Tails. Still, Nuala moaning and flailing around with Burt the Knob was hard to picture. "Well, anyway," I said, "we can't tell Bernice!" Then we laughed some more.

At the Buenavista we nodded at the dowdy Gardener lady behind the lobby desk, who was doing string knotwork and didn't look up. Then we climbed the stairs, avoiding the used needles and condoms. The Buenavista Condom was Amanda's name for this building, so I called it that now too. The mushroomy, spicy Buenavista smell was stronger today.

"Someone's got a gro-op," said Amanda. "It reeks of skunkweed." She was an authority: she'd lived out there in the Exfernal World, she'd even done some drugs. Not much though, she said, because you lost your edge with drugs, you should only buy them from people you trusted because anything could have anything in it, and she didn't trust anybody much. I'd nag her to let me try some, but she wouldn't. "You're a baby," she'd say. Or else she'd say she had no good contacts since she'd been with the Gardeners.

"There can't be a gro-op in here," I said. "This building's Gardener. It's only the pleebmobs who have gro-ops. It's just – kids smoke it in here, at night. Pleeb kids."

"Yeah, I know," said Amanda, "but this isn't smoke. It's more of a gro-op smell."

As we reached the fourth-floor level, we heard voices – men's voices, two of them, on the other side of the landing door. They didn't sound friendly.

"That's all I got," said one voice. "I'll have the rest tomorrow."

"Asshole!" said the other. "Don't jerk me around!" There was a thud, as if something had hit the wall; then another thud, and a wordless yell, of pain or anger.

Amanda poked me. "Climb," she said. "Fast!"

We ran up the rest of the stairs as quietly as we could. "That was serious," said Amanda when we'd reached the sixth floor.

"How do you mean?"

"Some trade going bad," said Amanda. "We never heard this. Now, act normal." She looked scared, which scared me too because Amanda didn't scare easily.

We knocked at Bernice's door. "Knock, knock," said Amanda.

"Who's there?" said Bernice's voice. She must've been waiting for us right inside the door, as if she was afraid we might not come. I found this sad.

"Gang," said Amanda.

"Gang who?"

"Gangrene," said Amanda. She'd adopted Shackie's password, and the three of us used it now.

When Bernice opened the door I had a glimpse of Veena the Vegetable. She was sitting on her brown plush sofa as usual, but she was looking at us as if she actually saw us. "Don't be late," she said to Bernice.

"She spoke to you!" I said to Bernice once she was out in the hall with the door closed behind her. I was trying to be friendly, but Bernice froze me out. "Yeah, so?" she said. "She's not a moron."

"Didn't say she was," I said coldly.

Bernice gave me a short glare. Even her glaring power wasn't what it used to be, ever since Amanda had come.

27

When we got to the vacant lot behind Scales for our Outdoor Classroom Predator-Prey demonstration, Zeb was sitting on a folding canvas campstool. There was a cloth bag at his feet with something in it. I tried not to look at the bag. "We're all here? Good," said Zeb. "Now. Predator-Prey Relations. Hunting and stalking. What are the rules?"

"Seeing without being seen," we chanted. "Hearing without being heard. Smelling without being smelled. Eating without being eaten!"

"You forgot one," said Zeb.

"Injuring without being injured," said one of the oldest boys.

"Correct! A predator can't afford a serious injury. If it can't hunt, it'll starve. It must attack suddenly and kill quickly. It must choose the prey that's at a disadvantage – too young, too old, too crippled to run away or fight back. How do we avoid being prey?"

"By not looking like prey," we chanted.

"By not looking like the prey *of that predator*," said Zeb. "A surfboarder looks like a seal, to a shark, from underneath. Try to imagine what you look like from the predator's point of view."

"Don't show fear," said Amanda.

"Right. Don't show fear. Don't act sick. Make yourself look as big as possible. That will deter the larger hunting animals. But we ourselves are among the larger hunting animals, aren't we? Why would we hunt?" said Zeb.

"To eat," said Amanda. "There's no other good reason."

Zeb grinned at her as if this was a secret only the two of them knew. "Exactly," he said.

Zeb lifted up the cloth bag, untied it, and reached his hand in. He left his hand inside for what seemed a very long time. Then he took out a dead green rabbit. "Got it in Heritage Park. Rabbit trap," he said. "Noose. You can use them for the rakunks too. Now we're going to skin and gut the prey."

It still makes me feel sick to think about that part. The older boys helped him – they didn't flinch, though even Shackie and Croze seemed a bit strained. They always did whatever Zeb said. They looked up to him. It wasn't only because of his size. It was because he had lore, and it was lore they respected.

"What if the rabbit isn't, like, dead?" Croze asked. "In the snare."

"Then you kill it," said Zeb. "Smash it on the head with a rock. Or take it by the hind legs and bash it on the ground." You wouldn't kill a sheep like that, he added, because sheep had hard skulls: you'd slit its throat. Everything had its own most efficient way of being killed.

Zeb went on with the skinning. Amanda helped with the part where the furry green skin turned inside out like a glove. I tried not to look at the veins. They were too blue. And the glistening sinews.

Zeb made the chunks of meat really small so everyone could try, and also because he didn't want to push us too far by making us eat big pieces. Then we grilled the chunks over a fire made with some old boards.

"This is what you'll have to do if worst comes to worst," said Zeb. He handed me a chunk. I put it into my mouth. I found I could chew and swallow if I kept repeating in my head, "It's really bean paste, it's really bean paste . . ." I counted to a hundred, and then it was down.

But I had the taste of rabbit in my mouth. It felt like I'd eaten a nosebleed.

That afternoon we had the Tree of Life Natural Materials Exchange. It was held in a parkette on the northern edge of Heritage Park, across from the SolarSpace boutiques. It had a sand pit and a swing-and-slide set for small kids. There was a cobb house too, made of clay and sand and straw. It had six rooms and curved doorways and windows, but no doors or glass. Adam One said it was ancient greenies who'd built it, at least thirty years ago. The pleebrats had sprayed their tags and messages all over the walls: *I LV pssys (BBQd). Sk my dk, it's organic! UR ded FKn GreeNeez!*

The Tree of Life wasn't just for Gardeners. Everyone in the Natmart Net sold there – the Fernside Collective, the Big Box Backyarders, the Golfgreens Greenies. We looked down on these others because their clothes were nicer than ours. Adam One said their trading products were morally contaminated, though they didn't radiate synthetic slave-labour evil the way the flashy items in the mallway did. The Fernsiders sold their overglazed ceramics, plus jewellery they'd made from paper clips; the Big Box Backyarders did knitted animals; the Golfgreeners made artsy handbags out of rolled paper from vintage magazines, and grew cabbages around the edges of their golf course. Big deal, said Bernice, they still spray the grass there so a few cabbages won't save their souls. Bernice was getting more and more pious. Maybe it was her substitute for not having any real friends.

A lot of upmarket trendies came to the Tree of Life. Affluents from the SolarSpace gated communities, Fernside showoffs, even people from the Compounds, coming out for a safe pleebland adventure. They claimed to prefer our Gardener vegetables to the supermarkette kinds and even to the so-called farmers' markets, where – said Amanda – guys in farmer drag bought stuff from warehouses and tossed it into ethnic baskets and marked up the prices, so even if it said Organic you couldn't trust it. But the Gardener produce was the real thing. It stank of authenticity: the Gardeners might be fanatical and amusingly bizarre, but at least they were ethical. That's how they talked while I was wrapping up their purchases in recycled plastic.

The worst thing about helping at the Tree of Life was that we had to wear our Young Bioneer neck scarves. This was humiliating, as the trendies would often bring their kids. These kids wore baseball caps with words on them and stared at us and our neck scarves and drab clothing as if we were freaks, whispering among themselves and laughing. I'd try to ignore them. Bernice would stomp up to them and say, "What're you staring at?" Amanda's mode was smoother. She'd smile at them, then take out her piece of glass with the duct tape and cut a line on her arm and lick the blood. Then she'd run her bloody tongue around her lips, and hold out her arm, and they'd back off fast. Amanda said if you want people to leave you alone you should act crazy.

The three of us were told to help at the mushroom booth. Usually it was Pilar and Toby there, but Pilar wasn't well so it was only Toby. She was strict: you had to stand up straight and be extra polite.

I checked out the affluents as they walked past. Some had pastel jeans and sandals, but others were overloaded with expensive skin – alligator slingbacks, leopard minis, oryx-hide handbags. They'd give you this defensive look: *I didn't kill it, why let it go to waste?* I wondered what it would be like to wear those things – to feel another creature's skin right next to your own.

Some of them had the new Mo'Hairs – silver, pink, blue. Amanda said there were Mo'Hair shops in the Sewage Lagoon that lured girls in, and once you were in the scalp-transplant room they'd knock you out, and when you woke up you'd not only have different hair but different fingerprints, and then you'd be locked in a membrane house and forced into bristle work, and even if you escaped you'd never be able to prove who you were because they'd stolen your identity. This sounded really extreme. And Amanda did tell lies. But we'd made a pact never to lie to each other. So I thought maybe it was true.

After an hour selling mushrooms with Toby we were told to go over to Nuala's booth to help with the vinegar. By this time we were feeling bored and silly, and every time Nuala bent over to get more vinegar from the box under the counter, Amanda and I made wiggly motions with our bums and sniggered under our breaths. Bernice was getting redder and redder because we weren't letting her in. I knew this was mean, but I couldn't somehow stop myself.

Then Amanda had to go to the violet porta-biolet, and Nuala said she needed a word with Burt, who was selling leaf-wrapped soap at the next booth. As soon as Nuala's back was turned, Bernice grabbed my arm and twisted it two ways at once. "Tell me!" she hissed.

"Let go!" I said. "Tell you what?"

"You know what! What's so funny with you and Amanda?"

"Nothing!" I said.

She twisted harder. "Okay," I said, "but you won't like it." Then I told her about Nuala and Burt and what they'd been doing in the Vinegar Room. I must have been longing to tell her anyway, because it all came out in a rush.

"That is a stinking lie!" she said.

"What's a stinking lie?" said Amanda, back from the porta-biolet.

"My father is not humping the Wet Witch!" hissed Bernice.

"I couldn't help it," I said. "She twisted my arm." Bernice's eyes were all red and watery, and if Amanda hadn't been there she would've hit me.

"Ren gets carried away," Amanda said. "The fact is, we don't know for sure. We just *suspect* that your father is humping the Wet Witch. Maybe he isn't. But you could understand him doing it, with your mother in a Fallow state so much. He must get very horny – that's why he's always groping little girls' armpits." She said all of this in a virtuous, Eve sort of voice. It was cruel.

"He's not," said Bernice. "He doesn't!" She was close to tears.

"If he is," said Amanda in her calm voice, "it's something you should be aware of. I mean, if I had a father, I wouldn't want him humping someone's generative organ, other than my mother's. It's a filthy habit – so unsanitary. You'd have to worry about his germy hands touching *you*. Though I'm sure he doesn't –"

"I really, really hate you!" said Bernice. "I hope you burn and die!"

"That's not very *forgiving*, Bernice," said Amanda in a reproachful voice.

"So, girls," said Nuala as she bustled towards us. "Any customers? Bernice, why are your eyes so red?"

"I'm allergic to something," said Bernice.

"Yes, she is," said Amanda solemnly. "She's not feeling well. Maybe she should go home. Or maybe it's the bad air. Maybe she should get a nose cone. Don't you think, Bernice?"

"Amanda, you are a very thoughtful girl," said Nuala. "Yes, Bernice dear, I do think you should leave right away. And we'll see about a nose cone for you, tomorrow, for the allergies. I'll walk you partway, dear." And she put her arm around Bernice's shoulders and led her away.

I couldn't believe what we'd just done. I had that sinking feeling in my stomach, like when you drop a heavy thing and you know it's going to land on your foot. We'd gone way too far, but I didn't know how to say that without Amanda thinking I was sermonizing. Anyway, there was no way of taking it back.

28

Right then a boy I'd never seen before came to our booth – a teenage boy, older than us. He was thin and dark-haired and tall, and he wasn't wearing the sort of clothes the affluents wore. Just plain black.

"How may I help you, sir?" said Amanda. We sometimes imitated SecretBurger wage-slaves when we were working the booths.

"I need to see Pilar," he said. No smile, nothing. "There's something wrong with this." He took a jar of Gardener honey out of his backpack. That was strange, because what could be wrong with honey? Pilar said it never went bad unless you got water in it.

"Pilar's not feeling well," I said. "You should talk to Toby about it – she's right over there, with the mushrooms."

He looked all around, as if he was nervous. He didn't seem to be with anyone else – no friends, no parents. "No," he said. "It has to be Pilar."

Zeb came over from the vegetable stand, where he was selling burdock roots and lamb's quarters. "Something wrong?" he said.

"He wants Pilar," said Amanda. "About some honey." Zeb and the boy looked at each other, and I thought I saw the boy give a small shake of his head.

"Would I do?" Zeb said to him.

"I think it should be her," said the boy.

"Amanda and Ren will take you over," said Zeb.

"What about selling the vinegar?" I said. "Nuala had to leave."

"I'll keep an eye on it," said Zeb. "This is Glenn. Take good care of him. Don't let them eat you alive," he said to Glenn.

We walked through the pleeb streets, heading to the Edencliff Rooftop Garden. "How come you know Zeb?" said Amanda.

"Oh, I used to know him," said the boy. He wasn't talkative. He didn't even want to walk beside us: after a block, he dropped a little behind.

We reached the Gardener building and climbed up the fire escape. Philo the Fog and Katuro the Wrench were up there – we never left the place empty, in case pleebrats tried to sneak in. Katuro was fixing one of the watering hoses; Philo was just smiling.

"Who is this?" sad Katuro when he saw the boy.

"Zeb told us to bring him here," said Amanda. "He's looking for Pilar."

Katuro nodded over his shoulder. "Fallows Hut."

Pilar was lying in a deck chair. Her chess game was set up beside her, the pieces all in place: she hadn't been playing. She didn't look well at all – she was kind of sunken in. Her eyes were closed, but she opened them when she heard us coming in. "Welcome, dear Glenn," she said, as if she was expecting him. "I hope you didn't have any trouble."

"No trouble," said the boy. He took out the jar. "Not good," he said.

"Everything's good," said Pilar. "In the big picture. Amanda, Ren, would you get me a glass of water?"

"I'll go," I said.

"Both of you," said Pilar. "Please."

She wanted us out of there. We left the Fallows Hut as slowly as we could. I wished I could hear what they were saying – it wouldn't be about honey. The way Pilar looked was frightening me.

"He's not pleeb," Amanda whispered. "He's Compound."

I thought that myself, but I said, "How can you tell?" The Compounds were where the Corps people lived – all those scientists and business people Adam One said were destroying old Species and making new ones and ruining the world, though I couldn't quite believe my real father in HelthWyzer was doing that; but in any case, why would Pilar even say hello to someone from there?

"I just have a feeling," said Amanda.

When we came back with the glass of water, Pilar had her eyes closed again. The boy was sitting beside her; he'd moved a few of her chess pieces. The white queen was boxed in: one more move and she'd be gone.

"Thank you," said Pilar, taking the glass of water from Amanda. "And thank you for coming, dear Glenn," she said to the boy.

He stood up. "Well, goodbye," he said awkwardly, and Pilar smiled at him. Her smile was bright but weak. I wanted to hug her, she looked so tiny and frail.

Going back to the Tree of Life, Glenn walked along beside us. "There's something really wrong with her," said Amanda. "Right?"

"Illness is a design fault," said the boy. "It could be corrected." Yes – he was definitely Compound. Only brainiacs from there talked like that: not answering your question up front, then saying some general kind of thing as if they knew it for a fact. Was that the way my real father had talked? Maybe.

"So, if you were making the world, you'd make it better?" I said. Better than God, was what I meant. All of a sudden I was feeling pious, like Bernice. Like a Gardener.

"Yes," he said. "As a matter of fact, I would."

29

The next day we went to pick up Bernice from the Buenavista Condos as usual. I think we were both feeling ashamed of ourselves because of what we'd done the day before – at least I was. But when we knocked on the door and said, "Knock, knock," Bernice didn't say, "Who's there?" She said nothing.

"It's Gang," Amanda called. "Gang grene!" Still nothing. I could almost feel her silence.

"Come on, Bernice," I said. "Open the door. It's us."

The door opened, but it wasn't Bernice. It was Veena. She was looking right at us, and she didn't seem in any way Fallow. "Go away," she said. Then she shut the door.

We looked at each other. I had a very bad feeling. What if we'd done some kind of permanent damage to Bernice, with our story about Burt and Nuala? What if it wasn't even true? It had just been a joke, at first. But it didn't seem like a joke any more.

Any other Saint Euell's Week we'd have gone to the Heritage Park to look for mushrooms with Pilar and Toby. It was exciting to go there because you never knew what you'd see. There'd be pleebland families having cookouts and family fights, and we'd hold our noses to avoid the stink of frizzling meat; there'd be couples thrashing around in the bushes, or homeless people drinking from bottles or snoring under the trees, or tangle-haired crazies talking to themselves or shouting, or druggies shooting up. If we got down as far as the beach, there might be girls in bikinis lying in the sun, and Shackie and Croze might say, *Skin cancer* to them, to get their attention.

Or there could be some CorpSeCorps guys on public-service patrol telling people to put their trash in the containers provided, though really – said Amanda – they were looking for small dealers doing business without cutting their mob friends in. Then you might hear the hot *zipzipzip* of a spraygun and some screams. Offering violence, they'd say to the bystanders as they dragged the guy away.

But our Heritage Park trip was cancelled that day because of Pilar being ill. So instead we had Wild Botanicals with Burt the Knob, in the vacant lot behind Scales and Tails.

We had our slates and chalk because we always drew the Wild Botanicals to help us memorize them. Then we'd wipe off our drawings, and the plant would be in our heads. There's nothing like drawing a thing to make you really see it, Burt would say.

Burt hunted around the vacant lot, picked something, held it up for us to see. "*Portulaca oleracea*," he said. "Common name, Purslane. Found cultivated and in the wild. Prefers disturbed earth. Notice the red stem, the alternate leaves. A good source of omega 3s." He paused, frowned at us. "Half of you aren't looking and the other half aren't drawing," he said. "This could save your lives! We're talking about sustenance here. *Sustenance.* What is sustenance?"

Blank stares, silence. "Sustenance," said the Knob, "is what sustains a person's body. It's food. Food! Where does food come from? Class?"

We recited together: "All food comes from the Earth."

"Right!" said Burt. "The Earth! And then most people buy it from the supermarkette. What would happen if suddenly there were no more supermarkettes? Shackleton?"

"Grow it on the roof," said Shackie.

"Suppose there weren't any roofs," said the Knob, beginning to go pink in the face. "Where would you get it then?" Blank stares again. "You'd *forage*," said the Knob. "Crozier, what do we mean by *foraging*?"

"Finding stuff," said Croze. "Stuff you don't pay for. Like, stealing." We laughed.

The Knob ignored this. "And where would you look for this *stuff*? Quill?"

"At the mallway?" said Quill. "In behind, like. Where they throw stuff out, like, old bottles, and . . ." He was kind of dim, Quill, but also he was acting dim. The boys did that to make the Knob lose it.

"No, no!" the Knob shouted. "There won't *be* anyone to throw stuff out! You've never been outside this pleeb, have you? You've never seen a *desert*, you've never been in a *famine*! When the Waterless Flood hits, even if you personally last it out you'll starve. Why? Because you haven't been paying any attention! Why do I waste my time on you?" Every time the Knob took a class, he'd tip over some invisible edge and start yelling.

"Well then," he said, winding down. "What is this plant? Purslane. What can you do with it? Eat it. Now then, keep on drawing. Purslane! Notice the oval shape of those leaves! Notice their shininess! Look at the stem! Memorize it!"

I was thinking, It can't be true. I didn't see how anyone – even Wet Witch Nuala – could do sex with Burt the Knob. He was so bald and sweaty. "Cretins," he was muttering to himself. "Why do I bother?"

Then he went very still. He was looking at something behind us. We turned around: Veena was standing there, beside the gap in the fence. She must have squeezed through. She was still in her slippers; her yellow baby blanket was draped over her head like a shawl. Beside her was Bernice.

They just stood there. They didn't move. Then two CorpSeMen came through the fence as well. They were Combat, in their shimmering grey suits that made them look like a mirage. They had their sprayguns out. I felt all the blood drain out of my face; I thought I was going to throw up.

"What's wrong?" shouted Burt.

"Freeze!" said one of the CorpSeMen. His voice was very loud because of the mike in his helmet. They moved forward.

"Stay back," Burt said to us. He looked as if he'd been tasered.

"Come with us, sir," said the first CorpSeMan when they'd reached us.

"What?" said Burt. "I haven't done anything!"

"Illegal growing of marijuana for black-market profit, sir," said the second one. "It would be safer not to resist arrest."

They walked Burt towards the gap in the fence. We all trailed silently along behind – we couldn't understand what was happening.

As they came up to Veena and Bernice, Burt held out his arms. "Veena! How did this happen?"

"You fucking degenerate!" she said to him. "Hypocrite! Fornicator! How dumb do you think I am?"

"What are you talking about?" said Burt in a pleading voice.

"I guess you thought I was so high on that poisonous weed of yours that I couldn't see straight," said Veena. "But I found out. What you're doing with that cow Nuala! Not that she's the worst of it. You twisted asshole!"

"No," said Burt. "I swear! I never really . . . I was just . . ."

I was looking at Bernice: I couldn't tell what she was feeling. Her face wasn't even red. It was blank, like a chalkboard. Dusty white.

Adam One stepped in through the gap in the fence. He always seemed to know if there was something unusual going on. Amanda said it was just like he had a phone. He laid his hand on Veena's yellow baby blanket. "Veena, dear, you've come out of your Fallow state," he said. "How wonderful. We've been praying for that. Now, what seems to be the matter?"

"Move out of the way, please, sir," said the first CorpSeMan.

"Why did you do this to me?" Burt howled at Veena as they pushed him forward.

Adam One took a deep breath. "This is regrettable," he said. "Perhaps it would be wise to reflect on our shared Human frailties . . ."

"You're an idiot," Veena said to him. "Burt's been running a major gro-op in the Buenavista, right under your sacred Gardener noses. He's been dealing right under your noses too, at that stupid market of yours.

Those cute bars of soap wrapped up in leaves – not all of it was soap! He's been making a killing!"

Adam One looked mournful. "Money is a terrible temptation," he said. "It is a sickness."

"You fool," Veena said to him. "Organic botanics, what a joke!"

"Told you there was a gro-op in the Buenavista," Amanda whispered to me. "The Knob's in very deep shit."

Adam One said we should all go home, so that's what we did. I felt really bad about Burt. All I could imagine was that Bernice had gone back that day after we'd been so mean to her at the Tree of Life, and told Veena about Burt and Nuala having sex, and also about the armpit-groping, and that had made Veena so jealous or angry that she'd got in contact with the CorpSeCorps and made an accusation. The CorpSeCorps encouraged you to do that – to turn in your neighbours and family members. You could even get money for it, said Amanda.

I hadn't meant any harm, or not that kind of harm. But now look what had happened.

I thought we should go to Adam One and tell him what we'd done, but Amanda said what good would that do, it wouldn't fix things, it would just land us in more trouble. She was right. But that didn't make me feel any better.

"Lighten up," said Amanda. "I'll steal something for you. What d'you want?"

"A phone," I said. "Purple. Like yours."

"Okay," said Amanda. "I'll take care of it."

"That's nice of you," I said. I tried to put a lot of energy into my voice so she'd know I appreciated it, but she could tell I was faking.

30

The next day, Amanda said she had a surprise that would cheer me up without fail. It was at the Sinkhole mallway, she said. And it really was a surprise, because when we got there Shackie and Croze were hanging around near the wrecked holospinner booth. I knew they both had a crush on Amanda – all the boys did – though she never spent time with them except in a group.

"Have you got it?" she said to them. They grinned at her shyly. Shackie had grown a lot lately: he was tall and rangy, with dark eyebrows. Croze had grown too, but sideways as well as up; he had the beginnings of a straw-coloured beard. Before this I hadn't thought too much about what they looked like – not in detail – but now I found myself seeing them in a different way.

"In here," they said. They seemed not scared exactly, but alert. They checked that no one was watching, and then we all crammed into the booth where people used to get their image spun out into the mallway. It was designed for just two, so we had to stand close together.

It was hot in there. I could feel the heat from our bodies, as if we were infected and burning with fever, and I could smell the dried-sweat and old cotton and grime and oily scalp smell from Shackie and Croze – which was what we all smelled like – mixed with their older-boy smell, a mushroom and wine-dregs blend; and the flowery smell of Amanda, with a musky undertone and a hint of blood.

I couldn't tell what I smelled like to them. They say you can never really smell your own smell because you're so used to yourself. I wished

I'd known about this surprise in advance, because then I could have used one of my saved-up rose soap ends. I hoped I didn't smell like dirty underwear or cooped-up feet.

Why do we want other people to like us, even if we don't really care about them all that much? I don't know why, but it's true. I found myself standing there and smelling all those smells, and hoping a lot that Shackie and Croze thought I was pretty.

"Here it is," Shackie said. He brought out a piece of cloth with something wrapped up in it.

"What is it?" I said. I could hear my own voice: girly and squeaky.

"It's the surprise," said Amanda. "They got some of that superweed for us. The stuff Burt the Knob was growing."

"No way!" I said. "You bought it? From the CorpSeCorps?"

"Lifted it," said Shackie. "We snuck in the back of the Buenavista – we've done that lots. The CorpSe guys were going in and out the front door, they didn't pay any attention to us."

"There's a loose set of bars on one of the cellar windows – we used to get in there and party in the stairwell," said Croze.

"They've put bags of it in the cellar," said Shackie. "They must've harvested all the gro-op rooms. You could get blasted just breathing."

"Show," said Amanda. Shackie unrolled the cloth: dried shredded leaves.

I knew how Amanda felt about doing drugs: you lost control of your mind, and that was risky because it gave other people the edge. Also you could do too much, like Philo the Fog, and then you wouldn't have any mind left to speak of so no one would care whether you lost control of it or not. And you should only smoke with people you trusted. Did she trust Shackie and Croze?

"Have you tried this stuff?" I whispered to Amanda.

"Not yet," Amanda whispered back. Why were we whispering? The four of us were so close together that Shackie and Croze could hear everything.

"Then I don't want to," I said.

"But I traded!" said Amanda. She sounded fierce. "I traded a lot!"

"I've done this shit," said Shackie. He used his toughest voice for *shit.* "It's awesome!"

"Me too, you feel like you're airborne," said Croze. "Like a fucking bird!" Shackie was already rolling the shredded leaves, already lighting up, already sucking in.

There was someone's hand on my bum, I didn't know whose. It was creeping up, trying to find a way in under my Gardener one-piece dress. I wanted to say, Stop that, but I didn't.

"Just give it a try," said Shackie. He took hold of my chin and stuck his mouth down on mine and blew me full of smoke. I coughed, and he did it again, and I felt very dizzy. Then I had a clear blinding-bright fluorescent image of the rabbit we'd eaten that week. It was glaring at me with its dead eyes, only the eyes were orange.

"That was too much," said Amanda. "She's not used to it!"

Then I felt sick to my stomach, and then I threw up. I think I must have hit all of them. Oh no, I thought, what an idiot. I don't know how long all of that lasted because time was like rubber, it stretched out like a long, long elastic rope or a huge piece of chewing gum. Then it snapped shut into a tiny black square and I passed out.

When I woke up I was sitting against the broken fountain in the mallway. I was still dizzy, though not so sick: it was more like floating. Everything seemed far away and translucent. Maybe I can stick my hand through the cement, I thought. Maybe everything's lacework – made of specks, with God in between, just like Adam One says. Maybe I'm smoke.

The mallway store window across from us was like a boxful of fireflies, like living sequins. There was a party going on in there, I could hear the music. Tinkly and strange. A butterfly party: they must be dancing on their spindly butterfly legs. If I could only stand up, I thought, I could dance too.

Amanda had her arm around me. "It's okay," she said. "You're fine." Shackie and Croze were still there, and they were sounding pissed off. Or Croze was, more than Shackie, because Shackie was almost as whacked as I was.

"So, when'll you pay up?" said Croze.

"It didn't work," said Amanda. "So, never."

"That wasn't the trade," said Croze. "The trade was, we bring the stuff. We brought it. So, you owe us."

"The trade was, Ren gets happy," said Amanda. "She didn't. End of story."

"No way," said Croze. "You owe us. Pay up."

"Make me," said Amanda. Her voice had that dangerous edge, the one she'd use on pleebrats when they got too close.

"Whatever," said Shackie. "Whenever." He didn't seem too bothered.

"You owe us two fucks," said Croze. "One each. We ran a big risk, we could've got killed!"

"Don't bug her," said Shackie. "I just want to touch your hair," he said to Amanda. "You smell like toffee." He was still flying.

"Piss off," said Amanda. And I guess they did, because the next time I looked for them they weren't there.

I was feeling more normal by then. "Amanda," I said. "I can't believe you traded with them." I wanted to say, For me, but I was afraid I'd cry.

"Sorry it didn't work," she said. "I only wanted you to feel better."

"I do feel better," I said. "Lighter." That was true, partly because I'd puked up a lot of water weight, but partly because of Amanda. I knew she used to do that kind of trade, for food, when she was so hungry after the Texas hurricane, but she'd told me she'd never liked it and it was strictly business, so she never did it any more because she didn't have to. And she didn't have to this time, but she'd done it anyway. I didn't know she liked me so much.

"Now they're mad at you," I said. "They'll get even." It didn't seem really important, though, because I was still high as a bee.

"I'm not worried," said Amanda. "I can take care of them."

MOLE DAY

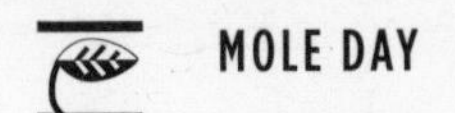

MOLE DAY

YEAR TWELVE.

OF THE LIFE UNDERGROUND.

SPOKEN BY ADAM ONE.

Dear Friends, dear Fellow Mammals, dear Fellow Creatures:

I point no fingers, for I know not where to point; but as we have just seen, malicious rumours can spread confusion. A careless remark can be as the cigarette butt casually tossed into the dumpster, smouldering until it bursts into flame and engulfs a neighbourhood. Do guard your words in future.

It is inevitable that certain friendships may lend themselves to undue comment. But we are not Chimpanzees: our females do not bite rival females, our males do not jump up and down on our females and hit them with branches. Or not as a rule. All pair-bondings are subject to stress and temptation – but let us not add to that stress nor misinterpret that temptation.

We miss the presence of our erstwhile Adam Thirteen, Burt, and his wife, Veena, and little Bernice. Let us forgive what needs to be forgiven, and put Light around them in our hearts.

Moving forward, we have identified an abandoned automobile repair establishment that can be turned into cozy homes, once our proposed Rat relocation has been carried out. I am sure the Rats of the FenderBender Body Shop will be very happy in the Buenavista once they have understood the food opportunities it has to offer.

You'll be pleased to know that though our Buenavista mushroom beds are lost to us, Pilar has kept some spawn on hand for each of our treasured species, and we will set up our mushroom beds in a cellar room at the Wellness Clinic until a damper location can be found.

Today we celebrate Mole Day, our Festival of Underground Life. Mole Day is a Children's festival, and our Children have been busily at work, decorating our Edencliff Rooftop Garden. The Moles with their little claws fashioned from hair combs, the Nematodes fashioned from transparent plastic bags, the Earthworms of stuffed pantyhose and string, the Dung Beetles – what a testimony to our God-given powers of creativity, through which even the useless and discarded may be redeemed from meaninglessness.

We are inclined to overlook the very small that dwell among us; yet, without them, we ourselves could not exist; for every one of us is a Garden of sub-visual life forms. Where would we be without the Flora that populate the intestinal tract, or the Bacteria that defend against hostile invaders? We teem with multitudes, my Friends – with the myriad forms of Life that creep about under our feet, and – I may add – under our toenails.

True, we are sometimes infested with nanobioforms we would prefer to be without, such as the Eyebrow Mite, the Hookworm, the Pubic Louse, the Pinworm, and the Tick, not to mention the hostile bacteria and viruses. But think of them as God's tiniest Angels, doing His unfathomable work in their own way, for these Creatures, too, reside in the Eternal Mind, and shine in the Eternal Light, and form a part of the polyphonic symphony of Creation.

Consider also His workers in the Earth! Without the Earthworms and Nematodes and Ants, and their endless tilling of the soil, without which it would harden into a cement-like mass, extinguishing all Life. Think of the antibiotic properties of the Maggots and of the various Moulds, and of the honey that our Bees make, and also of the Spider's web, so useful in the stopping of bloodflow from a wound. For every ill, God has provided a remedy in His great Medicine Cabinet of Nature!

Through the work of the Carrion Beetles and the putrefying Bacteria, our fleshly habitations are broken down, and returned to their elements to enrich the lives of other Creatures. How misguided were our ancestors in their preserving of corpses – their embalmings, their adornings, their encasings in mausoleums. What a horror – to turn the Soul's husk into an unholy fetish! And, in the end, how selfish! Shall we not repay the gift of Life by regifting ourselves to Life when the time comes?

When next you hold a handful of moist compost, say a silent prayer of thanks to all of Earth's previous Creatures. Picture your fingers giving each and every one of them a loving squeeze. For they are surely here with us, ever present in that nourishing matrix.

Now let us join our Buds and Blooms Choir in singing our traditional Mole Day Children's Hymn.

WE PRAISE THE TINY PERFECT MOLES

We praise the tiny perfect Moles
That garden underground;
The Ant, the Worm, the Nematode,
Wherever they are found.

They live their whole lives in the dark,
Unseen by Human sight;
The earth is like the air to them,
Their day is like our night.

They turn the soil and till it,
They make the plants to thrive;
The Earth would be a desert,
If they were not alive.

The little Carrion Beetles
That seek unlikely places
Return our Husks to Elements,
And tidy up our spaces.

And so for God's small Creatures
Beneath the field and wood,
Let us today give joyful thanks,
For God has found them good.

From *The God's Gardeners Oral Hymnbook*

31

TOBY. MOLE DAY

YEAR TWENTY-FIVE

While the Flood rages, you must count the days, said Adam One. You must observe the risings of the Sun and the changings of the Moon, because to everything there is a season. On your Meditations, do not travel so far on your inner journeys that you enter the Timeless before it is time. In your Fallow states, do not descend to a level that is too deep for any resurgence, or the Night will come in which all hours are the same to you, and then there will be no Hope.

Toby's been keeping track of the days on some old AnooYoo Spa-in-the-Park notepaper. Each pink page is topped with two long-lashed eyes, one of them winking, and with a lipstick kiss. She likes these eyes and smiling mouths: they're companions of a sort. At the top of each fresh page she prints the Gardener Feast Day or Saint's Day. She can still recite the entire list off by heart: Saint E.F. Schumacher, Saint Jane Jacobs, Saint Sigurdsdottir of Gullfoss, Saint Wayne Grady of Vultures; Saint James Lovelock, The Blessed Gautama Buddha, Saint Bridget Stutchbury of Shade Coffee, Saint Linnaeus of Botanical Nomenclature, The Feast of Crocodylidae, Saint Stephen Jay Gould of the Jurassic Shales, Saint Gilberto Silva of Bats. And the rest.

Under each Saint's Day name she writes her gardening notes: what was planted, what was harvested, what phase of the moon, what insect guests.

Mole Day, she writes now. *Year Twenty-five. Do the laundry. Gibbous Moon.* Mole Day was part of Saint Euell's Week. It wasn't such a good anniversary.

On the bright side, there should be some polyberries by now, ripe ones. The strength of the polyberry gene splice is that it produces at all seasons. Perhaps in the late afternoon she'll go down and pick them.

Two days back – on Saint Orlando Garrido of Lizards – she made an entry that wasn't about gardening. *Hallucination?* she'd written. She ponders this entry now. It did seem like a hallucination at the time.

It was after the daily thunderstorm. She was up on the roof, checking the rain barrel connections: the flow from the single tap she's kept open downstairs was blocked. She found the problem – drowned mouse clogging the intake – and was turning to go back down the stairs when she heard an odd sound. It was like singing, but not any singing she'd ever heard before.

She scanned with the binoculars. At first there was nothing, but then at the far end of the field a strange procession appeared. It seemed to consist entirely of naked people, though one man walking at the front had clothes on, and some sort of red hat, and – could it be? – sunglasses. Behind him there were men and women and children, every known skin colour; as she focused, she could see that several of the naked people had blue abdomens.

That was why she's decided it must have been a hallucination: the blueness. And the crystalline, otherworldly singing. She'd seen the figures for only a moment. They were there, then they'd vanished, like smoke. They must have gone in among the trees, to follow the walkway there.

Her heart had leapt with joy – she couldn't help it. She'd felt like running down the stairs, running outside, running after them. But it was far too much to hope for, other people – so many other people. Other people who looked so healthy. They couldn't possibly be real. If she allowed herself to be lured outside by such a siren mirage – lured into the pig-ridden forest – she wouldn't be the first person in history to have been destroyed by the overly optimistic projections of her own mind.

Confronted by too much emptiness, said Adam One, the brain invents. Loneliness creates company as thirst creates water. How many sailors have been wrecked in pursuit of islands that were merely a shimmering?

She takes her pencil and scratches out the question mark. *Hallucination*, it says now. Pure. Simple. No doubt about it.

She sets down her pencil, gathers her mop handle and her binoculars and the rifle, and trudges up the stairs to the rooftop to survey her domain. All is quiet this morning. No movement out there in the field – no large animals, no naked blue-tinged singers.

32

How long ago was that Mole Day, the last one Pilar was alive? Year Twelve, it must have been.

Right before it had come the disaster of Burt's arrest. After he'd been taken away by the CorpSeMen and Veena and Bernice had left the vacant lot, Adam One had called all the Gardeners together for an emergency meeting up on the Edencliff Rooftop. He'd told them the news, and when they'd grasped it, the Gardeners had gone into shock. The revelation was so painful, and so shameful! How had Burt managed to run a gro-op in the Buenavista without anyone suspecting?

Through trust, of course, thinks Toby. The Gardeners mistrusted everyone in the Exfernal World, but they trusted their own. Now they'd joined the long list of the religious faithful who'd woken one morning to find that the vicar had made off with the church building fund, leaving a trail of molested choirboys behind him. At least Burt hadn't done any choirboy molesting, or not as far as was known. There'd been gossip among the children – crude remarks of the kind children made – but they hadn't been about boys. Just girls, and just groping.

The only one of the Gardeners who hadn't been surprised and horrified by the gro-op was Philo the Fog, but he was never surprised or horrified by anything. "I'd like to try that shit, see if it's any good," was all he had to say.

Adam One had asked for volunteers to take in the families that had been so suddenly displaced – they couldn't go back to the Buenavista, he'd said, because it would be overrun with CorpSeMen, so they should consider their material possessions as lost to them. "If the building was on fire, you wouldn't run back into it to save a few baubles and trinkets," he said. "It is God's way of testing your attachment to the realm of useless illusion." The Gardeners weren't supposed to be bothered by that part: they'd gleaned their material possessions in junkyards and dumpsters so they could always glean others, went the theory. Nevertheless there was some weeping over a lost crystal glass, and a puzzling fuss about a broken waffle iron with sentimental value.

Adam One then asked all present not to talk about Burt and the Buenavista, and especially the CorpSeCorps. "Our enemies may be listening," he'd said. He'd been saying that more and more frequently: Toby sometimes wondered whether he was paranoid.

"Nuala, Toby," he'd said as the others were leaving. "A moment. Can you go by there and check?" he said to Zeb. "Though I don't suppose there's anything to be done."

"Nope," said Zeb cheerfully. "Not a fuckworth. But I'll take a look."

"Wear your pleebland clothes," said Adam One.

Zeb nodded. "The solarbiker outfit." He strolled away towards the fire-escape stairs.

"Nuala, my dear," said Adam One. "Can you cast any light? On what Veena said, about you and Burt?"

Nuala began sniffling. "I have no idea," she said. "It's such a lie! It's so disrespectful! It's so hurtful! How could she think such a thing, about me and . . . and Adam Thirteen?"

Not too hard, thought Toby, considering the way you rub up against pant legs. Nuala flirted with anything male. But Veena had been in a Fallow state while the flirting had been going on, so what had aroused her suspicion?

"None of us believes it, my dear," said Adam One. "Veena must have listened to some rumour-monger – perhaps an *agent provocateur* sent by our enemies to sow dissention among us. I will ask the Buenavista gatekeepers if Veena had any unusual visitors in recent days. Now, dear

Nuala, you should dry your tears and go to the Sewing Room. Our displaced congregation members will need many cloth items, such as quilts, and I know you're happy to be of use."

"Thank you," said Nuala gratefully. She gave him her only-you-understand-me look and hurried away towards the fire escape.

"Toby, my dear. Do you think you could see it in your heart to take over Burt's duties?" Adam One asked, once Nuala had gone. "The Garden Botanics, the Edible Weeds. We'd make you an Eve, of course. I've meant to do that for some time, but Pilar has so appreciated your help as her assistant, and I believe you've been happy in that role. I didn't want to steal you away from her."

Toby thought. "I'd be honoured," she said at last. "But I can't accept. To be a full-fledged Eve . . . it would be hypocritical." She'd never managed to repeat the moment of illumination she'd felt on her first day with the Gardeners, though she'd tried often enough. She'd gone on the Retreats, she'd done an Isolation Week, she'd performed the Vigils, she'd taken the required mushrooms and elixirs, but no special revelations had come to her. Visions, yes, but none with meaning. Or none with any meaning she could decipher.

"Hypocritical?" said Adam One, wrinkling his forehead. "In what way?"

Toby chose her words carefully: she didn't wish to hurt his feelings. "I'm not sure I believe in all of it." An understatement: she believed in very little.

"In some religions, faith precedes action," said Adam One. "In ours, action precedes faith. You've been acting as if you believe, dear Toby. *As if* – those two words are very important to us. Continue to live according to them, and belief will follow in time."

"That's not much to go on," said Toby. "Surely an Eve ought to be . . ."

Adam One sighed. "We should not expect too much from faith," he said. "Human understanding is fallible, and we see through a glass, darkly. Any religion is a shadow of God. But the shadows of God are not God."

"I wouldn't want to be a poor example," said Toby. "Children can spot faking – they'll see I'm just going through the motions. That might be harmful to what you're trying to accomplish."

"Your doubts reassure me," said Adam One. "They show how trustworthy you are. For every No there is also a Yes! Will you do one thing for me?"

"What thing?" said Toby cautiously. She didn't want the responsibilities of Evehood – she didn't want to close down her choices. She wanted to feel free to quit if she needed to. I've just been timeserving, she thought. Taking advantage of their goodwill. Such a fraud.

"Just ask for guidance," said Adam One. "Do an overnight Vigil. Pray for the strength to face your doubts and fears. I feel confident that a positive answer will be provided to you. You have gifts that should not be wasted. We would all welcome you as an Eve among us, I can assure you."

"All right," said Toby. "I can do that." For every Yes, she thought, there is also a No.

Pilar was the keeper of the Vigil materials and the other Gardener out-of-body voyaging substances. Toby hadn't spoken with her for several days because of her illness – a stomach virus, it was said. But in their conversation Adam One hadn't mentioned anything about this illness, so maybe Pilar was well again. Those bugs never lasted more than a week.

Toby sought out Pilar's tiny cubicle at the back of the building. Pilar was lying propped up on her futon; a beeswax candle flickered in a tin can on the floor beside her. The air was close, and smelled of vomit. But the bowl beside Pilar was empty, and clean.

"Dear Toby," said Pilar. "Come and sit beside me." Her little face was more like a walnut than ever, though her skin was pale, or as pale as brown skin could get. Greyish. Muddy.

"Are you feeling better?" said Toby, taking Pilar's sinewy claw in both of her own hands.

"Oh yes. Much better," said Pilar, smiling sweetly. Her voice was not strong.

"What was it?"

"I ate something that disagreed with me," said Pilar. "Now, what can I do for you?"

"I wanted to make sure you were all right," said Toby, who'd just discovered that this was true. Pilar looked so wan, so depleted. She recognized fear in herself: what if Pilar – who'd seemed eternal, who'd surely always been there, or if not always, at least for a very long time, like a boulder or an ancient stump – what if she were suddenly to vanish?

"That's very kind of you," said Pilar. She squeezed Toby's hand.

"And Adam One asked me to become an Eve."

"I suppose you said no?" said Pilar, smiling.

"That's right," said Toby. Pilar could usually guess what she was thinking. "But he wants me to do an overnight Vigil. To pray for guidance."

"That would be best," said Pilar. "You know where I keep the Vigil things. It's the brown bottle," she said as Toby lifted the rubber-band-and-string curtain in front of the storage shelves. "The brown one, to the right. Five drops only, and two from the purple one."

"Have I done this mix before?" asked Toby.

"Not this exact one. You'll get an answer of some kind, on this. It never fails. Nature never does betray us. You do know that?"

Toby knew no such thing. She measured the drops into one of Pilar's chipped teacups, then replaced the bottles. "Are you sure you're better?" she asked.

"I'm fine," said Pilar, "for the moment. And the moment is the only time we can be fine in. Now, you go along, Toby dear, and have a lovely Vigil. It's a gibbous moon tonight. Enjoy it!" Sometimes, when doling out the head trips, Pilar sounded like the supervisor of a kiddie carnival ride.

For the site of her Vigil, Toby chose the tomato section of the Edencliff Rooftop Garden. She posted the site on the Vigil sign-in slate, as required: those on Vigils sometimes went wandering away, and in tracing them it was helpful to know where they were supposed to have been.

Adam One had recently taken to placing gatekeepers on every floor, beside the landings. So I can't get down the Garden stairs without someone seeing me, thought Toby. Unless I fall off the roof.

She waited till dusk, then took the drops with a mix of Elderflower and Raspberry to disguise the taste: Pilar's Vigil potions always tasted like mulch. Then she sat down in meditation position, near a large tomato plant, which in the moonlight looked like a contorted leafy dancer or a grotesque insect.

Soon the plant began to glow and twirl its vines, and the tomatoes on it started to beat like hearts. There were crickets nearby, speaking in tongues: quarkit quarkit, ibbit ibbit, arkit arkit . . .

Neural gymnastics, thought Toby. She closed her eyes.

Why can't I believe? she asked the darkness.

Behind her eyelids she saw an animal. It was a golden colour, with gentle green eyes and canine teeth, and curly wool instead of fur. It opened its mouth, but it did not speak. Instead, it yawned.

It gazed at her. She gazed at it. "You are the effect of a carefully calibrated blend of plant toxins," she told it. Then she fell asleep.

33

The next morning Adam One came to see how Toby's Vigil had gone. "Did you get an answer?" he asked her.

"I saw an animal," said Toby.

Adam One was delighted. "What a successful outcome! Which animal? What did it say to you?" But before Toby could answer, he looked over her shoulder. "We have a messenger," he said.

In her hazy post-Vigil state, Toby thought he meant some kind of mushroom angel or plant spirit, but it was only Zeb, breathing hard from his climb up the fire escape. He was still wearing his pleeblander disguise: black fleather vest, grimy jeans, battered solarbike boots. He looked hungover.

"Were you up all night?" said Toby.

"You too, looks like," said Zeb. "I'll get shit for it back at the nest – Lucerne hates it when I work at night." He didn't seem too concerned about that. "You want to call a general meeting," he said to Adam One, "or hear the bad news first yourself?"

"Bad news first," said Adam One. "We may have to edit it for wider consumption." He nodded towards Toby. "She doesn't panic."

"Right," said Zeb. "Here's the story."

His sources of information were unofficial, he said: in pursuit of the truth, he'd been forced to sacrifice himself by spending an evening watching the girls gyrate at Scales and Tails, where the CorpSeCorps guys hung out when off-duty. He didn't like to get too close to the CorpSeMen, he said – he had a history of sorts, he might be recognized despite the alterations he'd had done to himself. But he knew a few of the girls, so he'd mined them for rumours.

"You paid them?" said Adam One.

"Nothing's free," said Zeb. "But I didn't pay too much."

Burt had indeed been running a gro-op in the Buenavista, he said. It was the usual method – unoccupied apartments, windows blacked out, electricity hijacked. Full-spectrum gro-lights, automatic sprinkler systems, all top of the line. But it wasn't just ordinary skunkweed, not even West Coast superweed: it was a stratospheric splice, with some peyote genes and psilocybins, and even a little ayahuasca – the good part, though they hadn't completely eliminated the part that made you puke your guts out. A lot of people who'd tried this would kill to do it again, and there wasn't much being made yet, so it was going for a very high price on the market.

It was a CorpSeCorps operation, naturally. The HelthWyzer labs had developed the splice, the CorpSeCorpsMen were the wholesalers. They ran it the way they ran everything illegal, through the pleebmobs. They'd thought it was a joke to get one of the Adams to front it, and to plant the gro-op in a building the Gardeners controlled. They'd been paying Burt well enough, but then he'd tried to cheat by selling on his own. He'd been getting away with it too, said Zeb, until the CorpSeCorps got an anonymous tip. Traced to a cellphone tossed into a dumpster. No DNA on it. Woman's voice, though. Very pissed-off woman.

That would be Veena, thought Toby. I wonder where she got the phone? Word had it that she'd taken Bernice to the West Coast, with the money the CorpSeCorps had paid her.

"Where is he now?" said Adam One. "Adam Thirteen? Former Adam Thirteen. Is he still alive?"

"Can't tell you," said Zeb. "No word on it."

"Let us pray," said Adam One. "He'll talk about us."

"If he was in that deep with them, he already has," said Zeb.

"Did he know about Pilar's tissue samples?" said Adam One. "And our contact in HelthWyzer? Our young courier with the honey jar?"

"No," said Zeb. "That was just you and me and Pilar. We never discussed it in Council."

"Fortunate," said Adam One.

"Let's hope he'll have an accident with a gutting knife," said Zeb. "You didn't hear any of this," he said to Toby.

"Fear not!" said Adam One. "Toby's truly one of us now. She's going to be an Eve."

"I didn't get an answer!" Toby protested. An animal yawn was not very definitive, as visions went.

Adam One smiled benignly. "You'll make the right decision," he said.

Toby spent the rest of the afternoon mixing up a scent combo that would be irresistible to rats, and could be laid down as a trail from the Fender-Bender Body Shop to the Buenavista Condos. The goal was to remove the rats from the former and rehouse them in the latter, without loss of life: the Gardeners didn't want to displace a fellow Species without offering them accommodation of equal value.

She used meat scraps from the stash Pilar kept for maggots, some honey, some peanut butter – she'd sent Amanda to buy that at a supermarkette. Some rancid cheese; beer dregs for the liquid element. When it was ready, she sent for Shackleton and Crozier and gave them their instructions.

"That is really putrid," said Shackleton, sniffing with admiration.

"Think you can stand it?" said Toby. "Because if you can't . . ."

"We'll do it," said Crozier, straightening his shoulders.

"Can I come too?" said little Oates, who'd followed them.

"No thumbsuckers," said Crozier.

"Be careful," said Toby. "We don't want to find you spraygunned in a vacant lot. Minus your kidneys."

"I know what I'm doing," said Shackleton proudly. "Zeb's gonna help us. We're wearing pleeb stuff – see?" He opened his Gardener shirt: underneath it was a black T-shirt that read, DEATH: A GREAT WAY TO LOSE WEIGHT! Underneath the slogan was a skull and crossbones, in silver.

"Those Corps guys are so dumb," said Crozier, grinning. He had a T-shirt too: STRIPPERS LOVE MY POLE. "We'll walk right past them!"

"Not a thumbsucker," said Oates, kicking Crozier in the shin. Crozier batted him on the side of the head.

"We're under their radar," said Shackleton. "They won't even see us."

"Pig-eater!" said Oates.

"Oates, that is enough language out of you," said Toby. "You can come and help me feed the worms. Off you go," she said to the other two. "Here's the bottle. Don't spill it inside FenderBender, and especially not on wood, or some unlucky people will have to live with it for a long time." She added, to Shackleton, "We're depending on you." It was good to let boys that age believe they were doing the jobs of men, so long as they didn't get carried away.

"Ciao, bedwetter," said Crozier.

"You totally stink," said Oates.

34

The next morning Toby was giving a class at the Wellness Clinic: Affective Herbs, for the twelve- to fifteen-year-olds. Manic Botanics, the kids called it, which was better than what they called some of the other subjects: Poop and Goop for violet biolet instruction, Guck and Muck for Compost-Pile Building.

"Willow," she said. "Analgesic. A-N-A-L-G-E-S-I-C, spell it on your slates." There was the squeaking of chalk – too much squeaking. "Stop that, Crozier," said Toby, without looking. Crozier was a chronic squeaker. Had she heard a whisper of *Dry Witch*? "I heard that, Shackleton," she said. The class was more restless than usual: aftershocks from the uproar caused by Veena. "Analgesic. What do we mean by that?"

"Painkiller," said Amanda.

"Correct, Amanda," said Toby. Amanda, always suspiciously well behaved in class, was even more so today. She was sly, Amanda. Too well versed in the ways of the Exfernal World. But Adam One believed the Gardeners had been of great benefit to her, and who was to say that Amanda was not undergoing a life change?

Still, it was unfortunate that Ren had been swept into Amanda's all-too-attractive orbit. Ren was overly pliable – she risked being always under somebody's thumb.

"What part of the Willow do we use to make the analgesic?" she went on. "The leaves?" said Ren. Too eager to please, the wrong answer anyway, and even more anxious than usual. Ren must be feeling the loss of Bernice, or maybe the guilt: how ruthlessly Bernice had been shouldered aside, once Amanda had appeared on the scene. They think we don't see them, thought Toby. They think we don't know what they're up to. Their snobberies, their cruelties, their schemes.

Nuala stuck her head in the door. "Toby, dear," she said, "could I have a word with you?" Her tone was lugubrious. Toby stepped out into the corridor.

"What's happened?" she said.

"You need to go and see Pilar," said Nuala. "Right now. She's chosen her time." Toby felt her heart contract. So Pilar had lied to her. No, not lied; just not told the whole truth. It had been something she'd eaten, but not by accident. Nuala squeezed Toby's arm to show deep sympathy. Get your moist palms off me, Toby thought, I'm not a man.

"Could you take my class?" she said. "Please. I'm teaching Willow."

"Of course, Toby dear," said Nuala. "I'll do 'The Weeping Willow' with them." This sugary song was a favourite of Nuala's; she'd composed it for small children. Toby could imagine the rolling eyes among these older kids. But since Nuala didn't really know much about botanicals, having them sing it would at least fill the time.

Toby hurried away to the sound of Nuala's voice: "Toby has been called away on an errand of mercy, so let us help her by singing the Weeping Willow song!" Her intense, slightly flat contralto rose above the lacklustre voices of the children:

Weeping willow, weeping willow, branches waving like the sea,
While I'm lying on my pillow, come and take my pain from me . . .

Hell would be an eternity of Nuala's lyrics, thought Toby. Anyway it wasn't the Weeping Willow, it was the White Willow, *salix alba*, with its available salicylic acid. That's what killed the pain.

Pilar was lying in her cubicle, on her bed, with her beeswax candle still burning in its tin container. She stretched out her thin brown fingers. "Dearest Toby," she said. "Thank you for coming. I wanted to see you."

"You did it yourself!" said Toby. "You didn't tell me!" She was so sad she was angry.

"I didn't want you to waste your time in worrying," said Pilar. Her voice had dwindled to a whisper. "I wanted you to have your nice Vigil. Now come and sit beside me, and tell me what you saw last night."

"An animal," said Toby. "Sort of like a lion, but not a lion."

"Good," whispered Pilar. "That's a good sign. You'll be helped with strength when you need it. I'm glad it wasn't a slug." She gave a tiny laugh; then her face contorted in pain.

"Why?" said Toby. "Why did you?"

"I got the diagnosis," said Pilar. "It's cancer. Very advanced. So, best to go now, while I still know what I'm doing. Why linger?"

"What diagnosis?" said Toby.

"I sent in some biopsy samples," said Pilar. "Katuro did it for me – took the tissue samples. We hid them in a jar of honey and smuggled them to the diagnostic labs at HelthWyzer West – under a different identity, of course."

"Who smuggled them?" said Toby. "Was it Zeb?"

Pilar smiled as if enjoying a private joke. "A friend," she said. "We have many friends."

"We could take you to a hospital," said Toby. "I'm sure Adam One would authorize –"

"Don't backslide, my Toby," said Pilar. "You know our views on hospitals. I might as well be thrown into a cesspool. Anyway, there's no cure for what I've taken. Now, please hand me that glass – the blue one."

"Not yet!" said Toby. How to postpone, delay? Keep Pilar with her.

"It's just water, and a little Willow and Poppy," Pilar whispered. "Deadens the pain without knocking you out. I want to stay awake as long as possible. I'm good for a while."

Toby watched while Pilar drank. "Another pillow," said Pilar.

Toby handed her one of the husk-filled sacks from the bottom of the bed. "You've been my family here," she said. "More than the others." She was finding it hard to talk, but she refused to cry.

"And you've been mine," said Pilar simply. "Remember to tend the Buenavista Ararat. Keep it renewed."

Toby didn't want to tell her that the Buenavista Ararat was lost to them because of Burt. Why upset her? She propped Pilar up with the pillow: she was strangely heavy. "What did you use?" she asked. Her throat was tightening.

"I've trained you well," said Pilar. Her eyes crinkled at the edges, as if the whole thing was a prank. "Let's see if you can guess. Symptoms: cramps and vomiting. Then a respite period during which the patient appears to improve. But meanwhile, the liver is slowly being destroyed. No antidote."

"One of the amanitas," said Toby.

"Clever girl," Pilar whispered. "The Death Angel, a friend in need."

"But it will be so painful," said Toby.

"Don't worry about that," said Pilar. "There's always the Poppy concentrate. It's the red bottle – that one. I'll let you know when. Now, listen to me carefully. This is my will. As we say, shrouds have no pockets – all earthly things must be passed from the dying to the living, and that includes our knowledge. I want you to have everything I've assembled here – all my materials. It's a good collection, and it confers great power. Guard it well and use it well. I trust you to do that. You're familiar with some of these bottles. I've made a paper list of the rest, which you must memorize and then destroy. The list is inside the green jar – that one. Do you promise?"

"Yes," said Toby. "I promise."

"Deathbed promises are sacred among us," said Pilar. "You know that. Don't cry. Look at me. I'm not sad."

Toby knew the theory: Pilar believed that she was donating herself to the matrix of Life through her own volition, and she also believed that this should be a matter for celebration.

But what about me? thought Toby. I'm being deserted. It was like the time her mother died, and then her father. How many times did she have to go through the process of being orphaned? Don't whine, she told herself sternly.

"I want you to be Eve Six," Pilar said. "In my place. No one else has the talent, and the knowledge. Can you do that for me? Promise?"

Toby promised. What else could she say?

"Good," Pilar whispered, breathing out. "Now, I think it's time for the Poppy. The red bottle, that's the one. Wish me well on my journey."

"Thank you for all you've taught me," said Toby. I can't stand this, she thought. I'm killing her. No: I'm helping her to die. I'm fulfilling her wishes.

She watched as Pilar drank.

"Thank you for learning," said Pilar. "I'm going to sleep now. Don't forget to tell the bees."

Toby sat beside Pilar until she stopped breathing. Then she pulled the coverlet up over her tranquil face and snuffed out the candle. Was it her imagination or had the candle flared up at the moment of Pilar's death as if a little surge of air had passed it? Spirit, Adam One would say. An energy that cannot be grasped or measured. Pilar's immeasurable Spirit. Gone.

But if Spirit wasn't material in any way, it couldn't influence a candle flame. Could it?

I'm getting as mushy as the rest of them, thought Toby. Addled as an egg. Next thing I'll be talking to flowers. Or snails, like Nuala.

But she went to tell the bees. She felt like an idiot doing it, but she'd promised. She remembered that it wasn't enough just to think at them: you had to say the words out loud. Bees were the messengers between this world and the other worlds, Pilar had said. Between the living and the dead. They carried the Word made air.

Toby covered her head – as was the custom, Pilar had claimed – and stood in front of the Rooftop's hives. The bees were flying around as usual, coming and going, bringing their leg-loads of pollen, waggling in their figure-eight semaphoric dances. From inside the hives came the humming of wings as they fanned the air, cooling it, ventilating the cells and passageways. One bee is all the bees, Pilar used to say, so what's good for the hive is good for the bee.

Several bees flew around her head, golden in their fur. Three lit on her face, tasting her.

"Bees," she said. "I bring news. You must tell your Queen."

Were they listening? Perhaps. They were nibbling gently at the edges of her dried tears. For the salt, a scientist would say.

"Pilar is dead," she said. "She sends you her greetings, and her thanks for your friendship over many years. When the time comes for you to follow her to where she has gone, she will meet you there." These were the words Pilar had taught her. She felt like such a dolt, saying them out loud. "Until then, I am your new Eve Six."

Nobody was listening, though if they had been they wouldn't have found anything odd, not up here on the Rooftop. Whereas down below at ground level they'd have labelled her as a crazy woman, wandering the streets, talking out loud to nothing.

Pilar used to bring the news to the bees every morning. Would Toby be expected to do the same? Yes, she would. It was one of the functions of the Eve Six. If you didn't tell the bees everything that was going on, Pilar said, their feelings would be hurt and they'd swarm and go elsewhere. Or they'd die.

The bees on her face hesitated: maybe they could feel her trembling. But they could tell grief from fear, because they didn't sting. After a moment they lifted up and flew away, blending with the circling multitudes above the hives.

35

Once she'd pulled herself together and arranged her face, Toby went to tell Adam One. "Pilar died," she said. "She took care of it herself."

"Yes, my dear. I know," said Adam One. "We discussed it. She used the Death Angel, and then the Poppy?" Toby nodded. "But – this is a delicate matter, and I am counting on your discretion – she didn't feel the Gardeners at large should be told the entire truth. Final self-journeying is a moral option only for the experienced and, I have to say, only for the terminally ill, as Pilar was; but it's not one we should make widely available – especially not to our young people, who are impressionable and prone to indulge in morbid sulking and false heroics. I trust you've taken charge of those medicine bottles of Pilar's? We wouldn't want any accidents."

"Yes," said Toby. I need to get a box made, she thought. A metal one. With a lock.

"And now you're Eve Six," said Adam One, beaming. "I'm so pleased, my dear!"

"You discussed that with Pilar too, I suppose," said Toby. The whole Vigil thing was just a stall, she thought. Keeping me on hold until Pilar could clinch the sale.

"It was her earnest desire," said Adam One. "She had such a deep love and respect for you."

"And I hope to be worthy of her," she said.

So the two of them had trapped her. What could she say? She found herself stepping into ritual as if into a pair of stone shoes.

Adam One called a general Gardeners meeting, at which he made a lying speech. "Unfortunately," he began, "our dear Pilar – Eve Six – passed away tragically earlier today after making a species identification error. She had many years of impeccable practice to her credit – but perhaps this was God's way of harvesting our beloved Eve Six for His greater purposes. Let me remind you of the importance of learning our mushrooms thoroughly; and do confine your mushrooming activities to well-known species, such as the Morels, the Shaggy Manes, and the Puffballs – those about which there cannot be any confusion.

"While she was alive, Pilar expanded our mushroom and fungus collection enormously, adding a number of wild specimens. Some of these can be an aid to meditation during your Retreats, but please, do not try them without taking informed advice, and watch for those telltale cups and rings – we do not want any more unfortunate incidents of this nature."

Toby felt outrage: how could Adam One disparage Pilar's mycological expertise? Pilar would never have made such a mistake: the older Gardeners must know that. But maybe it was only a way of talking, just as suicide used to be called "death by misadventure."

"I am happy to announce," Adam One continued, "that our worthy Toby has agreed to fill the position of Eve Six. This was Pilar's wish, and I'm sure you'll all agree that there is no one more suited to the position than she. I myself rely upon her completely for . . . for many things. Her great gifts include not only her extensive knowledge, but also her good sense, her fortitude in adversity, and her kind heart. This is why she was Pilar's choice." There was some subdued nodding and smiling in Toby's direction.

"Our beloved Pilar wished to be composted in Heritage Park," Adam One continued. "She herself thoughtfully selected the shrub she wished planted on top of her – a fine specimen of Elderberry – so that in time we may expect some foraging dividends. As you know, an unofficial composting is a risk, as it incurs heavy penalties – the Exfernal World believes that even death itself should be regimented and, above all, paid for – but we will prepare for this event with caution and carry it out with discretion. Meanwhile, those of you who desire to see Pilar for the last time may do so at her cubicle. If you wish to present a floral tribute, may I suggest the nasturtiums, which are plentiful at this season. Please do not pick any of the garlic flowers, as we are saving them for propagation."

There were some tears, and some outright sobbing from the children – Pilar had been well loved. Then the Gardeners filed away. Some smiled again at Toby to show they were pleased by her promotion. Toby herself stayed where she was, because Adam One was holding on to her arm.

"Forgive me, dear Toby," he said when the rest had gone. "I apologize for my excursion into fiction. I must sometimes say things that are not transparently honest. But it is for the greater good."

Toby and Zeb were chosen to select the location for Pilar's composting, and to pre-dig the hole. Time was of the essence, said Adam One: the Gardeners did not go in for refrigeration and the weather was warm, so if they didn't compost Pilar soon she was likely to undertake the process a little too rapidly herself.

Zeb had a couple of Heritage Park groundsman suits – green overalls and shirts, with the Park logo in white. The two of them put these on and set off with a couple of shovels and rakes and a mattock and a pitchfork rattling around in the back of their truck. It was news to Toby that the Gardeners had a truck, but they did. It was a compressed-air pickup, which they kept in a pet store over in the Sewage Lagoon. An abandoned pet store – not much call for pet pampering in the Lagoon, said Zeb, because if you did have a cat there it was likely to end up in someone else's deep fryer.

The Gardeners painted different things on their truck, said Zeb, according to need. At the moment it had a Heritage Park logo on it, impeccably forged. "There's a number of ex-graphic artists in the Gardeners," said Zeb. "Of course, there's a number of ex-everything."

They drove along through the Sinkhole, honking to get the pleebrats out of their path and shooing away any who tried to force-clean their windows. "Have you done this before?" Toby asked.

"By 'this,' you mean burying old ladies illegally in public parkland? Nope," said Zeb. "No Eves died on my watch until this. But there's a first time for everything."

"How dangerous is it?" said Toby.

"Guess we'll find out," said Zeb. "Course, we could just leave her in a vacant lot for the scavengers, but she might end up in a SecretBurger. Animal protein's getting very pricey. Or she could get sold to the garboil folks, they'll take anything. We're saving her from that: old Pilar was death on oil, it was contra to her religion."

"Not to yours?" said Toby.

Zeb chuckled. "I leave the finer points of doctrine to Adam One. I just use what I have to, to get where I need to go. C'mon, let's grab a Happicuppa." He swerved into a mallway lot.

"We're drinking Happicuppa?" said Toby. "Gen-mod, sun-grown, sprayed with poisons? It kills birds, it ruins peasants – we all know that."

"We're in deep cover," said Zeb. "You have to act the part!" He winked at her, then reached across her and opened the truck door. "Cut yourself some slack. I bet you used to be a babe until the Gardeners got to you."

Used to be, thinks Toby. That about sums up everything. Nevertheless she was pleased: she hadn't had a gender-weighted compliment for some time.

Happicuppa had once been a feature of such lunch breaks as she'd been able to snatch, back when she worked at SecretBurgers; it seemed a lifetime since she'd drunk any of the stuff. She ordered a Happicappuchino. She'd forgotten how delicious they could be. She drank it in sips: it could be years before she got another, if she ever did get one.

"We better go," said Zeb before she was quite finished. "We've got a hole to dig. Put your cap on, stick your hair up under it, that's how the girl parkies wear it."

"Hey, Park bitch," said a voice behind her. "Show us your shrub!" Toby was afraid to glance around. But Blanco was back in Painball again, Adam One had told her – that was the word on the street.

Zeb picked up on her fear. "If any guy bothers you, I'll hit him with the mattock," he said.

Back in the truck, they mowed their way through the pleebland streets until they reached the Heritage Parkland north gate. Zeb waved his forged pass at the gatekeepers and they drove through. The Park was officially pedestrian, so there were no vehicles other than theirs.

Zeb drove slowly, passing families of pleeblanders seated at the picnic tables with their barbecues going full blast. Rowdy groups of pleebrats were drinking and messing around. A rock bounced off the truck: the Heritage Parkies weren't armed, and the pleebrats knew that. There'd been swarmings and even fatalities, Zeb told her. Something about a bunch of trees made people think they could cut loose. "Wherever there's Nature, there's assholes," he said cheerfully.

They found a good location – a patch of open ground where the Elderberry shrub would get enough sunlight, and where they might not encounter too many tree roots while digging. Zeb set to work with the mattock, loosening the dirt; Toby shovelled. They'd put out a stand-alone sign: Planting Courtesy of HelthWyzer West. "If anyone asks, I've got the authorization," said Zeb. "Right here in my pocket. Didn't even cost that much."

When the hole was deep enough they packed up, leaving the sign in place.

Pilar's composting took place that afternoon. Pilar travelled to the site by truck, in a burlap sack labelled Mulch, with the Elderberry and a five-gallon water tank beside her. Nuala and Adam One marched the Buds and Blooms Choir through the Park, right past the burial spot, so anyone in the vicinity would be looking at them rather than at Zeb and Toby and their shrub planting. They were singing the "Mole Day Hymn" at the top of their lungs. When they came to the final verse, Shackleton and Crozier in their pleebrat T-shirt disguises jeered at them from the pathside. When Crozier tossed a bottle, the Buds and Blooms yelled and broke ranks and ran down the pathway. All the pleeblanders watched the chase with interest, hoping for violence. Zeb deftly slotted Pilar into the hole, still in her burlap sack, and positioned the Elderberry shrub on top of her. Toby shovelled and tamped; then they watered.

"Don't look mournful," Zeb told her. "Act like it's only a job."

There was another onlooker, a tall dark-haired boy. He wasn't distracted by the Buds and Blooms sideshow; he stood leaning against a tree, as if indifferent. He was wearing a black T-shirt with a slogan that said, THE LIVER IS EVIL AND MUST BE PUNISHED.

"You know that boy?" said Toby. The T-shirt looked wrong. If he was a real pleebrat it would have fit him better.

Zeb glanced over. "Him? Why?"

"He's taking an interest in us." CorpSeCorps, she thought? No. Surely too young.

"Don't stare," said Zeb. "He knew Pilar. I let him know we'd be here."

36

According to Adam One, the Fall of Man was multidimensional. The ancestral primates fell out of the trees; then they fell from vegetarianism into meat-eating. Then they fell from instinct into reason, and thus into technology; from simple signals into complex grammar, and thus into humanity; from firelessness into fire, and thence into weaponry; and from seasonal mating into an incessant sexual twitching. Then they fell from a joyous life in the moment into the anxious contemplation of the vanished past and the distant future.

The Fall was ongoing, but its trajectory led ever downward. Sucked into the well of knowledge, you could only plummet, learning more and more, but not getting any happier. And so it was with Toby, once she'd become an Eve. She could feel the Eve Six title seeping into her, eroding her, wearing away the edges of what she'd once been. It was more than a hair shirt, it was a shirt of nettles. How had she allowed herself to be sewn into it this way?

She knew more now, however. As with all knowledge, once you knew it, you couldn't imagine how it was that you hadn't known it before. Like stage magic, knowledge before you knew it took place before your very eyes, but you were looking elsewhere.

For instance: the Adams and Eves had a laptop. Toby had been shocked to discover this – wasn't such a device in direct contravention of Gardener principles? – but Adam One had reassured her: they never went online with it except with extreme precaution, they used it mostly for the storage of crucial data pertaining to the Exfernal World, and they took care to conceal such a dangerous object from the Gardener membership at large – especially the children. Nevertheless, they had one. "It's like the Vatican's porn collection," Zeb told her. "Safe in our hands."

They kept their laptop in a concealed wall compartment in the small room behind the vinegar barrels, which was also where they held the bi-weekly Adam and Eve meetings. There was a door to this room, but before Eveship had closed in around her Toby had been told there was only a closet behind it, used for bottle storage. There were indeed some shelves for empty bottles, but the whole shelf unit swung open to reveal the room's actual door. Both doors were kept locked: only the Adams and Eves had keys. Now Toby had a key too.

She ought to have realized the Adams and the Eves had some way of meeting together. They appeared to move and think as one, and they didn't use phones or computers, so how would they have made their group decisions except face to face? She must have supposed they exchanged information chemically, like trees. But no, nothing so vegetable: they sat around a table like any other conclave and hammered out their positions – theological as well as practical – as ruthlessly as medieval monks. And, as with the monks, there was increasingly much at stake. That was worrying to Toby, for the Corporations tolerated no opposition, and the Gardener stance against commercial activities in the larger sense might well come to be construed as that. So Toby was not wrapped in some otherworldly sheepfold-like cocoon, as she'd once supposed. Instead she was walking the edge of a real and potentially explosive power.

For the Gardeners, it seemed, were no longer a tiny localized cult. They were growing in influence: far from being confined to the Sinkhole Edencliff Rooftop Garden and its neighbouring rooftops and the other buildings they controlled, they had branches in different pleebs, and even in other cities. They also had cells of hidden Exfernal sympathizers embedded at every level, even within the Corporations themselves. The information provided by these sympathizers was indispensable, according to Adam One: by means of it, the intentions and movements of their enemies could be monitored, at least in part.

The cells were referred to as Truffles because they were underground, rare, and valuable, because you never could tell where they might appear next, and because pigs and dogs were employed to sniff them out. Not that the Gardeners had anything against actual Pigs and Dogs, Adam One made haste to explain – only against their enslavement by the forces of darkness.

Although they'd hidden their distress from the mass of the Gardeners, the Adams and Eves had been badly frightened by the arrest of Burt. Some claimed the CorpSeCorps would offer the age-old devil's bargain – information in exchange for your life. But the CorpSeCorps didn't need to make deals, Zeb said grimly, because once they got started on their Internal Rendition procedures a person would say anything. Who knew how many buckets of incriminating lies were being squeezed out of poor Burt, along with his blood, shit, and vomit?

So the Adams and Eves expected a CorpSeCorps raid on the Garden at any moment. They set their rapid-evacuation plans in place, and alerted the Truffle cells, who could be counted on to hide them. Then Burt had been discovered in the vacant lot behind Scales and Tails, with freezer burns on his skin and minus his vital organs.

"They want it to look like a mob hit," Zeb said at the Council meeting behind the Vinegar Room. "But it's not convincing. A mob would do more gratuitous mutilation. Fun stuff."

Nuala said it was disrespectful of Zeb to use the word *fun* in this context. Zeb said he was speaking ironically. Marushka Midwife, who rarely said anything, said that irony was overvalued. Zeb said he hadn't noticed such overvaluation much among the Gardeners. Rebecca – who was now a powerful new Eve – Eve Eleven of Nutriment Combining – said everyone should get a grip and bite their tongues. Adam One said that a house divided against itself could not stand.

A spirited debate then took place concerning the disposal of Burt's body. Burt had been an Adam, said Rebecca: he deserved to be illegally composted in the Heritage Park, like any other Adam or Eve. That would be fair. Philo the Fog – who was less foggy inside the Council Room than outside it – said this would be too dangerous: what if the CorpSeCorps had planted Burt's cadaver as bait and were watching to see who came to collect it? Stuart the Screw said the CorpSeCorps already knew Burt had been a Gardener, so what would they learn by that? Zeb said maybe dead Burt was a message from the CorpSeCorps to the pleebmobs, to tell them to tighten up their operations and root out maverick freeloaders.

Nuala said, well, if they couldn't compost poor Burt, maybe they could just go at night and sprinkle a spoonful of earth on him as a symbolic thing: she personally would feel a lot better in the Spirit if she could do that. Mugi said Burt was a meat-breath pig-eater who'd betrayed them, and he didn't know why they were even talking about this. Adam One said they should take a moment of silence and put Light around Burt in their hearts, and Zeb said they'd already put so much light around him the guy was probably burning like a suicide bomber in a fried-chicken franchise. Nuala said Zeb was being frivolous. Adam One said they should meditate overnight and perhaps the solution would arrive by visionary inspiration. Philo said in that case he'd toke up.

But the next day, Burt's corpse was no longer in the vacant lot: he'd been scooped by the early-bird garboil collectors, Zeb informed them, and was doubtless fuelling some Corps employee's cityvan. Toby asked how he was sure of that, and Zeb grinned and said he had connections among the pleebrat gangs who'd snitch on anyone if you paid them.

Adam One made a speech to the Gardener membership at large in which he outlined the fate of Burt, called him a victim seduced by the spirit of materialist greed whom they should pity rather than condemn, and asked them all to be extra vigilant and to report any overly curious tourists and especially any unusual activities.

But no unusual activities were reported. Months went by, then more months. The daily chores and teaching hours went on as usual, and the Saints' Days and Festivals kept their appointed rounds. Toby took up macramé, hoping it would cure her of idle daydreaming and fruitless desires, and increase her focus on the moment. The bees increased and multiplied, and Toby delivered the news to them every morning. The moon emerged from darkness, then plumped out, then dwindled. Several babies appeared, and an infestation of shiny green beetles, and a number of new Gardener converts. The sands of time are quicksands, said Adam One. So much can sink into them without a trace. And what a blessing when those things that sink away are needless worries.

APRIL FISH

APRIL FISH

YEAR FOURTEEN.

OF THE FOOLISHNESS WITHIN ALL RELIGIONS.
SPOKEN BY ADAM ONE.

Dear Friends, dear Fellow Creatures and Fellow Mortals:

What a fun-filled April Fish Day we have had, here on our Edencliff Rooftop Garden! This year's Fish lanterns, modelled on the phosphorescent Fish that adorn the depths of the Ocean, are the most effective yet, and the Fish cakes look delectable! We have Rebecca and her special helpers, Amanda and Ren, to thank for these toothsome confections.

Our Children always enjoy this day, as it allows them to make fun of their elders; and as long as that fun does not get out of hand, we elders welcome it, as it reminds us of our own childhoods. It never hurts us to remember how small we felt then, and how we depended on the strength, knowledge, and wisdom of our elders to keep us safe. Let us teach our Children tolerance, and loving-kindness, and correct boundaries, as well as joyful laughter. As God contains all things good, He must also contain a sense of playfulness – a gift he has shared with Creatures other than ourselves, as witness the tricks Crows play, and the sportiveness of Squirrels, and the frolicking of Kittens.

On April Fish Day, which originated in France, we make fun of one another by attaching a Fish of paper, or, in our case, a Fish of recycled cloth, to the back of another person and then crying out, "April Fish!" Or, in the original French, "Poisson d'Avril!" In anglophone countries, this day is known as April Fool's Day. But April Fish was surely first a Christian festival, as a Fish image was used by the early Christians as secret signals of their faith in times of oppression.

The Fish was an apt symbol, for Jesus first called as his Apostles two fishermen, surely chosen by him to help conserve the Fish population.

They were told to be fishers of men *instead of* being fishers of Fish, thus neutralizing two destroyers of Fish! That Jesus was mindful of the Birds, the Animals, and the Plants is clear from his remarks on Sparrows, Hens, Lambs, and Lilies; but he understood that most of God's Garden was under water and that it, too, needed tending. Saint Francis of Assisi preached a sermon to the Fish, not realizing that the Fish commune directly with God. Still, the Saint was affirming the respect due to them. How prophetic does this appear, now that the world's Oceans are being laid waste!

Others may take the Specist view that we Humans are smarter than Fish, and thus an April Fish is being marked as mute and foolish. But the life of the Spirit always seems foolish to those who do not share it: therefore we must accept and wear the label of God's Fools gladly, for in relation to God we are all fools, no matter how wise we may think we are. To be an April Fish is to humbly accept our own silliness, and to cheerfully admit the absurdity – from a materialist view – of every Spiritual truth we profess.

Please join me now in a Meditation on our Fish brethren.

Dear God, You who created the great and wide Sea, with its Creatures innumerable: we pray that You hold in your gaze those who dwell in Your underwater Garden, in which Life originated; and we pray that none may vanish from the Earth by Human agency. Let Love and aid be brought to the Sea Creatures in their present peril and great suffering; which has come to them through the warming of the Sea, and through the dragging of nets and hooks along the bottom of it, and through the slaughtering of all within it, from the Creatures of the shallows to the Creatures of the depths, the Giant Squid included; and remember your Whales, that You created on the fifth day, and set in the Sea to play therein; and bring help especially to the Sharks, that misunderstood and much-persecuted breed.

We hold in our minds the Great Dead Zone in the Gulf of Mexico; and the Great Dead Zone in Lake Erie; and the Great Dead Zone in the

Black Sea; and the desolate Grand Banks of Newfoundland, where the Cod once abounded; and the Great Barrier Reef, now dying and bleaching white and breaking apart.

Let them come to Life again; let Love shine upon them and restore them; and let us be forgiven for our oceanic murders; and for our foolishness, when it is the wrong kind of foolishness, being arrogant and destructive.

And help us to accept in all humility our kinship with the Fishes, who appear to us as mute and foolish; for in Your sight, we are all mute and foolish.

Let us sing.

OH LORD, YOU KNOW OUR FOOLISHNESS

Oh Lord, You know our foolishness,
And all our silly deeds;
You watch us scamper here and there,
Pursuing useless greeds.

We sometimes doubt that You are Love,
And we forget to thank;
We find the Sky an empty void,
The Universe a blank.

We fall into despondency,
And curse the hour that bore us;
We either claim You don't exist,
Or else that You ignore us.

So pardon us these vacant moods,
Our dour and gloomy sayings;
Today we own ourselves Your Fools,
And celebrate by playing.

We make a full acknowledgment
Of all in us that's vain –
Our petty strifes and tiny woes,
Our self-inflicted pain.

At April Fish we jest and sing
And laugh with childish glee;
We puncture pomp and puffed-up pride,
And smile at all we see.

Your starry World's beyond our thought,
And wondrous without measure;
We pray, among Your Treasures bright,
Your Fools You'll also treasure.

From *The God's Gardeners Oral Hymnbook*

37

REN

YEAR TWENTY-FIVE

I must have dozed off – being in the Sticky Zone makes you tired – because I was dreaming about Amanda. She was walking towards me in her khaki outfit through a wide field of dry grass with many white bones in it. There were vultures flying over her head. But she saw me dreaming her, and she smiled and waved at me, and I woke up.

It was too early to really go to sleep, so I did my toenails. Starlite liked the claw effect with spider-silk strengtheners, but I never used that because Mordis said it would be an image brainfry, like a bunny with spikes. So I stuck to the pastels. Shiny new toes make you feel all fresh and sparkling: if someone wants to suck your toes, those toes should be worth sucking. While the polish was drying I went to the intercom camera in the room I shared with Starlite. It cheered me up to connect with my own things – my dresser, my Robodog, my costumes on their hangers. I could hardly wait to be back in my normal life. Not that it was normal exactly. But I was used to it.

Then I surfed the Net, looking for the horoscope sites to see what sort of week was coming up, because I'd be out of the Sticky Zone very soon if my tests were clear. Wild Stars was my favourite: I liked it because it was so encouraging.

> The Moon in your sign, Scorpio, means your hormones are pumped this week! It's hot, hot, hot! Enjoy, but don't take this sexy flareup too seriously – it will pass.

You're working hard now at making your home a pleasure palace. Time to buy those new satin sheets and slip between them! You'll be pampering all your Taurean senses this week!

I was hoping that romance and adventure might be heading my way, once I got out of the Sticky Zone. And maybe travel, or spiritual quests – sometimes they had those. But my own horoscope wasn't so good:

Messenger Mercury in your sign, Pisces, means that things and people from the past will surprise you in the coming weeks. Be prepared for some quick transitions! Romance may take strange forms – illusion and reality are dancing closely together right now, so tread carefully!

I didn't like the sound of romance taking strange forms. I got enough of that at work.

When I checked in on the Snakepit again, it was really crowded. Savona was still on the trapeze, and Crimson Petal was up there too, in a Biofilm Bodysuit with extra genital ruffles so she looked like a giant orchid. Down below, Starlite was still working away on her Painballer customer. That girl could raise the dead, but he was so close to being unconscious that I didn't think she'd be getting a big tip out of him.

The CorpSeCorps minders were hovering, but suddenly they all looked in the direction of the entranceway, so I went to another camera and had a look myself. Mordis was over there, talking to a couple more CorpSeCorps guys. They had another Painballer in tow, who looked in even worse shape than the first three. More explosive. Mordis wasn't happy. Four of those Painballers – that was a lot to handle. And what if they were from different teams and just yesterday they were trying to disembowel each other?

Mordis was herding the new Painballer to the far corner. Now he was barking into his cell; now three backup dancers were hurrying over:

Vilya, Crenola, Sunset. Block the view, he must've told them. Use your tits, why in hell did God make them? There was a shimmering, a flurry of feathers, six arms twining around him. I could almost hear what Vilya was saying into the guy's ear: *Take two, honey, they're cheap.*

A signal from Mordis and the music got louder: loud music distracts them, they're less likely to rampage with their ears full of sound. Now the dancers were all over this guy like anacondas. Two Scales bouncers on standby.

Mordis was grinning: situation solved. He'd steer this one into the feather-ceiling rooms, dump in some alcohol, stick some girls on top of him, and he'd be what Mordis called one blitzed-out brain-dead squeeze-dried happy zombie. And now that we had BlyssPluss, he'd get multiple orgasms and wuzzy comfy feelings, with no microbe-death downside. The furniture breakage at Scales had tanked since they'd been using that stuff. They were serving it in chocolate-dipped polyberries, and in Soylectable olives – though you had to make sure not to overdo it, said Starlite, or the guy's dick might split.

38

In Year Fourteen, we had April Fish Day as usual. On that day you were supposed to act silly and laugh a lot. I pinned a fish onto Shackie, and Croze pinned a fish onto me, and Shackie pinned a fish onto Amanda. A lot of kids pinned fish onto Nuala, but nobody pinned a fish onto Toby because you couldn't get behind her without her knowing. Adam One pinned a fish onto himself to make some point about God. That little brat Oates ran around shouting, "Fish fingers" and poking his fingers into people from behind until Rebecca made him stop. Then he was sad, so I took him into the corner and told him the story about the Littlest Vulture. He was a sweet boy when he wasn't being a pest.

Zeb was away on one of his trips – he'd been going away more lately. Lucerne stayed home: she said she had nothing to celebrate, and it was a stupid festival anyway.

It was my first April Fish without Bernice. We'd always decorated a Fish Cake together when we were little, before Amanda arrived. We'd fight all the time about what to put on it. Once we'd made our cake green, with spinach for the green colour, with eyes of carrot rounds. It looked really toxic. Thinking about that cake made me want to cry. Where was Bernice now? I felt ashamed of myself, for being so unkind to her. What if she was dead, like Burt? If she was, it was partly my fault. Mostly my fault. My fault.

⦙⦙⦙

Amanda and I walked back to the Cheese Factory, and Shackie and Croze walked with us – to protect us, they said. Amanda laughed at that but said they could come with us if they liked. The four of us were more or less friends again, though every once in a while Croze would say to Amanda, "You still owe us," and Amanda would tell him to get knotted.

By the time we got back to the Cheese Factory it was dark. We thought we'd be in trouble for being so late – Lucerne was always warning us about the dangers of the street – but it turned out that Zeb was back, and already they were having a fight. So we went into the hall to wait it out, because their fights took up all the room in our place.

This fight was louder than usual. A piece of furniture toppled over, or was thrown: Lucerne, it must have been, because Zeb wasn't a thrower.

"What's it about?" I said to Amanda. She had her ear against the door. She was shameless about eavesdropping.

"I dunno," she said. "She's yelling too loud. Oh wait – she says he's having sex with Nuala."

"Not Nuala," I said. "He wouldn't!" Now I knew how Bernice must have felt when we'd said all that about her father.

"Men'll have sex with anything, given the chance," said Amanda. "Now she's saying he's a pimp at heart. And he despises her and treats her like shit. I think she's crying."

"Maybe we should stop listening," I said.

"Okay," said Amanda. We stayed with our backs against the wall, waiting until Lucerne would start wailing. As she always did. Then Zeb would stomp out and slam the door, and we might not see him for days.

Zeb came out. "See you around, Queens of the Night," he said. "Watch your backs." He was joking with us the way he liked to do, but there wasn't any fun behind it. He looked grim.

Usually after their fights Lucerne would go to bed and cry, but this night she started packing a bag. The bag was a pink backpack Amanda and I had gleaned. There wasn't much for Lucerne put into it, so quite soon she finished her packing and came into our cubicle.

Amanda and I were pretending to be asleep, on our husk-filled futons, under our blue-jean quilts. "Get up, Ren," Lucerne said to me. "We're going."

"Where?" I said.

"Back," she said. "To the HelthWyzer Compound."

"Right now?"

"Yes. Why are you looking like that? It's what you've always wanted." It's true that I'd longed for the HelthWyzer Compound, once. I'd been homesick for it. But ever since Amanda'd moved in, I hadn't been thinking about it too much.

"Amanda's coming too?" I said.

"Amanda's staying here."

I felt very cold. "I want Amanda to come," I said.

"Out of the question," said Lucerne. Something else had now happened, it seemed: Lucerne had cast off her paralyzing spell, the spell of Zeb. She'd stepped out of sex as if out of a loose dress. Now she was brisk, decisive, no nonsense. Had she been like that before, long ago? I could scarcely remember.

"Why?" I said. "Why can't Amanda come?"

"Because they won't let her in at HelthWyzer. We can get our identities back there, but she doesn't have one, and I certainly don't have the money to buy her one. They'll take care of her here," she added, as if Amanda was a kitten I was being forced to abandon.

"No way," I said. "If she's not coming, I'm not!"

"And where would you live, here?" said Lucerne with contempt.

"We'll stay with Zeb," I said.

"He's never home," said Lucerne. "You don't think they'd let two young girls camp out by themselves!"

"Then we can live with Adam One," I said. "Or Nuala. Or maybe Katuro."

"Or Stuart the Screw," said Amanda hopefully. This was desperate – Stuart was dour and a loner – but I grabbed the idea.

"We can help him make furniture," I said. I imagined the whole scenario – Amanda and me collecting pieces of junk for Stuart, sawing and hammering and singing as we worked, making herbal tea . . .

"You won't be welcome," said Lucerne. "Stuart is a misanthrope. He only tolerates you kids because of Zeb, and it's the same with all the others."

"We'll stay with Toby," I said.

"Toby has other things to do. Now that's enough. If Amanda can't find someone who'll take her in, she can always go back to the pleebrats. She belongs with them, anyway. You don't. Now, hurry up."

"I need to put on my clothes," I said.

"Fine," said Lucerne. "Ten minutes." She left the cubicle.

"What'll we do?" I whispered to Amanda as I started to dress.

"I don't know," Amanda whispered back. "Once you're in there she'll never let you out. Those Compounds are like castles, they're like jails. She won't ever let you see me. She hates me."

"I don't care what she thinks," I whispered. "I'll get out somehow."

"My phone," Amanda whispered. "Take it with you. You can phone me."

"I'll get you in somehow," I said. By this time I was crying silently. I slipped her purple phone into my pocket.

"Hurry up, Ren," said Lucerne.

"I'll call you!" I whispered. "My dad will buy you an identity!"

"Sure he will," said Amanda softly. "Don't take shit, okay?"

In the main room, Lucerne was moving fast. She dumped out the sickly looking tomato plant she'd been growing on the windowsill. Underneath the soil there was a plastic bag full of money. She must've been ripping it off, from selling stuff at the Tree of Life – the soap, the vinegar, the macramé, the quilts. Money was old-fashioned, but people still used it for small things and the Gardeners wouldn't take virtual money because they didn't allow computers. So she'd been stashing away her escape money. She hadn't been such a doormat as I'd thought.

Then she took the kitchen shears and cut off her long hair, straight across at neck level. The cutting made a Velcro sound – scratchy and dry.

She left the pile of hair in the middle of the dining-room table.

Then she took me by the arm and hauled me out of our place and down the stairs. She never went out at night because of the drunks and druggies on the street corners, and the pleebrat gangs and muggers. But right then she was white-hot with anger and filled with crackling energy: people on the street cleared out of our path as if we were contagious, and even the Asian Fusions and the Blackened Redfish left us alone.

It took us hours to get through the Sinkhole and the Sewage Lagoon, and then the richer pleebs. As we went along, the houses and buildings and hotels got newer looking, and the streets emptier of people. In Big Box we got a solarcab: we drove through Golfgreens and then past a big open space, and finally right up to the gates of the HelthWyzer Compound. It was so long since I'd seen that place it was like one of those dreams, where you don't recognize anything, yet also you do. I felt a little sick, but that might have been excitement.

Before we got into the cab, Lucerne had mussed up my hair and smeared dirt on her own face, and torn part of her dress. "Why'd you do that?" I said. But she didn't answer.

There were two guards at the HelthWyzer gateway, behind the little window. "Identities?" they said.

"We don't have any," said Lucerne. "They were stolen. We were forcibly abducted." She looked behind her, as if she was afraid someone was following us. "Please – you have to let us in, right away! My husband – he's in Nanobioforms. He'll tell you who I am." She started to cry.

One of them reached for the phone, pushed a button. "Frank," he said. "Main gate. Lady here says she's your wife."

"We'll need some cheek swabs, ma'am, for the communicables," said the second one. "Then you can wait in the holding room, pending bioform clearance and verification. Someone will be with you soon."

In the holding room we sat on a black vinyl sofa. It was five in the morning. Lucerne picked up a magazine – *NooSkins*, it said on the cover. *Why Live With Imperfection?* She riffled through it.

“Were we forcibly abducted?” I asked her.

“Oh, my darling,” she said. “You don’t remember! You were too young! I didn’t want to tell you – I didn’t want you to be frightened! They might have done something terrible to you!” Then she began to cry again, harder. By the time the CorpSeMan in the biosuit walked in, her face was all streaky.

39

Be careful what you wish for, old Pilar used to say. I was back at the HelthWyzer Compound and I was reunited with my father, just as I used to wish long ago. But nothing felt right. All that faux marble, and the reproduction antique furniture, and the carpets in our house – none of it seemed real. It smelled funny too – like disinfectant. I missed the leafy smells, of the Gardeners, the cooking smells, even the sharp vinegar tang; even the violet biolets.

My father – Frank – hadn't changed my room. But the four-poster bed and the pink curtains looked shrunken. It also looked too young for me. There were the plush animals I'd once loved so much, but their glass eyes looked dead. I stuffed them into the back of my closet so they wouldn't be able to look through me as if I was a shadow.

The first night, Lucerne ran a bath for me with fake-flower bath essence in it. The big white tub and the white fluffy towels made me feel dirty, and also stinky. I stank like earth – compost earth, before it's finished. That sour odour.

Also my skin was blue: it was the dye from the Gardener clothes. I'd never really noticed it because the showers at the Gardeners were so brief, and there weren't any mirrors. I hadn't noticed, either, how hairy I'd become, and that was more of a shock than my blue skin. I rubbed and rubbed at the blue: it wouldn't come off. I looked at my toes, where they stuck up out of the bath water. The toenails looked like claws.

"Let's put some polish on those," Lucerne said two days later, when she saw my feet in flip-flops. She was acting as if none of it had ever happened – not the Gardeners, not Amanda, and especially not Zeb. She was wearing crisp linen suits, she'd had her hair styled and streaked. She'd already had her own toes done – she'd wasted no time. "Look at all these colours I bought for you! Green, purple, frosted orange, and I got you some sparkly ones . . ." But I was angry with her, and I turned away. She was such a liar.

All those years I'd kept an outline of my father in my head, like a chalk line enclosing a father-shaped space. When I was little, I'd coloured it in often enough. But those colours had been too bright, and the outline had been too large: Frank was shorter, greyer, balder, and more confused-looking than what I'd had in mind.

Before he'd come to the HelthWyzer gatehouse to identify us, I'd thought he'd be overjoyed to find that we were safe and sound and not dead after all. But when he saw me, his face fell. Now I realize that he'd last known me when I was a small girl, so I was bigger than he expected, and probably bigger than he wanted. I was also shabbier – despite the drab Gardener clothes, I must have looked like one of the pleebrats he might have seen running around if he'd ever even been to the Sinkhole or the Sewage Lagoon. Maybe he was afraid I was going to pick his pockets or grab his shoes. He approached me as if I might bite, and put his arms awkwardly around me. He smelled of complex chemicals – the kind of chemicals used for cleaning off sticky things, like glue. A smell that could burn right down into your lungs.

On that first night I slept for twelve hours, and when I woke up I found that Lucerne had taken away my Gardener clothes and burnt them. Luckily I'd hidden Amanda's purple phone inside the plush tiger in my closet – I'd cut open the stomach. So the phone didn't get burnt.

I missed the smell of my own skin, which had lost its salty flavour and was now soapy and perfumy. I thought about what Zeb used to say about mice – if you take them out of the mouse nest for a while and then put them back, the other mice will tear them apart. If I went back to the Gardeners with my fake-flower smell, would they tear me apart?

Lucerne took me to the HelthWyzer In-clinic so I could be checked for head lice and worms, and for being interfered with. That meant a couple of fingers up you, front and back. "Oh my goodness," the doctor said when he saw my blue skin. "Are these bruises, dear?"

"No," I said. "It's dye."

"Oh," he said. "They made you dye yourself?"

"It's in the clothes," I said.

"I see," he said. Then he made an appointment for me with the In-clinic psychiatrist, who had experience with people who'd been snatched by cults. My mother would have to be at those appointments as well.

Which was how I found out what Lucerne was telling them. We'd been grabbed off the street while in SolarSpace doing some boutique shopping, but she couldn't say exactly where we'd been taken because she'd never been allowed to know. She said it wasn't the fault of the cult itself – it was one of the male members who'd been obsessed with her and wanted her for his personal sex slave, and had taken away her shoes to keep her captive. This was supposed to be Zeb, though she said she didn't know his name. I'd been too young to realize what was going on, she said, but I'd been a hostage – she'd had to do the bidding of this madman, service his every twisted whim, it was revolting the things he'd made her do – or my life would have been in danger. But she'd finally been able to share her plight with one of the other cult members – a sort of nun. She must have meant Toby. It was this woman who'd helped her to escape – brought her shoes, given her money, lured the madman away so Lucerne could make a dash for freedom.

It was no use asking me anything, she said. The cult members had been nice to me, and anyway they'd been duped. She'd been the only one who'd known the truth: it was a burden she'd had to carry alone. What woman who loved her child as much as she loved me wouldn't have done the same?

Before our psychiatry sessions, she'd squeeze my shoulder and say, "Amanda's back there. Keep that in mind." Meaning that if I told anyone she'd been lying her hair off she'd suddenly remember where she'd been imprisoned, and the CorpSeCorps would go in there with their spray-guns, and who knew what might happen? Bystanders got killed a lot in spraygun attacks. It couldn't be helped, said the CorpSeCorps. It was in the interests of public order.

For weeks Lucerne hovered around to make sure I wouldn't try to run away or else rat on her. But at last I got a chance to take out Amanda's purple phone and call. Amanda had texted me with the number of the new phone she'd lifted, so I'd know where to reach her – she thought ahead about everything. I sat inside my closet to make the call. It had a light inside, like all the closets in the house. The closet itself was as big as my former sleeping cubicle.

Amanda answered right away. There she was on the screen, looking the same as ever. I longed to be back at the Gardeners.

"I really miss you," I said. "I'm running away as soon as I can." But I didn't know when that would be, I said, because Lucerne was keeping my identity locked in a drawer, and I wouldn't be allowed past the gate-house without it.

"Can't you trade?" said Amanda. "With the guards?"

"No," I said. "I don't think so. It's different here."

"Oh. What happened to your hair?"

"Lucerne made me cut it."

"It looks okay," said Amanda. Then she said, "They found Burt dumped in the vacant lot, out behind Scales. He had freezer burns."

"He'd been in a freezer?"

"What was left. There were parts missing – liver, kidneys, heart. Zeb says the mobs will sell the parts, then keep the rest in the freezer until they need to send a message."

"Ren! Where are you?" It was Lucerne, in my room.

"I have to go," I whispered. I tucked the phone back into the tiger. "In here," I said. My teeth were chattering. Freezers were so cold.

"What are you doing in the closet, darling?" said Lucerne. "Come and have some lunch! You'll feel better soon!" She sounded chirpy: the crazier and more disturbed I acted, the better it was for her, because the less anyone would believe me if I told on her.

Her story was that I'd been traumatized by being stuck in among the warped, brainwashing cult folk. I had no way of proving her wrong. Anyway maybe I had been traumatized: I had nothing to compare myself with.

40

Once I'd adjusted enough – *adjusted* was the word they used, as if I was a bra strap – Lucerne said I had to go to school because it was bad for me to be moping around the house: I needed to get out and make a whole new life for myself, as she was doing. It was a risk for her – I was a walking cluster bomb, the truth about her might come popping out of my mouth at any time. But she knew I was judging her silently, and that annoyed her, so she really wanted me elsewhere.

Frank seemed to have believed her story, though he didn't seem to care about it one way or the other. I could see now why Lucerne had run off with Zeb: at least Zeb had noticed her. And he'd noticed me, as well, whereas Frank treated me like a window: he never looked at me, only through me.

Sometimes I dreamed about Zeb. He'd be wearing a bear suit, and the fur would unzip down the middle like a pyjama bag, and Zeb would step out. He'd smell comforting, in the dream – like rained-on grass, and cinnamon, and the salty, vinegary, singed-leaf smell of the Gardeners.

The school was called HelthWyzer High. On the first day I put on one of the new outfits that Lucerne had picked out for me. It was pink and lemon yellow – colours the Gardeners never would have allowed because they'd show the dirt and waste the soap.

My new clothes felt like a disguise. I couldn't get used to how tight they were compared to my old loose dresses, and how my bare arms stuck out from the sleeves and my bare legs came out from the bottom of the knee-length, pleated skirt. But this was what the girls at HelthWyzer High all wore, according to Lucerne.

"Don't forget your sunblock, Brenda," she said as I headed towards the door. She was calling me Brenda now: she claimed it was my real name.

HelthWyzer sent a student to be my guide – walk me to the school, show me around. Her name was Wakulla Price; she was thin, with glossy skin like toffee. She was wearing a pastel yellow top like mine, but she had pants on the bottom. She gazed at my pleated skirt, her eyes wide. "I like your skirt," she said.

"My mother bought it," I said.

"Oh," she said in a *sorry* voice. "My mother bought me one like that two years ago." So I liked her.

On the way to school, Wakulla said, *What does your dad do, when did you get here*, and so on, but she didn't mention any cults; and I said, *How do you like the school, who are the teachers*, and that got us safely there. The houses we were passing were all different styles, but with solarskins. They had the latest tech in the Compounds, which Lucerne had pointed out a lot. *Really, Brenda, they're so much more truly green than those purist Gardeners so you don't have to worry about how much hot water you're using, and isn't it time you took another shower?*

The high-school building was sparkling clean – no graffiti, no pieces falling off, no smashed windows. It had a deep green lawn and some shrubs pruned into round balls, and a statue: "Florence Nightingale," it said on the plaque, "The Lady of the Lamp." But someone had changed the *a* to a *u*, so it said The Lady of the Lump.

"Jimmy did that," said Wakulla. "He's my lab partner in Nanoforms Biotech, he's always doing dumb things like that." She smiled: she had really white teeth. Lucerne had been saying how dingy my own teeth were and I needed a cosmetic dentist. She was already planning to redecorate our entire house, but she had some alterations planned for me as well.

At least I didn't have any cavities. The Gardeners were against refined sugar products and were strict about brushing, though you had to use a frayed twig because they hated the idea of putting either plastic or animal bristles inside their mouths.

The first morning at that school was very strange. I felt as if the classes were in a foreign language. All the subjects were different, the words were different, and then there were the computers and the paper notebooks. I had a built-in fear of those: it seemed so dangerous, all that permanent writing that your enemies could find – you couldn't just wipe it away, not like a slate. I wanted to run into the washroom and wash my hands after touching the keyboards and pages; the danger had surely rubbed off on me.

Lucerne said that our so-called personal history – the forcible abduction and so on – would be kept confidential by the officials at the HelthWyzer Compound. But someone had leaked because the kids at the school all knew. At least they hadn't heard about Lucerne's sex-slave lust-mad pervert story. But I knew I'd lie about that if I had to, in order to protect Amanda, and Zeb, and Adam One, and even the ordinary Gardeners. We are all in one another's hands, Adam One used to say. I was beginning to find out what that meant.

At lunch hour a group gathered around me. Not a mean group, just curious. *So, you lived with a cult? Weird! How crazy were they?* They had a lot of questions. Meanwhile they were eating their lunches, and there was meat smell everywhere. Bacon. Fish sticks, 20 per cent real fish. Burgers – they were called WyzeBurgers, and they were made of meat cultured on stretchy racks. So no animals had actually been killed. But it still smelled like meat. Amanda would've eaten the bacon to show she hadn't been brainwashed by the leaf-eaters, but I couldn't go that far. I peeled the bun off my WyzeBurger and tried to eat that, but it stank of dead animal.

"Like, how bad was it?" said Wakulla.

"It was just a greenie cult," I said.

"Like the Wolf Isaiahists," said one kid. "Were they terrorists?" They all leaned forward: they wanted horror stories.

"No. They were pacifists," I said. "We had to work on this rooftop garden." And I told them about the slug and snail relocation. It sounded so strange to me, when I told it.

"At least you didn't eat them," said one girl. "Some of those cults, they eat road kill."

"The Wolf Isaiahists do, for sure. It was on the Web."

"You lived in the pleebs, though. Cool." Then I realized I had an edge, because I'd lived in the pleeblands where none of them had ever been except maybe on a school trip, or dragged along with their slumming parents to the Tree of Life. So I could make up whatever I liked.

"You were child labour," one boy said. "A little enviroserf. Sexy!" They all laughed.

"Jimmy, don't be so dumb," said Wakulla. "It's okay," she said to me, "he always says stuff like that."

Jimmy grinned. "Did you worship cabbages?" he went on. "Oh Great Cabbage, I kiss your cabbagey cabbageness!" He went down on one knee and grabbed a handful of my pleated skirt. "Nice leaves, do they come off?"

"Don't be such a meat-breath," I said.

"A what?" he said, laughing. "A meat-breath?"

Then I had to explain how that was a harsh name to call someone, among the extreme greens. Like pig-eater. Like slug-face. This made Jimmy laugh more.

I saw the temptation. I saw it clearly. I would come up with more bizarre details about my cultish life, and then I would pretend that I thought all these things were as warped as the HelthWyzer kids did. That would be popular. But also I saw myself the way the Adams and the Eves would see me: with sadness, with disappointment. Adam One, and Toby, and Rebecca. And Pilar, even though she was dead. And even Zeb.

How easy it is, treachery. You just slide into it. But I knew that already, because of Bernice.

⁂

Wakulla walked home with me, and Jimmy came too. He fooled around a lot – made jokes, expected us to laugh – and Wakulla did laugh, in a polite way. I could see that Jimmy had a big crush on her, though Wakulla told me later that she couldn't see Jimmy in any way other than as a friend.

Wakulla turned off halfway to go to her house, and Jimmy said he'd continue along with me because it was on the way. He was irritating when there was more than one other person: maybe he felt it was better to make a fool of yourself than to have other people do it for you. But when he wasn't putting on an act he was much nicer. I could tell he was sad underneath, because I was that way myself. We were sort of like twins in that way, or so I felt at the time. He was the first boy I'd ever really had for a friend.

"So, it must be weird for you, being here in a Compound, after the pleeblands," he said one day.

"Yeah," I said.

"Was your mom really tied to the bed by a deranged maniac?" Jimmy would come right out with stuff other people might think but would never say.

"Where did you hear that?" I said.

"Locker room," said Jimmy. So Lucerne's fable had seeped out.

I took a deep breath. "This is between us, right?"

"Cross my heart," said Jimmy.

"No," I said. "She wasn't tied to the bed."

"Didn't think so," said Jimmy.

"But don't tell that to anyone. I really trust you not to."

"I won't," said Jimmy. He didn't say, *Why not.* He knew that if everyone heard Lucerne had been bullshitting, people would know she hadn't been kidnapped, she'd merely cheated big time. What she'd done had been for love, or just sex. And she was back at HelthWyzer with her loser of a husband because the other guy had tossed her over. But she'd rather die than admit it. Or else she'd rather kill someone.

All this time I was going into my closet and taking the purple cellphone out of my tiger and phoning Amanda. We'd text each other with the best times to call, and if the connection was good we could see each other onscreen. I asked a lot of questions about the Gardeners. Amanda told me she wasn't staying with Zeb any more – Adam One said she was almost grown up so she had to sleep in one of the singles cubicles, and that was pretty boring. "When can you get back here?" she said. But I didn't know how I could manage to run away from HelthWyzer.

"I'm working on it," I said.

The next time we were on the phone she said, "Look who's here," and it was Shackie, grinning at me sheepishly, and I wondered if they'd been having sex together. I felt as if Amanda had scooped some glittery piece of junk I wanted for myself, but that was stupid because I had no feelings for Shackie whatsoever. I did wonder whether it had been his hand on my bum, that night I passed out in the holospinner. But most likely it was Croze.

"How's Croze?" I said to Shackie. "And Oates?"

"They're fine," Shackie mumbled. "When're you coming back? Croze really misses you! Gang, right?"

"Grene," I said. "Gangrene." I was surprised he'd still use that old kidstuff password, but maybe Amanda had put him up to it so I'd feel included.

After Shackie went offscreen, Amanda said they were partners – the two of them were boosting things from malls. But it was a fair trade: she got someone watching her back and helping her lift stuff and sell it, and he got sex.

"Don't you love him?" I said.

Amanda said I was a romantic. She said love was useless, because it led you into dumb exchanges in which you gave too much away, and then you got bitter and mean.

41

Jimmy and I started doing our homework together. He was really nice about helping me with the parts I didn't know. Because of all that memorizing we'd had to do at the Gardeners, I could stare at a lesson and then see everything inside my head, like a picture. So although it was hard for me and I felt I was way behind, I started to catch up quite fast.

Because he was two years ahead of me, Jimmy wasn't in any of my classes except for Life Skills, which was supposed to help you structure your life, once you had one. They mixed up the age groups in Life Skills so we could benefit from sharing our different life experiences, and Jimmy traded desks so he was sitting right behind me. "I'm your bodyguard," he whispered, which made me feel safe.

We went to my place to do our homework if Lucerne wasn't there; if she was, we went to Jimmy's. I liked Jimmy's place better because he had a pet rakunk – it was a new splice, half skunk but without the smell, half raccoon but without the aggression. Her name was Killer; she was one of the first ones they'd made. When I picked her up, she liked me right away.

Jimmy's mother seemed to like me as well, though the first time she saw me she looked at me very hard with her stern blue eyes and asked me how old I was. I liked her all right too, although she smoked too much, which made me cough. Nobody at the Gardeners smoked, or at least not cigarettes. She worked on a computer a lot, but I couldn't figure out what she did on it, because she didn't have a job. His father was hardly ever there – he was at the labs, figuring out how to transplant human stem cells and DNA into pigs, to grow new human pieces. I asked Jimmy what pieces, and he said kidneys, but maybe it was lungs too – in the future you'd be able to get your very own pig made, with second copies of everything. I knew what the Gardeners would think of that: they would think it was bad, because of having to kill the pigs.

Jimmy had seen these pigs: their nickname was pigoon, like pig balloon, because they were so big. The double-organ methods were proprietary secrets, he said: extra valuable. "Aren't you worried some foreign Corps will kidnap your dad and squeeze the secrets out of his brain?" I said. That was happening more often: they kept it out of the news, but there was gossip at HelthWyzer. Sometimes they got the kidnapped scientists back, sometimes they didn't. The security was getting tighter and tighter.

After doing our homework Jimmy and I would hang out at the HelthWyzer mall and play tame video games and drink Happicappuchinos. The first time, I told him Happicuppa was the brew of evil so I couldn't drink it, and he laughed at me. The second time I made an effort, and it tasted delicious, and soon I wasn't thinking too much about the evilness of it.

After a while Jimmy talked to me about Wakulla Price. He said she was the first girl he'd ever been in love with, but when he'd asked her to get serious with him she'd said they could only be friends. I knew that part already, but I said that was too bad, and Jimmy said he'd been a puddle of dog vomit for weeks and he still hadn't got over it.

Then he asked if I had a boyfriend back in the pleebs, and I said yes – which wasn't true – but since I had no way of getting back there I'd decided to forget about him because that was the best thing to do if you wanted someone you couldn't have. Jimmy was really sympathetic about my lost boyfriend, and he squeezed my hand. Then I felt guilty for telling such a lie; but I wasn't sorry about the squeezing.

By this time I had a diary – all the girls at school had them, it was a retro craze: people could hack your computer, but they couldn't hack a paper book. I wrote all of this down in my diary. It was like talking to someone. I didn't even think that writing things down was that dangerous any more: I guess that shows how far away from the Gardeners I'd grown already. I kept my diary in the closet, inside a stuffed bear, because I didn't want Lucerne snooping on me. The Gardeners were right about that part: reading someone else's secret words does give you power over them.

Then a new boy came to HelthWyzer High. His name was Glenn, and as soon as I saw him I knew he was the same Glenn who'd come to the Tree of Life on the Saint Euell's Week when Amanda and I had walked him over with that jar of honey to visit Pilar. I thought he gave me a little nod – did he recognize me? I hoped not, because I didn't want him to start talking about where he'd seen me last. What if the CorpSeCorps were still trying to track down Lucerne's pretend sex-slaver? What if they found Zeb through me and he ended up without his parts, in a freezer? That was a horrifying thought.

But surely even if he did remember me, Glenn wouldn't say anything because he wouldn't want them finding out about Pilar and the Gardeners and whatever he'd been doing with them. I was sure it was something illegal, or why would Pilar have sent Amanda and me away? It must have been to protect us.

Glenn acted like he didn't care about anybody, him and his black T-shirts. But after a while Jimmy started hanging out with him, and then I wasn't seeing so much of Jimmy.

"What do you do with that Glenn? He's creepy," I said one afternoon when we were doing our homework on the school library computers. Jimmy said they only played three-dimensional chess or online video games, at his place or else at Glenn's. I thought they were probably watching porn – most of the guys did, and a lot of girls too – so I asked what games. Barbarian Stomp, he said – that was a war game. Blood and Roses was like Monopoly, only you had to corner the genocide and atrocity market. Extinctathon was a trivia game you played with extinct animals.

"Maybe I could come over one day and play too," I said, but he didn't go for that. So I guessed that they really were watching porn.

Then a really bad thing happened: Jimmy's mother disappeared. Not kidnapped, they said: she'd gone on her own. I heard Lucerne talking about it to Frank: it seemed that Jimmy's mother had made off with a lot of crucial data, so the CorpSeCorps were all over Jimmy's house like a rash. And since Jimmy was such a buddy of mine, said Lucerne, they might soon be swarming all over us as well. Not that we had anything to hide. But it would be a nuisance.

I texted Jimmy right away and said how sorry I was about his mother, and was there anything I could do. He wasn't at school, but he texted me later that week, then came over to my place. He was very depressed. It was bad enough that his mother was gone, he said, but also the CorpSeCorps had asked his dad to help them with their inquiries, which meant that his dad was carted off in a black solarvan; and now two female CorpSers were snooping around the house and asking him a lot of stupid questions. Worst of all, Jimmy's mother had stolen Killer to let her loose in the wild – she'd left him a note about it. But the wild was totally wrong for Killer, because she'd be eaten by bobkittens.

"Oh Jimmy," I said. "That's terrible." I put my arms around him and hugged him: he was sort of crying. I started crying too, and we stroked each other carefully, as if both of us had broken arms or diseases, and then we slid tenderly into my bed, still holding on to each other as if we were drowning, and we started kissing each other. I felt I was helping Jimmy and he was helping me at the same time. It was like a feast day back at the Gardeners, when we'd do everything in a special way because it was in honour of something. That's what this was like: it was *in honour.*

"I don't want to hurt you," Jimmy said.

Oh Jimmy, I thought. I'm putting Light around you.

42

After that first time I felt very happy, as if I was singing. Not a doleful song, more like a bird song. I loved being in bed with Jimmy, it made me feel so safe to have his arms around me, and it was amazing to me how slippery and silky one skin felt against another skin. The body has a wisdom of its own, Adam One used to say: he'd been talking about the immune system, but it was true in another way. That wisdom wasn't merely like singing, it was like dancing, only better. I was in love with Jimmy, and I had to believe that Jimmy was just as in love with me.

I wrote in my diary: JIMMY. Then I underlined it in red and drew a red heart. I still distrusted writing enough not to put in everything that was happening, but each time we had sex I drew another heart and coloured it in.

I wanted to phone Amanda and tell her about it, even though Amanda had said once that people telling you about their sex was as boring as people telling you about their dreams. But when I went into my closet and took out my plush tiger, the purple phone was no longer there.

I felt cold all over. My diary was still inside the bear, where I'd hidden it. But I had no phone.

Then Lucerne came into my room. She said, didn't I know that any phone inside the Compound had to be registered, so people couldn't phone out industrial secrets? It was a crime to have an unregistered phone, and the CorpSeCorps could track such phones. Didn't I know that?

I shook my head. "Can they tell who was called?" I said. She said they could trace the number, which could be really bad news for the callers at both ends. She didn't say, *really bad news*, she said, *unfortunate consequences.*

Then she said that despite my obvious belief that she was a bad mother, she did have my best interests at heart. For instance, if she happened to find a purple phone with a frequently called number, she might leave a text message at that called number, such as "Dump it!!" So if they did locate that second phone, it would be inside a dumpster. And she herself would dispose of the purple one. And now she was going to play golf, and she hoped I would think very carefully about what she'd just said.

I did think very carefully. I thought, *Lucerne went out of her way to save Amanda. She must've known that's who I was phoning. But she hates Amanda. So really, Lucerne went out of her way to save Zeb: despite everything, she still loves him.*

Now that I was in love with Jimmy I had more sympathy for Lucerne and the way she used to behave around Zeb. I could see how you could do extreme things for the person you loved. Adam One said that when you loved a person, that love might not always get returned the way you wanted, but it was a good thing anyway because love went out all around you like an energy wave, and a creature you didn't even know would be helped by it. The example he used was of someone being killed by a virus and then eaten by vultures. I hadn't liked that comparison, but the general idea was true; because here was Lucerne, sending that text message because she loved Zeb, but as a side effect saving Amanda, which hadn't been her original intention. So Adam One was right.

But meanwhile I'd lost touch with Amanda. I felt very sad about that.

Jimmy and I still did our homework together. Sometimes we really did do it, when there were other people around. The rest of the time we didn't. It would take us about a minute to get out of our clothes and into each other, and Jimmy would be running his hands all over me and saying I was so slender, like a sylph – he liked words like that, not that I always knew what they meant. He said sometimes he felt like a child molester.

Later I'd write down some of the things he'd said, as if they were prophecies. *Jimmy is so great he said Im a silf.* I didn't care that much about spelling, only about the feeling.

I loved him so much. But then I made a mistake. I asked him if he was still in love with Wakulla or did he love me instead? I shouldn't have asked that. He waited too long to answer and then he said, Did it matter? I wanted to say yes, but instead I said no. Then Wakulla Price moved to the West Coast, and Jimmy got moody and went back to spending more time with Glenn than he spent with me. So that was the answer, and it made me very unhappy.

Despite that we were still having sex, though not very often – the red hearts in my diary were getting farther and farther apart. Then I saw Jimmy by accident at the mall with this foul-mouthed older girl called LyndaLee, who was rumoured to be going through all the boys at school, one by one but fast, like eating soynuts. Jimmy had his hand right on her ass, and then she pulled down his head and kissed him. It was a long, wet kiss. I felt sick to my stomach at the thought of Jimmy with her, and I remembered something Amanda once said about diseases, and I thought, Whatever LyndaLee's got, I've got too. And I went home and threw up, and cried, and then I got into my big white bathtub and had a warm bath. But it wasn't much comfort.

Jimmy didn't know I knew about him and LyndaLee. A few days later he asked if he could come over as usual, and I said yes. I wrote in my diary, *Jimmy you nosy brat I know your reading this, I hate it just because I fucked you doesn't mean I like you so STAY OUT!* Two red lines under *hate*, three under *stay out.* Then I left the diary on the top of my dresser. Your enemies could use your writing against you, I thought, but also you could use it against them.

After the sex I took a shower by myself, and when I came out, Jimmy was reading my diary, and said why did I hate him all of a sudden? So I told him. I used words I'd never said out loud before, and Jimmy said he was wrong for me, he was incapable of commitment because of Wakulla Price, she'd turned him into an emotional dumpster, but maybe he was destructive by nature since he messed up every girl he touched.

And I asked exactly how many that would be? I couldn't stand it that he would just include me in a big basket of girls, as if we were peaches or turnips. Then he said he really liked me as a person, which was why he was being honest with me, and I told him to get stuffed. So we broke up on bad terms.

The stretch of time after that was very dark. I wondered what I was doing on the Earth: no one would care much if I wasn't on it any more. Maybe I should cast away what Adam One called my husk and transform into a vulture or a worm. But then I remembered how the Gardeners used to say, *Ren, your life is a precious gift, and where there is a gift there is a Giver, and when you've been given a gift you should always say thank you.* So that was some help.

Also I could hear Amanda's voice: Why are you being so weak? Love's never a fair trade. So Jimmy's tired of you, so what, there's guys all over the place like germs, and you can pick them like flowers and toss them away when they're wilted. But you have to act like you're having a spectacular time and every day's a party.

What I did next wasn't good, and I'm still ashamed of it. I walked up to Glenn in the cafeteria – it took a lot of courage because Glenn was so cool he was practically frozen. And I asked him if he'd like to hang out with me. What I had in mind was that I'd have sex with Glenn, and Jimmy would find out and be wrecked. Not that I wanted sex with Glenn, it would be like shagging a salad server. Kind of flat and wooden.

Glenn said, "Hang out?" in a puzzled way. "Aren't you with Jimmy?" I said it was over, and anyway it was never serious because Jimmy was such a clown. Then I blurted out the next thing that came into my head.

"I saw you with the Gardeners, at the Tree of Life," I said. "Remember? I was the one who walked you over to see Pilar. With that honey?" He looked alarmed, and said we should get a Happicappuchino and talk.

We did talk. We talked a lot. We hung out in the mall so much that kids started saying we were a thing, but we weren't – it was never a romance. What was it then? I guess Glenn was the only person at HelthWyzer I could talk to about the Gardeners, and it was the same for him – that was the bond. It was like being in a secret club. Maybe Jimmy was never my twin at all – maybe it was Glenn. Which is a strange thought, because he was a strange guy. More like a cyborg, which was what Wakulla Price used to call him. Were we friends? I wouldn't even call it that. Sometimes he looked at me as if I was an amoeba, or some problem he was solving in Nanobioforms.

Glenn already knew quite a lot about the Gardeners, but he wanted to know more. What it was like to live with them every day. What they did and said, what they really believed. He'd get me to sing the songs, he'd want me to repeat what Adam One said in his Saint and Feast Day speeches: Glenn never laughed at them the way Jimmy would have if I'd ever done that for him. Instead he'd ask things like, "So, they think we should use nothing except recycled. But what if the Corps stopped making anything new? We'll run out." Sometimes he'd ask me more personal things, like "Would you eat animals if you were starving?" and "Do you think the Waterless Flood is really going to happen?" But I didn't always know the answers.

He'd talk about other things too. One day, he said that what you had to do in any adversarial situation was to kill the king, as in chess. I said people didn't have kings any more. He said he meant the centre of power, but today it wouldn't be a single person, it would be the technological connections. I said, you mean like coding and splicing, and he said, "Something like that."

Once he asked me if I thought God was a cluster of neurons, and if so, whether people having that cluster had been passed down by natural selection because it conferred a competitive edge, or whether maybe it was just a spandrel, such as having red hair, which didn't matter one way or another to your survival chances. A lot of the time I felt way out of my depth with him, so I'd say, "What do you think?" He always had an answer to that.

Jimmy did see us together at the mall, and he did seem taken aback; though not for long, because I caught him giving Glenn a thumbs-up, as if saying, *Go for it, buddy, be my guest!* As if I was his property and he was sharing.

Jimmy and Glenn graduated two years before I did and went off to college. Glenn went to Watson-Crick with all the brainiacs, and Jimmy went to the Martha Graham Academy, which was for kids with no math and science potential. So at least I didn't have to watch Jimmy at school any more, coming on to this or that new girl. But it was almost worse with Jimmy not there than with him there.

I put in the next two years somehow. My marks were poor, and I didn't think I'd get in anywhere for college – I'd end up as a minimum-wage meat slave, working at SecretBurgers or somewhere like that. But Lucerne pulled some strings. I heard her talking about it to one of her golf-club friends: "She's not stupid, but that cult experience ruined her motivation, so the Martha Graham Academy is the best we could do." So I'd be in the same space with Jimmy: that made me so nervous I felt sick.

The night before I left on the sealed bullet train, I reread my old diary, and then I knew what the Gardeners meant when they said, *Be careful what you write.* There were my own words from the time when I was so happy, except that now it was torture to read them. I took the diary down the street and around the corner and shoved it into a garboil dumpster. It would turn into oil and then all those red hearts I'd drawn would go up in smoke, but at least they would be useful along the way.

Part of me thought I would find Jimmy again at Martha Graham, and he would say it was me he'd loved all along, and could we get back together, and I'd forgive him and everything would be wonderful, the way it had been at first. But the other part of me realized that the chances of that were nothing. Adam One used to say that people can believe two opposite things at the same time, and now I knew it was true.

THE FEAST OF SERPENT WISDOM

THE FEAST OF SERPENT WISDOM

YEAR EIGHTEEN.

OF THE IMPORTANCE OF INSTINCTIVE KNOWING.

SPOKEN BY ADAM ONE.

Dear Friends, Fellow Mortals, Fellow Creatures:

Today is our Feast of Serpent Wisdom, and our Children have once again excelled in their decoration. We have Amanda and Shackleton to thank for the gripping mural of the Fox Snake ingesting a Frog – an apt reminder to us of the intertwined nature of the Dance of Life. For this Feast we traditionally feature the Zucchini, a Serpent-shaped vegetable. Thanks to Rebecca, our Eve Eleven, for her innovative Zucchini and Radish Dessert Slice. We are certainly looking forward to it.

But first I must alert you to the fact that certain individuals have been making unofficial inquiries about Zeb, our many-talented Adam Seven. In our Father's Garden there are many Species, and it takes all kinds to make an Ecosystem, and Zeb has chosen the non-violent option; so if questioned, do keep in mind that "I don't know" is always the best answer.

Our text for Serpent Wisdom is from Matthew 10:16: "Be ye therefore wise as Serpents, and harmless as Doves." To those former biologists among us who have made a study either of Serpents or of Doves, this sentence is puzzling. Serpents are expert hunters, paralyzing or strangling and crushing their prey, a gift that enables them to predate many Mice and Rats. Yet, despite their natural technology, one would not ordinarily call Serpents "wise." And Doves, though harmless to us, are extremely aggressive to other Doves: a male will harass and kill a less dominant male if occasion offers. The Spirit of God is sometimes pictured as a Dove, which simply informs us that this Spirit is not always peaceful: it has a ferocious side to it as well.

The Serpent is a highly charged symbol throughout the Human Words of God, though its guises are varied. Sometimes it is shown as an evil enemy of Humankind – perhaps because, when our Primate ancestors slept in trees, the Constrictors were among their few nocturnal predators. And for these ancestors – shoeless as they were – to step on a Viper meant certain death. Yet the Serpent is also equated with Leviathan, that great water-beast God made to humble Mankind, and also named to Job as an awe-inspiring example of His Inventiveness.

Among the Ancient Greeks, serpents were sacred to the god of healing. In other religions, the Serpent with its tail in its mouth refers to the cycle of Life, and to the beginning and end of Time. Because they shed their skins, Serpents have also symbolized Renewal – the Soul casting off its old self, from which it emerges resplendent. A complicated symbol, indeed. Therefore, how are we to be "wise as Serpents"? Are we to eat our own tails, or tempt people to wrongdoing, or coil around our enemies and squeeze them to death? Surely not – because in the same sentence, we are told to be as harmless as Doves.

Serpent Wisdom – I propose – is the wisdom of *feeling directly*, as the Serpent feels vibrations in the Earth. The Serpent is wise in that it lives in immediacy, without the need for the elaborate intellectual frameworks Humankind is endlessly constructing for itself. For what in us is belief and faith, in the other Creatures is inborn knowledge. No Human can truly know the full mind of God. The Human reason is a pin dancing on the head of an angel, so small is it in comparison to the Divine vastness that encircles us.

As the Human Words of God have put it, "Faith is the substance of things hoped for, the evidence of things not seen." That is the point: *not* seen. We cannot know God by reason and measurement; indeed, excess reason and measurement lead to doubt. Through them, we know that Comets and nuclear holocausts are among the possible tomorrows, not to mention the Waterless Flood, that we fear looms ever nearer. This fear dilutes our certainty, and through that channel comes loss of Faith; and then the temptation to enact malevolence enters our Souls; for if annihilation awaits us, why bother to strive for the Good?

We Humans must labour to believe, as the other Creatures do not. They *know* the dawn will come. They can sense it – that ruffling of the half-light, the horizon bestirring itself. Not only every Sparrow, not only every Rakunk, but every Nematode, and Mollusc, and Octopus, and Mo'Hair, and Liobam – all are held in the palm of His hand. Unlike us, they have no need for Faith.

As for the Serpent, who can tell where its head ends and its body begins? It experiences God in all parts of itself; it feels the vibrations of Divinity that run through the Earth, and responds to them quicker than thought.

This then is the Serpent Wisdom we long for – this wholeness of Being. May we greet with joy the few moments when, through Grace, and by the aid of our Retreats and Vigils and the assistance of God's Botanicals, we are granted an apprehension of it.

Let us sing.

GOD GAVE UNTO THE ANIMALS

God gave unto the Animals
A wisdom past our power to see:
Each knows innately how to live,
Which we must learn laboriously.

The Creatures need no lesson books,
For God instructs their Minds and Souls:
The sunlight hums to every Bee,
The moist clay whispers to the Mole.

And each one seeks its meat from God,
And each enjoys the Earth's sweet fare;
But none does sell and none does buy,
And none does foul its proper lair.

The Serpent is an arrow bright
That feels the Earth's vibrations fine
Run through its armoured shining flesh,
And all along its twining spine.

Oh, would I were, like Serpents, wise –
To sense the wholeness of the Whole,
Not only with a thinking Brain,
But with a swift and ardent Soul.

From *The God's Gardeners Oral Hymnbook*

43

TOBY. THE FEAST OF SERPENT WISDOM

YEAR TWENTY-FIVE

The Feast of Serpent Wisdom. Old Moon. Toby enters the Feast Day and the moon phase on her pink notepaper with the winky eyes and kissy lips. Old moon is a pruning week, said the Gardeners. Plant by the new, slash by the old. A good time to apply sharp tools to yourself, hack off any extraneous parts that might need trimming. Your head, for instance.

"A joke," she says out loud. She should avoid such morbid thoughts.

Today she will pare her fingernails. Toenails, as well: they shouldn't be permitted to run rampant. She could give herself a manicure: there are lots of cosmetic supplies in this place, whole shelves of them. AnooYoo Luscious Polish. AnooYoo Plum Skin Plumper. AnooYoo Fountain of Yooth Total Immersion: *Shed That Scaly Epidermis!* But why bother to polish or plump or shed? But why not bother? Either choice is equally pointless.

Do it for Yoo, AnooYoo used to croon. *The Noo Yoo.* I could have a whole new me, thinks Toby. Yet another whole new me, fresh as a snake. How many would that add up to, by now?

She trudges up the stairs to the rooftop, hoists her binoculars, surveys her visible realm. There's motion in the weeds, over by the forest edge: could it be the pigs? If so, they're keeping a low profile. Vultures are still clustering around the dead boar. There'll be lots of nanobioforms at work on it: it must be getting ripe by now.

Here's something different. Closer to the building, a clump of sheep is grazing. Five of them: three Mo'Hairs – a green one, a pink one, and a bright purple one – and two other sheep that appear to be conventional. The long hair of the Mo'Hairs isn't in good shape – there are clot-like snarls in it, and twigs and dry leaves. Onscreen, in advertisements, their hair had been shiny – you'd see the sheep tossing its hair, then a beautiful girl tossing a mane of the same hair. *More hair with Mo'Hair!* But they're not faring so well without their salon treatments.

The sheep clump together, lift their heads. Toby sees why: crouching low in the weeds, two liobams are on the hunt. Maybe the sheep smell them, but the scent must be confusing – part lion, part lamb.

The purple Mo'Hair is the most jittery. Don't look like prey, Toby thinks at it. Sure enough, it's the purple one the liobams go after. They cut it out from the group and chase it for a short distance. The pathetic beast is impeded by its coiffure – it looks like a purple fright wig on legs – and the liobams quickly pull it down. Finding the throat under all that hair padding takes them a while, and the Mo'Hair scrambles to its feet several times before the liobams finish it off. Then they settle down to eat. The other sheep have run awkwardly away in a muddle of bleating, but now they're grazing again.

She'd intended to do some gardening today, pick some greens: her stock of preserved and dried foods is waning like the moon. But she decides against it because of the liobams. Cats of all kinds will set ambushes: one frisks around in the open to distract your attention while another one slips quietly up behind.

In the afternoon she takes a nap. An old moon draws the past, said Pilar: whatever arrives from the shadows you must greet as a blessing. And the past does come back to her: the white frame house of her childhood, the ordinary trees, the woodland in the background, tinged with blue as if there's haze. A deer is outlined against it, standing rigid as a lawn ornament, ears pricked. Her father's digging with a shovel, over by the pile of picket fencing; her mother's a momentary glimpse at the kitchen window. Perhaps she's making soup. Everything tranquil, as if it would never end. But where is Toby in this picture? For it is a picture. It's flat, like a picture on a wall. She's not there.

She opens her eyes: tears on her cheeks. I wasn't in the picture because I'm the frame, she thinks. It's not really the past. It's only me, holding it all together. It's only a handful of fading neural pathways. It's only a mirage.

Surely I was an optimistic person back then, she thinks. Back there. I woke up whistling. I knew there were things wrong in the world, they were referred to, I'd seen them in the onscreen news. But the wrong things were wrong somewhere else.

By the time she'd reached college, the wrongness had moved closer. She remembers the oppressive sensation, like waiting all the time for a heavy stone footfall, then the knock at the door. Everybody knew. Nobody admitted to knowing. If other people began to discuss it, you tuned them out, because what they were saying was both so obvious and so unthinkable.

We're using up the Earth. It's almost gone. You can't live with such fears and keep on whistling. The waiting builds up in you like a tide. You start wanting it to be done with. You find yourself saying to the sky, *Just do it. Do your worst. Get it over with.* She could feel the coming tremor of it running through her spine, asleep or awake. It never went away, even among the Gardeners. Especially – as time wore on – among the Gardeners.

44

The Sunday after Serpent Wisdom Day was Saint Jacques Cousteau's Day. It was Year Eighteen – the year of rupture, though Toby did not yet know that. She remembers negotiating the Sinkhole streets on her way to the Wellness Clinic for the regular Sunday-evening Adams and Eves Council. She wasn't looking forward to it: lately those meetings had been sliding into squabbles.

The week before, they'd spent all their time on theological problems. The matter of Adam's teeth, for starters.

"Adam's *teeth*?" Toby had blurted. She needed to work on controlling such expressions of surprise, which might be read as criticism.

Adam One had explained that some of the children were upset because Zeb had pointed out the differences between the biting, rending teeth of carnivores and the grinding, munching teeth of herbivores. The children wanted to know why – if Adam was created as a vegetarian, as he surely was – human teeth should show such mixed characteristics.

"Shouldn't have brought it up," Stuart had muttered.

"We changed at the Fall," Nuala had said brightly. "We evolved. Once Man started to eat meat, well, naturally . . ."

That would be putting the cart before the horse, said Adam One; they could not achieve their goal of reconciling the findings of Science with their sacramental view of Life simply by overriding the rules of the former. He asked them to ponder this conundrum, and propose solutions at a later date.

Then they turned to the problem of the animal-skin clothing provided by God for Adam and Eve at the end of Genesis 3. The troublesome "coats of skins."

"The children are very worried about them," Nuala had said. Toby could understand why they'd been so dismayed. Had God killed and peeled some of his beloved Creatures to make these skin coats? If so, He'd set a very bad example to Man. If not, where had these skin coats come from?

"Maybe those animals died a natural death." That was Rebecca. "And God didn't see them going to waste." She was adamant about using up leftovers.

"Maybe very small animals," Katuro had said. "Short life spans."

"That is one possibility," Adam One had said. "Let it stand for now, until a more plausible explanation presents itself."

Early in her Eveship, Toby had asked if it was really necessary to split such theological hairs, and Adam One had said that it was. "The truth is," he'd said, "most people don't care about other Species, not when times get hard. All they care about is their next meal, naturally enough: we have to eat or die. But what if it's God doing the caring? We've evolved to believe in gods, so this belief bias of ours must confer an evolutionary advantage. The strictly materialist view – that we're an experiment animal protein has been doing on itself – is far too harsh and lonely for most, and leads to nihilism. That being the case, we need to push popular sentiment in a biosphere-friendly direction by pointing out the hazards of annoying God by a violation of His trust in our stewardship."

"What you mean is, with God in the story there's a penalty," said Toby.

"Yes," said Adam One. "There's a penalty without God in the story too, needless to say. But people are less likely to credit that. If there's a penalty, they want a penalizer. They dislike senseless catastrophe."

What would the topic be today? Toby wondered. Which fruit Eve ate from the Tree of Knowledge? It couldn't have been an apple, considering the state of horticulture at that time. A date? A bergamot? The Council had long been deliberating over that one. Toby had thought of proposing a strawberry, but then, strawberries didn't grow on trees.

As she walked, Toby was conscious, as always, of the others on the street. She could see in front of her and to the sides, despite her sunhat. She made use of pauses in doorways, of reflections in windows to check behind. But she could never shake the feeling that someone was sneaking up on her – that a hand would descend on her neck, a hand with red and blue veining and a bracelet of baby skulls. Blanco hadn't been seen in the Sewage Lagoon for some time – still in Painball, said some; no, overseas fighting as a mercenary, said others – but he was like smog: there were always some of his molecules in the air.

There was someone behind her – she could feel it, like a tingling between her shoulders. She stepped into a doorway, turned to face the sidewalk, then sagged with relief: it was Zeb.

"Hi, babe," he said. "Hot enough?"

He strolled along beside her, singing to himself:

Nobody gives a snot,
Nobody gives a snot,
That is why we're on the fucking spot,
Cause nobody gives a snot!

"Maybe you shouldn't sing," said Toby neutrally. It wasn't good policy to call attention to yourself on a pleeb sidewalk, especially not for Gardeners.

"Can't help it," said Zeb cheerfully. "God's fault. Wove music into the fabric of our being. Hears you better when you sing, so He's listening to this right now. I hope He's enjoying it," he added in a pious, mocking Adam One voice – a voice he was using a lot, though not when Adam One was around.

Lurking insubordination, thought Toby: he's tired of being the Beta Chimp.

Since becoming an Eve she'd gained much insight into Zeb's status among the Gardeners. Each Gardener Rooftop site and Truffle cell ran its own affairs, but every half-year they'd send delegates to a central convention, which for security reasons was never held in the same abandoned warehouse twice. Zeb was always a delegate: he was well equipped to make it through the more jagged pleebland neighbourhoods and around the CorpSeCorps checkpoints without being mugged, swarmed, spraygunned, or arrested. Maybe that was why he was allowed to stretch the Gardeners' rules the way he did.

Adam One seldom attended the conventions. The journey was hazardous, and the implication was that although Zeb was expendable, Adam One was not. In theory the Gardener fellowship had no overall head, but in practice its leader was Adam One, revered founder and guru. The soft hammer of his word carried a lot of weight at the Gardener conventions, and since he was rarely there to use that hammer himself, Zeb wielded it for him. Which must be a temptation: what if Zeb were to jettison Adam One's decrees and substitute his own? By such methods had regimes been changed and emperors toppled.

"You've had some bad news?" Toby asked Zeb now. The singing was the clue: Zeb was annoyingly upbeat whenever the news was bad.

"In point of fact," said Zeb. "We've lost contact with one of our insiders in Compoundland – our boy courier. He's gone dark."

Toby had learned about the boy courier once she'd become an Eve. He'd run Pilar's biopsy samples and brought her the fatal diagnosis – both of them concealed in a jar of honey. But that was all she knew: information was shared among the Adams and Eves, but only as much as was necessary. Pilar's death was years ago: the boy courier couldn't be much of a boy any longer.

"Gone dark?" she said. "How?" Had he had a pigmentation makeover? Surely not that.

"He used to be at HelthWyzer, but now he's graduated from high school and moved over to the Watson-Crick Institute, and he's fallen off our screen. Not that we have that much of a screen, as such," he added.

Toby waited. With Zeb, there was no point in pushing or fishing.

"Between us, right?" he said after a while.

"Of course," said Toby. I'm just an ear, she thought. A doggie-type faithful companion. A well of silence. Nothing more to it. After Lucerne had flown the coop four years ago she'd wondered briefly if there might be more, sometime, between her and Zeb. But nothing had come of that hankering. I'm the wrong body type, she thought. Too muscular. No doubt he likes the jiggle.

"Council doesn't know about this, okay?" said Zeb. "Him going dark will just make them nervous."

"I'll forget I heard it," said Toby.

"His dad was a friend of Pilar's – she used to be Botanic Splices, at HelthWyzer. I knew them both, at that time. But he got unhappy when he found out they were seeding folks with illnesses via those souped-up supplement pills of theirs – using them as free lab animals, then collecting on the treatments for those very same illnesses. Nifty scam, charging top dollar for stuff they caused themselves. Troubled his conscience. So the dad fed us some interesting data. Then he had an accident."

"Accident?" said Toby.

"Went off an overpass at rush hour. Blood gumbo."

"That's a bit graphic," said Toby. "For a vegetarian."

"Sorry about that," said Zeb. "Suicide, was the rumour."

"It wasn't, I take it," said Toby.

"We call it Corpicide. If you're Corp and you do something they don't like, you're dead. It's like you shot yourself."

"I see," said Toby.

"Anyway, back to our young guy. The mother was Diagnostics at HelthWyzer, he'd hacked her lab sign-in code, he could run stuff through the system for us. Genius hacker. The mom's married a top corp guy at HelthWyzer Central and the kid went with her."

"Where Lucerne is," said Toby.

Zeb ignored this. "Burned through their firewalls, cooked up a few onscreen identities, got back in touch. We heard from him for a while, but then nothing."

"Maybe he's lost interest," said Toby. "Or else they caught him."

"Maybe," said Zeb. "But he's a three-dimensional chess player, he likes a challenge. He's nimble. Also he's got no fear."

"How many like that do we have?" Toby asked. "In the Compounds?"

"Nobody that good at hacking," said Zeb. "This guy's one of a kind."

45

They reached the Wellness Clinic and entered the Vinegar Room. Toby moved around behind the three huge barrels, unlocked the bottle shelf, and swung it out so she could open the inner door. She could hear Zeb sucking in his stomach to squeeze past the barrels: he wasn't softly fat, but he was large.

The inner room was almost filled by a table patched together from old floorboards, with a motley collection of chairs. On one wall there was a recent watercolour – Saint E.O. Wilson of Hymenoptera – done by Nuala in one of her too frequent moments of artistic inspiration. The Saint was shown with the sun behind him, giving him a halo effect. On his face was an ecstatic smile, in his hand was a collecting jar containing several black spots. These were the bees, Toby supposed, or possibly the ants. As was often the case with Nuala's paintings of Saints, one of the arms was longer than the other.

There was a gentle knock, and Adam One slipped through the door. The rest followed in their turn.

Adam One was a different person behind the scenes. Not entirely different – no less sincere – but more practical. Also more tactical. "Let us say a silent prayer for the success of our deliberations," he began. The meetings always opened this way. Toby had some difficulty praying in the close confines of the hidden room: she was too aware of stomach rumblings, of the waftings of clandestine odours, of the creaks and shiftings of bodies. But then, she had some difficulty praying anyway.

The silent prayer seemed to be on a timer. As heads lifted and eyes opened, Adam One glanced around the room. "Is that a new picture?" he said. "On the wall?"

Nuala beamed. "It's Saint E.O.," she said. "Wilson. Of Hymenoptera."

"So like him, my dear," said Adam One. "Especially the . . . You are blessed with such talent." He coughed slightly. "Now to a pressing practical matter. We have just received a very special guest, originally from HelthWyzer Central, though she has been, shall we say, travelling. Despite all obstacles, she's brought us a gift of genome codes, for which we owe her, not only temporary asylum, but secure Exfernal placement."

"They're looking for her," said Zeb. "She shouldn't have come back to this country. We'll have to move her out as fast as possible. Through the FenderBender and over to the Street of Dreams, as usual?"

"If it's a clear path," said Adam One. "We can't take unnecessary risks. We can always keep her hidden in this meeting room, if we have to."

The ratio of women to men fleeing the Corporations was roughly three to one. Nuala said it was because women were more ethical, Zeb said it was because they were more squeamish, and Philo said it amounted to the same thing. Such fugitives often brought contraband information with them. Formulae. Long lines of code. Test secrets, proprietary lies. What did the Gardeners do with it all? Toby wondered. Surely they didn't sell it as industrial corp espionage material, though it would fetch a bundle from foreign rivals. As far as she could tell, they just held on to it; though it was possible that Adam One harboured a dream of restoring all the lost Species via their preserved DNA codes, once a more ethical and technically proficient future had replaced the depressing present. They'd cloned the mammoth, so why not all? Was that his vision of the ultimate Ark?

"Our new guest wants to send a message to her son," said Adam One. "She's worried about having left him at what may have been a crucial time in his life. Jimmy is this lad's name. I believe he's now at the Martha Graham Academy."

"A postcard," said Zeb. "We'll say it's from Aunt Monica. Get me the address, I'll relay it through England – one of our Truffle cellfolk has a trip there next week. The CorpSeCorps will read it, of course. They read all the postcards."

"She wants us to say that his pet rakunk was released into the wilds of Heritage Park, where it is living a free and happy life. Its name is – ah – Killer."

"Oh, Christ in a Zeppelin!" said Zeb.

"That language is uncalled for," said Nuala.

"Sorry. But they make it so fucking complicated," said Zeb. "That's the third pet rakunk message this month. Next it'll be gerbils and mice."

"I think it's touching," said Nuala.

"Guess some people anyway practise what they preach," said Rebecca.

Toby was assigned as minder to the new refugee. Her code name was the Hammerhead, because upon leaving HelthWyzer she was said to have taken her husband's computer apart with a home handyman's toolkit to disguise the extent of her data thefts. She was thin and blue-eyed, and far from calm. Like all Corp defectors, she thought she was the only one ever to have taken the momentous and heretical step of defying a Corp; and like all of them, she desperately wanted to be told what a good person she was.

Toby obliged. She said how brave the Hammerhead had been, which was true, and how smart she'd been to take a winding and devious path, and how much they appreciated the information she'd brought them. In reality she hadn't told them anything they didn't already know – it was that old human-to-pig neocortex transplant material – but it would have been less than kind to say so. We must cast a wide net, said Adam One, although some of the fish may be small. Also we must be a beacon of hope, because if you tell people there's nothing they can do, they will do worse than nothing.

Toby shrouded the Hammerhead in a dark blue Gardener dress, adding a nose cone to conceal her face. But the woman was nervous and fidgety, and kept asking if she could have a cigarette. Toby said no

Gardener smoked – not tobacco – so to be caught doing so would blow her cover. Anyway there weren't any cigarettes up on the Rooftop.

The Hammerhead paced the floor and gnawed her fingernails until Toby felt like hitting her. *We didn't ask you to come here and put all our necks in a noose over a teaspoonful of stale-dated crap,* she wanted to say. In the end she gave the woman some chamomile tea with Poppy in it, just to take her off the airwaves.

46

The next day was Saint Aleksander Zawadzki of Galicia. A minor saint but one of Toby's favourites. He'd lived in turbulent times – what times in Poland had ever not been turbulent? – but had followed his own peaceful and slightly dotty pursuits nonetheless, cataloguing the flowers of Galicia, naming its beetles. Rebecca liked him too: she'd put on her apron with the butterfly appliqués and made beetle biscuits for the small children's snack time, ornamenting each one with an *A* and a *Z*. The children had made up their own little song about him: *Alexsander, Alexsander, beetle up your nose! Blow it on your handkerchief, stick it on a rose!*

It was midmorning. The Hammerhead was still sleeping off the effects of yesterday's Poppy: Toby had overdone it, but she didn't feel too guilty, and now she had some time for her regular chores. She'd garbed up in her bee veil and gloves and lit the smudge in her bellows: as she'd explained to the bees, she intended to spend the morning extracting the full honeycombs. Before she'd begun the smoking, however, Zeb appeared.

"Crappy news," he said. "Your Painball buddy's out again." Like everyone at the Gardeners, Zeb knew the story of Toby's rescue from Blanco by Adam One and the Buds and Blooms – it was part of oral history. But he also sensed her fear. Though they'd never discussed it.

Toby felt an ice needle shoot through her. She lifted up her veil. "Really?"

"Older and meaner," said Zeb. "Twisted fuck should have been vulture pellets long ago. He must have friends in high places, though, because he's back managing SecretBurgers, over in the Sewage Lagoon."

"As long as he stays there," said Toby. She tried to make her voice sound strong.

"The bees can wait," said Zeb. He took her arm. "You need to sit down. I'll do a snoop. Maybe he's forgotten all about you."

He took Toby to the kitchen. "Sweetheart, you look beat," said Rebecca. "What's wrong?" Toby told her.

"Oh shit," said Rebecca. "I'll make you some Rescue Tea, you look like you need it. Don't you worry – that man's karma will kill him one day." But, thought Toby, *one day* was far too distant.

It was afternoon. Many of the general-membership Gardeners were gathered on the roof. Some were retying the tomatoes and climbing zucchinis that had blown over in the storm, a more violent one than usual. Others sat in the shade, working at their knitting, their knotting, their mending. The Adams and Eves were restless, as they always were when they were harbouring a runaway – what if the Hammerhead had been followed? Adam One had posted sentinels; he himself was standing over by the roof's edge in one-legged meditation pose, keeping an eye on the street below.

The Hammerhead had woken up, and Toby had set her to work picking snails off the lettuces; she'd told the rank-and-file Gardeners this was a new convert, and shy. They'd seen so many new converts come and go.

"If we have a visit," Toby said to the Hammerhead, "anything like an inspection, pull your sunhat down and go on with the snails. Act like background." She herself was smoking the bees, on the theory that it was best to carry on as usual.

Then Shackleton and Crozier and young Oates came pounding up the fire-escape stairs, followed by Amanda, then Zeb. They headed straight over to Adam One. He motioned to Toby with his chin: *join us.*

"There's been a scuffle in the Sewage Lagoon," said Zeb after they'd grouped around Adam One.

"Scuffle?" said Adam One.

"We were just looking," said Shackleton. "But he saw us."

"He called us fucking meat-stealers," said Crozier. "He was drunk."

"Not drunk: wasted," said Amanda with authority. "He tried to hit me, but I did a *satsuma*." Toby smiled a little: it was a mistake to underestimate Amanda. She was a tall sinewy Amazon by now, and she'd been studying Urban Bloodshed Limitation with Zeb. As had her two devoted henchmen. There were three if you counted Oates, though he was merely at the hopeless crush level.

"Who is 'he'?" said Adam One. "Where was this?"

"SecretBurgers," said Zeb. "We were checking it out – we heard Blanco was back."

"Zeb pulled an *unagi* on him," said Shackleton. "It was neat!"

"Did you have to actually go there?" said Adam One, a little peevishly. "We have other ways of . . ."

"Then the Asian Fusions swarmed him," said Oates excitedly. "They had bottles!"

"He pulled a killer knife," said Croze. "He notched a couple."

"I hope there was no lasting damage," said Adam One. "Much as we deplore the very existence of SecretBurgers, and the depredations of this – this unlucky individual, we want no violence."

"Booth overturned, meat thrown around. All he suffered was cuts and bruises," said Zeb.

"That is unfortunate," said Adam One. "It's true that we sometimes have to defend ourselves, and we've had trouble with this – with him before. But on this occasion, do I have the impression that we attacked first?" He frowned at Zeb. "Or provoked an attack? Is this correct?"

"Asshole had it coming," said Zeb. "We should be getting medals."

"Our way is the way of peace," said Adam One, frowning even more.

"Peace goes only so far," said Zeb. "There's at least a hundred new extinct species since this time last month. They got fucking eaten! We can't just sit here and watch the lights blink out. Have to begin somewhere. Today SecretBurgers, tomorrow that fucking gourmet restaurant chain. Rarity. That needs to go."

"Our role in respect to the Creatures is to bear witness," said Adam One. "And to guard the memories and the genomes of the departed. You can't fight blood with blood. I thought we'd agreed on that."

There was a silence. Shackleton and Crozier and Oates and Amanda were staring at Zeb. Zeb and Adam One were staring at each other.

"Anyway, it's too late now," said Zeb. "Blanco's raging."

"Will he cross pleebmob boundaries?" said Toby. "Raid us here, in the Sinkhole?"

"Mood he's in, no question," said Zeb. "Ordinary mob guys don't scare him any more. He's multiple-session Painball."

Zeb warned the assembled Gardeners, posted a line of watchers around the roof, and stationed the strongest gatekeepers at the bottom of the fire-escape stairs. Adam One protested, saying that to act like one's enemies was to descend to their level. Zeb said that if Adam One wanted to handle defence matters in some other way he was free to do so, but if not he should keep his nose out of it.

"There's movement," said Rebecca, who was watching. "Three of them coming, it looks like."

"Whatever you do," Toby told the Hammerhead, "don't cut and run. Don't do anything that calls attention." She went over to the roof's edge to look.

Three heavyweights were muscling along the sidewalk. They had baseball bats. No sprayguns. Not CorpSeCorps then, just pleeb thugs: payback for the wreckage at SecretBurgers. One of the three was Blanco – she could spot him from any angle. What would he do? Bash her to death on the spot, or drag her away to do it more slowly elsewhere?

"What is it, my dear?" said Adam One.

"It's him," said Toby. "If he sees me, he'll kill me."

"Be of good cheer," he said. "Nothing bad will be done to you." But since Adam One thought that even the most terrible things happened for ultimately excellent though unfathomable reasons, Toby did not find this reassuring.

Zeb told her she'd better get their special guest out of sight, just in case, so she took the Hammerhead to her own cubicle and gave her a calming drink, heavy on the chamomile, with a little Poppy. The Hammerhead drifted off to sleep, and Toby sat watching her and hoping the two of them wouldn't end up cornered. She found herself looking around for weapons. I suppose I could hit them with the Poppy bottle, she thought. But it's not very big.

Then she walked back out to the Rooftop. She was still in her bee gear. She adjusted her heavy gloves, took up her bellows, and lowered her veil. "Stand by me," she said to the bees. "Be my messengers." As if they could hear.

The fight didn't last long. Later, Toby heard Shackleton and Crozier and Oates enacting the full battle story for the younger children, who'd been hurried out of the way by Nuala. According to them, it had been epic.

"Zeb was brilliant," said Shackleton. "He had it all planned out! They must've thought since we're so pacifist and all, they could just . . . Anyway, it was like an ambush – we backed up the stairs, with them following."

"And then, and then," said Oates.

"And then, at the top, Zeb let the first guy lunge at him, and then he got the end of the guy's baseball bat and kind of flung it, and the guy almost crashed into Rebecca, and she had this two-pronged fork, and then he went screaming right over the edge of the roof."

"Like this!" said Oates, arms flailing.

"Then Stuart sprayed the next one with the plant hydrator," said Crozier. "He says it works on cats."

"Amanda did something to him. Didn't you?" Shackleton said to her fondly. "Like, some Bloodshed Limitation move, like a *hamachi*, or – I don't know what she did, but he went over the railing too. Did you kick him in the nuts or what?"

"I relocated him," said Amanda demurely. "Like a snail."

"Then the third one ran away," said Oates. "The biggest guy. With bees all over him. Toby did that, it was wicked. Adam One wouldn't let us go after him."

"Zeb says this won't be the end of it," said Amanda.

Toby had her own version, in which everything had moved both very fast and very slowly. She'd placed herself behind the hives, and then the three of them had been right there, just emerging from the stair-top. A pale-faced man with a dark chin and a baseball bat, a scarred Redfish type, and Blanco. Blanco had spotted her immediately. "I see you, stringy-assed bitch!" he'd yelled. "You're meat!" Her bee veil was no disguise. He had his knife out; he was grinning.

The first man had tangled with Rebecca and gone over the railing somehow, screaming on the way down, but the second one was still coming. Then Amanda – who'd been standing off to the side, looking ethereal and harmless – had raised her arm. Toby had seen a flash of light: was that glass? But Blanco was almost upon her: there was nothing between them but the hives.

She pushed the hives over – three of them. She was veiled, Blanco was not. The bees poured out, whining with anger, and went for him like arrows. He fled howling down the fire-escape stairs, flailing and slapping, trailing a plume of bees.

It took some time for Toby to set the hives back up. The bees were furious, and several Gardeners got stung. Toby apologized to the victims, and she and Katuro treated them with calamine and chamomile; but she apologized much more profusely to the bees, once she'd smoked them enough to make them drowsy: they'd sacrificed many of their own in the battle.

47

The Adams and Eves had a tense meeting in the hidden room behind the vinegar barrels. "That shit wouldn't attack without authorization," said Zeb. "It's the CorpSeCorps behind it – they're aware of some of the folks we've been helping out, so they're working up to branding us as terrorist fanatics, like the Wolf Isaiahists."

"Nope, it's personal," said Rebecca. "That man is mean as a snake, no disrespect to Snakes, and he was after Toby, is all. Once he's stuck his pole in some hole, he thinks it's his." When Rebecca got worked up, she tended to revert to her earlier vocabulary and then regret it. "No offence, Toby," she said.

"Surely the proximate cause is among us," said Adam One. "The young people provoked him. And Zeb. We should have let sleeping dogs lie."

"Dogs is right," said Rebecca. "No disrespect to Dogs."

"Two dead bodies on the sidewalk will hardly do our peaceful reputation any good," said Nuala.

"Accidents. They fell off the roof," said Zeb.

"And one got his throat cut and the other had his eye put out on the way down," said Adam One. "As any forensic investigation will show."

"Dangerous, brick walls," said Katuro. "Things stick. Nails. Broken glass. Sharp things."

"Maybe you'd like a few dead Gardeners better?" said Zeb.

"If your premise is correct," said Adam One, "and this is a CorpSeCorps plot, has it occurred to you that those three may have been sent to provoke exactly such an incident? To cause us to break the law, thus providing an excuse for reprisals?"

"What was our choice?" said Zeb. "Let them squash us like bugs? Not that we squash Bugs," he added.

"He'll come back," said Toby. "Whatever the reason, CorpSeCorps or not. As long as I stay here, I'll be a target."

"I think," said Adam One, "that it would be best for your safety, dear Toby, and also for the safety of the Garden, if we were to place you in one of our Truffle niches in the Exfernal World. You can be of much use to us there. We'll ask our pleebrat connections to spread the news that you are no longer among us. Perhaps your foe may then lack motivation, and we will be protected from aggression from that quarter, at least for the moment. How soon can we move her?" he asked Zeb.

"Consider it done," said Zeb.

Toby went to her sleeping cubicle and packed her most necessary items – the bottled extracts, the dried herbs, the mushrooms. Pilar's honey, the last three jars. She left some of each thing behind for whoever might be filling her empty Eve Six shoes.

She remembered her early desire to leave the Garden, out of boredom and claustrophobia, and the desire for what she used to think of as a life of her own; but now that she was actually going, it felt like an expulsion. No: more like a wrenching, a severing, a skin peeling off. She resisted the urge to drink some Poppy, to dull the edge. She had to stay alert.

Another hurt: she was failing Pilar. Would she have time to say goodbye to the bees, and if she didn't, would the hives die? Who would take over as beekeeper? Who had the skills? She covered her head with a scarf and hurried out to the hives.

"Bees," she said out loud. "I have news." Did the bees pause in mid-air, were they listening? Several came to investigate her; they lit on her face, exploring her emotions through the chemicals on her skin. She hoped they'd forgiven her for tipping their hives. "You must tell your

Queen I've had to leave," she said. "Nothing to do with you, you've performed your duties well. My enemy is forcing me to go. I'm sorry. I hope that when we meet again it will be under happier circumstances." She always found herself using a formal style with the bees.

The bees buzzed and fizzed; they appeared to be discussing her. She wished she could take them with her like a large, golden, furry collective pet. "I'll miss you, bees," she said. As if in answer, one of them started crawling up her nostril. She breathed it sharply out. Maybe we wear hats for these interviews, she thought, so they won't go into our ears.

She went back to her cubicle, where an hour later Adam One and Zeb joined her. "You'd better wear this, dear Toby," said Adam One. He was carrying a furzoot – a fluffy pink duck with flapping red rubbery feet and a smiling yellow plastic bill. "The nose cone's built in. It's the latest fabric. Mo'Hair NeoBiofur – it exhales for you. Or so the label claims."

The two of them waited on the other side of the cubicle curtain while Toby took off her sombre Gardener dress and put on the furzoot. NeoBiofur or not, it was hot in there. And dark. She knew she was looking out through a pair of round white eyes with big black pupils, but it felt like peering through a keyhole.

"Flap your wings," said Zeb.

Toby moved her arms up and down inside the zoot arms and the duck suit quacked. It sounded like an old man blowing his nose.

"If you want to make the tail wiggle, stamp your left foot."

"How do I talk?" said Toby. She had to say it again, louder.

"Through the right earhole," said Adam One.

Oh great, thought Toby. You quack with your foot, you talk through your earhole. I won't ask how to do any of the other bodily functions.

She changed back into her dress, and Zeb stuffed the furzoot into a duffle bag. "I'll drive you in the truck," he said. "It's right out front."

"We'll be in touch very soon, my dear," said Adam One. "I regret . . . it's unfortunate that . . . Keep the Light around . . ."

"I'll try," said Toby.

The Gardeners' forced-air truck now had a logo on it that said, PARTY TIME. Toby sat in the front with Zeb. The Hammerhead was in the back, disguised as a box of balloons: Zeb said he was killing two birds with one stone.

"Sorry," he added.

"For what?" Toby asked. Sorry that she was going? She felt a small pulse-beat.

"Killing two birds. Not good to mention bird murder."

"Oh. Right," said Toby. "It's okay."

"We'll send the Hammerhead down the line," said Zeb. "We've got connections among the bag-heavers for the sealed bullet train; she can go as cargo, we'll mark her as Fragile. We've got a Truffle cell in Oregon – they'll keep her out of sight."

"How about me?" said Toby.

"Adam One wants you closer to the Garden," said Zeb, "in case Blanco gets Painballed again and you can come back. We've got an Exfernal spot for you, but it'll take a few days to set up. Meanwhile, just hang out in your zoot. Street of Dreams, where they peddle the custom genes – that place is crawling with furzooters, nobody will notice you. Now, better scrunch down – we're going through the Sewage Lagoon."

Zeb delivered Toby to the FenderBender Body Shop, where the resident Gardeners whisked her out of the truck and stashed her in the former hydraulic-lift pit, which they'd covered with trapdoor flooring. There she breathed ancient engine-oil fumes and ate a sparse meal of damp soybits and mashed turnips, washed down with Sumac. She slept on an old futon, using her furzoot as a pillow. There was no biolet in there, only a rusted Happicuppa coffee can. *Use what's to hand* was a cherished Gardener motto.

Not all the members of the FenderBender rat colony had been successfully relocated to the Buenavista Condos, she discovered. But those remaining were not overtly hostile.

The next morning she began her spurious job – waddling along the Street of Dreams inside a wodge of fake fur, quacking at intervals and wiggling her tail, wearing a sandwich board, and handing out brochures. On the front of the board it said, UGLY DUCKLINGS TO LOVELY SWANS AT THE ANOOYOO SPA-IN-THE-PARK! *Goose Your Self-Esteem!* On the back, ANOOYOO! DO IT FOR YOO! On the brochures it said, *Epidermal enhancement! Lower cost! Avoid gene errors! Fully reversible!* AnooYoo didn't sell gene therapy – nothing so radical or permanent. Instead it sold more superficial treatments. Herbal elixirs, system cleansers, dermal mood lifts; vegetable nanocell injections, mildew-formula micromesh resurfacing, heavy-duty face creams, rehydrating balms. Iguana-based hue changes, microbial spot removal, flat-wart leech peels.

She handed out many brochures, but she also got hassled by some of the gene-shop owners: on the Street of Dreams it was dream eat dream. There were a number of other furzooters working the Street – a lion, a Mo'Hair sheep, two bears, and three other ducks. Toby wondered how many of them were really who they claimed to be: if she was hiding out in plain view, others in need of invisibility must have discovered the same solution.

If she'd been working for a genuine furzoot outfit as she'd done once before, she'd have clocked her hours at day's end, climbed out of her zoot, and pocketed the receipt for her e-pay. As it was, Zeb collected her in the pickup. Its logo now said, BIGZOOT – SAY IT WITH FURORE! She rolled herself into the back, still inside her zoot, and Zeb ferried her to another Gardener enclave – an abandoned bank in the Sewage Lagoon. The various banking corps had once paid the local pleebmob for protection, but soon their Tex-Mex identity-theft specialists were skipping in and out as freely as mice. Finally the banks had given up and decamped, because no employee's idea of a business day well spent was lying on the floor with duct tape over your mouth while an identity filcher hacked the accounts, gaining access with your cut-off thumb.

The old-fashioned bank vault was a much better place to spend the night than the hydraulic-lift pit had been. Cool, rat-free, no gas fumes; a lingering odour of the gently oxidizing paper money of yesteryear. But then Toby started wondering what would happen if someone inadvertently closed and locked the vault door and then forgot about her, so she didn't sleep very well.

The next day it was the Street of Dreams again. The duck costume was intolerable in the heat, one of her rubber feet was coming loose, and the nose-cone filter was dysfunctional. What if the Gardeners abandoned her and she was left to eddy around in the Dreams-land, transformed into a non-existent bird-animal and dehydrating herself to death, to be found one day in a welter of damp pink faux feathers, clogging up the drains?

But finally Zeb picked her up. He drove her to a clinic at the back of a Mo'Hair franchise outlet. "We're doing the hair and skin," he said. "You're going dark. And the fingerprints, and the voiceprint. Plus a bit of recontouring." The biotech for changing iris pigment was risky – there'd been some unpleasant bulging effects, said Zeb – so she'd have to use contacts. Green ones – he'd picked out the colour himself.

"Higher voice, or lower?" he asked her.

"Lower," said Toby, hoping she wouldn't come out a baritone.

"Good choice," said Zeb.

The doctor was Chinese, and very smooth. There'd be an anaesthetic, and a recuperation time in the recovery unit upstairs – top of the line, said Zeb – and once Toby found herself inside it, the place did seem very clean. They didn't do much cutting and stitching. Her fingertips lost their sensitivity – it would come back, said Zeb – and her throat was sore from the voicework, and her head itched a lot while the Mo'Hair scalp was bonding. The skin pigmentation was uneven at first, but Zeb told her it would be fine in six weeks: until then, she'd have to keep strictly out of the sun.

She spent the six weeks of seclusion at a Truffle cell in SolarSpace. Her contact, whose name was Muffy, collected Toby from the clinic in a very expensive all-electric coupé. "If anyone asks," Muffy said, "just tell them you're the new maid. I do have to apologize," she continued, "but we have to eat meat at our place, it's part of our cover. We feel terrible about it, but just about everyone in SolarSpace is a carnivore, and they're very big on barbecues – organic, naturally, and some of it's stretchy-rack-grown, you know, they grow just the muscle tissue, no brain, no pain – and it would be suspicious if we ducked it. But I'll try to keep the cooking smells away from you."

Too late for such a warning: Toby had already smelled something that came close to the aroma of the bone-stock soup her mother used to make. Though she was ashamed of herself, it made her hungry. Hungry, and also sad. Maybe sadness was a kind of hunger, she thought. Maybe the two went together.

In her little maid's room Toby read e-magazines, and practised sticking her contact lenses onto her eyeballs, and listened to music on a Sea/H/Ear Candy. It was a surreal interlude. "Think of yourself as a chrysalis," Zeb had told her before the transformation process had begun. Sure enough, she'd gone in as Toby and had come out as Tobiatha. Less angla, more latina. More alto.

She looked at herself – her new skin, her new abundant hair, her more prominent cheekbones. Her new almond-shaped green eyes. She'd have to remember to put those lenses in every morning.

The alterations hadn't made her stunningly beautiful, but that wasn't the object. The object was to make her more invisible. Beauty is only skin deep, she thought. But why did they always say *only*?

Still, her new look wasn't bad. The hair was a nice change, though the family cats were taking an interest in it, probably because of the faint lamb-like smell. When she woke up in the morning she was likely to find one of them sitting on her pillow, licking her hair and purring.

48

Once her scalp was firmly rooted to her head and her skin tone was uniform, Toby was ready to move into her new identity. Muffy explained to her what this was to be.

"We thought, the AnooYoo Spa-in-the-Park," she said. "They're heavy on the botanics there, so you'd fit right in, because of the mushrooms and the potions and all, Zeb told me – so you can get up to speed on their products really fast. They have an organic garden for the café, they pride themselves on that, with a compost heap and all of that; and they're doing some plant splice tryouts you might find interesting. As for the rest, it's like organizing anything else – product in, value added, product out. Supervising the books and the supplies, managing the staff – Zeb says you're really good with people. The procedural templates are already in place – you'll just need to follow them."

"The product would be the customers?" said Toby.

"That's right," said Muffy.

"And the value added?"

"It's an intangible," said Muffy. "They feel they look better afterwards. People will pay a lot of money for that."

"Do you mind telling me how you got me this position?" Toby asked.

"My husband's on the AnooYoo board," said Muffy. "Don't worry, I didn't lie to him. He's one of us."

Once installed at the AnooYoo Spa, Toby settled into her role as Tobiatha, the vaguely Tex-Mex but discreet and efficient manager. The days were placid, the nights were calm. True, there was an electric fence around the whole place and four gatehouses with guards, but the identi-checks were lax and the guards never bothered Toby. It wasn't a high-security posting. The Spa had no big secrets to defend, so the guards did nothing but monitor the ladies who were going in, frightened by the first signs of droop and pucker, then going out again, buffed and tightened and resurfaced, irradiated and despotted.

But still frightened, because when might the whole problem – the whole *thing* – start happening to them again? The whole signs-of-mortality thing. The whole *thing* thing. Nobody likes it, thought Toby – being a body, a thing. Nobody wants to be limited in that way. We'd rather have wings. Even the word *flesh* has a mushy sound to it.

We're not selling only beauty, the AnooYoo Corp said in their staff instructionals. We're selling hope.

Some of the customers could be demanding. They couldn't understand why even the most advanced AnooYoo treatments wouldn't make them twenty-one again. "Our laboratories are well on the way to age reversal," Toby would tell them in soothing tones, "but they aren't quite there yet. In a few years . . ."

If you really want to stay the same age you are now forever and ever, she'd be thinking, try jumping off the roof: death's a sure-fire method for stopping time.

Toby took pains to be a convincing manager. She ran the Spa efficiently, she listened carefully to both staff and customers, she mediated disputes when necessary, she cultivated efficiency and tact. Having been an Eve Six helped: through that experience she'd discovered a talent within herself for gazing solemnly as if deeply interested, while saying nothing. "Remember," she'd tell her staff, "every customer wants to feel like a princess, and princesses are selfish and overbearing." Just don't spit in their soup, she wanted to counsel, but that would have been going too far out of her Tobiatha character.

On the most aggravating days she amused herself by viewing the Spa as if it were a tabloid 'zine: *Socialite corpse found on lawn, toxic facial suspected. Amanita implicated in exfoliation death. Tragedy stalks the pool.* But why take it out on the ladies? They only wanted to feel good and be happy, like everything else on the planet. Why should she begrudge them their obsessions with their puffy veins and tummy flubber? "Think pink," she told her girls as per the AnooYoo Corp instructional template, and then she'd tell herself the same thing. Why not? It was a nicer colour than bilious yellow.

After a cautious pause, she began stashing away a few supplies – building her own private Ararat. She wasn't sure she believed in the Waterless Flood – as time passed, the Gardeners and their theories seemed more and more remote, more fanciful, more creative – in a word, loonier – but she believed in it enough to take the rudimentary precautions. She was in charge of Spa inventory, so stockpiling was easy. She'd simply retrieve empty product containers from the recycling bins, a few at a time – those for AnooYoo Intestinal Whisk were especially useful, as they were large and had tops that snapped on – and fill them with soybits or dried seaweed or powdered milk substitute or tins of soydines. Then she'd replace the tops and store the containers at the very backs of the stockroom shelves. A couple of other staff members had the storeroom door code, but as Toby was known to be a strict inventory-taker and to be tough on pilferers, no one was likely to make off with any of her refilled containers.

She had an office of her own, and in that office there was a computer. She knew the hazards of out-of-bounds usage – some AnooYoo Corp functionary might be monitoring her searches and messages and checking to make sure staff wasn't watching porno flicks on company time – so most days she scanned only for general news, hoping that way to pick up any word of the Gardeners.

There wasn't much. From time to time there'd be a story on subversive acts by fanatical greenies, but there was a number of such groups by now. She glimpsed some Gardener faces in the crowd during the Boston Coffee Party, when they were dumping Happicuppa beans into the harbour, but she might have been wrong about that. Several people were wearing T-shirts with G IS G on them for "God Is Green," which proved nothing: the Gardeners themselves hadn't worn such T-shirts, not in the old days.

The CorpSeCorps could have shut down the Happicuppa riots. They could have spraygunned the lot, plus any TV camerafolk who happened to be nearby. Not that you could shut down coverage of such events completely: people used their cameraphones. Still, why didn't the CorpSeCorps move in openly, blitz their opponents right in plain view, and impose overt totalitarian rule, since they were the only ones with weapons? They were even running the army, now that it had been privatized.

She'd once put this question to Zeb. He'd said that officially they were a private Corporation Security Corps employed by the brand-name Corporations, and those Corporations still wanted to be perceived as honest and trustworthy, friendly as daisies, guileless as bunnies. They couldn't afford to be viewed by the average consumer as lying, heartless, tyrannical butchers.

"The Corps have to sell, but they can't force people to buy," he'd said. "Not yet. So the clean image is still seen as a must."

That was the short answer: people didn't want the taste of blood in their Happicuppas.

Muffy, her Truffle-cell minder, kept in touch with Toby by checking herself in for AnooYoo treatments. Occasionally she'd bring news: Adam One was well, Nuala sent regards, the Gardeners were still expanding their influence, but the situation was unstable. Once in a while she'd bring in a female fugitive in need of a temporary hide. She'd dress the woman in clothes like hers – rich SolarSpace matron colours, pastel blue, creamy beige – and book her in for treatments. "Just pile on the mud and smother her in towels, and no one will notice a thing," she'd say, which turned out to be true.

One of these emergency guests was the Hammerhead. Toby recognized her – the fidgety hands, the intense blue martyr's eyes – but she didn't recognize Toby. So the Hammerhead hadn't made it to a quiet life in Oregon after all, thought Toby: she's still in the area, taking the risks, on the run all the time. Most likely she'd been sucked into the urban green-guerrilla scene; in which case her days were numbered, because the CorpSeCorps were said to be bent on eliminating all such activists. They'd have the samples from her old HelthWyzer identity, and once you were in their system you never got out of it except by turning up as a corpse with dental work and DNA that matched their records.

Toby ordered the Total Aromatics for the Hammerhead, and an extra Deep Pore Relax. She looked as if she needed them.

There was one serious hazard at the AnooYoo: Lucerne was a regular customer. She came every month, toting a Compound senior-level wife's wardrobe. She always had the Luscious Polish, the Plum Skin Plumper, and the AnooYoo Fountain of Yooth Total Immersion. She looked more stylish than she'd been at the Gardeners – not difficult, thought Toby, because in a plastic bag you'd be more stylish than a Gardener – but she also looked older and more desiccated. Her once-lush lower lip had developed a downward sag, despite all the collagen and plant extracts Toby knew had been pumped into it, and her eyelids were getting the crinkly texture of poppy petals. These signs of decline were gratifying to Toby, though it dismayed her to be burdened with such a petty and jealous emotion. *Give it up*, she told herself. *Just because Lucerne's turning into an old puffball doesn't mean you're a hot babe.*

It would of course be catastrophic if Lucerne were suddenly to burst out from behind a shrub or a shower curtain and shout out Toby's real name. So Toby took evasive action. She'd review the advance bookings so she'd know exactly when Lucerne was going to show up. Then she'd assign her most vigorous operatives – Melody with her big shoulders, Symphony with her firm hands – and keep herself out of Lucerne's sightline. But as Lucerne was usually prone and covered with brown goop and eye pads, she was unlikely to spot Toby; and even if she did see her, she'd be sure to look right through her. To women like Lucerne, women like Tobiatha were faceless.

What if I crept up on her during the Fountain of Yooth Total Immersion and gunned the lasers? Toby wondered. Or shorted the heat lamp? She'd melt like a marshmallow. A nematode snack. The Earth would cheer.

Dear Eve Six, said Adam One's voice. Such fantasies are unworthy of you. What would Pilar think?

One afternoon there was a knock at Toby's office door. "Come in," she said. It was a large man in a groundsman's green denim overall. He was whistling – surely – a familiar tune.

"I'm here to prune the lumiroses," he said. Toby looked up, drew her breath in sharply. She knew better than to say anything: her office could be crawling with bugs.

Zeb glanced back along the hallway, then stepped in and shut the door. He sat down at her computer, then took a Sharpie and wrote on her desk pad: *Watch what I do.*

The Gardeners? Toby wrote. *Adam One?*

Schism, Zeb wrote. *Own group now.* "Having any trouble with the plantings?" he said out loud.

Shackleton and Crozier? Toby wrote. *With you?*

Manner of speaking, Zeb replied. *Oates. Katuro, Rebecca. New ones too.*

Amanda?

Got out. Higher education. Art. Smart.

He'd pulled up a site: EXTINCTATHON. Monitored by MaddAddam. *Adam named the living animals, MaddAddam names the dead ones. Do you want to play?*

MaddAddam? Toby wrote on her desk pad. *Your group? You're plural?* She was elated: Zeb was here, beside her, in the flesh. After she'd thought for so long that she'd never see him again.

I contain multitudes, wrote Zeb. *Pick a codename. Life form, extinct.*

Dodo, Toby wrote.

Last fifty years, Zeb wrote. Not much time. *Pruning team waiting. Ask about aphids.*

"There's aphids on the lumiroses," Toby said. She was riffling through the old Gardener lists in her head – animals, fish, birds, flowers, clams, lizards, recently extinct. *Inaccessible Rail*, she wrote. That bird had gone ten years ago. *Can they hack this site?*

"We can take care of that," Zeb said. "Though there's supposed to be a built-in insecticidal deterrent . . . I'll take some samples. There's more than one way to skin a cat." *No*, he wrote. *Made our own virtual private networks. Quadrupally encrypted. Sorry about the cat-skinning ref. Here's your number.*

He wrote her new codename and a pass number on the pad. Then he typed his own number and code into the log-in space provided. *Welcome, Spirit Bear. Do you want to play a general game or do you want to play a Grandmaster?* said the screen.

Zeb clicked on Grandmaster. *Good. Find your playroom. MaddAddam will meet you there.*

Watch, he wrote on her pad. He entered a site advertising Mo'Hair transplants, skipped through a pixel gateway on the eye of a magenta-haired sheep, entered the blue percolating stomach of an ad for a Helth-Wyzer antacid, which led to the avid open mouth of a SecretBurger customer caught in mid-chomp. Then a wide green landscape unfolded – trees in the distance, a lake in the foreground, a rhino and three lions drinking. A scene from the past.

A line of type unscrolled across it: *Welcome to MaddAddam's playroom, Spirit Bear. You have a message.*

Deliver message, Zeb clicked.

The liver is evil and must be punished.

I hear you, Red-necked Crake, Zeb typed. *All is well.*

Then he closed the site and stood up. "Call me if there are any aphid recurrences," he said. "If you'd check our work from time to time and keep me informed, that would be good." He wrote on her pad: *The hair's great, babe. Love the slanty eyes.* Then he was gone.

Toby gathered up all the desk-pad pages. Luckily she had some matches to burn them with; she'd been hoarding matches for her Ararat, storing them in a container labelled Lemon Meringue Facial.

After Zeb's visit she felt less isolated. She'd log in to Extinctathon at irregular intervals and trace the path to the MaddAddam Grandmaster chatroom. Codenames and messages flitted across the screen: *Black Rhino to Spirit Bear: Newbies coming. Ivory Bill to Swift Fox: Fear no weevil. White Sedge and Lotis Blue: Micesplice a ten. Red-necked Crake to MaddAddam: Marshmallow hiways nice one!* She had no idea what most of these messages meant, but at least she felt included.

Sometimes there were e-bulletins that appeared to be CorpSeCorps classified information. Many of these were about strange outbreaks of new diseases, or peculiar infestations – the splice porcubeaver that was attacking the fan belts in cars, the bean weevil that was decimating Happicuppa coffee plantations, the asphalt-eating microbe that was melting highways.

Then the Rarity restaurant chain was obliterated by a series of lethal bombings. She saw the regular news, where these events were blamed on unspecified eco-terrorists; but she also read a detailed analysis on MaddAddam. It was the Wolf Isaiahists who'd done the bombings, they said, because Rarity had introduced a new menu item – liobam, a sacred animal for the Wolf Isaiahists. MaddAddam had added a P.S.: *Warning all God's Gardeners: They'll pin this on you. Go to ground.*

Shortly after that, Muffy came to the Spa unexpectedly. She was her usual elegant self; her manner gave nothing away. "Let's walk on the lawn," she said. When they were out in the open and away from any hidden mikes, she whispered, "I'm not here for a treatment. I just needed to tell you that we're going away, I can't say where. Don't worry. It's only urgent on the inside."

"Will you be all right?" Toby asked.

"Time will tell," said Muffy. "Good luck, dear Toby. Dear Tobiatha. Put Light around me."

She and her husband were listed as fatalities in an airship accident a week later. The CorpSeCorps were good at arranging high-class mishaps for highly placed suspects, Zeb had told her – people whose disappearance without a trace would cause a stir, up there among the Corps anointed.

Toby didn't go near the MaddAddam chatroom for months after that. She waited for the knock on the door, the shattering of glass, the *zipzip* of a spraygun. But nothing happened. When she finally screwed up the courage to enter MaddAddam again, there was a message for her:

Inaccessible Rail from Spirit Bear: The Garden is destroyed. Adams and Eves gone dark. Watch and wait.

POLLINATION DAY

POLLINATION DAY

YEAR TWENTY-ONE.

OF THE TREES, AND OF THE FRUITS IN THEIR SEASONS.
SPOKEN BY ADAM ONE.

Dear Friends and Fellow Mammals:

Today is a Feast day, but sadly we have no feast. Our flight was rapid: our escape narrow. Now, true to their nature, our enemies have laid waste to our Rooftop. But surely one day we will return to Edencliff and restore that blissful site to its former glory. The CorpSeCorps may have destroyed our Garden, but they have not destroyed our Spirit. Eventually, we shall plant again.

Why did the Corps strike? Alas, we were becoming too powerful for their liking. Many rooftops were blossoming as the rose; many hearts and minds were bent towards an Earth restored to balance. But in success lay the seeds of ruin, for those in power could no longer dismiss us as ineffectual faddists: they feared us, as prophets of the age to come. In short, we threatened their profit margins.

In addition, they linked us to the bio-attacks made on their infrastructures by the schismatic and heretical group calling itself MaddAddam. Last week's bombing attacks on the Rarity restaurant chain – though perpetrated by the Wolf Isaiahists alone – gave them an excuse to unleash a sweeping crackdown on all who have sided with God's Created Earth.

May they prove as blind in material vision as they have long been in Spiritual vision! For though our days of calling carnivores to open repentance on the pleebland streets are over, the lessons of Animal Camouflage have not been lost on us. Disguised to blend with the background, we thrive under the noses of our enemies. We have shed our plain vestments and swathed ourselves in mallway purchases. The monogrammed golf shirt, the lime green tank top, the striped pastel knit ensemble sported so courageously by Nuala – such is our defensive armour.

Some of you have chosen to allay suspicion by courageously eating the flesh of our fellow Creatures; but do not attempt feats beyond your strength, dear Friends. To bite into a SecretBurger and then choke on it will attract unwelcome scrutiny. If in doubts as to your limits, confine yourselves to a SoYummie ice cream. Such quasi-foods may be swallowed without undue strain.

Let us give thanks to the Fernside Truffle cell, which has made this Street of Dreams refuge available to us. The sign on our door proclaims, GREEN GENES, which purports to be a firm of botanic splice designers. The second sign – the one that says, CLOSED FOR RENOVATIONS – is our protection. If asked, say we've been having trouble with the contractor. That is always a plausible explanation.

Today is Pollination Day, on which we remember the contributions to forest preservation of Saint Suryamani Bhagat of India, Saint Stephen King of the Pureora Forest in New Zealand, and Saint Odigha of Nigeria, among so many others. This Festival is devoted to the mysteries of Plant Reproduction, especially that of those wondrous trees, the Angiosperms, with special emphasis upon the Drupes and the Pomaceous Fruits.

Legends of such Fruits have come down to us from the Ancients – the Golden Apples of the Hesperides, the similarly golden Apple of Discord. Some say that the Fruit of the Tree of Knowledge of Good and Evil was a fig, others prefer a date, yet others a pomegranate. It would have made sense for this foodstuff to have been truly evil – a meat object, such as a beefsteak. Why then a Fruit? Because our Ancestors were fruitivores, without a doubt, and only a Fruit would have tempted them.

The Fruit remains a deeply meaningful symbol for us, embodying the notions of healthful harvest, of rich culmination, and of new beginning, for within every Fruit is a seed – a potential new life. The Fruit ripens and falls and returns to the soil; but the Seed takes root, and grows, and brings forth more Life. As the Human Words of God have said, "By their Fruits ye shall know them." Let us pray that our Fruits be Fruits of Good, and not Fruits of Evil.

But a word of caution: we honour the Pollinating Insects, and in especial the Bees, but we are now informed that, in addition to the virus-resistant strain introduced after the recent honeybee die-off, the Corps have now developed a hybrid bee. It is not a genetic splice, my Friends. No: it is a greater abomination! Bees are seized while still in larval form, and micro-mechanical systems are inserted into them. Tissue grows around the insert, and when the full adult or "imago" emerges, it is a bee cyborg spy controllable by a CorpSeCorps operator, equipped to transmit, and thus to betray.

The ethical problems raised are troubling: Should we have recourse to insecticides? Is such a mechanized slave bee *alive*? If so, is it a true Creature of God or something else entirely? We must ponder the deeper implications, my Friends, and pray for guidance.

Let us sing.

THE PEACH OR PLUM

The Peach or Plum that spreads its boughs
Is beauteous at time of flower,
And Birds and Bees and Bats rejoice,
And sip its nectar hour by hour.

And Pollination then takes place:
For every Nut or Seed or Fruit,
A tiny golden particle
Has winged its way, and taken root.

Then swells the oval on the stem,
And slowly ripens, week by week –
Within it stored the nourishment
That Birds and Beasts and Men do seek.

And in each Seed or Fruit or Nut
Is coiled a silver infant Tree
That will arise if planted right,
Unfurling flowers, a joy to see.

When next you eat a golden Peach
And lightly throw away the pit,
Consider how it shines with Life –
God dwelling in the midst of it.

From *The God's Gardeners Oral Hymnbook*

49

REN

YEAR TWENTY-FIVE

Adam One used to say, If you can't stop the waves, go sailing. Or else, What can't be mended may still be tended. Or else, Without the light, no chance; without the dark, no dance. Which meant that even bad things did some good because they were a challenge and you didn't always know what good effects they might have. Not that the Gardeners ever did any dancing, as such.

So I decided to perform a Meditation, which would be one way of dealing with the fact that there was nothing to do inside the Sticky Zone. If nothing's the problem, work with nothing, Philo the Fog would say. Turn off your mind chatter. Open up your inner eye, your inner ear. See what you can see. Hear what you can hear. Back at the Gardeners, what I'd see would be the pigtails of the girl in front of me and what I'd hear would be the snoring of Philo, because when he was leading Meditation he always went to sleep.

I wasn't much more successful now. I could hear the thump, thump of the bass line coming from the Snakepit and the humming of the mini-fridge, I could see the lights of the street making blurry patterns through the glass bricks of the window, but none of this was spiritually enlightening. So I stopped doing the Meditation and turned on the news.

There was another minor epidemic, they were saying, but nothing to get alarmed about. Viruses and bacteria were always mutating, but I knew the Corporations could always invent treatments for them, and anyway whatever this bug was I didn't have it myself because I'd been in isolation with a double virus barrier protecting me. I was in the safest place I could be.

I switched back to the Snakepit. A fight had broken out. It must have been the Painballers – the three who'd come in first and the other one.

As I watched, the CorpSeCorps minders moved in. They got one of the Painballers down on the floor, used their tasers on him. The bouncers were fighting now too – one of them staggered backwards, clutching his eye; then another one hit the bar. It didn't usually take this long to get things under control. Savona and Crimson Petal were still up on the trapezes trying to carry on, but the pole girls were scurrying off the stage. Then they ran back onto it again: the exits behind must be blocked. Oh no, I thought. Then a bottle flew into the camera and smashed it.

I went to another camera, but my hands were shaking and I'd forgotten the key-in, and by the time I'd turned it on and got it focused the Snakepit was a lot emptier. The lights were still on and the music was playing, but the room was a shambles. The customers must have all run out. Savona was lying on the bar: I could tell it was her by the sparkly costume, even though it was half torn off. Her head was bent at a strange angle and there was blood all over her face. Crimson Petal was hanging from the trapeze; one of the ropes was around her neck, and between her legs was the glint of a bottle – someone must have shoved it up her. Her frills and ruffles were ripped to shreds. She looked like a limp bouquet.

Where was Mordis?

A dark flailing bundle tumbled across the screen: a shadow dance, a kinky ballet. There was the *bam!* of a door slammed back, and then something that sounded like hooting. Then sirens, in the distance. Feet running.

Then there was shouting in the hallway outside the Sticky Zone and the videoscreen from outside my door lit up, and on it was Mordis, close up, staring in at me with one eye. The other one was closed. His face looked chewed.

"Your name," he whispered.

Then an arm grabbed him around the throat, pulled his head back. One of the Painballers. I could see his hand, holding a slice of bottle: red and blue veins. "Open the fucking door, asshole," he said. "Bitch in heat! Time to share!"

Mordis was howling. What they wanted from him was the door code. "The numbers, the numbers," they were saying.

I saw Mordis for one more instant. There was a gurgling, and he was gone. In his place was the Painballer – a faceful of scars.

"Open up and we'll let your buddy live," he said. "We won't hurt you." But he was lying because Mordis was already dead.

Then there was more shouting, and then the CorpSeMen must have tasered him, because he howled in his turn and vanished from the screen, and there was a thudding sound like someone kicking a sack.

I went to the Snakepit camera: more CorpSeMen, in riot gear, a swarm of them. They were pushing and dragging the Painballers out the door – one dead one, three still alive. It would be back to Painball for them – they should never have been let out, not ever.

Then I realized what would happen. The Sticky Zone was a fortress. No one could get in without the door code, and nobody but Mordis knew that code. That's what he always said. And hadn't told it: he'd saved my life.

But now I was locked inside, with no one to let me out. *Oh please*, I thought. *I don't want to be dead.*

50

I told myself not to panic. SeksMart would send a cleaning crew, and they'd realize I was in there, and they'd get someone to work on the lock. They wouldn't leave me in there to starve and dry up like a mummy: when they reopened Scales they'd need me. It wouldn't be at all the same without Mordis – already I missed him – but at least I would have a function. I wasn't only a disposable, I was talent. That's what Mordis always said.

So it was just a matter of waiting it out.

I took a shower – I felt dirty, as if those Painballers really had got in, or as if I had the blood of Mordis all over me.

Then I did another Meditation, a real one. *Put Light around Mordis*, I prayed. *Let him go into the Universe. May his Spirit go in peace.* I pictured him flying up out of his demolished body in the form of a small, brown beady-eyed bird.

The next day, two bad things happened. First, I turned on the news. The minor epidemic they'd been talking about earlier wasn't behaving in the usual way – a local outbreak, one they could contain. Now it was an emergency. They showed a map of the world, with the hotspots lighting up in red – Brazil, Taiwan, Saudi Arabia, Bombay, Paris, Berlin – it was like watching the planet being spraygunned. It was an eruptive plague, they said, and the thing was spreading fast – no, not even spreading, breaking out at the same time in cities far apart, which wasn't the normal pattern. Ordinarily the Corps would have called for lies and cover-ups, and we'd hear something like the real story only in rumours, so the fact that all this was right out there on the news showed how serious it was – the Corps couldn't keep the lid on.

The news jockeys were trying to keep calm. The experts didn't know what the superbug was, but it was a pandemic for sure, and a lot of people were dying fast – just sort of melting. As soon as they said, "No need for panic," in that eerie calm tone with those glued-on smiles, I could tell it was really serious.

The second bad thing was that some guys in biosuits came into the Snakepit and stuffed the dead people into body bags and took them out. But they didn't check out the second floor, although I screamed and screamed. I guess they couldn't hear me because the Sticky Zone walls were thick and the Snakepit music was still going and it must have drowned me out. That was lucky for me, because if I'd left the Sticky Zone right then I'd have caught what everyone else was catching. So it wasn't really a bad thing, but it felt like it at the time.

The next day the news was even worse. The plague was spreading, and there was rioting and looting and killing going on, and the CorpSeCorps had just more or less vanished: they must've been dying too.

And a few days after that, there wasn't any more news.

Now I was really scared. But I told myself that although I couldn't get out, nobody else could get in, and I'd be okay as long as the solar didn't break down. It would keep the water flowing and the minifridge running, and the freezer, and the air filters. Air filtering was a plus, because it would soon be smelling very bad out there. And I would take one day at a time and see what came of it.

I knew I'd have to be practical, or I'd lose hope and slide into a Fallow state and maybe never come out of it. So I opened the minifridge and the freezer and counted all the stuff inside – the Joltbars and energy drinks and snacks, and the frozen ChickieNobs and the faux fish. If I ate only a third of every meal instead of half, and saved the rest instead of tossing it down the chute, I'd have enough for at least six weeks.

I'd been trying to call Amanda, but she hadn't answered. All I could do was leave text messages: CUM 2 SCLS. My hope was that she'd get the texts and realize something was wrong, and then she'd come to Scales and figure out how to unlock the door. I'd kept my cellphone turned on all the time in case she called, but now when I tried to phone or even text I got NO SERVICE. Once I did get a short message – IM OK – but the channels must have been jammed with frantic people trying to reach their families, because I didn't get anything more.

Then I guess the calling must have thinned out as people died, and I was able to get through. No picture, just her voice. "Where are you?" I said, and she said, "Nicked a solarcar. Ohio."

"Don't go into the cities," I said. "Don't let anyone touch you." I wanted to tell her what I'd been learning from the news, but she'd faded out. After that I couldn't even get a signal. The relay towers must have gone down.

You create your own reality, the horoscopes always said, and the Gardeners said that too. So I tried to create the reality of Amanda. Now she was in her khaki desert-girl outfit. Now she'd stopped to have a drink of water. Now she was digging up a root and eating it. Now she was walking again. She was coming towards me, hour by hour. She wouldn't get the sickness, and no one would kill her, because she was so smart and strong. She was smiling. Now she was singing. But I knew I was just making it up.

51

I hadn't seen Amanda except on the phone for such a long time, not since I'd started working at Scales. Before that, there had been a period when I hadn't even known where she was. I'd lost touch when Lucerne had thrown out my purple phone, back when I'd still been living inside the HelthWyzer Compound. At that time I thought I'd never see Amanda again – that she was gone out of my life forever.

That was what I still believed as I sat on the bullet train on my way to the Martha Graham Academy. I was feeling very alone and sorry for myself: I hadn't lost only Amanda, I'd lost everything in my life that had any meaning. The Adams and the Eves, or some of them, such as Toby and Zeb. Amanda. But most of all, Jimmy. I was over the worst of the hurt he'd caused me, but there was a dull ache. He'd been so sweet to me, then he'd shut me out as if I wasn't really there. That was a cold and miserable feeling. I was so depressed that I'd even given up the idea that I might get together with Jimmy again, at Martha Graham: it seemed like a far-fetched daydream.

By the time I was on that bullet train it had been a long time since I'd been in love with Jimmy. No: it had been a long time since Jimmy had been in love with me – when I was being honest and not only angry and sad, I knew that I was still in love with Jimmy. I'd slept with other boys, but I'd just been going through the motions. I was going to Martha Graham partly to get away from Lucerne, but also I had to do something so I might as well get an education. That's how they talked about it, as if an education was a thing that you got, like a dress. I didn't care what happened to me one way or the other, I just felt grey.

That was not at all the Gardener way of thinking. The Gardeners said the only real education was the education of the Spirit. But I'd forgotten what that meant.

Martha Graham was an artistic school named after a famous ancient dancer, so dance courses were featured at it. Since I had to take something I took Dance Calisthenics and Dramatic Expression – you didn't need any background or math for those. I figured I could get a job in one of the Corps, leading the in-corp noon-hour exercise programs that the better ones had. Tone to Music, Yoga for Middle Management – one of those.

The Martha Graham campus was like the Buenavista Condos – it had been classy once, but now it was falling apart, and had mould issues, and the ceilings leaked. I couldn't eat the stuff in the cafeteria because who knew what was in it – I still had a lot of trouble with animal protein, especially if it might be organs and noses. But I felt more at home there than I had in the HelthWyzer Compound, because at least Martha Graham wasn't so shiny and fake-looking and it didn't smell of chemical cleaning products. Or any cleaning products at all.

Every freshperson at Martha Graham had to share a suite. The roommate I was given was called Buddy the Third; I didn't see much of him. He was in Football, but the Martha Graham team always got pulverized and Buddy the Third was drunk or stoned a lot as a result. I'd lock the door on my side of our shared bathroom because the guys on the football team were known for date rape and I didn't think Buddy would even bother with the date part of it, but I could hear him in there throwing up in the mornings.

There was a Happicuppa franchise on campus, and I'd go there for breakfast because they had vegan muffins, I wouldn't have to listen to

Buddy puking, and I could use their washroom, which stank less than mine. One day I was walking up to the Happicuppa, and there was Bernice. I recognized her right away. I was really startled to see her. It was shocking – like a jolt of electricity. All the guilt I'd once felt about her but had more or less forgotten came flooding back.

She was wearing a green T-shirt with a big G on it and holding a sign that said, A HAPPICUPPA IS A CRAPPICUPPA. There were two other kids with the same T-shirt, but different signs: BREW OF EVIL, DON'T DRINK DEATH. I could see from the outfits and facial expressions that they were extreme fanatic ultra-greens, and they were picketing the place. This was the year when there were all the Happicuppa riots – I'd seen them onscreen.

Bernice wasn't any prettier than she used to be. If anything, she was chunkier, and her scowling was fiercer. She didn't spot me, so I had a choice: I could have gone right past her and into the Happicuppa, pretending I hadn't seen her, or I could have turned around and slid away. But I found myself going right back into Gardener mode, remembering all those teachings about taking responsibility and if you killed a thing you had to eat it. And I had killed Burt, in a way. Or I felt I had.

So I didn't dodge it. Instead I went right up to her and said, "Bernice! It's me – Ren!"

She jumped as if I'd kicked her. Then she focused on me. "So I see," she said in a sour voice.

"Let me buy you a coffee," I said. I must've been really nervous to say that because why would Bernice want a coffee from a place she was picketing?

She must have thought I was making fun of her because she said, "Piss off."

"Sorry," I said. "I didn't mean it that way. How about a water, then? We could drink it over there, by the statue." The statue of Martha Graham was a sort of mascot: it showed her being Judith, holding up the head of her enemy Holofernes, and the students had painted the head's neck stump red and stuck steel wool under Martha's armpits. There was a flat base right underneath the Holofernes head where you could sit.

She gave me another scowl. "You are so backslidden," she said. "Bottled water is evil. Don't you know anything?"

I could have called her a bitch and just walked away from everything. But this was my one chance to put things right, at least with myself. "Bernice," I said, "I want to make you an apology. So just tell me what you can drink, and I'll get some of it, and we'll go someplace and drink it."

She was still grumpy – no one could hold a grudge like her – but after I'd said we needed to put Light around it, which must've triggered off the better Gardener part of her, she said there was this organic mix in a recyclable carton made of pressed kudzu leaves, you could get it at the campus supermarkette, and she still had some picketing to do, but by the time I came back with the stuff she could take a break.

We sat underneath the head of Holofernes with the two boxes of liquid mulch I'd bought, and the taste brought back my early days at the Gardeners – how unhappy I'd been at first, and how Bernice had stuck up for me then. "Didn't you go to the West Coast?" I asked her. "After all that . . ."

"Yeah," she said. "Well, I'm back here now." She said that Veena had backslidden and joined an entirely different religion called the Known Fruits, who claimed it was a mark of God's favour to be rich because *By their fruits ye shall know them*, and *fruits* meant bank accounts. Veena had gone into a HelthWyzer vitamin-supplements franchise, and had quickly expanded to five outlets, and was doing very well. Bernice said the West Coast was perfect for that because although they all did stuff like yoga and said it was Spiritual, they were really just twisted, fish-crunching, materialistic body-worshippers out there, with facelifts and bimplants and genework and totally warped values.

Veena had wanted Bernice to take Business at college, but Bernice had stayed a Gardener by faith, so they'd fought about it; and Martha Graham was a compromise because it had courses in How to Profit from Holistic Healing. Which was what Bernice was taking.

I couldn't picture Bernice healing anything, because I couldn't picture her wanting to heal anything. Grinding dirt into your cut was more her style. But I said that was really interesting.

I told her what I was taking, but I saw she didn't care. So I told her about my roommate, Buddy the Third, and she said the entire Martha Graham Academy was filled with people like that – Exfernals frittering away their time on Earth without one serious thought in their heads except drinking and getting laid. She'd had a roommate like that at first, plus he'd been an animal-murderer because he'd worn leather sandals. Though they'd been fleather. But they'd looked like leather. So she'd burnt them. And thank God she didn't have to share a bathroom with him any more, because she could hear him doing sexual things with girls practically every night, like some degenerate bonobo/rabbit splice.

"Jimmy!" she said. "What a meat-breath!"

When I heard the name Jimmy I thought, It can't be the same one, but then I thought, Oh yes it can. While this was running through my head, Bernice said why didn't I move into the room adjoining hers since now that Jimmy had moved out it was empty.

I'd wanted to make it up with her but not that much. So I launched into what I needed to say. "I'm very sorry about Burt," I said. "Your dad. About him dying like that. I feel so responsible."

She looked at me as if I was crazy. "What're you talking about?" she said.

"That time I told you he was having sex with Nuala, and you told Veena, and she blew up and called the CorpSeCorps? Well, I don't think he was having sex with Nuala. Me and Amanda – we kind of made it up because we were being mean. I feel terrible about it, and I'm really sorry. I don't think he ever did anything worse than girls' armpits."

"At least Nuala was a grown-up," said Bernice. "But he didn't stop at the armpits. With the girls. He was a degenerate, just like my mother said. He used to tell me I was his favourite little girl, but not even that was true. So I told Veena. That's why she ratted him out. So you can stop feeling so self-important." I got the old glare, though this time with red watery eyes. "You're just lucky it was never you."

"Oh," I said. "Bernice, I'm really sorry."

"I don't want to talk about this any more," said Bernice. "I prefer to spend my time in more productive ways." She said would I come and stencil Happicuppa protest signs with her, and I said I'd already skipped one class that day, but maybe some other time. She gave me that slitty-eyed look that said she could tell I was wriggling out of something. Then I asked her what her old roommate Jimmy had actually looked like, and she said why was that any of my business?

She was right back into her bossy mode, and I knew that if I hung around with her much longer I'd be nine years old again, and she'd have the same hold on me, only more so because however awful things might be for me in my life they'd always be worse in hers, and she'd have a victim hammerlock on me. I said I really had to run, and she said, "Yeah, right," and then she said I hadn't changed at all, I was still just as much of a simpy lightweight as I'd ever been.

Years later – when I was already working at Scales and Tails – I saw onscreen that Bernice had been spraygunned in a raid on a Gardeners safe house. That was after the Gardeners had been outlawed. Though being outlawed wouldn't have stopped Bernice; she was a person with the courage of her convictions. I had to admire her for that – for the convictions, and also for the courage – because I never really felt I had either one.

There was a close-up of her dead face, looking more gentle and peaceful than I'd ever seen her look in life. Maybe that was the real Bernice, I thought – kind and innocent. Maybe she was truly like that inside, and all the fighting we used to do and all her sharp and unpleasant edges – that was her way of struggling to get out of the hard skin she'd grown all over herself like a beetle shell. But no matter how she hit out and raged, she'd been stuck in there. That thought made me feel so sorry for her that I cried.

52

Before that conversation with Bernice when she'd talked about her former roommate, I'd been half expecting to see Jimmy – in a classroom, at the Happicuppa, or just walking somewhere. But now I felt he must be very close by. He was right around the corner, or on the other side of a window; or I'd wake up one morning and there he would be, right beside me, holding my hand and looking at me the way he used to do when we first got together. It was like being haunted.

Maybe I've imprinted on Jimmy, I thought. Like a baby duck hatching out of an egg and the first thing it sees is a weasel, so that's what it follows around for the rest of its life. Which is likely to be short. Why did it have to be Jimmy who was the very first person I'd fallen in love with? Why couldn't it have been someone with a better character? Or at least a less fickle person. A more serious person, not so given to playing the fool.

The worst thing about it was that I couldn't get interested in anyone else. There was a hole in my heart that only Jimmy could fill. I know that's a country-and-western thing to say – I'd heard enough of that kind of worldly music on my Sea/H/Ear Candy by then – but it's the only way I can explain it. And it isn't that I wasn't aware of Jimmy's faults, because I was.

I did see Jimmy eventually, of course. The campus wasn't huge, so it was bound to happen sooner or later. I saw him in the distance, and he saw me, but he didn't come rushing over. He stayed in the distance. He didn't even wave, he looked away as if he hadn't seen me. So if I'd been waiting for the answer to the question I was always asking myself – Does Jimmy still love me? – I had it now.

Then I met a girl in Dance Calisthenics – Shayluba somebody – who'd been with Jimmy for a while. She said it was great at first, but he started saying how he was really bad for her, he was incapable of commitment because of the girlfriend he'd had in high school. They were too young, it ended badly, and he'd been an emotional dumpster ever since, but maybe he was destructive by nature since he messed up every girl he touched.

"Was her name Wakulla Price?" I asked.

"No, actually," said Shayluba. "It was you. He pointed you out."

Jimmy, what a fraud and bullshitting liar you are, I thought. But then I thought, What if it's true? What if I'd crapped up Jimmy's life just as much as he'd crapped up mine?

I tried to forget all about him. But somehow I couldn't. Beating myself up over Jimmy had become a bad habit with me, like biting your nails. Every once in a while I'd see him drifting past in the distance, which was like having just one cigarette when you're trying to quit – it starts you off again. Not that I was ever a smoker.

I'd been at Martha Graham for almost two years when I got some really terrible news. Lucerne called me and said that my biofather, Frank, had been kidnapped by a rival Corp somewhere to the east of Europe. The Corps over there were always trying to poach on our Corps – their undercover thugs were even more cut-throat than ours, and they had an advantage because they were better at languages and could pretend to be immigrants. We couldn't do that to them, because why would we immigrate there?

They'd bagged Frank right inside the Compound – in the men's room of his lab building, said Lucerne – and shipped him out in a Zizzy Froots delivery van; then they'd carted him across the Atlantic Ocean in an airship wrapped up in gauze bandages and disguised as a patient recovering from a facelift. Worse, they'd sent back a DVD of him in a drugged-looking state, confessing that HelthWyzer had been sticking a slow-acting but incurable gene-spliced disease germ inside their supplements so they could make a lot of money on the treatments. It was blackmail pure and simple, said Lucerne – they'd trade Frank for a couple of the formulas they wanted, most notably the ones for the slow-acting diseases; and, in addition, they wouldn't make the incriminating DVD public. But otherwise, they'd said, Frank's head would have to kiss his body goodbye.

HelthWyzer had done a cost-benefit analysis, said Lucerne, and they'd decided the disease germs and formulas were worth more to them than Frank was. As for the adverse publicity, they could squelch it at source, since the media Corps controlled what was news and what wasn't. And the Internet was such a jumble of false and true factoids that no one believed what was on it any more, or else they believed all of it, which amounted to the same thing. So HelthWyzer wasn't going to pay up. They said they regretted Lucerne's loss, but it wasn't their policy to give in to blackmail demands, as that would encourage more kidnappings, which were numerous enough as it was.

Therefore Lucerne had lost her top-wife position at HelthWyzer, and the house along with it, and under the circumstances, which were unfortunate, she'd decided to move to the CryoJeenyus Compound and take up housekeeping with a very nice man she'd met through the golf club, whose name was Todd. And she certainly hoped I wouldn't go overboard with grief about Frank the way I went overboard on all my other emotions.

CryoJeenyus. What a scam that place was. You paid to get your head frozen when you died in case someone in the future invented a way to regrow a body onto your neck, though the kids at HelthWyzer used to joke that they didn't freeze anything but head shells because they'd already scooped out the neurons and transplanted them into pigs. They made a lot of gruesome jokes like that at HelthWyzer High, though you never knew whether they were actually jokes.

The upshot was – Lucerne continued – that money was tight. Todd wasn't a senior vice-president, he was only an accounts manager and he had three young children of his own to support who would have to take priority over me, and she could hardly ask Todd to pay for me in addition to everything else he was paying for. So I would have to stop coasting along at college, and leave Martha Graham, and take responsibility for myself.

I was out of the nest in one swift kick. Not that I was ever in much of a nest: I'd always been on the edge of the ledge with Lucerne.

This is Irony, I thought. I'd learned about Irony in Dance Theatrics. There was Lucerne, who'd told a slanderous whopper about being kidnapped, and now poor Frank, my biofather, really had been kidnapped, and probably murdered as well. It was clear that Lucerne didn't feel much of anything about that. As for me, I didn't know what to feel.

Before the spring term exams the various Corps set up interview booths in the main hallway. Not the serious Corps, the science ones – they wouldn't bother recruiting at Martha Graham, they wanted numbers people – but the more frivolous ones. I wasn't eligible for these interviews because I wasn't graduating that year, but I decided to go anyway and take a chance. I wouldn't get any of the jobs on offer, but maybe they'd take me on as a floor scrubber. I'd done some floor scrubbing at the Gardeners, though naturally I couldn't say that or I'd get stamped as a fanatical greenie weirdo.

My Dance Calisthenics teacher said I should talk to Scales and Tails. I was a good enough dancer, and Scales was part of SeksMart now, which was a legitimate Corp with health benefits and a dental plan, so it wasn't like being a prostitute. A lot of girls went into it, and some of them met nice men that way and did very well in life afterwards. So I thought I might try for it. I wasn't likely to get anything better without a degree. Even a Martha Graham degree was a lot better than none. And I didn't want to end up as a meat barista at some place like SecretBurgers.

That day I managed to line up five interviews. I had butterflies in my stomach, but I sucked it up and smiled, and talked my way in, even though I wasn't on the graduating list. I could have done six – CryoJeenyus was looking for a Comfort Girl to sooth the relatives who were getting the heads of their loved ones and sometimes their dead pets frozen – but I couldn't work there because of Lucerne. I didn't ever want to see her again, not only because of what she'd done to me but also because of how she'd done it. Like firing the maid.

I saw the hiring teams from Happicuppa, and ChickieNobs, and Zizzy Froots, and Scales and Tails, and finally AnooYoo. The first three didn't want me, but I did get an offer from Scales and Tails. Each Corp had a team doing the interviewing, and Mordis was part of the Scales team – there were some SeksMart higher-ups there too, but he was the man on the ground so it was really his call. I did a routine from Dance Calisthenics, and Mordis said I was exactly what he was looking for, such talent, and if I came to Scales he'd make sure I wouldn't regret it. "You can be whoever you want," he said. "Act it out!" So I almost signed up.

But the AnooYoo booth was right next to Scales, and on that team there was a woman who reminded me a lot of Toby at the Gardeners, though she was darker and had different hair, her eyes were green, and her voice was huskier. She took me a little aside and asked me if I was in trouble, and I found myself explaining that for family reasons I had to leave college. I'd do any kind of a job, I said; I was willing to learn. When she asked me what family reasons I blurted out about my father being kidnapped and my mother not having any money. I could hear my voice going trembly: it wasn't all acting.

Then she asked me what my mother's name was. I told her, and she nodded: she'd take me on at the AnooYoo Spa as an apprentice, and I could live right on the premises, and they'd train me. I'd be working with women, not with men who'd be drunk and violent as they often were at Scales, even if it did have a dental plan; and I wouldn't have to wear a Biofilm Bodysuit and let strange men touch me. It would be a healing atmosphere, and I'd be helping people.

This woman really did look like Toby, and strangely enough, the name on her tag was Tobiatha. That was like a sign to me – that I'd be really safe there, and welcomed, and also wanted. So I said yes.

Mordis gave me his card anyway, and said that if I changed my mind he'd take me on at Scales, any time, no questions asked.

53

The AnooYoo Spa was located in the middle of the Heritage Park. I'd heard a lot about it because Adam One had been so against it – he'd said that many Creatures and also Trees had been destroyed to build a pavilion to vanity. Sometimes on Pollination Day he'd preach a whole sermon about it. But in spite of that, I felt happy there. They had roses that glowed in the dark, and big pink butterflies in the daytime and beautiful kudzu moths at night, and a swimming pool, although staff couldn't use it, and fountains, and their own organic vegetable garden. The air was better there than it was in the middle of the city so you didn't have to wear nose cones so much. It was like a comforting dream. They put me to work in the laundry room folding the sheets and towels, and I liked that because it was peaceful: everything was pink.

On my third day there, Tobiatha came across me as I was carrying a stack of clean towels to one of the rooms and said she'd like to talk to me. I thought maybe I'd done something wrong. We walked out onto the lawn, and she told me to keep my voice down. Then she said that she could tell I'd partly recognized her, and she had certainly recognized me. She'd hired me because I'd been a Gardener, and now that they'd been outlawed and the Garden destroyed we had a duty to look after one another. She could see I was in trouble, beyond not having any money. What was the matter?

I started to cry because I hadn't known about the Garden. It was a shock: I must have had it in my mind that I could go back there if things got really bad. She took me to sit down beside one of the fountains – so the rushing water would blot out our voices in case there were any directional microphones, she said – and I told her about HelthWyzer, and how I'd been in touch with the Gardeners through Amanda before I'd lost my cell, and I didn't know anything about the Garden after that. I didn't say anything about being in love with Jimmy and how he'd broken my heart, but I did tell about Martha Graham, and about Lucerne cutting me off in that abrupt way after my father had been kidnapped.

Then I said I had no direction in life, and I felt numb inside, like an orphan. She said all of that must be very disturbing; she'd had a difficult time too when she'd been my age, and something similar had happened to her, about her father.

This new version of Toby wasn't nearly as hardass as she'd been when she was Eve Six. She was mellower. Or maybe I was older.

She looked around and lowered her voice. Then she told me she'd had to leave the Edencliff Rooftop Garden in a hurry and get some alterations done on herself because she'd been in danger there, so I'd have to be very careful not to tell anyone who she was. She'd taken a risk with me, and she hoped she could trust me, and I said she could. Then she warned me that Lucerne came to the Spa sometimes, and I should be aware of that and try to keep out of her sightline.

Finally she said that if anything should happen – some crisis – and she wasn't around, I should know that she'd put together a dried-foods Gardener-style Ararat, right in the AnooYoo Spa supply room; she told me the door code in case I might ever need to get in. Though she hoped it would never be necessary.

I thanked her very much, and then I asked if she knew where Amanda was. I'd really like to see her again, I said. She was about my only real friend. Toby said she might be able to find out.

We didn't talk often after that – Toby said it would look suspicious, even though she didn't know who might be watching – but we'd exchange a few words and nods. I felt she was guarding me – protecting me with some space-alien type of force field. Though of course I was only making that up.

![section break]

One day, after I'd been there for nearly a year, Toby said she'd located Amanda through mutual acquaintances on the Internet. What she told me was surprising, though not too surprising when I thought about it. Amanda had become a bioartist: she did art involving Creatures or parts of Creatures arranged outdoors on a giant scale. She was living near the western entrance of the Heritage Park, and if I wanted to see her, Toby could arrange a pass for me and get me driven there in one of the pink AnooYoo minivans.

I threw my arms around Toby and hugged her, but she said I should watch that – a laundry-room girl hugging the manager. Then she said I shouldn't get too involved with Amanda: Amanda had a tendency to go too far, she didn't know the limits of her own strength. I wanted to ask her what she meant, but she was walking away.

On the day of the visit, Toby told me that Amanda had been alerted that I was coming; but the two of us should wait until I was inside the door before hugging or shrieking or other demonstrations. She gave me a basket of AnooYoo products to deliver, as an excuse in case anyone stopped the van and asked where I was going. The driver would wait for me: I would have only an hour, because it would look odd for an AnooYoo girl to be wandering around in the Exfernal too long.

I said maybe I should go in disguise, and she said no, because the guards would ask questions. So I had to put on my pink AnooYoo top-to-toe over my work smock and cotton pants and go off with my pink basket, like Little Pink Riding Hood.

I got delivered to Amanda's falling-apart condo by the AnooYoo minivan, as planned. I did remember what Toby had said. I waited until I was inside the door, where Amanda was waiting, and then we both said, "I can't believe it!" and held on to each other. But not for long; Amanda had never been much of a hugger.

She was taller than when I'd last seen her in the flesh. She'd got a tan – even through the sunblock and hats – from doing so much outdoors art, she said. We went into her kitchen, which had a lot of her designs pinned up on the walls, and some bones here and there; and we had a beer each. I've never liked drinking alcohol that much, but this was special.

We started talking about the Gardeners – Adam One, and Nuala, and Mugi the Muscle and Philo the Fog, and Katuro, and Rebecca. And Zeb. And Toby, though I didn't say she was now Tobiatha and managing the AnooYoo Spa. Amanda told me why Toby had to leave the Gardeners. It was because Blanco from the Sewage Lagoon was after her. Blanco had the street rep of snuffing anyone who'd annoyed him, especially women.

"Why her?" I said. Amanda said she'd heard it was some old sexual thing; which was puzzling, she said, because sexual things and Toby had never fitted together, which was most likely why we kids had called her the Dry Witch. And I said maybe Toby had been wetter than we'd thought, and Amanda laughed, and said obviously I still believed in miracles. But now I knew why Toby was hiding out with a different identity.

"Remember how we used to say, *Knock knock, who's there*? You and me and Bernice?" I said. The beer was creeping up on me.

"Gang," said Amanda. "Gang who?"

"Gang grene," I said, and we both snorted with laughter, and some of the beer went up my nose. Then I told her about running into Bernice, and how she'd been as crabby as ever. We laughed about that too. But we didn't mention dead Burt.

I said, "What about the time you arranged that superweed treat for me with Shackie and Croze, and we all went into the holospinner booth, and I threw up?" So we laughed some more.

She told me she had two roommates, who were artists as well; and also, for the first time in her life, she had a live-in boyfriend. I asked if she was in love with him, and she said, "I'll try anything once."

I asked what he was like, and she said really sweet, though moody at times because he was still getting over some teen-lust girlfriend.

And I said what was his name, and she said, "Jimmy – maybe you knew him at HelthWyzer High, he must have been there about the same time you were."

I got a very cold feeling. She said, "That's him on the fridge, two pictures down, on the right." It was Jimmy all right, with his arm around Amanda, grinning like an electrocuted frog. I felt as if she'd stuck a nail right into my heart. But there was no point in spoiling things for Amanda by telling her that. She hadn't done it on purpose.

I said, "He looks really cute, and now I have to go because it's time for the driver." She asked if there was anything wrong, and I said no. She gave me her cellphone number and said next time I came to visit she'd make sure Jimmy was there, and we'd all have spaghetti.

It would be nice to believe that love should be dished out in a fair way so that everyone got some. But that wasn't how it was going to be for me.

I went back to the AnooYoo Spa feeling totally dumped out and hollow. Then, just after I got back, when I was carting the towels around to the rooms, I almost ran right into Lucerne. It was her time to have her face lifted again: Toby had warned me about it each time she came so I could lower my profile and evade her, but because of Amanda and Jimmy it had gone right out of my head.

I smiled at her in the neutral way we'd been trained. I think she recognized me, but she blew me off like I was a piece of lint. Although I hadn't ever wanted to see her or talk to her, it was a very bad feeling to know that she didn't want to see me or talk to me either. It was like being erased off the slate of the universe – to have your own mother act as if you'd never been born.

At that moment I understood that I couldn't stay at AnooYoo. I needed to be on my own, apart from Amanda, apart from Jimmy, apart from Lucerne, even apart from Toby. I wanted to be someone else entirely, I didn't want to owe anyone anything, or be owed anything either. I wanted no strings, no past, and no questions asked. I was tired of asking questions.

I found the card Mordis had given me, and left a note for Toby thanking her for everything, and saying that for personal reasons I couldn't work at the Spa any longer. I still had the day pass I'd used for Amanda, so I left right then. Everything was ruined and destroyed, and there was no safe place for me; and if I had to be in an unsafe place it might as well be an unsafe place where I was appreciated.

When I got to Scales, I had to talk my way past the bouncers because they didn't believe I was really looking for a job there. But finally they called Mordis, and he said oh yes, he remembered me – I was the little dancer. Brenda, wasn't it? I said yes, but he could call me Ren – I already felt that comfortable with him. He asked if I was really serious about the job, and I said I was; and he said there was a minimum undertaking because they didn't want to waste the training, so would I be willing to sign a contract?

I said maybe I was too sad for the job: didn't they want a more upbeat personality in their girls? But Mordis smiled with his shiny black-ant eyes and said, as if he was patting me: "Ren. Ren. Everyone's too sad for everything."

54

So I did go to work at Scales after all. In some ways it was a relief. I liked having Mordis for a boss because at least it was clear what pleased him. He made me feel safe, maybe because he was the closest thing to a father I was ever going to get: Zeb had vanished into thin air and my real father hadn't found me very interesting, and in addition he was dead.

But Mordis said I was really something special – I was the answer to every dream, wet ones included. It was so encouraging to be doing something I was good at. I didn't like the other parts of the job that much, but I did like the trapeze dancing, because nobody could touch you then. You were up in the air, like a butterfly. I used to picture Jimmy looking at me, and thinking that it was really me he'd loved all along, not Wakulla Price or LyndaLee or any of the others, or even Amanda, and that I was dancing just for him.

I do know how useless this was.

After going to Scales, I was only in touch with Amanda by phone. She was away a lot, doing her art projects; also I didn't want to see her in person. I'd feel uncomfortable because of Jimmy, and she'd pick up on that feeling and ask about it, and I'd either lie or tell her; and if I told her she'd be angry, or maybe just curious; or she'd think I was being stupid. There was a hard side to Amanda.

Jealousy is a very destructive emotion, Adam One used to say. It's part of the stubborn Australopithecine heritage we're stuck with. It eats away at you and deadens your Spiritual life, but also it leads you to hatred, and causes you to harm others. But Amanda was the last person I'd ever want to harm.

I tried to visualize my jealousy as a yellowy-brown cloud boiling around inside me, then going out through my nose like smoke and turning into a stone and falling down into the ground. That did work a little. But in my visualization a plant covered with poison berries would grow out of the stone, whether I wanted it to or not.

Then Amanda broke up with Jimmy. She let me know about it in a roundabout way. She'd already told me about her outdoor art landscape installation series called The Living Word – how she was spelling words out in giant letters, using bioforms to make the words appear and then disappear, just like the words she used to do with ants and syrup when we were kids. Now she said, "I'm up to the four-letter words." And I said, "You mean the dirty ones, like *shit*?" And she laughed and said, "Worse ones than that." And I said, "You mean the c-word and the f-word?" and she said, "No. Like *love*."

And I said, "Oh. So Jimmy didn't work out." And she said, "Jimmy can't be serious." So I knew he must've cheated on her, or something like that.

"I'm sorry," I said. "Are you really pissed off at him?" I tried to keep the happiness out of my own voice. *Now I can forgive her*, I thought. But really there was nothing to forgive her for because she hadn't done anything hurtful to me on purpose.

"Pissed off?" she said. "You can't be pissed off with Jimmy." I wondered what she meant by that, because I was certainly pissed off with Jimmy. Though I still loved him.

Maybe that's what love is, I thought: it's being pissed off.

After a while, Glenn started coming to Scales – not every night, but often enough to get discounts. I hadn't seen him since HelthWyzer – he'd been with the brainiacs, doing science at the Watson-Crick Institute – but now he was a top guy at the Rejoov Corp. He wasn't shy about bragging, though with Glenn it was more like stating a fact, the way you'd say, "It's going to rain." What I picked up from listening in on his conversations with the Mr. Bigs and his funders was that he was in charge of a really important initiative called the Paradice Project. They'd built a special dome for it, with its own air supply and quadruple security. He'd assembled a team of the best brains available, and they were working night and day.

Glenn was vague about what they were working on. *Immortality* was a word he used – Rejoov had been interested in it for decades, something about changing your cells so they'd never die; people would pay a lot for immortality, he said. Every couple of months he'd claim they'd made a breakthrough, and the more breakthroughs he made, the more money he could raise for the Paradice Project.

Sometimes he'd say he was working on solutions to the biggest problem of all, which was human beings – their cruelty and suffering, their wars and poverty, their fear of death. "What would you pay for the design of a perfect human being?" he'd say. Then he'd hint that the Paradice Project was designing one, and they'd dump more money on him.

For the finales of these meetings he'd rent the feather-ceiling room and order up the drinks and the drugs and the Scalies – not for himself, but for the guys he'd bring with him. Sometimes he'd even entertain the top CorpSeMen. They were sinister, those guys. I never had to do the Painballers, but I had to do the CorpSeMen, and they were my least favourite clients. It was like they had machine parts in behind their eyes.

Occasionally Glenn would rent two or three Scalies for the whole evening, not for sex but for some very strange things. Once he wanted us to purr like cats so he could measure our vocal cords. Another time he wanted us to sing like birds so he could record us. Starlite complained to Mordis that this wasn't what we were paid for, but Mordis only said, "So, he's a loony. You've seen those before. But he's a rich loony and he's harmless, so just humour him."

I was part of the threesome the night he gave us a sort of quiz. What would make us happy? he wanted to know. Was happiness more like excitement, or more like contentment? Was happiness inside or outside? With trees, or without? Did it have running water nearby? Did too much of it get boring? Starlite and Crimson Petal tried to figure out what he wanted to hear so they could tell the right lies. "No," I said. I knew what Glenn was like. "He's a geek. He wants us to say what we honestly feel." Which confused them a lot.

He never asked us about sadness, though. Maybe he thought he knew enough about that.

Then he started bringing a woman – an Asian Fusion body type with a foreign accent. He said she wanted to familiarize herself with Scales because ReJoov had picked us as one of their prime test venues, and she'd be explaining a new product to us – the BlyssPluss pill, which would solve every known problem connected with sex. We had been awarded the privilege of introducing it to our clients. This woman had a ReJoov executive title – Senior VP Satisfaction Enhancement – though her real job was Glenn's main plank.

I could tell she'd been one of us: a girl for rent, of one kind or another. It was obvious if you knew the signs. She was acting all the time, giving nothing away about herself. I'd watch them onscreen: I was curious because Glenn was such a cold fish, but he could have sex all right, just like a human being. This girl had more moves than an octopus, and her plankwork was astonishing. Glenn acted like she was the first, last, and only girl on the planet. Mordis used to watch them too, and he said Scales would pay this girl top dollar. But I told him he couldn't afford her: she was way out of his price range.

The two of them had pet names for each other. She'd call him Crake, he'd call her Oryx. The other girls found it strange – the two of them being lovey-dovey – because it was so out of character for Glenn. But I thought it was kind of nice.

"That Russian or something?" Crimson Petal asked me. "Oryx and Crake?"

"I guess," I said. They were extinct animal names – every Gardener had to memorize a ton of those – but if I said it the girls would wonder why I knew.

The first time Glenn came to Scales I recognized him right away, but of course he didn't recognize me, in my Biofilm Bodysuit and with green sequins all over my face, and I didn't let on. Mordis told us not to forge personal bonds with the customers, because if they wanted a relationship they could get one elsewhere. He said that Scales customers didn't care about your life history, they just wanted epidermis and fantasy. They wanted to be carried away to Never-Never Land, where they could have sinful experiences they'd never, never be able to have at home. Dragon ladies winding around them, snake women slithering over them. So we should save our private emotional crap for people who actually cared about us, like the other Scalies.

One night Glenn arranged an evening of extra-special treatment – for an extra-special guest, he said. He ordered up the feather room with the green bedspread, plus the most powerful Scales and Tails martinis – "kicktails," they called them – plus two Scalies, me and Crimson Petal. Mordis picked us because Glenn said this extra-special guest preferred the slender body type.

"Does he want the schoolgirl sailor suit thing?" I asked; sometimes that's what "slender body type" meant. "Do I need to bring my skipping rope?" If so I'd have to change, because right then I was in full glitter.

"This guy's already so shitfaced he doesn't know what he wants," Mordis said. "Just give him your all, baby bunny. We want to see the high-number tips. Make those multiple zeroes shoot right out of his ears."

When we got to the room, the guy was lying on the green satin bedspread as if he'd been thrown from a plane, but happy about it, because he had a whole-body grin.

It was Jimmy. Sweet, ruinous Jimmy. Jimmy, who'd trashed my life.

My heart flipped over. Oh shit, I thought. I'm not up to this. I'm going to lose it and start crying. I knew he wouldn't know it was me: I was covered in glitz, and he was flying so high he was almost blind. So I just slid into the usual act and started in on his buttons and Velcro. We Scalies used to call it "peeling the shrimp." "Oh, nice abs," I whispered. "Honey, just lie back."

Did I hate this or love it? Why did it have to be one or the other? As Vilya always said about her boobs, *Take two, they're cheap.*

Now he was trying to pull the scales off my face, so I had to keep taking his hands and putting them elsewhere. "Are you a fish?" he was saying. He didn't seem to know.

Oh Jimmy, I thought. What's left of you?

SAINT DIAN, MARTYR

SAINT DIAN, MARTYR

YEAR TWENTY-FOUR.

OF PERSECUTION.
SPOKEN BY ADAM ONE.

Dear Friends, dear Faithful Companions:

Our Edencliff Rooftop Garden blooms now only in our memories. On this Earthly plane it is now a desolation – a swamp or a desert, depending on rainfall. How changed is our situation from our former green and salad days! How shrunk, how dwindled are our numbers! We are driven from one refuge to another, we are hounded and pursued. Some former Friends have renounced our creeds, others have borne false witness against us. Yet others have tried extremism and violence, and have been murderously spraygunned in the course of raids carried out against them. We remember in this connection our dear former Child, Bernice. Let us put Light around her.

Some have been mutilated and tossed into vacant lots to sow panic among us. Yet others have disappeared, snatched from their places of refuge, to vanish into the prisons of the Exfernal Powers, denied trial, forbidden even to know the names of their accusers. Their minds may already have been destroyed by drugs and torture, their bodies melted into garboil. Because of unjust Laws, we cannot learn the whereabouts of these, our fellow Gardeners. We can only hope that they will die in unwavering Faith.

Today is Saint Dian's Day, consecrated to interspecies empathy. On this day we invoke Saint Jerome of Lions, and Saint Robert Burns of Mice, and Saint Christopher Smart of Cats; also Saint Farley Mowat of Wolves, and the Ikhwan al-Safa and their *Letter of the Animals*. But especially Saint Dian Fossey, who gave her life while defending the Gorillas from ruthless exploitation. She laboured for a Peaceable Kingdom, in which all

Life would be respected; yet malignant forces combined to destroy both her and her gentle Primate companions. Her murder was horrific; and equally horrific were the malicious rumours spread about her, both during her lifetime and after it. For the Exfernal Powers kill both in deed and in word.

Saint Dian embodies an ideal we hold dear: loving care for all other Creatures. She believed that these deserve the same tenderness we would show to beloved friends and kinfolk, and in this she is a revered model for us. She is buried among her Gorilla Friends, on the mountain she tried to protect.

Like many martyrs, Saint Dian did not live to see the fulfilment of her labours. At least she has been spared the knowledge that the Species for which she gave her life is no more. Like so many others, it has been wiped from the face of God's Planet.

What is it about our own Species that leaves us so vulnerable to the impulse to violence? Why are we so addicted to the shedding of blood? Whenever we are tempted to become puffed up, and to see ourselves as superior to all other Animals, we should reflect on our own brutal history.

Take comfort in the thought that this history will soon be swept away by the Waterless Flood. Nothing will remain of the Exfernal World but decaying wood and rusting metal implements; and over these the Kudzu and other vines will climb; and Birds and Animals will nest in them, as we are told in the Human Words of God: "They shall be left together unto the Fowls of the mountains, and to the Beasts of the Earth; and the Fowls shall summer upon them, and all the Beasts of the Earth shall winter upon them." For all works of Man will be as words written on water.

As we crouch together in this dim cellar, speaking softly behind darkened windows, worried lest we have been infiltrated, or that listening devices or cyborg insects are nearby, or the vindictive functionaries of the CorpSeCorps may even now be speeding towards us, we have more need than ever of our resolve. We pray that the Spirit of Saint Dian may inspire us, and help us to stand firm in the moment of trial. Fear not, says that Spirit, even if the worst shall come: for we shelter in the wings of a yet greater Spirit.

An hour before dawn, we must move out of this hiding place, singly and in twos or threes. Be silent then, my Friends; be invisible; merge with your own shadows. And with Grace we will prevail.

We cannot sing, for fear of being overheard, but:

Let us whisper.

TODAY WE PRAISE OUR SAINT DIAN

Today we praise our Saint Dian,
Whose blood for bounteous Life was spilled –
Although she interposed her Faith,
One Species more was killed.

For all around the misty hills
She tracked the wild Gorilla bands,
Until they learned to trust her Love,
And take her by the hand.

The timid giants, huge and strong,
She held in her courageous arms;
She guarded them with anxious care,
Lest they should come to harm.

They knew her as their Friend and kin,
Around her they would feast and play –
And yet cruel Murderers came by night,
And slew her where she lay.

Too many violent hands and hearts!
Dian, too sadly few like you –
For when a Species dies from Earth,
We die a little too.

Among the green and misty hills,
Where once the shy Gorillas gathered,
Your kindly Spirit wanders still,
In watchfulness, forever.

From *The Gods' Gardeners Oral Hymnbook*

55

REN

YEAR TWENTY-FIVE

You create your own world by your inner attitude, the Gardeners used to say. And I didn't want to create the world out there: the world of the dead and dying. So I sang some old Gardener hymns, especially the happy ones. Or I danced. Or I played the songs on my Sea/H/Ear Candy, though I couldn't help thinking that now there'd be no more new music.

Say the Names, Adam One would tell us. And we'd chant these lists of Creatures: Diplodocus, Pterosaurus, Octopus, and Brontosaurus; Trilobite, Nautilus, Ichthyosaurus, Platypus. Mastodon, Dodo, Great Auk, Komodo. I could see all the names, as clear as pages. Adam One said that saying the names was a way of keeping those animals alive. So I said them.

I said other names too. Adam One, Nuala, Zeb. Shackie, Croze, and Oates. And Glenn – I just couldn't picture anyone so smart being dead.

And Jimmy, despite what he'd done.

And Amanda.

I said those names over and over, in order to keep them alive.

Then I thought about what Mordis had whispered, at the end. *Your name*, he'd said. It must have been important.

I counted the food I had left. Four weeks' worth, three weeks, two. I marked off the time with my eyebrow pencil. If I ate less, I could make it last longer. But if Amanda didn't come soon, I'd be dead. I couldn't really imagine it.

Glenn used to say the reason you can't really imagine yourself being dead was that as soon as you say, "I'll be dead," you've said the word *I*, and so you're still alive inside the sentence. And that's how people got the idea of the immortality of the soul – it was a consequence of grammar. And so was God, because as soon as there's a past tense, there has to be a past before the past, and you keep going back in time until you get to *I don't know*, and that's what God is. It's what you don't know – the dark, the hidden, the underside of the visible, and all because we have grammar, and grammar would be impossible without the FoxP2 gene; so God is a brain mutation, and that gene is the same one birds need for singing. So music is built in, Glenn said: it's knitted into us. It would be very hard to amputate it because it's an essential part of us, like water.

I said, in that case is God knitted in as well? And he said maybe so, but it hadn't done us any good.

His explanation of God was a lot different from the Gardeners' explanation. He said "God is a Spirit" was meaningless because you couldn't measure a Spirit. Also he'd say *Use your meat computer* when he meant *Use your mind.* I found that idea repulsive: I hated the idea of my head being full of meat.

I kept thinking I could hear people walking around in the building, but when I scanned the rooms I couldn't see anyone moving. At least the solar was still working.

I counted the food again. Five days left, and that was stretching it.

56

I first spotted Amanda as a shadow on the videoscreen. She came into the Snakepit carefully, hugging the wall: the lights were still on, so she wasn't groping in the dark. The music was still blaring and thumping, and once she'd looked around to make sure the place was empty she went over behind the stage and switched it off.

"Ren?" I heard her say.

Then she went offscreen. After a pause the videocam mike in the hallway picked up her soft footsteps, and then I could see her. And she could see me. I was crying so much with relief I couldn't speak.

"Hi," she said. "There's a dead guy right outside the door. He's gross. I'll be back." Mordis was who she meant – he'd never been taken away. She told me later that she got him onto a shower curtain and dragged him down the hall and bundled him into an elevator, what was left of him. The rats had been having a party, she said, not just at Scales but anywhere even close to urban. She'd put on the gloves of someone's Biofilm Bodysuit before touching him – even though she was daring, Amanda didn't take stupid risks.

After a while she was back on my screen. "So," she said. "Here I am. Stop crying, Ren."

"I thought you'd never get here," I managed to say.

"That's what I thought too," she said. "Now. How does the door open?"

"I don't have the code," I said. I explained about Mordis – how he was the only one who'd known the Sticky Zone numbers.

"He never told you?"

"He said why would we need to know the codes? He changed them every day – he didn't want them leaking out because crazies might get in. He just wanted to protect us." I was trying hard not to panic: there was Amanda, outside the door, but what if she couldn't do anything?

"Any clue?" she said.

"He did say something about my name," I said. "Just before he – before they – Maybe that's what he meant."

Amanda tried. "Nope," she said. "Well then. Maybe it's your birthday. Month and day? Year?"

I could hear her punching in numbers, swearing gently to herself. After what seemed a long time, I heard the clunk of the lock. The door swung open, and there she was, right in front of me.

"Oh, Amanda," I said. She was sunburned, tattered, and grimy, but she was real. I reached out my arms to her, but she stepped back and away.

"It was a simple A equals One code," she said. "It was your name, after all. Brenda, only backwards. Don't touch me, I might have germs. I need to shower."

While Amanda was taking her shower in my Sticky Zone bathroom I propped the door open with a chair because I didn't want it to swing shut and lock both of us inside. The air outside my room smelled awful compared with the filtered air I'd been breathing: rotting meat, and also smoke and burnt chemicals, because there'd been fires and nobody to put them out. It was lucky that Scales hadn't caught fire and burned down with me inside it.

After Amanda had taken a shower I took one too, so I'd be as clean as her. Then we put on the green Scales dressing gowns Mordis kept for his best girls and sat around eating Joltbars from the minifridge and microwaving ChickieNobs, and drinking some beers we'd found downstairs, and telling each other the stories of why it was that we were still alive.

57

TOBY. SAINT KAREN SILKWOOD

YEAR TWENTY-FIVE

Toby wakes up suddenly, her blood rushing in her head: *katoush*, *katoush*, *katoush*. She knows at once that something in her space has changed. Someone's sharing her oxygen.

Breathe, she tells herself. Move as if swimming. Don't smell like fear.

She lifts the pink sheet off her damp body as slowly as she can, sits up, looks carefully around. Nothing large, not in this cubicle: there isn't room. Then she sees it. It's only a bee. A honeybee, walking along the sill.

A bee in the house means a visitor, said Pilar; and if the bee dies, the visit will not be good. I mustn't kill it, Toby thinks. She folds it carefully in a pink washcloth. "Send a message," she says to it. "Tell those in the Spirit world: 'Please send help soon.'" Superstition, she knows that; yet she feels oddly encouraged. Though maybe the bee is one of the transgenics they let loose after the virus wiped out the natural bees; or it may even be a cyborg spy, wandering around with no one left to control it. In which case it will make a very poor messenger.

She slips the washcloth into the pocket of her top-to-toe: she'll take the bee up to the roof, release it there, watch it set off on its errand to the dead. But in slinging the rifle over her shoulder by the strap she must have crushed the pocket, because when she unwraps the bee it looks less than alive. She shakes the cloth over the railing, hoping the bee will fly. It moves through the air, but more like a seed than an insect: the visit will not be a good one.

She walks to the garden side of the roof, looks over. Sure enough, the bad visit has already occurred: the pigs have been back. They've dug under the fence, then gone on a rampage. Surely it was less like a feeding frenzy than a deliberate act of revenge. The earth is furrowed and trampled: anything they haven't eaten they've bulldozed.

If she were a cryer, she'd cry. She lifts her binoculars, scans the meadow. At first she doesn't see them, but then she spots two pinkish-grey heads – no, three – no, five – lifting above the weedy flowers. Beady eyes, one per pig: they're looking at her sideways. They've been watching for her: it's as if they want to witness her dismay. Moreover, they're out of range: if she shoots at them she'll waste the bullets. She wouldn't put it past them to have figured that out.

"You fucking pigs!" she yells at them, "Fuck-pigs! Pig-faces!" Of course, for them none of these names would be insults.

What now? Her supply of dried greens is tiny, her goji berries and chia are almost gone, her plant protein is finished. She was counting on the garden for all of that. Worst of all, she's out of fats: she's already eaten the last of the Shea and Avocado Body Butter. There's fat in Joltbars – she still has some of those – but not enough to last for long. Without lipids your body eats your fat and then your muscles, and the brain is pure fat and the heart is a muscle. You become a feedback loop, and then you fall over.

She'll have to resort to foraging. Go out into the meadow, the forest: find protein and lipids. The boar will be putrid by now, she can't eat that. She could shoot a green rabbit, maybe; but no, it's a fellow mammal and she isn't up to that kind of slaughter. Ant larvae and eggs, or grubs of any kind, for starters.

Is that what the pigs want her to do? Go outside her defensive walls, into the open, so they can jump her, knock her down, then rip her open? Have a pig-style outdoor picnic. A pig-out. She has a fair idea of what that would look like. The Gardeners weren't squeamish about describing the eating habits of God's various Creatures: to flinch at these would be hypocritical. No one comes into the world clutching a knife and fork and a frying pan, Zeb was fond of saying. Or a table napkin. And if we eat pigs, why shouldn't pigs eat us? If they find us lying around.

No point in trying to repair the garden. The pigs would just wait until there was something worth destroying, and then destroy it. Maybe she should build a rooftop garden, like the old Gardener ones: then she'd never have to go outside the main building. But she'd have to haul the soil up all those stairs, in pails. Then there's the watering in the dry seasons and the drainage in the wet seasons: without the Gardeners' elaborate systems the thing would be impossible.

There are the pigs, peering at her above the daisies. They have a festive air. Are they snorting in derision? Certainly there's some grunting going on, and some juvenile squealing, as there used to be when the topless bars in the Sewage Lagoon closed at night.

"Assholes!" she screams at them. It makes her feel better to scream. At least she's talking to someone other than herself.

58

REN

YEAR TWENTY-FIVE

The worst, said Amanda, was the thunderstorms – she thought she was dead a couple of times, the lightning came so close. But then she'd lifted a rubber mat from a mallway hardware store to crouch on, and she'd felt safer after that.

She'd avoided people as much as possible. She abandoned the solarcar in upstate New York because the highway was too jammed with scrap metal. There'd been some spectacular crashes: the drivers must have started dissolving right inside their cars. "Blood hand lotion," she said. There'd been about a million vultures. Some people would have been freaked out by them, but not Amanda – she'd worked with them in her art. "That highway was the biggest Vulture Sculpture you could imagine," she said. She wished she'd had a camera.

After ditching the solarcar she'd walked for a while and then lifted another solar, a bike this time – easier to get through the metal snarls. When in doubt she'd kept to the urban fringes, or else the woods. She'd had a couple of close calls because other people must've had the same idea – she'd almost tripped over a few bodies. Good thing she hadn't actually touched them.

She'd seen some living people. A couple of them had seen her too, but by then everyone must have known this bug was ultra-catching, so they'd stayed far away from her. Some of them were in the last stages, wandering around like zombies; or they were already down, folded in on themselves like cloth.

She slept on top of garages whenever she could, or inside abandoned buildings, though never on the main floor. Otherwise, in trees: the ones with sturdy forks. Uncomfortable but you got used to it, and best to be above ground level because there'd been some strange animals around. Huge pigs, those lion/lamb splices, packs of wild dogs on the prowl – one pack had almost cornered her. Anyway you were safer from the zombie people, up in trees: you wouldn't want a clot on legs to fall on top of you in the darkness.

What she was telling was gruesome, but we laughed a lot that night. I guess we should have been mourning and wailing, but I'd already done that, and anyway what good would it be? Adam One said we should always look on the positive side, and the positive side was that we were still alive.

We didn't talk about anyone we knew.

I didn't want to sleep in my Sticky Zone room because I'd been there long enough, and we couldn't use my old room either because the husk of Starlite was still in it. Finally we chose one of the client facilities, the one with the giant bed and the green satin bedspread and the featherwork ceiling. That room looked elegant if you didn't think too much about what it had been used for.

The last time I'd seen Jimmy had been in that room. But having Amanda there was like an eraser: it smudged that earlier memory. It made me safer.

We slept in the next morning. Then we got up and put on our green dressing gowns and went into the Scales kitchen where they used to make the bar snacks. We microwaved some frozen soybread out of the main freezer and had that for breakfast, with instant Happicuppa.

"Didn't you think I must be dead?" I asked Amanda. "And so maybe you shouldn't bother coming here?"

"I knew you weren't dead," said Amanda. "You get a feeling when someone's dead. Someone you know really well. Don't you think?"

I wasn't sure about that. So I said, "Anyway, thanks." Whenever you thanked Amanda for something she pretended not to hear; or else she'd say, "You'll pay me back." That's what she said now. She wanted everything to be a trade, because giving things for nothing was too soft.

"What should we do now?" I said.

"Stay here," said Amanda. "Until the food's gone. Or if the solar shuts off and the stuff in the freezers begins to rot. That could get ugly."

"Then what?" I said.

"Then we'll go somewhere else."

"Like where?"

"We don't need to worry about that now," said Amanda.

Time got stretchy. We'd sleep as long as we wanted, then get up and have showers – we still had water because of the solar – and then eat something out of the freezers. Then we'd talk about things we'd done at the Gardeners – old stuff. We'd sleep some more when it got too hot. Later we'd go into the Sticky Zone rooms and turn on the air conditioning and watch DVDs of old movies. We didn't feel like going outside the building.

In the evenings we'd have a few drinks – there were still some unbroken bottles behind the bar – and raid the expensive tinned foods Mordis kept for the high-roller clients and also for his best girls. Loyalty Snacks, he called them; he'd dish them out when you'd gone the extra mile, though you never knew in advance what that extra mile would be. That's how I got to eat my first caviar. It was like salty bubbles.

There was no more caviar left at Scales for me and Amanda, though.

59

TOBY. SAINT ANIL AGARWAL

YEAR TWENTY-FIVE

Here comes famine, thinks Toby. Saint Euell, pray for me and for all who starve in the midst of plenty. Help me to find that plenty. Send animal protein quickly.

In the meadow the dead boar is entering the afterlife. Gases are rising from it, fluids are seeping away. The vultures have been at it; the crows are hanging around on the perimeter like runts at a street fight, grabbing what they can. Whatever's going on out there, maggots are a part of it.

When in extreme need, Adam One used to say, begin at the bottom of the food chain. Those without central nervous systems must surely suffer less.

Toby gathers the necessary items – her pink top-to-toe, her sunhat, her sunglasses, a water bottle, a pair of surgical gloves. The binoculars, the rifle. Her mop-handle cane, for balance. She finds a plastic snap-top and punches some holes in the lid, adds a spoon, and stows everything in a plastic gift bag with the winky-eye AnooYoo Spa logo on it. A packsack would be better, it would leave her hands free. There used to be some packsacks around here – the ladies took them on strolls, with picnic sandwiches in them – but she can't remember where she put them.

There's still some AnooYoo All-Natural SolarNix in stock. It's stale-dated and smells rancid, but she spreads it on her face anyway, then sprays her ankles and wrists with SuperD in case of mosquitoes. She has a good long drink of water, then visits the violet biolet: if panic arises, at least she won't piss herself. Nothing worse than sprinting in a wet top-to-toe. She hangs the binoculars around her neck, then goes up to the roof for a last double-check. No ears in the meadow, no snouts. No furry golden tails.

"Quit stalling," she tells herself. She has to leave immediately so she can get back before the afternoon rainstorm. Stupid to get struck by lightning. Any death is stupid from the viewpoint of whoever is undergoing it, Adam One used to say, because no matter how much you've been warned, Death always comes without knocking. Why now? is the cry. Why so soon? It's the cry of a child being called home at dusk, it's the universal protest against Time. Just remember, dear Friends: What am I living for and what am I dying for are the same question.

A question – Toby says to herself very firmly – that I will not ask myself just now.

She puts on the surgical gloves and slings the AnooYoo bag over her shoulder, and lets herself out. She goes first to the ruined garden, where she salvages one onion and two radishes, and spoons a layer of damp earth into the plastic snap-top. Then she crosses the parking lot and walks past the silent fountains.

It's been a long time since she's been this far away from the Spa buildings. Now she's in the meadow: it's a big space. The light is dazzling, even though she has the broad hat and the sunglasses on.

Don't panic, she tells herself. This is how mice feel when they venture onto the open floor, but you aren't a mouse. The weeds catch at her top-to-toe and tangle her feet as if to hold her back and keep her with them. There are little thorns in them somewhere, little claws and traps. It's like pushing through a giant piece of knitting: knitting done with barbed wire.

What's this? A shoe.

Not to think about shoes. Not to think about the mouldering handbag she's just glimpsed nearby. Stylish. Red fleather. A tatter of the past that hasn't yet been drawn down into the earth. She doesn't want to step on any of these remnants, but it's hard to see down through the nets and meshes of the ensnaring weeds.

She moves forward. Her legs are tingling, the way flesh does when it knows it's about to be touched. Does she really think a hand will come up from among the clover and sow thistles and grab her by the ankle?

"No," she says out loud. She stops to calm her heart, and to reconnoiter. The wide brim of the hat impedes her view: she swivels her whole body like an owl's head – to left, to right, behind, then to the front again. All around her is a sweet scent – the tall clover's in bloom, the Queen Anne's lace, the lavender and marjoram and lemon balm, self-seeded. The field hums with pollinators: bumblebees, shining wasps, iridescent beetles. The sound is lulling. Stay here. Sink down. Go to sleep.

Nature full strength is more than we can take, Adam One used to say. It's a potent hallucinogen, a soporific, for the untrained Soul. We're no longer at home in it. We need to dilute it. We can't drink it straight. And God is the same. Too much God and you overdose. God needs to be filtered.

Ahead of her in the middle distance is the line of dark trees that marks the edge of the forest. She feels it drawing her, luring her in, as the depths of the ocean and the mountain heights are said to lure people, higher and higher or deeper and deeper, until they vanish into a state of rapture that is not human.

See yourself as a predator sees you, Zeb once taught. She places herself behind the trees, looking out through the filigree of leaves and branches. There's an enormous wild savannah, and in the middle of it a small soft pink figure, like an embryo or an alien, with big dark eyes – alone, unprotected, vulnerable. Behind this figure is its dwelling, an absurd box made of straw that only looks like bricks. So easy to blow down.

The smell of fear comes to her, from herself.

She lifts the binoculars. The leaves are moving a little, but only in the breeze. Walk forward slowly, she tells herself. Remember what you came to do.

After what seems a long time she reaches the dead boar. A horde of glittering green and bronze flies dithers in the air above it. At her approach the vultures lift their red, featherless heads, their boiled-looking necks. She waves her mop handle at them and they scrabble away, hissing with indignation. Some of them spiral upwards, keeping an eye on her; others flap towards the trees and settle their dust-rag feathers, waiting.

There are fronds scattered about, on top of the boar's carcass and beside it. Fern fronds. Such ferns don't grow in the meadow. Some are old and dry and brown, some quite fresh. Also flowers. Are those rose petals, from the roses by the driveway? She'd heard of something like this; no, she read it as a child, in a kid's book about elephants. The elephants would stand around their dead ones, sombrely, as if meditating. Then they'd scatter branches and earth.

But pigs? Usually they'd just eat a dead pig, the same way they'd eat anything else. But they haven't been eating this one.

Could the pigs have been having a funeral? Could they be bringing memorial bouquets? She finds this idea truly frightening.

But why not? says the kindly voice of Adam One. We believe the Animals have Souls. Why then would they not have funerals?

"You're mad," she says out loud.

The smell of decaying flesh is rank: it's hard to keep from gagging. She lifts a fold of her top-to-toe, clamps it over her nose. With the other hand she pokes at the dead boar with her stick: maggots boil forth. They're like giant grey rice.

Just think of them as land shrimp, says the voice of Zeb. Same body plan. "You're up to this," she tells herself. She has to set down the rifle and the mop handle in order to do the next part. She scoops up the twirling white maggots with the spoon and transfers them to the plastic snap-on. She drops some; her hands are shaking. There's a buzzing in her head like tiny drills, or is it only the flies? She makes herself slow down.

Thunder in the distance.

She turns her back on the forest, heads back across the meadow. She doesn't run.

Surely the trees have moved closer.

60

REN

YEAR TWENTY-FIVE

One day we were drinking champagne and I said, "Let's do our nails, they're a wreck." I thought maybe it would cheer us up. Amanda laughed and said, "Nothing wrecks your nails like a lethal pandemic plague," but we did our nails anyway. Amanda's were an orangey-pink shade called Satsuma Parfait, mine were Slick Raspberry. We were like two kids with fingerpaints, having a party. I love the smell of nail polish. I know it's toxic, but it smells so clean. Crisp, like starched linen. It did make us feel better.

After that we had some more champagne, and I had another party idea, so I went upstairs. There was only one room with a person in it – Starlite, in our old bedroom. I felt terrible about her, but I'd stuffed sheets all around the door so no more smell could get out, and I hoped the microbes would get on with the job so she could be transformed into something else really fast. I took the Biofilm Bodysuits and costumes from Savona's empty room and Crimson Petal's, and brought them downstairs in a giant armful, and we started trying them on.

The Biofilms needed to be sprayed with water and lubricant skin-food – they were dried out – but once we'd done that they slid on as usual, and you could feel the pleasant suction as their layers of living cells bonded with your skin, and then the warm, tickly feeling as they started to breathe. Nothing in but oxygen, nothing out but your natural excretions, said the labels. The face unit even did your nostrils for you. A lot of the Scales customers would have preferred membrane and bristle work if it was completely safe, but at least with the Biofilms they could relax, because they knew they weren't planking a fester.

"This feels great," said Amanda. "It sort of gives you a massage."

"Recommended for the complexion," I said, and we laughed some more. Then Amanda put on a flamingo outfit with pink feathers and I put on a peagret one, and we turned on the music and the coloured spotlights and got up on the stage and danced. Amanda was still a great dancer, she could really shake those feathers. But I was better than her by then, because of all the training I'd had, and the trapeze work; and she knew it. And that pleased me.

That was stupid of us, the whole dancing event: we'd cranked the music up really loud, and it was going right out through the open door, and if there was anyone in the neighbourhood they'd be sure to hear it. But I wasn't thinking about that. "Ren, you're not the only person on the planet," Toby used to say when I was little. It was a way of telling us to have consideration. But now I really did think I was the only person on the planet. Or me and Amanda. So there we were in our flamingo-pink and peagret-blue costumes and our fresh nail polish, dancing on the Scales stage together with the music turned up, whump whump babadedump, bam bam kabam, singing along as if we didn't have a care in the world.

Then the number came to the end, and we heard clapping. We stood there as if frozen. I felt a chill shoot through me: I had a flash of Crimson Petal hanging from the trapeze rope with a bottle shoved up her, and I couldn't breathe.

Three guys had come in – they must have snuck in very carefully – and there they were. "Don't run," said Amanda to me in a quiet voice. Then she said, "You alive or dead?" She smiled. "Because if you're alive, maybe you'd like a drink?"

"Nice dancing," said the tallest one. "How come you didn't get this bug?"

"Maybe we did." said Amanda. "Maybe we're contagious and we just don't know it yet. Now I'm turning down the stage lights so we can see you."

"Anyone else here?" said the tallest one. "Like, any guys?"

"None that I know of," said Amanda. She'd dimmed the lights. "Take off your face," she said to me. She meant the green sequins, the Biofilm. She went down the steps from the stage. "There's some Scotch left, or we could make you a coffee." She was peeling off her own Biofilm headpiece, and I knew what she was thinking: Make direct eye contact, like Zeb taught us. Don't turn away, they're more likely to swarm you from behind. And the less we looked like sparkly birds rather than people, the less likely we'd be mangled.

Now I could see the three of them better. A tall one, a shorter one, another tall one. They were in camouflage suits, very dirty ones, and they looked as if they'd been out in the sun too much. The sun, the rain, the wind.

Then all of a sudden I knew. "Shackie?" I said. "Shackie! Amanda, it's Shackie and Croze!"

The tall one turned his face towards me. "Who the fuck are you?" he said. Not angry, just kind of stunned.

"It's Ren," I said. "Is that little Oates?" I started to cry.

All five of us moved towards each another like a slow-motion football huddle on TV, and then we were hugging each other. Just hugging and hugging, and holding on.

There was some orange-coloured juice in the freezer, so Amanda mixed up mimosas with the champagne that was left. We opened some salted soynuts, and microwaved a pack of faux fish, and all five of us sat at the bar. The three boys – I still thought of them as boys – practically inhaled the food. Amanda made them drink some water, but not too fast. They weren't starving – they'd been breaking into supermarkettes and even into houses, living off what they could glean, and they'd even snared a couple of rabbits and broiled the chunks, the way we'd done it back at the Gardeners in Saint Euell Week. Still, they were thin.

Then we told one another about where we'd all been when the Waterless Flood hit. I told about the Sticky Zone, and Amanda told about the cow bones in Wisconsin. Dumb luck for both of us, I said – that we hadn't been with other people when the thing got going. Though Adam One used to say no luck was dumb because luck was just another name for miracle.

Shackie and Croze and Oates nearly hadn't made it. They'd been shut up in the Painball Arena. Red Team, said Oates, showing me his thumb tattoo; he seemed proud of it. "They put us in there because of what we'd been doing," said Shackie. "With MaddAddam."

"Mad Adam?" I said. "Like Zeb, at the Gardeners?"

"More than Zeb. It was a bunch of us – him and us, and some others," said Shackie. "Top scientists – gene-splicers who'd bailed out of the Corps and gone underground because they hated what the Corps were doing. Rebecca and Katuro were in it – they helped distribute the product."

"We had a website," said Croze. "We could share our info that way, in the hidden chatroom."

"Product?" said Amanda. "You were pushing superweed? Cool!" She laughed.

"No way. We were doing bioform resistance," said Croze importantly. "The splicers put the bioforms together and Shackie and me and Croze and Rebecca and Katuro had top identities – insurance and real estate, stuff like that you could travel with. So we'd take the bioforms to the locations and let them loose."

"We'd plant them," said Oates. "Like, you know, time bombs."

"Some of those suckers were really cool," said Shackie. "The microbes that ate the asphalt, the mice that attacked cars . . ."

"Zeb figured if you could destroy the infrastructure," said Croze, "then the planet could repair itself. Before it was too late and everything went extinct."

"So this plague, was it a MaddAddam thing?" said Amanda.

"No way," said Shackie. "Zeb didn't believe in killing people, not as such. He just wanted them to stop wasting everything and fucking up."

"He wanted to make them think," said Oates. "Though some of those mice got out of control. They got confused. Attacked shoes. There were foot injuries."

"Where is he now?" I asked. It would be so comforting if Zeb was there: he'd know what we should do next.

Shackie said, "We only talked to him online. He flew solo."

"CorpSeCorps nabbed our MaddAddam splicers, though," said Croze. "Tracked us down. I figure some creep in our chatroom was a plant."

"They shot them?" Amanda asked. "The scientists?"

"Don't know," said Shackie, "but they didn't end up with us in Painball."

"We were only in there a couple of days," said Oates. "In Painball."

"Three of us, three of them. The Gold team – they were beyond vicious. One of them – remember Blanco, from the Sewage Lagoon? Rip off your head and eat it? Lost some weight, but it was him all right," said Croze.

"You're joking," said Amanda. She looked – not frightened exactly. But concerned.

"Tossed in for trashing Scales – killed some people, sounded proud of it. Said Painball was like home to him, he'd done it so much."

"Did he know who you were?" said Amanda.

"Definitely," said Shackie. "Yelled at us. Said it was payback time for that brawl on the Edencliff Rooftop – he'd slit us like fish."

"What brawl on the Edencliff Rooftop?" I said.

"You'd gone by then," said Amanda. "How did you get out?"

"Walked," said Shackie. "We were figuring out how to kill the other team before they killed us – they gave you three days to plan, before the Start gong – but all of a sudden there were no guards. They were just gone."

"I'm really tired," said Oates. "I need to sleep." He put his head down on the bar.

"Guards were still there, it turned out," said Shackie. "In the gatehouse. Only they were kind of melted."

"So we went online," said Croze, "The news was still working. Big disaster coverage, so we figured we shouldn't go out and mingle. We locked ourselves into one of the guardhouses – they had some food in there."

"Problem was, the Golds were in the guardhouse on the other side of the gate. We kept thinking they'd whack us when we were sleeping."

"We took turns staying awake, but it was too much strain, just waiting. So we forced them out," said Croze. "Shackie went through a window at night and cut their water lines."

"Fuck!" said Amanda with admiration. "Really?"

"So they had to leave," said Oates. "No water."

"Then we ran out of food and we had to leave too," said Shackie. "We thought maybe they'd be waiting for us, but they weren't." He shrugged. "End of story."

"Why did you come here?" I said. "To Scales."

Shackie grinned. "This place had a reputation," he said.

"A legend," said Croze. "Even though we didn't think there'd be any girls still left in it. We could at least see it."

"Something to do before you die," said Oates. He yawned.

"Come on, Oatie," said Amanda. "Let's put you to bed."

We took them upstairs and ran each of them through a Sticky Zone shower, and they came out a lot cleaner than when they went in. We gave them towels and they dried off, and then we tucked them into beds, one in each room.

It was me who took care of Oates – gave him his towel and soap, and showed him the bed where he could sleep. I hadn't seen him for such a long time. When I left the Gardeners he was just a little kid. A little brat – always getting into trouble. That's how I remembered him. But cute, even then.

"You've grown a lot," I said. He was almost as tall as Shackie. His blond hair was all damp, like a dog that's been swimming.

"I always thought you were the best," he said. "I had a huge crush on you when I was eight."

"I didn't know," I said.

"Can I kiss you?" he said. "I don't mean in a sexy way."

"Okay," I said. And he did, he gave me the sweetest kiss, beside my nose.

"You're so pretty," he said. "Please keep your bird suit on." He touched my feathers, the ones on my bum. Then he gave this shy little grin. It reminded me of Jimmy, the way he was at first, and I could feel my heart lurch. But I tiptoed out of the room.

"We could lock them in," I whispered to Amanda out in the hallway.

"Why would we do that?" said Amanda.

"They've been in Painball."

"So?"

"So, all Painball guys are unhinged. You don't know what they'll do, they just go crazy. Plus, they might have the germ. The plague thing."

"We hugged them," said Amanda. "We've already got every germ they've got. Anyway, they're old Gardener."

"Which means?" I said.

"Which means they're our friends."

"They weren't exactly our friends back then. Not always."

"Relax," said Amanda. "Those guys and me did lots of stuff together. Why would they hurt us?"

"I don't want to be a time-share meat-hole," I said.

"That's pretty crude," said Amanda. "It's not them you should be afraid of, it's the three Painball guys who were in there with them. Blanco's not a joke. They must be out there somewhere. I'm putting my real clothes back on." She was already peeling off her flamingo suit, pulling on her khaki.

"We should lock the front door," I said.

"The lock's broken," said Amanda.

Then we heard voices coming along the street. They were singing and yelling, the way men did at Scales when they're more than drunk. Stinking drunk, smashing-up drunk. We heard the crash of glass.

We ran into the bedrooms and woke up our guys. They put on their clothes very fast, and we took them to the second-floor window that overlooked the street. Shackie listened, then peered cautiously out. "Oh shit," he said.

"Is there another door in this place?" Croze whispered. His face was white, despite his sunburn. "We need to get out. Right now."

We went down the back stairs and slipped out the trash door, into the yard where the garboil dumpsters were, and the bins for empty bottles. We could hear the Gold Teamers bashing around inside the Scales building, demolishing whatever hadn't been demolished already. There was a giant smash: they must have pulled down the shelving behind the bar.

We squeezed through the gap in the fence and ran across the vacant lot to the far corner and down the alleyway there. They couldn't possibly see us, yet I felt as if they could – as if their eyes could pierce through brick, like TV mutants.

Blocks away, we slowed to a walk. "Maybe they won't figure it out," I say. "That we were there."

"They'll know," said Amanda. "The dirty plates. The wet towels. The beds. You can tell when a bed's just been slept in."

"They'll come after us," said Croze. "No question."

61

We turned corners and went up alleyways to mix up our tracks. Tracks were a problem – there was a layer of ashy mud – but Shackie said the rain would wash away our marks, and anyway the Gold Team weren't dogs, they wouldn't be able to smell us.

It had to be them: the three Painballers who'd smashed up Scales, that first night of the Flood. The ones who'd killed Mordis. They'd seen me on the intercom. That's why they'd come back to Scales – to open up the Sticky Zone like an oyster in order to get at me. They would have found tools. It might have taken a while, but they'd have done it in the end.

That thought gave me a very cold feeling, but I didn't tell the others about it. They had enough to worry about anyway.

There was a lot of trash cluttering the streets – burnt things, broken things. Not only cars and trucks. Glass – a lot of that. Shackie said we had to be careful which buildings we went into: they'd been right near one when it collapsed. We should stay away from the tall ones because the fires could have eaten away at them, and if the glass windows fell on you, goodbye head. It would be safer in a forest than in a city now. Which was the reverse of what people used to think.

It was the small normal things that bothered me the most. Somebody's old diary, with the words melting off the pages. The hats. The shoes – they were worse than the hats, and it was worse if there were two shoes the same. The kids' toys. The strollers minus the babies.

The whole place was like a doll's house that had been turned upside down and stepped on. Out of one shop there was a trail of bright T-shirts, like huge cloth footprints, going all along the sidewalk. Someone must have smashed in through the window and robbed the place, though why did they think a bundle of T-shirts was going to do them any good? There was a furniture store spewing chair arms and legs and leather cushions onto the sidewalk, and an eyeglasses place with high-fashion frames, gold and silver – nobody had bothered to take those. A pharmacy – they'd trashed it completely, looking for party drugs. There were a lot of empty BlyssPluss containers. I'd thought it was just at the testing stage, but that place must have been selling it black market.

There were bundles of rag and bone. "Ex-people," said Croze. They were dried out and picked over, but I didn't like the eyeholes. And the teeth – mouths look a lot worse without lips. And the hair was so stringy and detachable. Hair takes years to decay; we learned that in Composting, at the Gardeners.

We hadn't had any time to grab food from Scales, so we went into a supermarkette. There was junk all over the floor, but we found a couple of Zizzy Froots and some Joltbars, and in another place there was a solar-freezer that was still running. It had soybeans and berries – we ate those right away – and frozen SecretBurger patties, six to a box.

"How're we going to cook them?" asked Oates.

"Lighters," said Shackie. "See?" On the counter there was a rack of lighters in the shape of frogs. Shackie tried one: the flame shot out of its mouth, and it said Ribbit.

"Take a handful," said Amanda.

By this time we were near the Sinkhole, so we headed for the old Wellness Clinic because it was a place we knew. I hoped there'd be some Gardeners left inside it, but it was empty. We had a picnic in our old classroom: we made a fire out of broken desks, though not a big fire because we didn't want to send any smoke signals to the Gold Painballers, but we had to open the windows because we were coughing too much. We broiled the SecretBurgers and ate them, and half of the soybeans – we didn't bother cooking those – and drank the Zizzy Froots. Oates kept making the frog lighter say Ribbit until Amanda told him to stop because he was wasting fuel.

The adrenalin of running away had worn off by then. It was sad to be back in the place where we'd been children: even if we hadn't liked it all the time, I felt so homesick for it now.

I guess this is what the rest of my life will be like, I thought. Running away, scrounging for leftovers, crouching on floors, getting dirtier and dirtier. I wished I had some real clothes, because I was still in my peagret outfit. I wanted to go back to the T-shirt place to see if there was anything left inside the store that wasn't damp and mouldy, but Shackie said it was too dangerous.

I thought maybe we should have sex: it would have been a kind and generous thing to do. But everyone was too tired, and also we were shy with one another. It was the surroundings – though the Gardeners weren't there in their bodies, they were there in Spirit, and it was hard to do anything they'd have disapproved of if they'd seen us doing it when we were ten.

We went to sleep in a pile, on top of one another, like puppies.

The next morning when we woke up there was a huge pig standing in the doorway, staring in at us and sniffing the air with its wet, sluggy-looking nose. It must have come in the door and all the way down the hall. It turned and went away when it saw us looking at it. Maybe it smelled the burger patties being cooked, said Shackie. He said it was an enhanced splice – MaddAddam had known about those – and that it had human brain tissue in it.

"Oh yeah," said Amanda, "and it's doing advanced physics. You're bullshitting us."

"Truth," said Shackie, a little sulky.

"Too bad we don't have a spraygun," said Croze. "Long time since I had bacon."

"None of that language," I said in a Toby voice, and we all laughed.

Before we left the Wellness Clinic we went into the Vinegar Room, for a last look at it. The big barrels were still there, though someone had taken an axe to them. There was a smell of vinegar, and also a toilet smell: people had been using a corner of the room for that, and not long ago either. The little closet door where they used to keep the vinegar bottles was standing open. There weren't any bottles; but there were some shelves. They were at a strange angle, and Amanda went over and took an edge and pulled, and the shelves swung out.

"Look," she said. "There's a whole other room in here!"

We went in. There was a table that took up most of the room, and some chairs. But the most interesting thing was a futon, like our old Gardener ones, and a bunch of empty food containers – soydines, chickenpeas, dried gojiberries. Over in one corner was a dead laptop.

"Somebody else made it through," said Shackie.

"Not a Gardener," I said. "Not with a laptop."

"Zeb had a laptop," said Croze. "But he'd stopped being a Gardener."

We left the Wellness Clinic without any clear plan. It was me who said we should go to the AnooYoo Spa: there might be food in the Ararat that Toby put together in the storeroom; she'd told me the doorcode. Also there could still be something growing in the garden. I even wondered if maybe Toby was hiding out there, but I didn't want to get any hopes up, so I didn't say that.

We thought we were being really careful. We couldn't see anybody anywhere. We went into the Heritage Park and headed towards the Spa's west gatehouse, staying on the forest pathway, under the trees – we felt less visible that way.

We were going single file. Shackie was at the front of the line, then Croze, then Amanda, then me; Oates was at the very back. Then I had a cold feeling, and I looked behind me, and Oates wasn't there. I said, "Shackie!"

And then Amanda lurched sideways, right off the path.

Then there was a dark patch like going through brambles – everything painful and tangled. There were bodies on the ground, and one of them was mine, and that must have been when I got hit.

When I woke up again, Shackie and Croze and Oates weren't there. But Amanda was.

I don't want to think about what happened next.

It was worse for Amanda than for me.

PREDATOR DAY

PREDATOR DAY

YEAR TWENTY-FIVE.

OF GOD AS THE ALPHA PREDATOR.
SPOKEN BY ADAM ONE.

Dear Friends, dear Fellow Creatures, dear Fellow Mortals:

Long ago, we celebrated Predator Day on our lovely Edencliff Rooftop Garden. Our Children would don their faux-fur Predator ears and tails, and at sunset we'd light candles inside the Lions and Tigers and Bears fashioned from perforated tin cans, and the burning-bright eyes of these Predator images would sparkle upon our Predator Day feast.

But today our Festival must be held in the inner Gardens of our Minds. We are fortunate to have even these, for the Waterless Flood has now rolled over our city, and indeed over the entire Planet. Most were taken by surprise, but we relied on Spiritual guidance. Or, to put it in a materialistic way: we knew a global pandemic when we saw one.

Let us give thanks for this Ararat in which we have been sheltering over the past months. It is not perhaps the Ararat we would have chosen, situated as it is in the cellars of the Buenavista Condo Complex, which were dank even at the time of Pilar's mushroom beds, and are even danker now. But we are blessed that so many of our Rat relatives have donated their protein to us, thus enabling us to remain on this Earthly plane. It is also fortunate that Pilar had built an Ararat in this very cellar, hidden behind a concrete block marked with a tiny bee symbol. How providential that so many of her supplies retained their freshness! Though unhappily not all.

But these resources are now exhausted, and we must either move or starve. Let us pray that the outer world is Exfernal no more – that the Waterless Flood has cleansed as well as destroyed, and that all the world is now a new Eden. Or, if it is not a new Eden yet, that it will be one soon. Or so we trust.

⁝

On Predator Day we celebrate, not God the loving and gentle Father and Mother, but God the Tiger. Or God the Lion. Or God the Bear. Or God the Wild Boar. Or God the Wolf. Or even God the Shark. Whatever the symbol, Predator Day is devoted to the qualities of terrifying appearance and overwhelming strength, which, since they are at times desired by us, must also belong to God, as all good things belong to Him.

As Creator, God has put a little of Himself into each of His Creatures – how could it be otherwise? – and therefore the Tiger, the Lion, the Wolf, the Bear, the Boar, and the Shark – or, on the miniscale of things, the Water Shrew and the Praying Mantis – are in their way reflections of the Divine. Human societies through the ages have known this. On their flags and coats of arms, they have not placed prey Animals such as Rabbits and Mice, but Animals capable of inflicting death, and when they invoked God as defender, was it not these qualities upon which they called?

Thus on Predator Day we meditate on the Alpha Predator aspects of God. The suddenness and ferocity with which an apprehension of the Divine may appear to us; our smallness and fearfulness – may I say, our Mouselikeness – in the face of such Power; our feelings of individual annihilation in the brightness of that splendid Light. God walks in the tender dawn Gardens of the mind, but He also prowls in its night Forests. He is not a tame Being, my Friends: he is a wild Being, and cannot be summoned and controlled like a Dog.

Human Beings may well have killed the last Tiger and the last Lion, but their Names are cherished by us; and as we say those Names, we hear behind them the tremendous Voice of God at the moment of their Creation. God must have said to them: My Carnivores, I command you to fulfil your appointed task of culling your Prey Species, lest these multiply overmuch, and exhaust their food supply, and sicken, and die out. Go forth, therefore! Leap! Run! Roar! Lurk! Spring! For I delight in your dread hearts, and in the gold and green jewels of your eyes, and in your well-fashioned sinews, and in your scissor teeth and your scimitar claws, which I Myself have bestowed upon you. And I give you My Blessing, and pronounce you Good.

For they do seek their meat from God, as Psalm 104 so joyfully puts it.

As we prepare to leave our sheltering Ararat, let us ask ourselves: Which is more blessed, to eat or to be eaten? To flee or to chase? To give or to receive? For these are at heart the same question. Such a question may soon cease to be theoretical: we do not know what Alpha Predators may lurk without.

Let us pray that if we must sacrifice our own protein so it may circulate among our fellow Species, we will recognize the sacred nature of the transaction. We would not be Human if we did not prefer to be the devourers rather than the devoured, but either is a blessing. Should your life be required of you, rest assured that it is required by Life.

Let us sing.

THE WATER-SHREW THAT RENDS ITS PREY

The Water-Shrew that rends its Prey
Acts purely out of Nature's need;
It does not stop to plot its course,
But simply does the deed.

The Leopard pouncing in the night
Is kin to soft domestic Puss –
They love to hunt, and hunt to love,
Because God made them thus.

And who can say if joy or fear
Are each in other's lasting debt?
Does every Prey enjoy each breath
Because of constant threat?

But we are not as Animals –
We cherish other Creatures' lives;
And so we do not eat their flesh
Unless dread Famine drives.

And if dread Famine drives us on,
And if we yield to tempting Meat,
May God forgive our broken Vows,
And bless the Life we eat.

From *The God's Gardeners Oral Hymnbook*

62

TOBY. SAINT NGANEKO MINHINNICK OF MANUKAU

YEAR TWENTY-FIVE

A red sunrise, meaning rain later. But there's always rain later.

Mist rising.

Oodle-oodle-ooo. Oodle-oodle-oo. Chirrup, twareep. Aw aw aw. Ey ey ey. Hoom hoom baroom.

Mourning dove, robin, crow, bluejay, bullfrog. Toby says their names, but these names mean nothing to them. Soon her own language will be gone out of her head and this will be all that's left in there. Ooodle-oodle-oo, hoom hoom. The ceaseless repetition, the song with no beginning and no end. No questions, no answers, not in so many words. Not in any words at all. Or is it all one huge Word?

Where has this notion come from, out of nowhere and into her head?

Tobeee!

So much like someone calling her. But it's only birdsong.

She's up on the roof, cooking her daily portion of land shrimp in the cool of the morning. Don't scorn the lowly table of Saint Euell, says the voice of Adam One. The Lord provides, and sometimes what He provides is land shrimp, says Zeb. Rich in lipids, a good source of protein. How do you think bears get so fat?

Best to cook outside, because of the smoke and heat. She's using her Saint Euell–inspired hobo stove, made of a bulk-sized body-butter can: hole in the bottom for dry sticks and the draft, hole on the side for smoke. The maximum heat for the minimum fuel. No more than needed. The land shrimp sizzle on the top.

Suddenly there's a racket of crows: they're excited about something. Not alarm calls, so not an owl. More like astonishment: *Aw Aw! Look! Look! Look at that!*

Toby scrapes the crispy land shrimp off the top of her tin can onto her plate – to waste food is to waste Life, says Adam One – then douses the fire with her pot of rainwater and hits the rooftop, flat on her belly. Lifts the binoculars. The crows are flying around above the treetops, a flock of them. Six or seven. *Aw! Aw! Look! Look! Look!*

Two men come out from among the trees. They aren't singing, and they aren't naked and blue: they have clothes on.

There are still people, Toby thinks. Alive. Maybe one of them is Zeb, come in search of her: he must have guessed she'd still be here, still be holed up, still holding out. She blinks: are these tears? She wants to rush downstairs and out into the open, hold out her arms in welcome, laugh with happiness. But caution restrains her, and she crouches down behind the air-conditioning exhaust unit and peers through the rooftop railings.

It could be a trick of the senses. Is she seeing things again?

The men are in camouflage gear. The one in front has a weapon of some kind – a spraygun, perhaps. Surely not Zeb: wrong shape. Neither of them is. There's another person with them – man or woman? Tall, in a khaki outfit. Head hanging down; hard to tell which. Hands held together in front, as if in prayer. One of the men has this person by the arm or elbow. Pushing or pulling.

Then another man emerges from the shadows. He's leading a huge bird on a leash – no, on a rope – a bird with blue-green iridescent plumes like a peagret. But this bird has the head of a woman.

I must be hallucinating again, thinks Toby. Because no matter what the gene splicers could do, they couldn't do this. The men and the bird-woman look real and solid enough, but then, hallucinations do.

One of them has a burden slung over his shoulder. At first she thinks it's a sack, but no, it's a haunch of something. It has fur. Golden fur. Is it a liobam? A shiver of horror runs through her: sacrilege! They've killed an Animal on the Peaceable Kingdom list!

Think clearly, Toby orders herself. First of all, since when are you a fanatical Peaceable Kingdom Isaiahist? Second, if these men are real and not just runoff from an addled brain, they've been killing things. Killing and butchering large Creatures, in which case they have lethal weapons and they've started at the top of the food chain. They're a menace, they'll stop at nothing, and I ought to shoot them before they get as far as me. Then I can free the large bird or whatever it is, before they kill it as well.

Anyway, if they aren't real, it won't matter if I shoot them. They'll just dissolve like smoke.

Then the one leading the bird-woman looks up. He must have seen Toby, because he begins to shout, waving his free arm. Light glints from a knife. The other two men look, and then they all start trotting towards the Spa. The bird creature has to keep up with them because of the rope, and now Toby can see that the feathers are a costume of some kind. It's a woman. No wings. A noose around her neck.

Not a hallucination, then. Real. Real evil.

She centres the knife man in her scope and shoots at him. He staggers backwards and yells and stumbles. But she isn't fast enough, so although she squeezes off a couple more, she misses the other two.

Now the wounded man's up again, limping, and all of them are running back to the trees. The bird woman's running with them. Not that she has a choice, because of the rope. Then she falls down and vanishes into the weeds.

Behind the others, the green tree-leaves open, swallow. Gone now. All of them. She can't spot the place where the woman tumbled: the weeds are too tall. Should she go out and look for her? No. It could be a decoy. There'd be three against her one.

She watches for a long time. The crows must be following them – the men, the one in khaki. *Aw aw aw aw.* A trail of sound, off into the distance.

Will they be back? They'll be back, thinks Toby. They know I'm in here, they'll guess I must have food in order to have stayed alive this long. Also I shot one of them: they'll want revenge, it's only human. They'll be vindictive, like the pigs. But they won't come soon, because they know I have a rifle. They'll have to plan.

63

TOBY. SAINT WEN BO DAY

YEAR TWENTY-FIVE

No men. No pigs either. No liobams.

No bird woman.

Maybe I lost my mind, thinks Toby. Not lost. Temporarily misplaced.

It's bath time; she's up on the roof. She pours rainwater from her collection of smaller bowls and pans into the largest bowl, soaps herself, hands and face only: she won't risk the vulnerability of a full bath, because who knows who may be peering? She's in the midst of sponging off the suds when she hears the crows making a commotion, close by. *Aw aw aw!* This time it sounds like laughing.

Toby! Toby! Help me!

Was that my name? thinks Toby. She looks over the railing, sees nothing. But the voice comes again, right close to the building.

Is it a trap? A woman calling out to her, a man's arm around her throat, a knife to the jugular?

Toby! It's me! Please!

She blots herself with a towel, slides into her top-to-toe, shoulders the rifle, makes her way down the stairs. Opens the door: no one. But the voice again, so near. *Oh please!*

Left corner: nobody. Right corner, nobody again. She's just outside the garden gate when a woman comes around the building. She's hobbling, she's thin and beat up; her long hair's across her face, matted with dirt and dried blood. She's wearing a spangled body suit, with damp, tattered blue feathers.

The bird woman. Some freak from a sex circus. She's bound to be infected, a walking plague. If she touches me, thinks Toby, I'm dead.

"Keep away from me!" she shouts. She backs up against the garden fence. "Fuck off out of here!"

The woman sways on her feet. She has a gash on her leg, and her bare arms are scratched and bleeding – she must have run through brambles. All Toby can think of is the fresh blood: boiling with microbes and viruses.

"Piss off! Get away!!"

"I'm not sick," says the woman. Tears are running down her face. But they'd all said that in their despair. They'd said it, pleading, holding up their hands for help, for comfort, and then they'd turned into pink porridge. Toby had watched them from the roof.

They'll be drowning. Don't let them clutch you. Don't let yourself be that last straw, my Friends, says Adam One.

The rifle. She fumbles with the strap: it's caught in the fabric of her top-to-toe. How to fend off this festering hotspot? Yelling's no good without a weapon. Maybe I could bang her on the head with a stone, thinks Toby. But she doesn't have a stone. A good kick in the solar plexus, then wash my feet.

You are an uncharitable person, says the voice of Nuala. You have scorned God's Creatures, for are not Human beings God's Creatures too?

From under the mat of hair the woman pleads: "Toby! It's me!" She crumples, falls to her knees. Then Toby sees it's Ren. Beneath all the dirt and mangled glitz, it's only little Ren.

64

Toby hauls Ren inside the Spa building and dumps her on the floor while she locks the door behind them. Ren is still crying hysterically, in great gulping sobs.

"Never you mind," says Toby. She takes Ren under the arms and pulls her upright, and they stumble down the hall into one of the treatment cubicles. Ren's a dead weight, but she's not very heavy, and Toby manages to hoist her onto a massage table. She smells of sweat and earth, and blood somewhere, and another smell: something's decaying.

"Stay here," says Toby unnecessarily: Ren isn't going anywhere. She's lying back on the pink pillow with her eyes closed. One of those eyes is black and blue. AnooYoo Soothing Aloe Eye Pads, thinks Toby. With Extra Arnica. She breaks open a packet and applies them, and adds a pink sheet, tucked in at the sides so Ren won't fall off the table. There's a cut on Ren's forehead, another on her cheek: nothing too serious, she'll deal with those later.

She goes into the kitchen, boils up some water in the Kelly kettle. Most likely Ren's dehydrated. She pours hot water into a cup, adds a little of her cherished honey, a pinch of salt. Some dried green onions from her dwindling stash. Carries the cup into Ren's cubicle, takes off the eye pads, sits her up.

Ren's eyes are huge in her thin, bruised face. "I'm not sick," she says, which is untrue: she's burning with fever. But there's more than one kind of sickness. Toby checks the symptoms: no blood oozing from the pores, no froth. Still, Ren could be a plague carrier, an incubator; in which case, Toby's already infected.

"Try to drink," says Toby.

"I can't," says Ren. But she does manage to get some of the water down. "Where's Amanda? I need to get dressed."

"It's okay," says Toby. "Amanda's nearby. Now try to sleep." She eases Ren back down. So Amanda's in this story somewhere, she thinks. That girl was always trouble.

"I can't see," says Ren. She's trembling all over.

Back in the kitchen, Toby pours the rest of the boiled water into a bowl: she needs to clean away those bedraggled feathers and sequins. She carries the bowl and a pair of scissors and a bar of soap and a stack of pink washcloths into Ren's cubicle, folds back the sheet, and cuts away the grubby outfit. It isn't cloth, it's some other substance, underneath the feathers. Stretchy. Almost like skin. She soaks the patches where it's stuck on so she can peel them off more easily. The crotch has been torn away. Cripes, thinks Toby, what a mess. Later she'll make a poultice.

There are abrasions around the neck – rope burns, no doubt. The gash on the left leg is what's festering. Toby's as gentle as she can be, but Ren winces and yelps. "That fucking hurts!" she says. Then she throws up the salt-and-sugar water.

After she's wiped away the filth, Toby starts washing the leg wound. "How did you get this?" she asks.

"I don't know." Ren is whispering. "I fell down."

Toby cleans out the gash and puts some honey on it. Antibiotics in it, Pilar used to say. There ought to be a first-aid kit, somewhere in the Spa. "Hold still. You don't want gangrene," she says to Ren.

Ren giggles. "Knock, knock," she says, "Gang grene."

The dirty covering's all stripped away, and Ren has been sponged. "I'll give you some Willow and Chamomile," Toby says. And Poppy, she thinks. "You need to sleep." Ren will be safer on the floor than on the table: she makes a nest of pink towels, eases her down onto it, adds extra padding because Ren can't make it to the bathroom, she's too weak. She's hot as an ember.

Toby brings the Willow mixture in a small glass. Ren swallows, her throat moving like a bird's. Nothing comes up.

There's no use trying the maggots yet. Ren needs to be coherent for that, able to obey instructions: no scratching, for instance. The first thing is to get the temperature down.

While Ren sleeps, Toby sorts through her store of dried mushrooms. She chooses the immune-system boosters: reishi, maitake, shitake, birch polypore, zhu ling, lion's mane, coryceps, ice man. She puts them in boiled water to soak. Then in the afternoon she prepares a mushroom elixir – the simmering, the straining, the cooling – and gives Ren thirty drops of it.

The cubicle stinks. Toby lifts Ren up, rolls her to the side, pulls out the soiled towels, wipes Ren off. She's put on rubber gloves for the purpose: if dysentery's going around she has no wish to catch it. She smoothes down clean towels, rolls Ren back. Her arms flop, her head wilts; she's muttering.

This is going to be a lot of work, thinks Toby. And when Ren recovers – if she recovers – there will be two people eating instead of one. So the food stash will be gone twice as quickly. What's left of it. Which isn't much.

Maybe the fever will get the better of Ren. Maybe she'll die in her sleep.

Toby considers the powdered Death Angels. It wouldn't take much. Just a little, in Ren's weakened condition. Put her out of her misery. Help her to fly away on white, white wings. Maybe it would be kinder. A blessing.

I am an unworthy person, Toby thinks. Merely to have such an idea. You've known this girl since she was a child, she's come to you for help, she has every right to trust you. Adam One would say that Ren is a precious gift that has been given to Toby so that Toby may demonstrate unselfishness and sharing and those higher qualities the Gardeners had been so eager to bring out in her. Toby can't quite see it that way, not at the moment. But she'll have to keep trying.

Ren sighs and groans and flails. She's having a bad dream.

When it's dark, Toby lights a candle and sits beside her, listening to her breathe. In out, in out. Pause. In. Then out. Raggedy. At intervals she feels Ren's forehead. Cooler? There must be a thermometer in the building; in the morning she'll look for it. She takes her pulse: rapid, irregular.

Then she nods off in her chair, and the next thing she knows she wakes up in the dark with a smell of singeing. She winds up her flashlight: the candle has fallen over, and a corner of Ren's pink sheet is smouldering. Luckily it's damp.

That was terminally stupid, Toby tells herself. No more candles unless I'm fully awake.

65

TOBY. SAINT MAHATMA GANDHI DAY

YEAR TWENTY-FIVE

In the morning Ren feels cooler. Her pulse is stronger, and she can even hold the cup of warm water in her own two trembling hands. Toby's put mint in it this morning, as well as the honey and salt.

Once Ren has gone to sleep again, Toby hauls the dirty sheets and towels up to the roof to wash them. She's brought her binoculars, and while the sheets and towels are soaking she scans the Spa grounds.

Pigs far away, over in the southwest corner of the meadow. Two Mo'Hairs, a blue one and a silver one, grazing quietly together. No liobams. Dogs barking somewhere. Vultures flapping around the pig funeral site.

"Get away from there, you archeologists," says Toby. She's feeling light-headed, almost giddy – in the mood to tell herself jokes. Three huge pink butterflies circle her head, alight on the damp sheets. Maybe they think they've found the biggest pink butterfly of all. Maybe it's a love affair. Now they have their thin tongues unrolled, licking. Not love, then: salt.

Some will tell you Love is merely chemical, my Friends, said Adam One. Of course it is chemical: where would any of us be without chemistry? But Science is merely one way of describing the world. Another way of describing it would be to say: where would any of us be without Love?

Dear Adam One, thinks Toby. He must be dead. And Zeb – dead also, despite wishful thinking. Though maybe not; because if I'm alive – more to the point, if Ren's alive – then anyone at all could be alive too.

She stopped listening on her wind-up radio months ago because the silence was so discouraging. But just because she's heard no one doesn't mean no one's there. Which had been among Adam One's hypothetical proofs for the existence of God.

Toby washes Ren's infected leg, applies more honey. Ren eats a little, drinks a little. More mushroom elixir, more Willow. After much rummaging, Toby locates a Spa first-aid kit; there's a tube of antibiotic cream, but it's stale-dated. No thermometer. Who ordered this crap? she thinks. Oh yes. I did.

Anyway maggots are better.

In the afternoon she lifts the maggots from the plastic snap-top, rinses them in tepid water. Then she transfers them to a sheet of gauze from the first-aid kit, applies another sheet over the top, and tapes the maggot-filled envelope over the wound. It won't take long for the maggots to eat through the gauze: they know what they like.

"This will tickle," she tells Ren. "But they'll make you better. Try not to move your leg."

"What are they?" says Ren.

"They're your friends," says Toby. "But you don't need to look."

Her homicidal impulse of the night before is gone: she will not drag dead Ren out into the meadow for the pigs and vultures. Now she'd like to cure her, cherish her, for isn't it miraculous that Ren is here? That she's come through the Waterless Flood with only minor damage? Or fairly minor. Just to have a second person on the premises – even a feeble person, even a sick person who sleeps most of the time – just this makes the Spa seem like a cozy domestic dwelling rather than a haunted house.

I've been the ghost, thinks Toby.

66

TOBY. SAINT HENRI FABRE, SAINT ANNA ATKINS, SAINT TIM FLANNERY, SAINT ICHIDA-SAN, SAINT DAVID SUZUKI, SAINT PETER MATTHIESSEN

YEAR TWENTY-FIVE

It takes the maggots three days to clean the wound. Toby watches them carefully: if they run out of dead tissue, they'll start in on living flesh.

By the second morning Ren's fever has gone, though Toby continues the mushroom drops just to make sure. Ren's eating more now. Toby helps her up the stairs to the roof and sits her down on the imitation-wood bench, in the early morning light. The maggots are photophobic: light drives them into the deepest corners of the wound, which is where they need to be.

No movement out there in the meadow. No sounds from the forest.

Toby tries asking Ren where she's been ever since the Flood hit, and how she escaped it, and how she got here, why she'd been dressed in those blue feathers; but she only tries once because Ren starts crying. All she'll say is, "I've lost Amanda!"

"Never mind," says Toby. "We'll find her."

On the fourth morning Toby removes the maggot plaster: the wound is clean, and healing. "Now to get your muscles back in shape," she tells Ren.

Ren starts walking, up and down the stairs, along the corridors. She's gained a little weight: Toby's been feeding her the last few jars of AnooYoo Lemon Meringue Facial, which has a lot of sugar in it and nothing toxic that Toby can think of. She leads Ren through some exercises from Zeb's old Urban Bloodshed Limitation classes – the *satsuma*, the *unagi*. Centred like a Fruit, sinuous like an Eel. She needs the refresher herself; she's out of practice.

After a few days Ren tells her story, or a little of her story. It comes out in short clumps of words punctuated by long periods of staring into space. She tells about being locked in at Scales, and how Amanda came all the way from the Wisconsin desert and figured out the door code. Then Shackie and Croze and Oates appeared from nowhere, just like magic, and she was so happy – they'd been saved by being in Painball when the plague broke out. But then three horrible men from the Painball Gold Team came to Scales, and she and Amanda and the boys ran away. She'd said they should come to AnooYoo because Toby might be there, and they'd almost made it – they were walking along through the trees, and then blackout. She can't get any farther than that.

"What did they look like?" says Toby. "Did they have any . . ." She wants to say "distinguishing marks," but Ren shakes her head, meaning that that subject is closed. "I have to find Amanda," she says, wiping away tears. "I really have to. They'll kill her."

"Here, blow your nose," says Toby, handing her a pink washcloth. "Amanda's very clever." It's best to talk as if Amanda is still alive. "She's very resourceful. She'll be all right." She's about to say that women are in short supply and therefore Amanda will surely be preserved and rationed, but she thinks better of it.

"You don't understand," says Ren, crying harder. "There's three of them, they're Painball – they're not really human. I have to find her."

"We'll look," Toby says, to be soothing. "But we don't know where they – where she's gone."

"Where would you go?" says Ren. "If you were them?"

"Maybe east," says Toby. "To the sea. Where they could fish."

"We can go there."

"When you're strong enough," says Toby. They have to move somewhere else anyway: the food supply's shrinking fast.

"I'm strong enough now," says Ren.

Toby scours the garden, unearths one more lone onion. She digs up three burdocks from the near edge of the meadow, and some Queen Anne's lace – the spindly white proto-carrot roots. "Do you think you could eat a rabbit?" she asks Ren. "If I cut it up very small and make it into soup?"

"I guess so," said Ren. "I'll try."

Toby's almost ready for the switch to full-blown carnivore herself. There's the sound of the rifle shot to worry about, but if there are still Painballers lurking in the forest they already know she has a gun. No harm in reminding them.

There are often green rabbits near the swimming pool. Toby shoots at one of them from the rooftop, but she can't seem to hit it. Is conscience twisting her aim? Maybe she needs a bigger target, a deer or a dog. She hasn't seen the pigs lately, or any of the sheep. Just as she was getting all set to eat them, they're gone.

She locates the packsacks on a laundry-room shelf. She hasn't been down there since the pumps stopped working, and the air's thick with mildew. Luckily the packsacks aren't cotton but impenetrable synthetic. She takes them up to the roof, sponges them off, leaves them in the hot sun to dry.

She lays out her available supplies on the kitchen counter. Don't carry so much weight that you burn more calories than you can eat, says the voice of Zeb. Tools are more important than food. Your best tool is your brain.

The rifle, of course. Ammunition. Trowel, for digging roots. Matches. Barbecue lighter, which won't last long but it might as well be used up. Pocket knife with scissors and tweezers. Rope. Two sheets of plastic, handy in rain. Windup flashlight. Gauze bandages. Duct tape. Plastic snap-top containers. Cloth bags for wild edibles. Cooking pot. The Kelly kettle. Toilet paper – a luxury item, but she can't resist. Two medium-sized Zizzy Froots from a Spa minibar, raspberry flavour: junk food, but food, since it has calories in it. The bottles can be used later, for water.

Spoons, metal, two; cups, plastic, two. The remaining sunblock. The last SuperD bug spray. Binoculars: heavy but necessary. The mop handle. Sugar. Salt. The last of the honey. The last Joltbars. The last soybits.

The syrup of Poppy. The dried mushrooms. The Death Angels.

The day before they leave, she cuts her hair short. It's a shorn look – it reminds her of Joan of Arc on a bad day – but she doesn't want a hair handle growing out of her head, all the better to grab you by and slash your throat. She cuts Ren's hair as well. They'll be cooler that way, she tells her.

"We should bury the hair," says Ren. She wants it out of sight for some reason Toby can't fathom.

"Why don't we put it on the roof?" says Toby. "That way the birds can make nests out of it." She doesn't intend to waste her body's calories digging a hair burial site.

"Oh. Okay," says Ren. This idea seems to please her.

67

TOBY. SAINT CHICO MENDES, MARTYR

YEAR TWENTY-FIVE

They leave the Spa building just before dawn. They're dressed in pink cotton exercise outfits, the loose pants and the T-shirt top with the kissy mouth and the winky eye on the front. Pink canvas sport shoes, of the kind the ladies wore to do their rope skipping and weight training. Broad pink hats. They smell of SuperD, and of rancid SolarNix. In their packsacks are their pink top-to-toes, for when the sun gets too high. If only everything weren't so pink, thinks Toby – like baby clothes or girly birthday parties. Not an adventurous colour. Terrible choice for camouflage.

She knows the situation is grave, as the news used to say – of course it is. But nonetheless she feels cheerful, almost giggly. As if she's a little drunk. As if they're just going on a picnic. It must be a surge of adrenalin.

The eastern horizon is brightening; mist rises from the trees. Dew shimmers on the lumirose bushes, mirroring the faint eerie light of their flowers. The sweetness of the damp meadow breathes all around them. The birds are beginning to stir and chirp; the vultures on the bare branches are spreading their wings to dry. A peagret flaps towards them from the south, sails over the meadow, then swoops in for a landing on the edge of the green-scummed swimming pool.

It occurs to Toby that she may never see this vista again. Amazing how the heart clutches at anything familiar, whimpering, *Mine! Mine!* Did she enjoy her enforced stay in the AnooYoo Spa? No. But it's her home territory now: she's left her skin flakes all over it. A mouse would understand: it's her nest. *Farewell* is the song Time sings, Adam One used to say.

Somewhere dogs are barking. She's heard them at intervals over the past months, but today they sound closer. She doesn't much like this. With nobody to feed them, any dogs left by now are sure to have turned wild.

She'd climbed up to the rooftop before they left, scanned the fields. No pigs, no Mo'Hairs, no liobams. Or none in plain view. How little I've ever been able to see, she thinks. The meadow, the driveway, the swimming pool, the garden. The edge of the forest. She'd like to avoid going in there, among the trees. Nature may be dumb as a sack of hammers, Zeb used to say, but it's smarter than you.

Look, she thinks at the forest, with its hidden pigs and liobams. And Painballers too, for all she knows. Don't push me. I may be pink, but I've got a rifle. Bullets too. Longer range than a spraygun. So back off, assholes.

The Spa grounds and its woodland perimeter are separated from the surrounding Heritage Park by a chain-link fence topped with electrified barbed wire, though the electricity won't be functional now. Four gates, east, west, north, and south, with winding driveways connecting them. It's Toby's plan to spend the night at the eastern gatehouse. That's not too far for Ren to walk: she's still not strong enough for heroic trekking. The next morning they can begin to make their way gradually towards the sea.

Ren still believes they'll find Amanda. They'll find her, and Toby will shoot the Gold Painballers with her rifle, and then Shackleton and Crozier and Oates will reappear from wherever they've been hiding. Ren's not yet free of the effects of her illness. She wants Toby to fix and cure everything, as if she herself were still a child; as if Toby were still Eve Six, with magic adult powers.

They pass the crashed pink minivan and, around a curve in the road, two other vehicles – a solarcar, a jeep-sized garboil guzzler. Judging from the blackened wreckage, both must have burned. There's a rusty, sweetish odour mixed in with the charred smell.

"Don't look inside," Toby tells Ren as they walk past.

"It's okay," Ren says. "I saw a lot of stuff like that in the pleebs, when we were coming here from Scales."

Farther along there's a dog – a spaniel, recently dead. Something's torn it open; there's a scribble of entrails, a buzzing of flies, but no vultures yet. Whatever it was will surely return to its kill: predators don't waste. Toby eyes the roadside bushes: the vines are growing almost audibly, shutting out sight. What a lot of kudzu. "We should walk faster," she says.

But Ren can't walk faster. She's tired, her packsack's too heavy. "I think I'm getting a blister," she says. They stop under a tree for a drink of Zizzy Froot. Toby can't shake the feeling that something's crouched up in the branches, waiting to leap on them. Can liobams climb? She forces herself to slow down, to breathe deeply, to take her time.

"Let's see your blister," she says to Ren. It's not a blister yet. She tears a strip off her top-to-toe, winds it around Ren's foot. The sun's at ten. They put on their top-to-toes and Toby smears their faces with more SolarNix, then sprays them again with SuperD.

Ren begins to limp before they've reached the next curve in the road.

"We'll cut across the meadow," says Toby. "It's shorter that way."

SAINT RACHEL AND ALL BIRDS

SAINT RACHEL AND ALL BIRDS

YEAR TWENTY-FIVE.

OF THE GIFTS OF SAINT RACHEL; AND OF THE FREEDOM OF THE SPIRIT.
SPOKEN BY ADAM ONE.

Dear Friends, dear Fellow Creatures and Fellow Mortals:

What a cause for rejoicing is this rearranged world in which we find ourselves! True, there is a certain – let us not say *disappointment.* The debris left by the Waterless Flood, like that left by any receding flood, is not attractive. It will take time for our longed-for Eden to appear, my Friends.

But how privileged we are to witness these first precious moments of Rebirth! How much clearer the air is, now that man-made pollution has ceased! This freshly cleansed air is to our lungs as the air up there in the clouds is to the lungs of Birds. How light, how ethereal they must feel as they soar above the trees! For many ages, Birds have been linked to the freedom of the Spirit, as opposed to the heavy burden of Matter. Does not the Dove symbolize Grace, the all-forgiving, the all-accepting?

It is in the spirit of that Spirit of grace that we welcome among us three fellow Mortal companions on our journey – Melinda, Darren, and Quill. They have miraculously escaped the Waterless Flood by having been providentially sequestered: Melinda in a hilltop yoga and weight-loss establishment, Darren in a hospital isolation ward, and Quill in a place of solitary incarceration. We rejoice that these three appear not to have been exposed to viral contamination. Although not of our Faith – or not still of our Faith in the case of Quill and Melinda – they are our fellow Creatures; and we are happy to aid them at this common time of trial.

We are grateful also for this temporary abode, which, though it is a former Happicuppa franchise, has sheltered us from the grilling sun and the gruelling storm. Thanks to the skills of Stuart – in especial, his acquaintance with chisels – we have gained entrance to the storeroom, thereby procuring access to much Happicuppa product: the dried milk substitute, the vanilla-flavoured syrup, the moccachino mix, and the single-serving packets of sugar, both raw and white. You all know my view of refined sugar products, but there are times when the rules must bend. Thank you to Nuala, our indomitable Eve Nine, for the skill with which she has whipped up a sustaining brew for our refreshment.

We remember on this Day that the Happicuppa Corp was in direct contravention to the Spirit of Saint Rachel. Its sun-grown, pesticide-sprayed, rainforest-habitat-destroying coffee products were the biggest threat to God's feathered Creatures in our times, just as DDT was the biggest threat to them in the times of Saint Rachel Carson. It was in the Spirit of Saint Rachel that some of our more radical former members joined the militant campaign against Happicuppa. Other groups were protesting its treatment of indigenous workers, but those ex-Gardeners were protesting its anti-Bird policies. Although we could not condone the violent methods, we did endorse the intention.

Saint Rachel dedicated her life to the Feathered Ones, and thus to the welfare of the entire Planet – for as the Birds sickened and died out, did this not indicate the growing illness of Life itself? Imagine God's sorrow as he viewed the distress of His most exquisite and tuneful feathered Creations!

Saint Rachel was attacked by the powerful chemical corps of her day, and scorned and pilloried for her truth-telling, but her campaign did at last prevail. Sadly, the anti-Happicuppa campaign did not meet with equal success, but that problem has now been solved by a greater power: Happicuppa has not survived the Waterless Flood. As the Human Words of God put it, in Isaiah 34, "From generation to generation it shall lie waste. . . . But the Cormorant and the Bittern shall possess it. . . . There shall the great Owl make her nest, and lay, and hatch, and gather under her shadow; there shall the Vultures also be gathered, every one with her mate."

And so it has come to pass. Even now, my Friends, the rainforest must be regenerating!

Let us sing.

WHEN GOD SHALL HIS BRIGHT WINGS UNFOLD

When God shall His bright wings unfold
And fly from Heaven's blue,
He first will as a Dove appear
Of pure and sparkling hue.

Then next the Raven's form He'll take,
To show there's beauty too
In any Bird that He did make,
The oldest and the new.

He'll sail with Swans, with Hawks He'll glide,
With Cockatoo and Owl,
The chorus of the dawn He'll sing,
He'll dive with Waterfowl.

As Vulture He will next appear,
The Holy Bird of yore,
Who Death does eat, corruption too,
And thus does Life restore.

Under His wings we'll sheltered be:
From fowler's nets He'll save;
His Eye will note the Sparrow's fall,
And mark the Eagle's grave.

For those who Avian blood do shed
In idle sport and play
Are murderers of God's Holy Peace
That blessed the Seventh Day.

From *The God's Gardeners Oral Hymnbook*

68

REN. SAINT CHICO MENDES, MARTYR

YEAR TWENTY-FIVE

We walk through the shimmering meadow. There's a humming like a thousand tiny vibrators; huge pink butterflies float all around. The clover scent is very strong. Toby probes in front of her with her mop handle. I try to pay attention to where I'm putting my feet, but the ground is lumpy and I trip, and when I look down it's a boot. Beetles scurry out.

There's some animals up ahead. They weren't there a minute ago. I wonder if they were lying down in the grass and then stood up. I hang back, but Toby says, "It's okay, they're just Mo'Hairs."

I've never seen a live one before, only online. They stand there looking at us with their jaws moving sideways. "Would they let me pat them?" I say. They're blue and pink and silver and purple; they look like candy, or sunny-day clouds. So cheerful and peaceful.

"I doubt it," says Toby. "We need to walk faster."

"They're not afraid of us," I say.

"They should be," says Toby. "Come on. Let's go."

The Mo'Hairs watch us. When we're closer to them, they turn in a group and move slowly away.

At first Toby says we're going to the eastern gatehouse. Then after we walk for a while on the paved road, she says it's farther than she thought. I start to feel dizzy because it's so hot, especially inside the top-to-toe, so Toby says we'll head for the trees at the far side of the meadow because it will be cooler in there. I don't like the trees, it's too dark in there, but I know we can't stay out in the meadow.

It is shadier under the trees, but not cooler. It's dank, and there's no breeze, and the air is thick, as if it has more air stuffed into it than other air does. But at least we're out of the sun, so we take off our top-to-toes and walk along the pathway. There's that rich deep smell of rotting wood, the mushroomy smell I remember from the Gardeners, when we'd go to the Park for Saint Euell's. The vines have been moving in over the gravel, but a lot of the branches are broken back and stepped on, and Toby says that someone else has come this way; not today though, because the leaves have wilted.

There's crows up ahead, making a racket.

We come to a stream, with a little bridge. The water's rippling over stones, and I can see minnows in it. On the far bank there are signs of digging. Toby stands still, turns her head to listen. Then she crosses the bridge and looks at the hole that's been dug. "Gardeners," she says, "or someone smart."

The Gardeners taught that you should never drink right from a stream, especially one near a city: you should make a hole beside it, so the water would be filtered at least a little. Toby has an empty bottle, the one we've been drinking from. She fills it from the water hole so only the top layer of water runs into the bottle: she doesn't want any drowned worms.

Up ahead, off in a small clearing, there's a patch of mushrooms. Toby says they're Sweet Tooth – hydnum repandum – and they used to be a fall variety, when we still had fall. We pick them, and Toby puts them into one of the cloth bags she's brought, and hangs the bag outside her pack so the mushrooms won't get squashed. Then we continue on.

We smell the thing before we see it. "Don't scream," says Toby.

This is what the crows have been cawing about. "Oh no," I whisper.

It's Oates. He's hanging from a tree, twisting slowly. The rope is passed under his arms and knotted at the back. He doesn't have any clothes on except for his socks and shoes. This makes it worse, because he's less like a statue that way. His head is thrown back, too far because his throat has been cut; crows flap around his head, scrabbling for footholds. His blond hair's all matted. There's a gaping wound in his back, like those on the bodies they used to dump in vacant lots after a kidney theft. But these kidneys wouldn't have been stolen for transplants.

"Somebody has a very sharp knife," says Toby.

I'm crying now. "They killed little Oatie," I say. "I feel sick." I crumple down onto the ground. Right now I don't care if I die here: I don't want to be in a world where they'd do this to Oates. It's so unfair. I'm gulping air in huge gasps, crying so hard I can barely see.

Toby takes hold of my shoulders, and pulls me up, and shakes me. "Stop that," she says. "We don't have time for it. Now come on." She pushes me ahead of her along the path.

"Can't we at least cut him down?" I manage to say. "And bury him?"

"We'll do that later," says Toby. "But he's not in his body any more. He's in Spirit now. Shhh, it's okay." She stops and puts her arms around me and rocks me to and fro, then pushes me gently forward again. We need to reach the gatehouse before the afternoon thunderstorm, she says, and the clouds are moving in fast from the south and west.

69

TOBY. SAINT CHICO MENDES, MARTYR

YEAR TWENTY-FIVE

Toby feels bludgeoned – that was brutal, it was horrifying – but she can't show her feelings to Ren. The Gardeners would have encouraged mourning – within limits – as part of the healing process, but there isn't the space for it now. The storm clouds are yellowy green, the lightning's ferocious: she suspects a twister. "Hurry," she says to Ren. "Unless you want to be blown away." For the last fifty metres they hold hands and run, heads down, into the wind.

The gatehouse is retro Tex-Mex, with rounded lines and pink adobe-style solarskin: all it lacks is a chapel tower and some bells. Already there's kudzu clambering up the walls. The wrought-iron gate is standing open. In the ornamental garden with its ring of whitewashed stones – WELCOME TO ANOOYOO spelled out in petunias, but now invaded by purslane and sow thistles – something has been rooting. The pigs, most likely.

"There's some legs," says Ren. "Over there by the gate." Her teeth are chattering: she's still in shock.

"Legs?" says Toby. She feels affronted: how many demi-bodies does she have to encounter in one day? She goes over to the gate to look. The legs aren't human, they're Mo'Hair legs – a complete set of four; just the lower legs, the skinny parts. A little hair still on them, lavender in colour. There's a head as well, though not a Mo'Hair head: it's the head of a liobam, the golden fur scruffy, the eye sockets empty and crusted. The tongue's gone, as well. Liobam tongue, once an expensive gourmet feature at Rarity.

Toby walks back to where Ren stands quivering, hands to her mouth.

"They're Mo'Hair," she says. "I'll make them into soup. With our nice mushrooms."

"Oh, I can't eat anything," says Ren in a doleful voice. "He was just a – he was a boy. I used to carry him around." The tears are rolling down her cheeks. "Why did they do that?"

"You have to eat," says Toby. "It's your duty." Duty to what? she wonders. Your body is a gift from God and you must honour that gift, said Adam One. But right now she feels no such conviction.

The gatehouse door is open. She looks through the window into the reception area – nobody – and propels Ren inside: the storm's coming fast. She flicks a light switch: no power. There's the usual bulletproof check-in window, a blank-faced document scanner, the fingerscan and iris cameras. You'd stand there knowing that you had five wall-mounted sprayguns pointed at your back and controlled from the inside room where the guards used to slouch.

She shines her flashlight through the counter window into the darkness of the inner space. Desks, filing cabinets, trash. Over in the corner, a shape: large enough to be someone. Someone dead, someone asleep, or – worst case – someone who's heard them coming and is pretending to be a garbage bag. Then, once they're at ease, there'd be some sneaking up and baring of canines, some slashing and rending.

The door to the inner room's ajar: she sniffs the air. Mildew, of course. What else? Excrement. Decaying meat. Other noxious undertones. She wishes she had the nose of a dog, to sort one smell from another.

She pulls the door closed. Then she goes outside despite the rain and wind and hauls in the biggest stone from the ornamental flower-garden border. Not enough to stop a strong person, but it might slow down someone weak, or ill. She doesn't wish to be leapt on from behind by a carnivorous mound of tatters.

"Why are you doing that?" says Ren.

"Just in case," says Toby. She doesn't elaborate. Ren is shaky enough as it is: one more horror and she could collapse.

The full force of the storm hits. A thicker darkness howls around them; thunder hollows out the air. In the lightning, Ren's face comes and goes, her eyes closed, her mouth a frightened O. She clutches Toby's arm as if about to topple from a cliff.

After what seems like a long time, the thunder trundles away. Toby goes outside to inspect the Mo'Hair legs. Her skin's prickling: those legs didn't walk there by themselves, and they're still quite fresh. No sign of a fire: whoever killed the animal didn't cook the rest here. She notes the cut marks: Mister Sharp Knife has passed this way. How close might he be?

She looks both ways along the road, strewn now with ripped-off leaves. No movement. The sun's back now. Steam rises. Crows in the distance.

She uses her own knife to scrape much of the hairy skin from one of the Mo'Hair legs. If she had a large cleaver she could hack it into pieces small enough for her cooking pot. Finally she places one end on the top of the step leading up to the gatehouse and the other on the pavement and hits it with a rock. Now there's the problem of a fire. She could spend a long time rummaging among the trees for dry wood and still come up empty-handed. "I need to go through that door," she says to Ren.

"Why?" says Ren weakly. She's huddled in the empty front room.

"There's stuff we can burn," says Toby. "To make a fire. Now listen. There might be someone in there."

"A dead person?"

"I don't know," says Toby.

"I don't want any more dead people," says Ren fretfully. There may not be much choice about that, thinks Toby.

"Here's the rifle," she says. "This is the trigger. I want you to stand right here. If anyone but me comes out that door, shoot. Don't hit me by mistake. Okay?" If she herself gets whacked in there, at least Ren will have a weapon.

"Okay," says Ren. She takes the rifle awkwardly. "But I don't like it."

This is crazy, Toby thinks. She's jumpy enough to shoot me in the back if I sneeze. But if I don't check that room out, no sleep tonight and maybe a slit throat in the morning. And no fire.

She goes in with her flashlight and her mop handle. Papers litter the floor, smashed lamps. There's broken glass, crunching underfoot. The smell is stronger now. Flies buzzing. The hairs on her arms lift, the blood rushes in her head.

The bundle on the floor is definitely human, covered with some sort of gruesome blanket. Now she can see the dome of a bald head, some wisps of hair. She pokes at the blanket with the mop handle, keeping the beam of light on the bundle. A moan. She pokes again, harder: there's a feeble twitching of cloth. Now there are the slits of eyes, and a mouth, lips crusted and blistered.

"Fuckin' hell," says the mouth. "Who in fuck are you?"

"Are you sick?" says Toby.

"Asshole shot me," says the man. His eyes are blinking in the light. "Turn that fuckin' thing off." No sign of blood leaking out of his nose or mouth or eyes: with any luck, he doesn't have the plague.

"Shot you where?" says Toby. The bullet must have been hers, from that time in the meadow. A hand scrabbles forth: red and blue veins. Although he's shrivelled and filthy, his eyes sunken with fever, this is Blanco, no doubt of it. She ought to know, she's had the close-up view.

"Leg," he says. "Went bad on me. Fuckers dumped me here."

"Two of them?" says Toby. "Did they have a woman with them?" She makes her voice level.

"Gimme some water," says Blanco. There's an empty bottle in the corner, near his head. Two bottles, three. Gnawed ribs: the lavender Mo'Hair? "Who else is out there?" he rasps. His breath's coming hard. "More bitches. I heard more."

"Let me see your leg," says Toby. "I may be able to help." He won't be the first person ever to have shammed injury.

"I'm fuckin' dying," says Blanco. "Turn off that light!" Toby sees various courses of action rippling across his forehead in waves of little frowns. Does he know who she is? Will he try to jump her?

"Take the blanket off," says Toby, "and I'll get you some water."

"Take it off yourself," croaks Blanco.

"No," says Toby. "If you don't want help I'll just lock you in."

"Lock's broken," he says. "Asshole skinny bitch! Gimme some water!"

Toby pinpoints the other smell: whatever else is wrong with him, he's decaying. "I've got a Zizzy Froot," she says. "You'll like that better." She backs out through the door and closes it behind her, but not before Ren's had a look.

"It's him," she whispers. "The third one, the worst one!"

"Take a deep breath," says Toby. "You're perfectly safe. You've got the rifle, he doesn't. Just keep it pointed at that door."

She digs into her packsack, finds the remaining Zizzy Froot, drinks a quarter of the warm, sugary, fizzy liquid: *Waste not.* Then she fills the bottle up with Poppy and adds a generous dollop of powdered amanitas for good measure. The white Death Angel, granter of dark wishes. If there's two bad choices take the lesser evil, Zeb would say.

She pushes the door open with her mop handle and shines the flashlight in. Sure enough Blanco is shoving himself across the floor, grinning with the effort. In one hand is his knife: most likely he was hoping to get near enough so he could grab her by the ankles when she went in. Take her down with him, or use her as a bargaining chip to get hold of Ren.

Mad dogs bite. What else is there to know?

"Here you are," she says. She rolls the bottle towards him. His knife falls with a clink as he grabs for the bottle, unscrews it with shaking hands, guzzles. Toby waits to make sure it all goes down. "Now you'll feel better," she says gently. She closes the door.

"He'll get out!" says Ren. She's ashen.

"If he gets out, we'll shoot him," says Toby. "I've given him some painkillers to calm him down." Silently she says the words of apology and release, the same as she would for a beetle.

She waits until the Poppy has taken hold, then re-enters the room. Blanco's snoring heavily: if the Poppy doesn't finish him, the Death

Angels will. She lifts the blanket: his left thigh is a mess – decaying cloth and decaying flesh all simmering together. It takes a lot of self-restraint for her not to throw up.

Then she sorts through the room for flammables, gathering what she can – paper, some remnants of a smashed chair, a stack of CDs. There's a second floor, but Blanco's blocking the door to what must be the stairway and she's not ready to get that close to him yet. She searches under the trees for dead branches: with the barbecue lighter and the paper and the CDs, they catch eventually. She makes bone soup with the Mo'Hair leg, adding the mushrooms and some purslane from the flower bed; they eat it sitting in the smoke of the fire, because of the mosquitoes.

They sleep on the flat roof, using a tree to climb up. Toby drags the packsacks up too, and the other three Mo'Hair legs, so nothing can steal them during the night. The rooftop's pebbly, and wet as well: they lie on the two sheets of plastic. The stars are brighter than bright; the moon's invisible. Just before they go to sleep, Ren whispers, "What if he wakes up?"

"He'll never wake up," says Toby.

"Oh," says Ren in a tiny voice. Is that admiration of Toby, or simply awe in the face of death? He wouldn't have lived, Toby tells herself, not with a leg as bad as that. Attempting to treat it would have been a waste of maggots. Still, she's just committed a murder. Or an act of mercy: at least he didn't die thirsty.

Don't kid yourself, babe, says the voice of Zeb in her head. You had vengeance in mind.

"May his Spirit go in peace," she says out loud. Such as it is, the fuck-pig.

70

TOBY. SAINT RACHEL AND ALL BIRDS

YEAR TWENTY-FIVE

Toby wakes just before dawn. In the distance there's a liobam, its odd plaintive roar. Dogs barking. She moves her arms, then her legs: she's stiff as a slab of cement. The dampness of the mist goes right into the marrow.

Here comes the sun, a hot rose lifting out of peach-coloured clouds. The leaves on the overhanging trees are covered with tiny droplets that shine in the strengthening pink light. Everything looks so fresh, as if newly created: the stones on the rooftop, the trees, the spiderwebbing slung from branch to branch. Sleeping Ren seems luminous, as if silvered all over. With the pink top-to-toe tucked around her oval face and the mist beading her long eyelashes, she's frail and otherworldly, as if made of snow.

The light hits Ren directly, and her eyes open. "Oh shit, oh shit," she says. "I'm late! What time is it?"

"You're not late for anything," says Toby, and for some reason both of them laugh.

Toby scouts with the binoculars. To the east, where they'll be going, there's no movement, but to the west there's a group of pigs, the biggest gathering of them she's seen to date – six adults, two young. They're strung out along the roadside like round flesh pearls on a necklace; they have their snouts down, snuffling along as if they're tracking.

Tracking us, thinks Toby. Maybe they're the same pigs: the grudge-bearing pigs, the funeral-holding pigs. She stands up, waves the rifle in the air, shouts at them: "Go away! Piss off!" At first they just stare, but when she brings the rifle down and aims it at them they lollop off into the trees.

"It's almost like they know what a rifle is," says Ren. She's a lot steadier this morning. Stronger.

"Oh, they know," says Toby.

They clamber down the tree, and Toby lights the Kelly kettle. Although there's no sign of anyone around, she doesn't want to risk making a bigger fire. She's worried about the smoke – will anyone smell it? Zeb's rule was: Animals shun fire, humans are drawn to it.

Once the water has boiled she makes tea. Then she parboils more of the purslane. That will warm them up enough for their early walking. Later they can have more Mo'Hair soup, from the three legs remaining.

Before they leave, Toby checks the gatehouse room. Blanco's cold; he smells even worse, if that's possible. She rolls him onto the blanket and drags him out to the rooted-up earth of the flower bed. Then she finds his knife on the floor where he dropped it. It's sharp as a razor; with it she slits his filthy shirt up the front. Hairy fishbelly. If she was being thorough, she'd open him up – the vultures would thank her – but she remembers the sickening reek of innards from the dead boar. The pigs will take care of it. Maybe they'll view Blanco as an atonement offering to them and forgive her for shooting their fellow pig. She leaves the knife among the flowers. Good tool, but bad karma.

She heaves the wrought-iron gate shut behind them; the electronic lock's non-functional, so she uses some of her rope to tie it shut. If the pigs decide to follow, the gate won't deter them for long – they can dig under – but it may give them pause.

Now she and Ren are outside the AnooYoo grounds, walking along the weed-bordered road that leads through the Heritage Park. They come to some picnic-table clearings; the kudzu is crawling over the trash barrels and barbecues, the tables and benches. In the sunlight, which is hotter by the minute, butterflies waft and spiral.

Toby takes her bearings: downhill, to the east, must be the shore and then the sea. To the southwest, the Arboretum, with the creek where the Gardener children used to launch their miniature Arks. The road leading to the SolarSpace entrance ought to join in somewhere around here. Nearby is where they'd buried Pilar: sure enough, there's her Elderberry, quite tall now, and in flower. Bees buzz around it.

Dear Pilar, thinks Toby. If you were here today you'd have something wise to tell us. What would it be?

Up ahead they hear bleating, and five – no, nine – no, fourteen Mo'Hairs scramble up the bank and out onto the road. Silver, blue, purple, black, a red one with its hair in many braids – and now there's a man. A man in a white bedsheet, belted around the waist. It's a biblical getup: he even has a long staff, for sheep-prodding no doubt. When he sees them he stops and turns, watching them quietly. He's got sunglasses on; he's also got a spraygun. He holds it casually by his side, but lets it be clearly seen. The sun's behind him.

Toby stands still, her scalp and arms tingling. Is this one of the Painballers? He'd turn her into a sieve before she could even get the rifle aimed: the sun's in his favour.

"It's Croze!" says Ren. She runs towards him with her arms outstretched, and Toby certainly hopes she's right. But she must be, because the man lets her throw her arms around him. He drops his spraygun and his staff on the ground and clutches Ren tightly, while the Mo'Hairs amble about munching flowers.

71

REN. SAINT RACHEL AND ALL BIRDS

YEAR TWENTY-FIVE

"Croze!" I say. "I can't believe it! I thought you were dead!" I'm talking into his bedsheet because we're holding on so tight I'm smushed up against him. He doesn't say anything – maybe he's crying – so I say, "I bet you thought I was dead too," and I feel him nod.

I let go and we look at each other. He tries a grin. "Where'd you get the bedsheet?" I say.

"There's a lot of beds around," he says. "These things are better than pants, you don't get so hot. Did you see Oates?" He sounds worried.

I don't know what to say. I don't want to spoil this time by telling him about something so unhappy. Poor Oates, hanging in a tree with his throat cut and his kidneys missing. But then I look at his face and realize I've misunderstood: it's me he's worried about, because he already knows about Oates. He and Shackie were up ahead of us on the path. They'd have heard me shout, they'd have hidden. Then they would have heard the screaming, all sorts of screaming. Then, later – because of course they would have come back to check – they would have heard the crows.

If I say no, he'll most likely pretend that Oates is still alive, so as not to upset me. "Yes," I say. "We did see him. I'm sorry."

He looks at the ground. I think of how I can change the subject. The Mo'Hairs have been nibbling all around us – they want to stay close to Croze – so I say, "Are those your sheep?"

"We've started herding them," he says. "We've got them kind of tamed. But they keep getting out." Who is *we*, I'd like to ask; but Toby comes up, so I say, "This is Toby, remember?" and Croze says, "No shit! From the Gardeners?"

Toby gives him one of her dry little nods and says, "Crozier. You've certainly grown," as if it's a school reunion. It's hard to throw her off balance. She sticks out her hand and Croze shakes it. It's so strange – Croze in a bedsheet, looking like Jesus though his beard isn't exactly flowing, and Toby and me in our pink outfits with the winking eyes and lipstick mouths; and Toby with three purple Mo'Hair legs sticking up out of her packsack.

"Where's Amanda?" he says.

"She's not dead," I say too quickly. "I just know she isn't." He and Toby trade a look over my head, as if they don't want to tell me my pet bunny got run over. "What about Shackleton?" I say, and Croze says, "He's okay. Let's go back to the place."

"What place?" says Toby, and he says, "The cobb house. Where we used to have the Tree of Life Exchange. Remember?" he says to me. "It's not too far."

The sheep are heading that way anyway. They seem to know where they're going. We follow along behind them.

The sun's so hot by now that it's boiling inside our top-to-toes. Croze has part of his bedsheet draped over his head; he looks a lot cooler than me.

It's noon when we reach the old Tree of Life parkette. The plastic swings are gone, but the cobb house is the same – even the spraypainted pleeb tags are there – except they've been building onto it. There's a fence made of poles and planks and wire and a lot of duct tape. Croze opens the gate, and the sheep go in and file towards a pen in the yard.

"I got the sheep," Croze calls, and a man with a spraygun comes out through the house door, and then two more men. Then four women – two young, one a bit older, and an older one, maybe as old as Toby. Their clothes aren't Gardener clothes, but they aren't new and they aren't pretty. Two of the men are wearing bedsheets, the third has cut-offs and a shirt. The women have long cover-ups, like top-to-toes.

They stare at us. Not friendly: anxious. Croze says our names. "You sure they're not infected?" says the first man, the one with the spraygun.

"No way," says Croze. "They were isolated the whole time." He looks at us for confirmation, and Toby nods. "Friends of Zeb," Croze adds. "Toby and Ren." Then he tells us, "This is MaddAddam."

"What's left of us," says the shortest man. He says their names: his is Beluga, and the other three are Ivory Bill, Manatee, and Zunzuncito. The women are Lotis Blue, Swift Fox, White Sedge, and Tamaraw. We don't shake hands: they're still nervous about us and our germs.

"MaddAddam," says Toby. "Good to meet you. I followed some of your work online."

"How'd you get in?" Ivory Bill says to Toby. "To the playroom?" He's eyeing her antique rifle as if it's made of gold.

"I was Inaccessible Rail," says Toby.

They look at one another. "You," says Lotis Blue. "You were Inaccessible! The secret lady!" She laughs. "Zeb would never tell us who you were. We thought you were some hot bimbo he had." Toby gives her a thin little smile.

"He said you were solid, though," says Tamaraw. "He insisted on that."

"Zeb?" says Toby, as if she's talking to herself. I know she wants to ask if he's still alive, but she's afraid to.

"MaddAddam was a great caper," says Beluga. "Until we got snatched."

"So-called drafted by fucking ReJoov," says White Sedge, the youngest woman. "Crake, that little bastard." She's brown-skinned but she has kind of an English accent, so it comes out *bahstahd*. They're a lot friendlier now that Toby's told them she was really somebody else.

I'm confused. I look up at Croze, and he says, "It was that thing we were doing, the bioresistance thing. Why they put us in Painball. These are the scientists they scooped. Remember I told you? At Scales?"

"Oh," I say. But I'm still not clear. Why did ReJoov scoop them? Was it a brain kidnapping, like what happened to my father?

"We had visitors," Ivory Bill says to Croze. "After you went for the sheep. Two guys, with a woman and a spraygun and a dead rakunk."

"Really," says Croze. "That's major."

"Said they were Painball, like we should respect that," says Beluga. "They wanted to trade the woman for spraygun cells and Mo'Hair meat – the woman and the rakunk."

"I bet it was them got our purple Mo'Hair," says Croze. "Toby found the legs."

"Rakunk! Why would we trade for that?" says White Sedge indignantly. "We're not stahving!"

"We should've shot them," says Manatee. "But they were holding the woman in front."

"What was she wearing?" I say, but they ignore me.

"We said no trade," says Ivory Bill. "Tough for the girl. But they're desperate for cells, which means they're running out. So we'll deal with them later."

"It's Amanda," I say. They could have saved her. Though I don't blame them for not trading: you can't give spraycells to guys who'll use them to kill you. "What about Amanda?" I say. "Shouldn't we go and get her?"

"Yeah – we need to get everyone together now that the Flood's over," says Croze. "Like we've said." He's backing me up.

"Then we can, you know, rebuild the human race," I say. I know it sounds stupid, but it's the only thing I can think of. "Amanda could really help us – she's so good at everything." But they just smile at me sadly as if they know it's hopeless.

Croze takes my hand and walks me away from them. "You mean that?" he says. "About the human race?" He smiles. "You'll have to have babies."

"Maybe not just yet," I say.

"Come on," he says. "I'll show you the garden."

They have a cookhouse, and some violet porta-biolets over in one corner, and some solar they're fixing up. There's no shortage of parts for just about everything back in the pleebs, though you have to look out for falling buildings.

Their vegetable garden is in behind: they don't have a lot of stuff planted yet. "We get pig attacks," he says. "They dig under the fence. We shot one of them, so maybe the others got the point. Zeb says they're superpigs, because they're spliced with human brain tissue."

"Zeb?" I say. "Is Zeb alive?" I feel dizzy all of a sudden. All of these dead people, coming alive again – it's overwhelming.

"Sure," says Croze. "Are you all right?" He puts his arm around me, to keep me from falling down.

72

TOBY. SAINT RACHEL AND ALL BIRDS

YEAR TWENTY-FIVE

Ren and Crozier have wandered off behind the cobb house. No harm, thinks Toby. Young love, no doubt. She's telling Ivory Bill about the third man – the dead one. Blanco. He listens carefully. "Plague?" he asks. An infected bullet wound, she says. She doesn't add the Poppy and the Death Angels.

While they're talking, another woman comes around from behind the house. "Hey, Toby," she says. It's Rebecca. Older, less plump, but still Rebecca. Solid. She takes hold of Toby's shoulders. "You're too thin, sweetheart," she says. "Never mind. We've got bacon. Fatten you up for sure."

Bacon is not a concept that Toby can grasp right now. "Rebecca," she says. She wants to add, "Why are you alive?" but this is – increasingly – a meaningless question. Why are any of them alive? So she merely says, "Wonderful."

"Zeb said you'd make it. He always said that. Hey. Gimme a smile!"

Toby doesn't like the past tense. It has a deathbed smell. "When did he say it?" she asks.

"Heck, he says it most days. Now come on in the kitchen, eat something. Tell me where you've been."

Zeb's alive then, thinks Toby. Now that it's true she feels she's always known it. She also doubts it – it won't really be true until she sees him. Touches him.

They have coffee – dandelion roots, roasted, Rebecca says proudly – and some baked burdock root with herbs, and a slice of – could it be cold pork? "Those pigs are a nuisance," says Rebecca. "Too smart by half." She eyes Toby challengingly. "Needs must when the devil drives," she says. "Anyways, at least we know what's in it – not like at SecretBurgers."

"It's delicious," Toby says truthfully.

After their snack, Toby hands over the three remaining Mo'Hair legs, not that fresh but Rebecca says they'll be fine for stock. Then they plunge right into history. Toby runs through her time in the AnooYoo Spa, and tells about the arrival of Ren; Rebecca describes her fake identity selling life insurance in gated communities out west while planting MaddAddam's inventive bioforms, and how she got the last bullet train east – a risk, lot of folks coughing but she wore a nose cone and gloves – and then holed up in the Wellness Clinic, along with Zeb and Katuro. "In our old meeting room, remember?" she says. "Our Ararat supplies were still there."

"And Katuro?" says Toby.

"Doing fine. Had a germ of some kind, but not the bad one; he's over it now. He's off with Zeb and Shackleton, and Black Rhino. They're looking for Adam One and the rest of them. Zeb says if anyone could get through, they could."

"Really? There's a chance?" says Toby. *Did he look for me?* she wants to ask. Probably not. He'd have thought she'd do fine on her own. And she had, hadn't she?

"We've been listening on the windup shortwave, 24/7, and sending too. Couple of days ago we finally got an answer," says Rebecca.

"It was him?" Toby's prepared to believe anything now. "Adam One?"

"We just heard the one voice. All it said was, 'I'm here, I'm here.'"

"Let's hope," says Toby. And she does hope; or she tries to.

There's the barking of dogs outside, and a confusion of shouting. "Shit. Dog attack," says Rebecca. "Bring that gun."

The MaddAddams with sprayguns are already at the fence. Big dogs and small ones, maybe fifteen, bounding towards them wagging their tails. The spraygunners begin shooting. Before Toby can fire, seven of the dogs are dead and the rest have run away.

"Watson-Crick splices," says Ivory Bill. "They're not really dogs, they only look like it. They'll tear out your throat. Used them in prison moats and such – you couldn't hack them, not like an alarm system code – but they got loose during the Flood."

"Are they breeding?" says Toby. Will they have to fight off wave after wave of these non-dogs, or are they few in number?

"Lord knows," says Ivory Bill.

Lotis Blue and White Sedge go out to make sure the dogs are dead. Then Tamaraw and Swift Fox and Rebecca and Toby join them, and they skin and butcher, with the spraygunners standing guard in case the other dogs come back. Toby's hands remember how to do this from long ago. The smell is the same too. A childhood smell.

The dog skins are laid aside, the meat's cut up and put into a pot. Toby feels a little sick. But she also feels hungry.

73

REN. SAINT RACHEL AND ALL BIRDS

YEAR TWENTY-FIVE

I ask Croze if I should be helping to skin the dogs, but Croze says there's enough people doing it and I look tired, so why don't I lie down on his bed, inside the cobb house? The room is cool and smells the cobb-house way I remember, so I feel safe. Croze's bed is just a platform, but it has a silver Mo'Hair fleece on it with a sheet, and Croze says, Sleep tight and then goes away, and I take off my AnooYoo top and pants because it's getting too hot, and the Mo'Hair is soft and silky, and I go to sleep.

When the afternoon thunderstorm wakes me up, Croze is curled around behind me, and I can tell he's worried and sad; so I turn around and then we're hugging each other, and he wants to have sex. But all of a sudden I don't want to have sex without loving the person, and I haven't really loved anybody in that way since Jimmy; certainly not at Scales, where it was just acting, with other people's kinky scripts.

Also there's a dark place in me, like ink spilled into my brain – I can't think about sex, in that place. It has brambles in it, and something about Amanda, and I don't want to be there. So I say, "Not yet." And even though Croze used to be kind of crude he seems to understand, so we just hold on to each other and talk.

He's full of plans. They'll build this, they'll build that; they'll get rid of the pigs, or else tame them. After the two Painballers are dead – he personally will take care of that – he'll take me, and Amanda and Shackie too, and we'll all go down to the beach and do some fishing. As for the MaddAddam group – Bill and Sedge and Tamaraw and Rhino, all them – they're really smart, so they'll have the communications going in no time.

"Who are we going to communicate with?" I ask, and Croze says there must be others out there. Then he tells me about the MaddAddams – how they were working with Zeb, but then the CorpSeCorps tracked them down through a MaddAddam codenamed Crake, and they ended up as brain slaves in a place called the Paradice Project dome. It was a choice between that and being spraygunned, so they took the jobs. Then when the Flood came and the guards vanished, they deactivated the security and walked out, but that wasn't too hard for them because they're all brainiacs.

He's told me some of this before, but he hasn't said *Paradice Project* or *Crake*. "Just a minute," I say. "That's what they were working on inside the dome? Immortality?"

Yes, Croze says: they were all helping Crake with his big experiment: some kind of perfectly beautiful human gene splice that could live forever. They were the ones who'd done the heavy lifting on the BlyssPluss pill too, but they weren't allowed to take it themselves. Not that they were tempted: it gave you the best sex ever, but it had serious side effects, such as death.

"That's how the pandemic plague got started," Croze says. "They said Crake ordered them to put it in the supersex pill." I felt lucky all over again that I'd been in the Sticky Zone because I might've gulped down the BlyssPluss pill secretly even though Mordis said no drugs for Scalies. It sounded so great, like a whole other reality.

"Who'd do a thing like that?" I say. "A poison sex pill?" It was Glenn, it must have been. That's the sort of stuff he was telling the ReJoov Mr. Bigs, at Scales. He didn't tell about the poison part, of course. I remembered those nicknames, Oryx and Crake. I'd thought it was just sex talk, with Glenn and his main plank: a lot of people used animal names at such times. Panther and Tiger and Wolverine, Pussycat and Doggie-wog. So, not sex talk: codenames. Or maybe both.

For one split second I think about saying all this to Croze – how I know quite a lot about this Crake from a former life. But then I'd have to tell about what I used to do at Scales – not just the trapeze dancing or even Glenn making us purr and sing like birds, but the other things, the feather-ceiling room things. Croze wouldn't want to hear about that: guys hate to picture other guys doing sex things with you that they want to do themselves.

So instead I ask, "What about the splice people? The perfect ones? Did they actually make them?" Glenn always wanted everything to be more perfect.

"Yeah, they made them," says Croze, as if it's an everyday thing, making people.

"I guess those people died along with everyone else," I say.

"Nope," says Croze. "They're living down by the shore. They don't need clothes, they eat leaves, they purr like cats. Not my idea of perfect." He laughs. "Perfect is more like you!"

I let that go by. "You're making this up," I say.

"No, I swear," says Croze. "They get these huge – their dicks turn blue. Then they have group sex with these blue-assed women. It's wicked!"

"It's a joke, right?" I say.

"Seen them myself," says Croze. "We aren't supposed to go near them in case we mess them up. But Zeb says we can look at them from a distance, like the zoo. He says they're not dangerous – it's us that's dangerous to them."

"When can I see them?"

"Once we take care of those Painballers," says Croze. "I'd have to go with you, though. There's another guy down there – sleeps in a tree, talks to himself, crazy as a bag of snakes, no offence to snakes. We leave him alone – figure he might be infected. I wouldn't want him bothering you."

"Thanks," I say. "This Crake, in the Paradice Project dome. What did he look like?"

"Never saw him," says Croze. "Nobody said."

"Did he have a friend?" I asked. "Inside the dome thing?" When Glenn brought Jimmy to Scales that time, they were definitely into something together.

"Rhino says he wasn't much on friends. But he did have some pal of his in there, plus his girlfriend – the two of them were supposed to be planning the marketing. Rhino says the guy was a waste of time. Told a lot of stupid jokes, drank too much."

That would be Jimmy all right, I thought. "Did he make it out?" I say. "Out of the dome? With the blue people?"

"How would I know? Anyway, who gives a shit?" says Croze.

I do. I don't want Jimmy to be dead. "That's kind of harsh," I say.

"Hey, be cool," says Croze. He puts his arm around me, lets his hand fall onto my breast, as if by accident. I take it off. "Okay," he says in a disappointed voice. He kisses my ear.

The next thing I know Croze is waking me up. "They're back," he says. He hurries out and I put my clothes on, and when I go outside Zeb is there in the yard, and Toby's got her arms around him. Katuro's there; and the man they call Black Rhino, who's even kind of black. Shackie's there too, grinning over at me. He hasn't heard yet about the two Painballers and Amanda. Croze will have to tell him. If I do he'll ask me questions, and I only have bad answers.

I go slowly over to Zeb – I'm feeling shy – and Toby lets go of him. She's smiling – not a thin smile, a real one – and I think, *She can still be pretty sometimes.* "Little Ren. You grew up," Zeb says to me. He's greyer than the last time I saw him. He smiles, and squeezes my shoulder briefly. I remember him singing in our shower, back at the Gardeners; I remember the times he was nice to me. I'd like him to be proud of me for making it through, even though that part was mostly luck. I'd like him to be more surprised and happy that I'm alive. But he must have a lot on his mind.

Zeb and Shackie and Black Rhino have sprayguns and packsacks, and now they start opening up the packsacks and taking things out. Tins of soydines, a couple of bottles – looks like booze – a handful of Joltbars. Three cellpacks, for the sprayguns.

"From Compounds," Katuro says. "Gates open on a lot of them. Looters have been through."

"CryoJeenyus was locked up tight," says Zeb. "Guess they thought they could tough it out inside."

"Them and all the frozen heads they had in there," says Shackie.

"I doubt anyone got out," says Black Rhino. I'm sorry to hear that, because Lucerne must have been inside that Compound, and despite how she acted later, she was my mother once, and I used to love her. I look over at Zeb, because maybe he did too.

"You find Adam One?" says Ivory Bill.

Zeb shakes his head. "We looked in the Buenavista," Zeb says. "They must've been there for some time – them, or someone. There were all the signs. Then we tried a few more Ararats, but nothing. They must have moved on."

"Did you tell him someone was living in the Wellness Clinic?" I say to Croze. "In that little room in behind the vinegar barrels? With the laptop?"

"Yeah, I did," says Croze. "It was him. And Rebecca and Katuro."

"We did see that crazy guy, limping along and talking to himself," says Shackie. "The one who sleeps in a tree, down by the shore. He didn't see us, though."

"You didn't shoot him?" says Ivory Bill. "In case he's catching?"

"Why waste the ammo?" says Black Rhino. "He won't last long."

When the sun's low we make a fire outside in the yard and have nettle soup with chunks of meat in it – I'm not sure what kind – and burdock, and some Mo'Hair-milk cheese. I'm expecting them to begin the meal with "Dear Friends, we are the only people left on Earth, let us give thanks" or some Gardener thing like that, but they don't; we just have the dinner.

After we've finished, they talk about what to do next. Zeb says they have to find Adam One and the Gardeners before anything or anyone else gets to them. He'll go to the Sinkhole tomorrow to check out the Edencliff Rooftop and some of the Truffle safe houses, and other places they might've gone. Shackie says he'll go with him, and Black Rhino and Katuro say the same. The others need to stay and defend the cobb house against the dogs and pigs, and also the two Painballers in case they come back.

Then Ivory Bill tells Zeb about Toby and how Blanco's dead now, and Zeb looks at Toby and says, "Well done, babe." It's kind of shocking to hear Toby called a babe: sort of like calling God a studmuffin.

I work up my courage and say we need to find Amanda and get her away from the Painballers. Shackie says he'll vote for that, and I think he means it. Zeb says he's very sorry, but we have to understand that it's an either/or choice. Amanda's just one person and Adam One and the Gardeners are many; and if it was Amanda, she'd decide the same thing. Then I say, "Okay, I'll go alone then," and Zeb says, "Don't be silly," as if I'm still eleven.

Then Croze says he'll go with me, and I squeeze his hand for thank you. But Zeb says he's needed at the cobb house, they can't do without him. If I wait until he and Shackie and Rhino and Katuro get back, he says, they'll send three guys with me, with sprayguns, which will give us a much better chance.

But I say there isn't enough time, because if those Painballers want to trade Amanda, it means they're tired of her and they could kill her at any minute. I know how it works, I say. It's like Scales, with the temporaries – she's a disposable – so I really have to find her right now, and I know it's dangerous, but I don't care. Then I start crying.

Nobody says anything. Then Toby says she'll go with me. She'll take her own rifle – she's not a bad shot, she says. Maybe the Painballers have used up their last spraygun cell, which would lengthen the odds.

Zeb says, "That's not such a good idea." Toby pauses, then says it's the best idea she can come up with because she can't let me wander off into the woods by myself: it would be like murder. And Zeb nods and says, "Be very careful." So it's settled.

The MaddAddams hang up some duct-tape hammocks in the main room for Toby and me. Toby's still talking with Zeb and the rest of them, so I go to bed first. With a Mo'Hair rug the hammock's quite comfortable; and though I'm worrying a lot about how to find Amanda and what will happen then, I finally manage to sleep.

When we get up the next morning, Zeb and Shackie and Katuro and Black Rhino have already left, but Rebecca tells Toby that Zeb's drawn a map for her in the sand of the old kids' sandbox, with the cobb house and the shore marked on it, so she'll know the directions. Toby studies it for a long time with an odd expression on her face – a sad kind of smile. But maybe she's just memorizing it. Then she wipes it away.

After breakfast Rebecca gives us some dried meat, and Ivory Bill gets two lighter hammocks for us because it's not safe to sleep on the ground, and we refill our water bottles from the well they've dug. Toby leaves a bunch of stuff behind – her bottles of Poppy, her mushrooms, her maggot container, all the medical stuff – but she takes her cooking pot and her knife and the matches and some rope, because we don't know how long we'll be gone. Rebecca hugs her and says, "Watch your back, sweetheart," and then we set out.

We walk and walk; at noon we stop to eat. Toby's listening all the time: too many birdcalls of the wrong kind, such as crows – or else no bird calls at all – means *Look out*, she says. But all we're hearing is background cheeping and chirping. "Bird wallpaper," says Toby.

We keep walking, and eat again, and walk some more. There are so many leaves; they steal the air. Also they make me nervous because of the last time we walked in a forest and found Oates hanging.

When it gets dark, we choose some big-enough trees and string up the hammocks and climb in. But it's hard for me to sleep. Then I hear singing. It's beautiful, but it's not like normal singing – it's clear, like glass, but with layers. It's like bells.

The singing fades away, and I think maybe I was imagining things. And then I think, it must have been the blue people: that must be how they sing. I picture Amanda among them: they're feeding her, taking care of her, purring to heal her and comfort her.

It's make-believe. Wishful thinking, I know I shouldn't do it: I should face reality. But reality has too much darkness in it. Too many crows.

The Adams and the Eves used to say, *We are what we eat*, but I prefer to say, *We are what we wish*. Because if you can't wish, why bother?

SAINT TERRY
AND ALL WAYFARERS

SAINT TERRY AND ALL WAYFARERS

YEAR TWENTY-FIVE.

OF THE WANDERING STATE.
SPOKEN BY ADAM ONE.

Dear Friends, dear Fellow Creatures, Fellow Sojourners on this dangerous road that is now our pathway through life:

How long it has been since our last Saint Terry's Day on our beloved Edencliff Rooftop Garden! We did not realize then how much better those times were, compared with the dark days we are living through now. Then, we enjoyed the prospect from our peaceful Garden, and though that prospect was one of slums and crime, yet we viewed it from a space of restoration and renewal, flourishing with innocent Plants and industrious Bees. We raised our voices in song, sure that we would prevail, for our aims were worthy and our methods without malice. So we believed, in our innocence. Many woeful things have happened since, but the Spirit that moved us then is present still.

Saint Terry's Day is dedicated to all Wayfarers – prime among them Saint Terry Fox, who ran so far with one mortal and one metallic leg; who set a shining example of courage in the face of overwhelming odds; who showed what the human body can do in the way of locomotion without fossil fuels; who raced against Mortality, and in the end outran his own Death, and lives on in Memory.

On this day we remember, too, Saint Sojourner Truth, guide of escaping slaves two centuries ago, who walked so many miles with only the stars to guide her; and Saints Shackleton and Crozier, of Antarctic and Arctic fame; and Saint Laurence "Titus" Oates of the Scott Expedition, who hiked where no man had ever hiked before, and who sacrificed himself during a blizzard for the welfare of his companions. Let his immortal last words be an inspiration to us on our journey: "I am just going outside and may be some time."

The Saints of this day are all Wayfarers. They knew so well that it is better to journey than to arrive, as long as we journey in firm faith and for selfless ends. Let us hold that thought in our hearts, my Friends and fellow Voyagers.

It is fitting that we remember those whom we have lost so far on our journey. Darren and Quill have succumbed to an illness, the early symptoms of which are cause for grave apprehension. At their own request we have left them behind us. We thank them for showing such praiseworthy concern for those of us who remain healthy.

Philo has entered a Fallow state, and is at peace on top of a parking garage, a location that reminds him perhaps of our own dear Rooftop.

We should not have allowed Melissa to lag so far behind us. Via the conduit of a wild dog pack, she has now made the ultimate Gift to her fellow Creatures, and has become part of God's great dance of proteins.

Put Light around her in your hearts.

Let us sing.

THE LONGEST MILE

The last mile is the longest mile –
'Tis then we weaken;
We lose the strength to run the race,
We doubt Hope's beacon.

Shall we turn back from this dark Road,
Footsore and weary,
When deep Despair has drained our Faith,
And all seems dreary?

Shall we give up the narrow path,
The plodding byway –
Chose swift transport and false delight:
Destruction's highway?

Shall Enemies erase our Life,
Our Message bury?
And shall they quench in war and strife
The Torch we carry?

Take heart, oh dusty Travellers:
Though you may falter,
Though you be felled along the way,
You'll reach the Altar.

Race on, race on, though eyes grow dim,
And faint the Chorus;
God gives us Nature's green applause –
Such will restore us.

For in the effort is the Goal,
'Tis thus we're treasured:

He knows us by our Pilgrim Soul –
'Tis thus we're measured.

From *The God's Gardeners Oral Hymnbook*

74

REN. SAINT TERRY AND ALL WAYFARERS

YEAR TWENTY-FIVE

When I wake up, Toby's already sitting in her hammock doing some arm stretches. She smiles at me: she's smiling more lately. Maybe she does it now to encourage me. "What day is today?" she says.

I think for a moment. "Saint Terry, Saint Sojourner," I say. "All Wayfarers."

Toby nods. "We should do a short Meditation," she says. "The path our feet will travel on today will be a dangerous one; we'll need inner peace."

When any of the Adams or the Eves tells you to do a Meditation, you don't say no. Toby climbs out of her hammock, and I stand watch in case of surprises while she goes into the Lotus: she's quite flexible for someone her age. But when it's my turn, although I bend myself into the shape just like rubber, I can't do the Meditation properly. I can't manage the first three parts: the Apology, the Gratitude, the Forgiveness – and especially not the Forgiveness, because I don't know who I need to forgive. Adam One would say I'm too fearful and angry.

So I think about Amanda, and everything she did for me, and how I never did anything for her. Instead I allowed myself to feel jealous of her about Jimmy, though Jimmy was in no way her fault. Which wasn't fair. I have to find her, and get her away from whatever may be happening to her. Though maybe she's already hanging in a tree with parts of her cut out, like Oates.

But I don't want to picture that, so instead I imagine myself walking towards her because that's what I'll have to do.

It is not only the body that travels, Adam One used to say, it is also the Soul. And the end of one journey is the beginning of another.

"I'm ready now," I say to Toby.

We eat some of the dried Mo'Hair meat and drink some water, and cache the hammocks under a bush so we won't have to carry them. We should take the packsacks, though, says Toby, with the food and stuff. Then we look around to make sure we haven't left any obvious traces of ourselves. Toby checks the rifle. "I'll only need two bullets," she says.

"If you don't miss," I say. One for each Painballer: I picture the bullets moving through the air, straight into – what? An eye? A heart? It makes me flinch.

"I can't afford to miss," she says. "They've got a spraygun."

Then we rejoin the pathway and continue on in the direction of the sea, towards where I heard the voices coming from in the night.

After a while we hear those voices, but they aren't singing, just talking. There's the smell of smoke – a wood fire – and children laughing. It's Glenn's made-on-purpose people. It has to be.

"Walk slowly," she says in a low voice. "The same rules as for animals. Stay very calm. If we have to leave, back away. Don't turn and run."

I don't know what I'm expecting, but it isn't what I see. There's a clearing, and in the clearing there's a fire, and around the fire there are people, maybe thirty of them. They're all different colours – black, brown, yellow, and white – but not one of them is old. And not one of them has any clothes on.

A nudist camp, I think. But that's only a joke I make to myself. They're too good-looking – way too perfect. They look like ads for the AnooYoo Spas. Bimplants and totally waxed – no body hair at all. Resurfaced. Airbrushed.

Sometimes you can't believe in a thing until you actually see it, and these people are like that. I didn't quite believe that Glenn had really done it; I didn't believe what Croze told me, even though he'd actually seen these people. But now here they are, right in front of me. It's like seeing unicorns. I want to hear them purr.

When they spot us – first one of the children, then a woman, then all of them – they stop whatever they're doing and turn to stare at us, all together. They don't look frightened or threatening: they look interested but placid. It's like being stared at by the Mo'Hairs, and they're chewing like the Mo'Hairs as well. Whatever they're eating is green: a couple of the kids are amazed enough by us that they keep their mouths open.

"Hello," says Toby. To me she says, "Stay here." She steps forward. One of the men stands up – he'd been squatting beside the fire – and moves out in front of the rest.

"Greetings," he says. "Are you a friend of Snowman?"

I can hear Toby pondering her choices: Who is Snowman? If she answers yes, will they think she's an enemy? What if she answers no?

"Is Snowman good?" says Toby.

"Yes," the man says. He's taller than the others, and seems to be their spokesman. "Snowman is very good. He is our friend." The rest nod, still chewing.

"Then we are his friends too," says Toby. "And we are your friends as well."

"You are like him," says the man. "You have an extra skin, like his. But you have no feathers. Do you live in a tree?"

"Feathers?" says Toby. "On his extra skin?"

"No, on his face," says the man. "Another came, like Snowman. With feathers. And one with him, who had short feathers. And a woman who smelled blue but did not act blue. Perhaps the woman with you is like that?"

Toby nods as if she understands all of this. Maybe she does. I can't ever tell exactly what she understands.

"She smells blue," says another man. "That woman with you."

All the men are now sniffing in my direction, as if I'm a flower or maybe a cheese. A number of them have sprouted huge blue erections. Croze warned me about this, but I've never seen anything like it, even at Scales, where some of the clients went in for body paint and extenders. Several of these men are giving out a strange humming sound, like the kind you make by rubbing your finger around the rim of a crystal glass.

"But the other woman that came was frightened when we sang to her and offered her flowers, and signalled to her with our penises," says the chief one.

"Yes. The two men were frightened also. They ran away."

"How tall was she?" says Toby. "The woman. Taller than this one?" She points to me.

"Yes. Taller. She was not well. Also she was sad. We would have purred over her and made her better. Then we could have mated with her."

It must be Amanda, I think. So she's still alive, they haven't killed her yet. *Hurry up!* I want to shout. But Toby's not going anywhere yet.

"We wished her to choose which four of us she would copulate with," says the main one. "Perhaps the woman with you will choose. She smells very blue!" At this, the men all smile – they have brilliantly white teeth – and their penises point at me and wag from side to side like the tails of happy dogs.

Four? All at once? I don't want Toby to shoot any of these men – they seem so gentle, and they're very good-looking – but also I don't want those bright-blue penises anywhere near me.

"My friend isn't really blue," says Toby. "It's just her extra skin. It was given to her by a blue person. That's why she smells blue. Where did they go? These two men and the woman?"

"They went along the shore," says the main one. "And then, this morning, Snowman went to find them."

"We could look under her extra skin and see how blue she is."

"Snowman has a hurt foot. We purred over it, but it needs more purring."

"If Snowman was here, he would find out about the blue. He would tell us how we should act."

"Blue should not be wasted. It is a gift from Crake."

"We wanted to go with him. But he told us to stay here."

"Snowman knows," says one of the women. So far the women have been taking no part in the conversation, but now they all nod and smile.

"We must go now and help Snowman," says Toby. "He is our friend."

"We will come with you," says another man – a shorter one, yellow in tone, with green eyes. "We will help Snowman too." Now that I notice, they all have green eyes. They smell like citrus fruits.

"Snowman often needs our help," says the tall man. "His smell is weak. It has no power. And this time he is sick. He is sick in his foot. He is limping."

"If Snowman told you to stay here, you must stay here," says Toby. They look at one another: something's worrying them.

"We will stay here," says the tall man. "But you must come back soon."

"And bring Snowman," says one of the women. "So we can help him. Then he can live in his tree again."

"And give him a fish. A fish makes him happy."

"He eats it," says one of the children, making a face. "He chews it up. He swallows it. Crake said he has to."

"Crake lives in the sky. He loves us," says a short woman. They seem to think this Crake is God. Glenn as God, in a black T-shirt – that's pretty funny, considering what he was really like. But I don't laugh.

"We could give you a fish too," says the woman. "Would you like a fish?"

"Yes. Bring Snowman," says the tall man. "Then we will catch two fish. Three. One for you, one for Snowman, one for the woman who smells blue."

"We'll do our best," says Toby.

This seems to puzzle them. "What is 'best'?" says the man.

We step out from under the trees, into the open sunlight and the sound of the waves, and walk over the soft dry sand, down to the hard wet strip above the water's edge. The water slides up, then falls back with a gentle hiss, like a big snake breathing. Bright junk litters the shore: shards of plastic, empty cans, broken glass.

"I thought they were going to jump me," I say.

"They smelled you," says Toby. "They smelled the estrogen. They thought you were in season. They only mate when they turn blue. It's like baboons."

"How do you know all that?" I say. Croze told me about the blue penises but not about the estrogen.

"From Ivory Bill," says Toby. "The MaddAddams helped to design that feature. It was supposed to make life simpler. Facilitate mate selection. Eliminate romantic pain. Now we should keep very quiet."

Romantic pain, I think. I wonder what Toby knows about that?

There's a line of deserted high-rises standing in the offshore water: I remember them from our Gardener trips to the Heritage Park beach. It was dry land out there before the sea levels rose so much, and all the hurricanes: we'd learned that in school. Gulls are soaring and settling on the flat roofs.

We can get eggs there, I think. And fish. Jacklight, Zeb taught us, if you're desperate. Make a torch, the fish will swim to the light. There's a few crab holes in the sand, small ones. Nettles growing farther up the beach. You can eat seaweed too. All those Saint Euell things.

I'm wishing again: planning lunch, when in the back of my head is just plain fear. We can never do it. We'll never get Amanda back. We'll be killed.

Toby's found some tracks in the wet sand – several people with shoes or boots, and the place where they took the shoes off, maybe to wash their feet, and then where they put the shoes back on and headed up towards the trees.

They could be in among those trees right now, looking out. They could be watching us. They could be aiming.

On top of those tracks is another set. Barefoot. “Someone limping,” whispers Toby, and I think, It must be Snowman. The crazy man who lives in a tree.

We slip our packsacks off and leave them where the sand ends and the grass and weeds begin, under the first trees. Toby says we don’t need them weighing us down: we need our arms free.

75

TOBY. SAINT TERRY AND ALL WAYFARERS

YEAR TWENTY-FIVE

So, God, thinks Toby. What's Your view? Supposing You exist. Tell me now, please, because this may be the end of it: once we tangle with the Painballers, we don't have a cat's chance in a bonfire, the way I see it.

Are the new people Your idea of an improved model? Is this what the first Adam was supposed to be? Will they replace us? Or do You intend to shrug your shoulders and carry on with the present human race? If so, you've chosen some odd marbles: a clutch of one-time scientists, a handful of renegade Gardeners, two psychotics on the loose with a nearly dead woman. It's hardly the survival of the fittest, except for Zeb; but even Zeb's tired.

Then there's Ren. Couldn't you have picked someone less fragile? Less innocent? A little tougher? If she were an animal, what would she be? Mouse? Thrush? Deer in the headlights? She'll fall apart at the crucial moment: I should have left her back there on the beach. But that would prolong the inevitable, because if I go down, so will she. Even if she runs, it's too far back to the cobb house: she'll never make it, and even if she outruns them she'll get lost. And who's going to protect her from the dogs and pigs, in the wild woods? Not the blue folks back there. Not if the Painballers have a spraygun that works. Much worse for her if she doesn't die immediately.

The Human moral keyboard is limited, Adam One used to say: there's nothing you can play on it that hasn't been played before. And, my dear Friends, I am sorry to say this, but it has its lower notes.

She stops, checks the rifle. Safety off.

Left foot, right foot, quietly along. The faint sounds of her feet on the fallen leaves hit her ears like shouts. How visible, how audible I am, she thinks. Everything in the forest is watching. They're waiting for blood, they can smell it, they can hear it running through my veins, *katoush.* Above her head, clustering in the treetops, the crows are treacherous: *Hawhawhaw!* They want her eyes, those crows.

Yet each flower, each twig, each pebble, shines as though illuminated from within, as once before, on her first day in the Garden. It's the stress, it's the adrenalin, it's a chemical effect: she knows this well enough. But why is it built in? she thinks. Why are we designed to see the world as supremely beautiful just as we're about to be snuffed? Do rabbits feel the same as the fox teeth bite down on their necks? Is it mercy?

She pauses, turns, smiles at Ren. Do I look reassuring? she wonders. Calm and in control? Do I look as if I know what the hell I'm doing? I'm not up to this. I'm not fast enough, I'm too old, I'm rusty, I don't have the whiplash reflexes, I'm weighed down with scruples. Forgive me, Ren. I'm leading you to doom. I pray that if I miss we both die quickly. No bees to save us this time.

What Saint should I call upon? Who has the resolution and the skill? The ruthlessness. The judgment. The accuracy.

Dear Leopard, dear Wolf, dear Liobam: lend me your Spirits now.

76

REN. SAINT TERRY AND ALL WAYFARERS

YEAR TWENTY-FIVE

As soon as we hear voices we go forward very silently. Heel on the ground, said Toby, then roll forward on the foot, other heel on the ground. That way nothing dry snaps.

The voices are men. We can smell the smoke from their fire, and another smell: charred meat. I realize how hungry I am: I can feel myself drooling. I try to think about this hunger instead of being scared.

We peer through the leaves. It's them all right: the one with the longer dark beard, the one with the light stubbly beard and the shaved head that's growing in. I remember everything about them, and I feel like throwing up. It's hate and fear grabbing at my stomach and sending tendrils through my whole body.

But now I see Amanda, and I feel so light all of a sudden. As if I could fly.

Her hands are free, but there's a rope around her neck, with the other end tied to the leg of the dark-bearded guy. She's still wearing her khaki desert-girl outfit, though it's filthier than ever. Her face is smudged with dirt, her hair is dull and stringy. She has a purple bruise under one eye, and there are other bruises on the bare parts of her arms. She still has some of the orange nail polish on her fingers from Scales. Seeing it makes me want to cry.

She's only skin and bones. But the two of them don't look so fat themselves.

I feel myself breathing fast. Toby takes hold of my arm and gives it a squeeze. That means *Keep calm.* She turns her brown face towards me and smiles a shrunken-head smile; the edges of her teeth glint through her lips, the muscles of her jaws tighten, and all of a sudden I feel sorry for those two men. Then she lets go of my arm and lifts the rifle, very slowly.

The two men are sitting cross-legged, broiling chunks of meat on sticks over the coals. Rakunk meat. The black-and-white-striped tail is on the ground, over to the side. There's a spraygun on the ground too. Toby must have seen it. I can hear her thinking: If I shoot one of them, will I have time to shoot the other one before he can shoot me?

"Maybe it's some fuckin' savages thing," the dark-bearded one is saying. "Blue paint."

"Nah. Tattoos," says the shorthair.

"Who'd get their dick tattooed?" says the bearded one.

"Savages will tattoo anything," says the other. "It's some cannibal thing."

"You been watching too many dumb movies."

"Bet they'd human-sacrifice her in about two minutes," says the bearded one. "After they all had sex with her." They look over at Amanda, but she's staring at the ground. The bearded one jerks the rope. "We're talkin' to you, bitch," he says. Amanda raises her head.

"A sex toy you can eat," says the shorthair, and the two of them laugh. "You see the bimplants on those bitches, though?"

"Not bimplants, they were real. Way to find out, cut them open. The fake ones've got, like, some kind of gel in them. Maybe we could go back there, do a trade," says the bearded one. "With the savages. They get this one, they seem to want her so much, stick their blue dicks into her, and we get some of those hot babes of theirs. Fuckin' good deal!"

I see Amanda as they see her: used up, worn out. Worthless.

"Why trade?" says the shorthair. "Why not just go back and shoot the fuckers?"

"Not enough juice in this thing to shoot all of them. Cellpack's really low. They'd figure that out, they'd rush us. Tear us apart and eat us."

"We got to get farther away," says the shorthair, alarmed now. "Thirty of them, two of us. What if they sneak up on us in the dark?"

There's a pause while they think about this. My skin is crawling all over, I hate them so much. I wonder why Toby's waiting. Why doesn't she just kill them? Then I think, she's old Gardener – she can't do it, not in cold blood. It's against her religion.

"Not too bad," says the bearded one, lifting a skewer from the coals. "We can bag another one of these tasty little suckers tomorrow."

"We gonna feed her?" says the shorthair. He's licking his fingers.

"Give her some of yours," says the bearded one. "She's no use to us dead."

"No use to *me* dead," says the shorthair. "You're such a pervert you'd plank a fuckin' corpse."

"Speaking of which, your turn first. Get the pump primed. I hate a dry fuck."

"It was me first yesterday."

"So, we arm-wrestle?"

Then suddenly there's a fourth person in the clearing – a naked man, but not one of the green-eyed beautiful ones. This one is emaciated and scabby. He has a long scraggly beard, and he looks very crazy. But I know him. Or I think I know him. Is it Jimmy?

He's carrying a spraygun, and he has it aimed it at the two men. He's going to shoot them. He has that kind of maniac focus.

But he'll shoot Amanda too, because the dark-bearded guy sees him and scrambles up onto his knees and pulls Amanda in front of him, one arm around her neck. The shorthair ducks in behind them. Jimmy hesitates, but he doesn't lower the spraygun.

"Jimmy!" I scream from inside the shrubbery. "Don't! That's Amanda!"

He must think the bushes are talking to him. His face turns. I come out from behind the leaves.

"Great! The other bimbo," says the bearded one. "Now we'll have one each!" He's grinning. The shorthair crouches forward, reaches for their spraygun.

Toby steps into the clearing. She has the rifle up and aimed. "Don't touch that," she says to the shorthair. Her voice is strong and clear but dead flat even. She must sound scary to him, and look it too – skinny, tattered, teeth bared. Like a TV banshee, like a walking skeleton; like someone with nothing to lose.

The shorthair freezes. The one holding Amanda doesn't know which way to turn: Jimmy's in front of him, but Toby's off to the side. "Back off! I'll break her neck," he says to all of us. His voice is very loud: that means he's afraid.

"I might care about that, but he doesn't," Toby says, meaning Jimmy. To me: "Get that spraygun. Don't let him grab you." To the shorthair: "Lie down." To me: "Watch your ankles." To the bearded one: "Let go of her."

This is very fast, but at the same time slowed down. The voices are coming from far away; the sun's so bright it hurts me; the light crackles on our faces; we glare and sparkle, as if electricity's running all over us like water. I can almost see into the bodies – everyone's bodies. The veins, the tendons, the blood flowing. I can hear their hearts, like thunder coming nearer.

I think I might faint. But I can't, because I need to help Toby. I don't know how, but I run over. So close I can smell them. Rancid sweat, oily hair. Snatch up their spraygun.

"Around behind him," Toby tells me. To the Painballer: "Hands behind your head." To me: "Shoot him in the back if you don't see those hands quick." She's talking as if I know how to work this thing. To Jimmy, she says, "Easy now," as if he's a big frightened animal.

All this time Amanda has kept still, but when the dark-bearded one lets go of her she moves like a snake. She pulls the rope noose up and over her head and whips the guy across the face with it. Then she kicks him in the nuts. I can tell she doesn't have a lot of strength left, but she uses all she has, and when he doubles over on the ground she kicks the other one. Then she grabs a stone and whacks each of them over the head, and there's blood. Then she drops the stone and hobbles over to me. She's crying, big gulping sobs, and I know it must have been very terrible, those days when I wasn't there, because it takes more than a lot to make Amanda cry.

"Oh, Amanda," I say to her. "I'm so sorry."

Jimmy's swaying on his feet. "Are you real?" he says to Toby. He looks so bewildered. He rubs his eyes.

"As real as you," says Toby. "You'd better tie them up," she says to me. "Do a good job. When they come out of it they're going to be very angry."

Amanda wipes her face on her sleeve. Then we start knotting the two of them together, the hands behind the backs, a loop around each neck. We could use more rope, but it will do for now.

"Is it you?" says Jimmy. "I think I've seen you before."

I walk towards him, slowly and carefully because he still has his gun. "Jimmy," I say. "It's Ren. Remember me? You can put that down. It's okay now." It's how you'd say it to a child.

He lowers the spraygun and I wrap my arms around him and give him a long hug. He's shivering, but his skin's burning hot.

"Ren?" he says. "Are you dead?"

"No, Jimmy. I'm alive, and so are you." I smooth back his hair.

"I'm such a mess," he says. "Sometimes I think everyone's dead."

SAINT JULIAN AND ALL SOULS

SAINT JULIAN AND ALL SOULS

YEAR TWENTY-FIVE.

OF THE FRAGILITY OF THE UNIVERSE.

SPOKEN BY ADAM ONE.

My dear Friends, those few that now remain:

Only a little time is left to us. We have used some of that time to make our way up here, to the site of our once-flourishing Edencliff Rooftop Garden, where in a more hopeful era we spent such happy days together.

Let us take this opportunity to dwell, for one final moment, on the Light.

For the new moon is rising, signalling the beginning of Saint Julian and All Souls. All Souls is not restricted to Human Souls: among us, it encompasses the Souls of all the living Creatures that have passed through Life, and have undergone the Great Transformation, and have entered that state sometimes called Death, but more rightly known as Renewed Life. For in this our World, and in the eye of God, not a single atom that has ever existed is truly lost.

Dear Diplodocus, dear Pterosaur, dear Trilobite; dear Mastodon, dear Dodo, dear Great Auk, dear Passenger Pigeon; dear Panda, dear Whooping Crane; and all you countless others who have played in this our shared Garden in your day: be with us at this time of trial, and strengthen our resolve. Like you, we have enjoyed the air and the sunlight and the moonlight on the water; like you, we have heard the call of the seasons and have answered them. Like you, we have replenished the Earth. And like you, we must now witness the end of our Species, and pass from Earthly view.

As always on this day, the words of Saint Julian of Norwich, that compassionate fourteenth-century Saint, remind us of the fragility of our Cosmos – a fragility affirmed anew by the physicists of the twentieth century, when Science discovered the vast spaces of emptiness that lie, not only within the atoms, but between the stars. What is our Cosmos but a snowflake? What is it but a piece of lace? As our dear Saint Julian so beautifully said, in words of tenderness that have echoed down through the centuries:

> ... He showed me a little thing, the quantity of a hazel nut, lying in the palm of my hand ... as round as any ball. I looked at it and thought, What may this be, and I was answered generally thus: It is all that is made. I marvelled how it might last. For I thought it might fall suddenly to nothing, for little cause; and I was answered in my understanding: It lasts and ever shall, for God loves it. And so has everything its being, through the love of God.

Do we deserve this Love by which God maintains our Cosmos? Do we deserve it as a Species? We have taken the World given to us and carelessly destroyed its fabric and its Creatures. Other religions have taught that this World is to be rolled up like a scroll and burnt to nothingness, and that a new Heaven and a new Earth will then appear. But why would God give us another Earth when we have mistreated this one so badly?

No, my Friends. It is not this Earth that is to be demolished: it is the Human Species. Perhaps God will create another, more compassionate race to take our place.

For the Waterless Flood has swept over us – not as a vast hurricane, not as a barrage of comets, not as a cloud of poisonous gasses. No: as we suspected for so long, it is a plague – a plague that infects no Species but our own, and that will leave all other Creatures untouched. Our cities are darkened, our lines of communication are no more. The blight and ruin of our Garden is now mirrored by the blight and ruin that have emptied the streets below. We need not fear discovery now: our old enemies cannot pursue us, occupied as they must be by the hideous torments of their own bodily dissolution, if they are not already dead.

We should not – indeed we cannot – rejoice at that. For yesterday the plague took three of us. Already I sense within myself those changes that I see reflected in your own eyes. We know only too well what awaits us.

But let our going out be brave and joyous! Let us end with a prayer for All Souls. Among these are the Souls of those who have persecuted us; those who have murdered God's Creatures, and extinguished His Species; those who have tortured in the name of Law; who have worshipped nothing but riches; and who, to gain wealth and worldly power, have inflicted pain and death.

Let us forgive the killers of the Elephant, and the exterminators of the Tiger; and those who slaughtered the Bear for its gall bladder, and the Shark for its cartilage, and the Rhinoceros for its horn. May we forgive them freely, as we may hope to be forgiven by God, who holds our frail Cosmos in His hand, and keeps it safe through His endless Love.

This Forgiveness is the hardest task we shall ever be called upon to perform. Give us the strength for it.

I would like us all to join hands now.

Let us sing.

THE EARTH FORGIVES

The Earth forgives the Miner's blast
That rends her crust and burns her skin;
The centuries bring Trees again,
And water, and the Fish therein.

The Deer at length forgives the Wolf
That tears his throat and drinks his blood;
His bones return to soil, and feed
The trees that flower and fruit and seed.

And underneath those shady trees
The Wolf will spend her restful days;
And then the Wolf in turn will pass,
And turn to grass the Deer will graze.

All Creatures know that some must die
That all the rest may take and eat;
Sooner or later, all transform
Their blood to wine, their flesh to meat.

But Man alone seeks Vengefulness,
And writes his abstract Laws on stone;
For this false Justice he has made,
He tortures limb and crushes bone.

Is this the image of a god?
My tooth for yours, your eye for mine?
Oh, if Revenge did move the stars
Instead of Love, they would not shine.

We dangle by a flimsy thread,
Our little lives are grains of sand:
The Cosmos is a tiny sphere
Held in the hollow of God's hand.

Give up your anger and your spite,
And imitate the Deer, the Tree;
In sweet Forgiveness find your joy,
For it alone can set you free.

From *The God's Gardeners Oral Hymnbook*

77

REN. SAINT JULIAN AND ALL SOULS

YEAR TWENTY-FIVE

The new moon's rising now, out over the sea: Saint Julian and All Souls has begun.

I loved Saint Julian's when I was little. Each of us kids would make our own Cosmos, out of stuff we'd gleaned. Then we'd stick glittery things onto it and hang it on a string. The Feast that night was round foods, like radishes and pumpkins, and the whole Garden would be decorated with our shining worlds. One year we made the Cosmos balls out of wire and put candle ends inside them: that was really pretty. Another year we tried to make Divine Hands for holding the Cosmos balls, but the yellow plastic housework gloves we came up with looked very strange, like zombie hands. Anyway you don't picture God as wearing gloves.

We're sitting around the fire – Toby and Amanda and me. And Jimmy. And the two Gold Team Painballers, I have to include them. The light flickers on all of us and makes us look softer and more beautiful than we really are. But sometimes it makes us darker and scarier too, when the faces go into shadow and you can't see the eyes, only the eye sockets. Deep pools of blackness welling out of our heads.

My body hurts all over, but at the same time I feel so joyful. We're lucky, I think. To be here. All of us, even the Painballers.

After the mid-day heat and the thunderstorm I went back to the beach for our packsacks and brought them to the clearing, along with some wild mustard greens I'd found along the way. Toby took out her cooking pot, and the cups, and her knife, and her big spoon. Then she made soup with the leftovers from the rakunk and the rest of Rebecca's meat, some of her dried botanicals. When she put the bones of the rakunk into the water she spoke the words of apology and asked for its pardon.

"But you didn't kill it," I said to her.

"I know," she said. "But I wouldn't feel right unless somebody did this."

The Painballers are tied to a nearby tree with the rope and also some braided strips torn from Toby's once-pink top-to-toe. I did the braiding: if there's one thing the Gardeners taught you, it was craft uses for recycled materials.

The Painballers aren't saying much. They can't be feeling great, not after being pounded by Amanda. They must also be feeling stupid. I would be if I were them. Dumb as a box of hair – as Zeb would say – for letting us creep up on them like that.

Amanda must be still in shock. She's crying gently, off and on, and twisting the raggedy ends of her hair. The first thing Toby did – once the Painballers were safely roped up – was to give her a cup of warm water with honey, for dehydration, with some of her lamb's-quarters powder stirred in.

"Don't drink it all at once," she said. "Just little sips." Once Amanda's electrolyte levels were back up, said Toby, she could start to deal with whatever else about Amanda needed fixing. The cuts and bruises, to begin with.

Jimmy's in bad shape. He has a high fever, and a festering sore on his foot. Toby says that if only we can get him back to the cobb house, she can use maggots – those might work in the long run. But Jimmy may not have the long run.

Earlier she spread some honey on his foot, and fed him a spoonful of it, as well. She can't give him any Willow or Poppy, because she left those back at the cobb house. We wrapped him up in Toby's top-to-toe, but he keeps unwrapping himself. "We need to find him a bedsheet or something," Toby says. "For tomorrow. And figure some way of keeping it on him or he'll broil to death in the sun."

Jimmy doesn't recognize me at all, or Amanda either. He keeps talking to some other woman, who appears to be standing by the fire. "Owl music. Don't fly away," he says to her. There's such longing in his voice. I feel jealous, but how can I be jealous of some woman who isn't there?

"Who are you talking to?" I ask him.

"There's an owl," he says. "Calling. Right up there." But I don't hear any owl.

"Look at me, Jimmy," I say.

"The music's built in," he says. "No matter what." He's gazing up into the trees.

Oh Jimmy, I think. Where have you gone?

The moon's moved westward. Toby says the bone soup has boiled enough. She adds the mustard greens I collected, waits a minute, then ladles out. We've got only two cups – we'll have to take turns, she says.

"Not them too?" said Amanda. She won't look at the Painballers.

"Yes," said Toby. "Them too. This is Saint Julian and All Souls."

"What happens to them?" says Amanda. "Tomorrow?" At least she's taking an interest in something.

"You can't just let them loose," I say. "They'll kill us. They murdered Oates. And look what they did to Amanda!"

"I'll consider that problem," says Toby, "later. Tonight is a Feast night." She dips the soup into the cups, then looks around the firelight circle. "Some feast," she says in her dry-witch voice. She laughs a little. "But we're not finished yet! Are we?" She says this last thing to Amanda.

"Kaputt," says Amanda. Her voice is so small.

"Don't think about it," I say, but she begins to cry again, softly: she's in a Fallow state. I put my arms around her. "I'm here, you're here, it's okay," I whisper.

"What is the point?" says Amanda, not to me but to Toby.

"This is not the time," says Toby in her old Eve voice, "for dwelling on ultimate purposes. I would like us all to forget the past, the worst parts of it. Let us be grateful for this food that has been given to us. Amanda. Ren. Jimmy. You, too, if you can manage it." This to the two Painballers.

One of them mutters something like *Fuck off*, but he doesn't say it very loudly. He wants some of the soup.

Toby continues on as if she hasn't heard. "And I would like us to remember those who are gone, throughout the world but most especially our absent friends. Dear Adams, dear Eves, dear Fellow Mammals and Fellow Creatures, all those now in Spirit – keep us in your view and lend us your strength, because we are surely going to need it."

Then she takes a sip from the cup and passes it to Amanda. The other cup she gives to Jimmy, but he can't hold it right and he spills half of the soup into the sand. I crouch down beside him to help him drink. Maybe he's dying, I think. Maybe in the morning he'll be dead.

"I knew you'd come back," he says, this time to me. "I knew it. Don't turn into an owl."

"I'm not an owl," I say. "You're out of your mind. I'm Ren – remember? I just want you to know that you broke my heart; but anyway, I'm happy you're still alive." Now that I've said it, something heavy and smothering lifts away from me, and I truly do feel happy.

He smiles at me, or at whoever he thinks I am. A blistery little grin. "Here we go again," he says to his sick foot. "Listen to the music." He tilts his head to the side; his expression is rapturous. "You can't kill the music," he says. "You can't!"

"What music?" I say, because I don't hear anything.

"Quiet," says Toby.

We listen. Jimmy's right, there is music. It's faint and far away, but moving closer. It's the sound of many people singing. Now we can see the flickering of their torches, winding towards us through the darkness of the trees.

ACKNOWLEDGEMENTS

The Year of the Flood is fiction, but the general tendencies and many of the details in it are alarmingly close to fact. The God's Gardeners cult appeared in the novel *Oryx and Crake*, as did Amanda Payne, Brenda (Ren), Bernice, Jimmy the Snowman, Glenn (alias Crake), and the MaddAddam group. The Gardeners themselves are not modelled on any extant religion, though some of their theology and practices are not without precedent. Their saints have been chosen for their contributions to those areas of life dear to the hearts of the Gardeners; they have many more saints, as well, but they are not in this book. The clearest influence on Gardener hymn lyrics is William Blake, with an assist from John Bunyan and also from *The Hymn Book of the Anglican Church of Canada and the United Church of Canada*. Like all hymn collections, those of the Gardeners have moments that may not be fully comprehensible to non-believers.

The music for the hymns came about by fortunate coincidence. Singer and musician Orville Stoeber of Venice, California, began composing the music to several of these hymns to see what might happen, and then got swept away. The extraordinary results can be heard on the CD, *Hymns of the God's Gardeners*. Anyone who wishes to use any of these hymns for amateur devotional or environmental purposes is more than welcome to do so. Visit them at www.yearoftheflood.com, www.yearoftheflood.co.uk, or www.yearoftheflood.ca.

The name Amanda Payne originally appeared as that of a character in *Oryx and Crake*, courtesy of an auction for the Medical Foundation for the Care of Victims of Torture (U.K.). Saint Allan Sparrow of Clean Air was sponsored by an auction run by CAIR (CommunityAIR, Toronto). The name Rebecca Eckler appears thanks to a benefit auction for *The Walrus* magazine (Canada). My thanks to all name donors.

My gratitude as always to my enthusiastic and loyal but hard-pressed editors, Ellen Seligman of McClelland & Stewart (Canada), Nan Talese of Doubleday (U.S.A.), and Alexandra Pringle and Liz Calder of Bloomsbury (U.K.), as well as Louise Dennys of Vintage/Knopf Canada, LuAnn Walter of Anchor (U.S.A.), Lennie Goodings of Virago (U.K.), and Maya Mavjee of Doubleday Canada. Also to my agents, Phoebe Larmore (North America) and Vivienne Schuster and Betsy Robbins of Curtis Brown (U.K.); and to Ron Bernstein; and to all my other agents and publishers around the world. Thanks also to Heather Sangster for her heroic job of copy-editing; and to my exceptional office support staff, Sarah Webster, Anne Joldersma, Laura Stenberg, and Penny Kavanaugh; and to Shannon Shields, who helped as well. Also to Joel Rubinovitch and Sheldon Shoib; and to Michael Bradley and Sarah Cooper. Also to Coleen Quinn and Xiaolan Zhang, for keeping my writing arm moving.

Special thanks to the dauntless early readers of this book: Jess Atwood Gibson, Eleanor and Ramsay Cook, Rosalie Abella, Valerie Martin, John Cullen, and Xandra Bingley. You are highly valued.

And finally, my special thanks to Graeme Gibson, with whom I've celebrated so many April Fish, Serpent Wisdom, and All Wayfarers' Feasts. It's been a fine long journey.

A NOTE ON THE AUTHOR

Margaret Atwood is the author of more than thirty books of fiction, poetry and critical essays.

In addition to the classic *The Handmaid's Tale*, her novels include *Cat's Eye*, which was shortlisted for the Booker Prize in 1989, *Alias Grace*, which won the Giller Prize in Canada and the Premio Mondello in Italy in 1996, and *The Blind Assassin*, winner of the Booker Prize in 2000. Her most recent novel, *Oryx and Crake*, was shortlisted for the Man Booker Prize in 2003 and the Orange Prize in 2004. She was awarded the Prince of Asturias Prize for Literature in 2008.

Margaret Atwood lives in Toronto, Canada.

A NOTE ON THE TYPE

The text of this book is set in Epic Thin, one of six weights in a contemporary and versatile font family, with many subtleties in its construction. Epic is a true workhorse and is effective both as a readable text face and one that is visually interesting when used in display.